Night's Fall
The Four Realms
Book One

KRISTEN ASHLEY

ROCK CHICK
PRESS

Night's Fall

THE FOUR REALMS SERIES BOOK ONE

KRISTEN
NEW YORK TIMES BESTSELLING AUTHOR
ASHLEY

This book is a work of fiction. Any reference to historical events, real people, or real places are used fictitiously. Other names, characters, places, and incidents are products of the author's imagination. Any resemblance to actual events, locales, or persons, living or dead, is coincidental.

Copyright© 2025 by Kristen Ashley

All rights reserved, including the right to reproduce this book or portions thereof in any form whatsoever. In accordance with the U.S. Copyright Act of 1976, the scanning, uploading, and electronic sharing of any part of this book without the permission of the publisher is unlawful piracy and theft of the author's intellectual property. Thank you for your support of the author's rights. If you would like to use material from this book (other than for review purposes), prior written permission must be obtained. Please address Rock Chick Press, 4340 East Indian School Road, Suite 21-413, Phoenix, Arizona, 85016, USA.

Cover Image: Pixel Mischief Design

ACKNOWLEDGMENTS

Thank you to JD Robb for writing the absolutely fabulous In Death series and offering a masterclass in making future/sci-fi interesting, exciting and accessible. Diving into the amazing world of Eve and Roarke was the inspiration behind the Four Realms. Even if this book is not crime/suspense/romance, I hope it's the homage it was intended to be.

CHAPTER 1
THE PINK AND BLACK CLUB

"You can pay me back whenever," Catla announced graciously.

Sitting across from Catla in the back of her father's LuxeCraft (or...one of them), Gayliliel and I could do nothing but stare at our friend in shock.

I should have expected something like this the minute Cat started pressing for a night out.

She'd couched it in the whole "I know what happened to you was awful, but you can't hide away from life forever" routine.

However expected something like this was, this particular something was very un-Cat-like.

That being, spring it on us at the definition of the last minute and think we'd pay for it.

On this thought, the cab filled with Gayle's fae energy, which meant I had no choice.

I had to take control of this burgeoning situation and speak first.

"Cat, entry into the Black Room is very expensive."

I communicated this in as reasonable a tone as I could muster, considering everyone knew entry into the hyper-exclusive, VIP Black Room of the ridiculously famous and trendy Pink and Black Club wasn't expensive. It was cripplingly steep. Cat knew it most of all, since she'd paid for it.

Gayle's family had wealth, like Cat's. Not as much, but she came from money.

That said, Gayle made her own way like most human children did when the time came, and considering her father was human (it was Gayle's mom who was fae), that was the expectation.

Regardless, Gayle would have struck out on her own anyway. It was just who she was. Case in point, Gayle had started working at age fifteen, intent to get a head start. As such, now, she didn't do too badly.

But she couldn't afford the Black Room of the P&B Club.

Very few could.

This unlike Cat, whose mother was human, but her father was demon, and they were loaded. They not only had money, they had status. So much, they even hobnobbed with royalty.

Demons did things differently, especially for their daughters. Although Catla worked, she also received an additional allowance (a hefty one) from her family, which afforded her the opportunity to live the high life and dress to impress.

Not to mention, a monthly line of credit that was more than I'd ever made in an entire year.

My family, straight shifters on both sides, came from modest means.

Even if we didn't, I'd escaped their dysfunction years ago. There had been no support from that quarter since, well...

I was born.

They'd kept me clothed and fed with a roof over my head, I'd give them that.

However, I'd gone no contact the minute I could. That being at seventeen, the age of majority for a shifter. But even before, I was as no contact as I could get still living in the same house with them.

"And we didn't agree to it," Gayle cut in, not speaking reasonably but instead, heatedly.

"And it's really not in my budget," I continued. *Ever*, I did not say.

"You can pay me back in installments or something," Cat allowed.

I could feel Gayliliel bristling, not a good thing for a dark fae, and before I could intervene, she asked, "So, if you go out and buy me a pair of Eduardo Navasco shoes I don't want and can't afford, and give them to me, you'd expect me to pay you back for them?" Gayle asked.

"That's hardly the same." Cat flicked out an elegant hand. "You're here, aren't you? No one forced this on you."

"Yes, I'm here because I thought we were going to the Pink Room," Gayle shot back. "Or, at most, the Blue Room."

The Pink Room was where everyone could get in, if you were chosen by the doorman. The cover charge was more expensive than most, but it wasn't outlandish.

The Blue Room was one room deeper into the club. It required a charge that was not nominal. As such, although I'd been to the Pink Room, I'd never been in there.

The Black Room required a charge that, as noted, was astronomical. It also required connections. But since Cat's people, the Truelocks, were *The Truelocks*, all she undoubtedly had to do was say her name, give her credit code, and we were in.

Cat crinkled her adorable snub nose at the very idea of mingling in the Pink Room, and when Gayle mentioned Blue, she didn't look any happier.

Gayle didn't miss it, nor did she like it.

"The little people can be fun. You should know,"—she flapped a hand between herself and me—"since you hang out with us."

She wasn't the "little people."

But I was.

"No demon would be caught dead in the Pink Room," Cat retorted.

She was very correct. When I'd been there before, I'd gone with Gayle, or one of our other friends, Monique. Never Cat.

And there it was.

Recently, Catla had been husband hunting at the decree of her father.

And Cat was hunting for a demon, or at least a half one, also at the decree of her father.

Demon females married early, in their twenties, or the upper crust did, with the Truelocks occupying the uppermost part of the upper crust that wasn't titled aristocracy.

Cat was turning thirty-one on her next birthday, a day that was only two months away. But since she'd passed the thirty mark, Mr. Truelock had been becoming increasingly displeased with his daughter's live-life-have-fun-and-spend-money-until-you-drop lifestyle.

"I cannot believe you did this," Gayliliel said quietly but in a razor-sharp tone. "Especially tonight."

I tensed at the deterioration of her voice.

Cat didn't miss the edge either, and I could feel her demon rearing, which meant, if the situation didn't shift, things were about to get ugly.

"Did what?" she demanded.

"You making it all about you the first time Laura goes out after—" Gayle abruptly stopped speaking.

At that, things shifted.

They very much did.

This shift for me meant I had the familiar sensation of my chest compressing at the reminder of what that "after" Gayle was referring to meant.

At least it wasn't so bad anymore. I could still breathe. Three months ago, when it happened, it felt like I couldn't.

Cat glared at Gayle.

Gayle appeared contrite and avoided my eyes.

I sighed.

"You can say it," I whispered into the loaded silence of the car. "It happened. I can't pretend it didn't."

Even if I wished I could.

But I lived with it every day.

Or more to the point, without it.

It took everything I had not to fall into the habit I'd acquired and lift my hand to rub my chest like I could soothe the beast who wasn't there anymore.

Or she was, but she was still gone.

Annnnnnd...

Yeah.

Remembering the enormity of my loss, I felt like I couldn't breathe.

I forced air into my lungs.

I was so busy trying to get oxygen, I didn't hide the fact I couldn't, thus neither of my friends missed it.

"Well done," Cat sniped at Gayle.

"You started it with this ridiculous Black Room business," Gayle sniped back.

"Girls—" I tried to intervene.

It was always a crapshoot if my attempts at intervention would work, but this time when I rolled the dice, I failed.

"Not everyone is husband hunting. Fae have mates. So do shifters," Gayle pointed out. "We don't have to go on the prowl."

"Lucky you," Cat snapped. "As you know, it's not so easy for us demons."

"Not lucky *or* easy," Gayle slapped back. "My mate could live in Land's End, and I'll never meet him."

This was true.

Same for shifters.

In your everyday life, if you weren't lucky enough to run across the one who was meant for you, something that rarely happened, eventually, you had to quest.

Which meant, unlike what Gayle just asserted, we *did* have to go on the prowl in order to meet our mate, and it was much more of a thing than what Cat had to do.

In fact, many fae and shifters took a year from work (this was, fortunately, legally mandated for employers to allow us to do), if not longer, in order to travel the Four Realms in hopes of running across the one who was meant to be ours.

You could, of course, contract a witch to narrow down the search area for you, but witches who could successfully track mates were few and far between, and that meant they were insanely expensive. That said, witches who scammed desperate fae and shifters were a dime a dozen.

And if you didn't find him or her, you'd just have to make do, something no one wanted, because living without your true mate was like living without a limb. You could do it, but it would suck.

"But you can take your time, make a holiday of it," Cat stated. "I *have* to *make* a connection or Dad's going to—"

Now it was Cat cutting herself off.

"Your dad's going to what?" I asked.

She turned her head to look out the window, the long, copper waves of her hair floating over the alabaster skin of her bare shoulder.

"Oh shit," Gayle mumbled, watching Cat closely.

She turned to me (by the by, the waves of her gorgeous chestnut hair also floated enchantingly over *her* bare shoulders).

I stretched my lips at her. She bugged out her moss-green eyes at me.

"You two can stop pulling faces," Catla said into our exchange.

We both looked to her to see her attention on us.

"Okay, so I messed up," Cat went on to explain, and her gaze moved to me. "I wanted to make a big thing of it, us finally talking you into going out after…what happened to you."

I was attacked. Randomly. Viciously. And when I was, my beast was murdered inside me. She's still inside me, part of my soul, there but gone forever. I'm alive, but I'm still only one half of a whole. That's what happened to me.

But I could see how they couldn't say it.

I remembered their faces when I woke up in the hospital. They'd had the news before I did. I remembered the weeks after. The concern. The care. The sadness. The powerlessness.

I remembered all of it.

It was like what was done to me was done to everyone I loved, even if they weren't shifters and couldn't really understand.

They were my friends, and any friend feels the pain another friend is experiencing.

"And it was going to be my gift, you know, like a celebration, the three of us going out again. *You* going out with Gayle and me again," Cat continued.

Aw. She was so sweet.

"So you got us into the Black Room to make a thing of it, and then your dad got the credit notice," Gayle deduced.

Oh dang.

Part of Mr. Truelock's displeasure was manifesting in him tightening the reins on Cat's spending. He'd already decreased her allowance. Now it looked like he was aiming at her credit line.

"Did you tell him you were taking Laura out?" Gayle asked.

At the question, abruptly, Cat lost it.

"You know, I shouldn't have to explain myself," she bit off. "That money, Truelock money, *our* money, he didn't toil and break his back to earn it. We're a *First Family*, for the gods' sakes. Yes, Dad works, but the vast majority of Truelock wealth was inherited. It's *always* inherited."

She was not wrong.

She was also not done ranting.

"And he didn't have to rush out and make a connection. He has a penis. Therefore, he could decide when he'd find his mate and he could wait until he was a hundred and twenty if he felt like it. I mean, he didn't even get married to Mom until he was *forty-two*." She shook her head and those coppery locks I envied slid gloriously against the pale skin I also envied. "This whole thing is bullshit. Demon patriarchal *bullshit*. I mean, it's not like we're driving around in *cars* anymore. We've progressed! At least the humans, fae and shifters have. But oh no. Not us demons."

Gayliliel and I exchanged a glance, because we both agreed this was very true.

Shifters had their patriarchal bullshit as well, and it could get extreme, even more extreme than the demon kind.

But fortunately, they didn't push a female to wed before her thirties like she couldn't get on with her life without a mate attached to her. And more fortune (at least for me), I'd cut ties with my patriarch, so I didn't have to worry about it.

Fae and humans, they tended not to get mired in all of that crap.

"You know what?" Cat asked, and she didn't wait for our answer. She told us what. "Screw it. Dad adores Laura. If he knew what tonight was about, he wouldn't have jumped my shit about it. So I'll tell him and he'll back off. And then I'll tell him I'll find my mate when I find my mate and he can just live with it."

Gayle gasped at this proclamation.

Knowing Mr. Truelock, I got worried and instantly reached forward to grab Cat's hand. "Don't do anything rash," I advised.

"He'll totally cut you off," Gayle put in.

He totally would.

Cat pulled her hand from mine and waved it in front of her face angrily. "Screw that too. If he does, he does. I have a job. I'll get by."

"You can't even afford your flat without his—"

I kicked the side of Gayle's foot with my own, and she shut up.

Cat turned to gaze out the window again, muttering, "Rena's a mess."

Oh boy.

It was all coming out now.

Rena was Cat's cousin. Rena married less than a year ago. Rena's husband was a dick. And Rena had gotten the same strongarm tactics from her father to find a connection as Cat was now getting.

Cat continued muttering. "She pretty much hates Dagon."

We all pretty much hated Dagon, though I knew between the three of us, "pretty much" wasn't part of what we felt for him. He was arrogant, self-absorbed and condescending.

Though, he was gorgeous.

Their wedding had been an exercise in awkwardness with liberal mix-ins of embarrassment and moments of pure outrage.

The traditional wedding cake at a demon wedding had black frosting over a blood red cake. And during the cutting, Dagon rubbed his slice all over Rena's face, neck, chest, and even got some in her hair. When he was done, she looked like she got in a bar fight while the bar was burning down around her. And she lost.

Enough said.

"The seal is broken now," I remarked. "So I'm all in to be your wingman to help you find your connection. A *good* one."

I wasn't. I didn't even want to be out tonight.

But I was sure Cat didn't want to sleep on my couch for the week after I got home from the hospital following my attack. Only for her to go home for a week when Gayle took over. Then Cat came back. They did this for six weeks, and probably would still be doing it if I hadn't put my foot down that they had to get on with their lives, and I did too.

They got on with their lives.

I returned to work (much of which I could do at home, at least when we weren't on set, so that wasn't a big deal) but didn't really get on with mine.

Hence, our night out.

Although, even before, I was more of a homebody. That said, Cat had been right when she insisted it was time to leave my couch. I was in danger of becoming my couch, I was spending so much time on it.

"Me too," Gayle put in. "Though, I can't be hitting the Black Room every Saturday."

"You don't have to," Cat said in a small voice that broke my heart. "We'll figure it out so Dad will lay off and it won't cost a fortune for us to go out. And just to say, you guys are the best."

"You're better than the best," I replied. "So tell your dad that I'm over it." I wasn't, but fake it 'til you make it, right? "And now that I am, we are so totally on the case."

"We so totally are," Gayle agreed.

For a second, it looked like Cat might start crying, something that freaked me out. Demons rarely cried, and for the vast majority of halves, the demon was dominant.

Though humans did.

Of course, she got a lock on it, and she managed this by sweeping me from my pink high-heeled sandals that had straps that crisscrossed up my calves to my frothy, girlie-pink, short cocktail dress.

"Shut up," I said before she could give me stick for wearing pink.

"You shut up," she returned, her lips tipping up.

"Dudes like pink," Gayliliel chimed in. "It's all feminine and girlish and goofy and makes you seem vulnerable, like someone they need to protect. They get into that shit."

"It's not goofy," I declared.

Gayle ignored me and advised Cat, "You should try wearing it. Maybe you'll run into an alpha demon whose protection gene activates seeing you all pink and defenseless."

Cat instantly looked nauseous.

I burst out laughing, not at Cat's expression (okay, maybe a little at her expression), but at the idea of her wearing pink.

One could definitely say pink was *not* a demon color (case in point, she was wearing a slinky black number right now).

Fae, definitely. It was just that Gayle was not a pink kind of female (case for that point, Gayle was in a barely-there, deep violet number).

I totally was all about pink.

In fact, my beast had been…

"Gods, no. My skin would catch fire," Cat decreed, horror dripping from each word, fortunately taking me from my train of thought.

That was when Gayle started laughing, and I felt relief.

Drama averted; we were back.

Again, Cat's attention turned out the window. "Do you think the prince will be there?"

I felt my heart skip at the possibility.

This was one of the reasons why the Black Room was so expensive *and* exclusive. The True Heir of Night's Fall, Prince Aleksei, went there on occasion. In fact, it was rumored he owned the Pink and Black Club, among many of his other financial ventures.

If he was there and I got one shot at looking at him, live and in person, I'd take a second job to pay Cat back for the opportunity.

"I think he's probably lying low," Gayle said. "You know, after that whole Princess Anna debacle."

"Their engagement was totally ludicrous," I groused, and my grousing was only part to do with my lifelong crush on the handsome heir apparent of the Starknight Dynasty, and how devastated I was when it was announced Aleksei was to wed the glorious Anna, Princess Royal of Dawn's Break. I was this regardless of how preposterous it was that I'd feel that devasted, since I had no shot and never would.

It was mostly due to my affront that he was a shifter, and she was not.

It wasn't like shifters didn't mingle breeds, we did. Even the royal family had non-shifters in their lineage.

It was the fact that *I* was a shifter, or I had been (I was one in ancestry only now), and that made me feel somehow connected to him. It felt almost like a personal affront when they got engaged. And yeah, I know, that was ridiculous too.

Nevertheless, that was how I felt.

The only bright light in the months since my attack was when it was announced the engagement was off.

I wasn't the only one who celebrated this event. It was a surprise a spontaneous parade didn't happen, so many females in Night's Fall were beyond delighted the prince was a free agent again. Even if none of us had that first chance in any ever after.

"I wonder what happened with those two," Cat mused. "Everyone says she's all that and a bag of chips."

"Did you just say 'all that and a bag of chips?'" Gayle teased.

"Well, how would you put it?' Cat asked.

"She's sweetness and light and peace and ethereality, and on top of that, painfully beautiful, so, yeah. It's a real mystery why that didn't work."

"Hardly," Cat scoffed. "Can you imagine how boring she'd be?"

Gayle snorted. "I hear you. That has to be it. She was fine to look at, but have a couple of dinners with her floating around being an earthbound angel and constantly exuding utter perfection, and it'd be an endless snoozefest. A shifter needs some fire. A shifter like Aleksei needs an inferno."

And with that, not that I ever had a chance, I was out.

I was quiet. In certain situations, I could be shy. I was mostly an introvert, unless I was around people I knew, but even then, I was more of a listener than a talker. I didn't like attention. And I preferred cooking at home, snuggling in to watch some display, reading a book or taking a hot bath and drinking a glass of wine to being out on the town or off on an adventure.

Even when I went on holiday, I found a cottage or cabin somewhere and did all the stuff I preferred to do at home. I just did it without it having to be interrupted by work.

I wasn't ethereality and utter perfection.

I also wasn't fire.

I was just...*me*.

"She's probably been crying in her meditation studio or isolation aquarium for the past month," Catla surmised gleefully, as a female was wont to do when another female, especially one born with more than you had, was brought down a peg.

I couldn't say Princess Anna was more attractive than Cat. Their looks were very different.

But she was Princess Royal of a peaceful, affluent realm. She had magic (seeing as she was a witch) and natural beauty, nothing enhanced. She was rolling in family money. And she was, well...ethereality and utter perfection.

Hard not to hold some jealousy for a chick like that.

"Wouldn't you be, if you lost all the lusciousness that is Prince Aleksei?" Gayliliel asked.

"She was picced cavorting with Dolph Windstalker on the beach on Tyball's Gate. I saw the images on the social tapes this morning," I told them. I then added, "Oh, and she decided against donning the top of her bikini. And yes, her breasts are as perfect as everything else about her."

"She...*what*?" Cat was aghast.

"I'd say she isn't utter perfection, considering how richly petty that is,"

I declared, loyal, as ever, to the prince. "Aleksei has barely been seen in public since the break. And she's topless, on the beach on a party island off Land's End with a hunky screen star who usually dates shifters who are barely majority. Blech."

Cat's eyes narrowed on me. "Have you met Windstalker?"

Like I wouldn't tell her if I met Dolph Windstalker while working one of my gigs.

I shook my head. "Never. But I haven't heard good things."

"Men that handsome tend not to promote people hearing good things about them," Cat muttered.

"Well, if Anna ever thought they'd make up, she killed that fantasy," Gayle noted. "Not that Aleksei's the kind of guy to change his mind. Outside realizing the female he asked to marry him wasn't the female for him, that is."

"That was *so* out of character," Cat put in. "I think I was more surprised he changed his mind at all, much less that he changed it about her."

"Seems he dodged a bullet," Gayle remarked.

"He totally did," I declared. "It's obvious, as he got to know her, as it came closer to the wedding actually happening and her hooks were sinking deeper into him, she thought he couldn't get away, or at least not change his mind, since that's not his style. And both realms would want to avoid the scandal. Maybe because of all that, she let the mask drop. Maybe who she pretended to be was all about the Starknight and Dayrise houses unifying, and once that seemed a foregone conclusion, he got a sense of the real her and wanted nothing to do with it. You should have seen the comments on those pics with Windstalker. She was not faring well," I shared.

"That's pretty out of character too," Gayle mumbled.

"Or maybe it's not," I stated.

"Well, Aleksei isn't a waffler," Cat said. "This is a PR fiasco for Anna, and it was before those pics were put on the tapes. This means the stupidity of the Windstalker move is undeniable. Everyone was already speculating it was something about her or something she did that made Aleksei beg off. Now, they'll be certain of it."

"It's always the female's fault," Gayle griped.

"Yeah, so I either champion her for saying, 'fuck it, instead of licking my wounds, I'm gonna lick this hot wolf shifter,' or I think she's an idiot, for the same reason," Cat replied.

The craft stopped, and we all turned our heads to peer out the window.

What we saw was the glistening black façade, including the equally glistening black double doors, and a line of people down the pavement, queued along a black velvet rope attached to shiny black posts.

No sign.

None needed.

Such was the allure of the Pink and Black Club.

"We're here," Cat whispered with excitement.

The instant she did, my stomach performed an odd, and profound, drop. I blinked at the strength of the sensation but put it down to breaking the seal of going out and being in the world for the first time since my attack. The first time after my beast was murdered. The first time since the nightmare any shifter feared the worst happened to me.

I drew in a deep breath and let it out, much preferring the idea of simply gliding on and continuing to gab with my gals, perhaps going through a flyby to get something fried and awful for us while we did it.

But I told myself it wasn't going to be that bad. A few drinks. More girl talk. Once they started flirting, I could start people watching.

Then I could be at home with my cats, wearing my pajamas, with a tub of stem ginger frozen custard, a cup of tea, and maybe a Dolph Windstalker flick (he was a terrible actor, and possibly a terrible person, but he wasn't hard on the eyes).

A couple of hours.

Maybe three.

And then I could be out of these uncomfortable shoes, and equally uncomfortable dress, and this would be over.

I could do it.

Cat's dad's pilot opened the door, and that sensation in my stomach happened again, this time deeper, almost painful, but also curiously, maybe even impossibly...*pleasurable.*

What in the realms was that?

Cat got out. Gayle got out.

I sat in the craft.

They turned to look in at me.

Dang.

I guess I had no choice.

Time to do it.

I got out too.

CHAPTER 2

PHANTOM

If the stomach thing was weird, the minute I put my stiletto-heeled sandal to the pavement was weirder.
I felt flush all over.
Right, this wasn't good.
Was I having some sort of panic attack?
Before I could decide, Gayle encouragingly tucked her arm through mine, pulled me fully from the craft and forward while Cat waved something on her Palm unit at one of the doormales.
He jutted his chin to another doormale, who broke off and guided us down the pavement.
We followed, and as for my part, I did it deep breathing and concentrating on the chill autumn-is-right-around-the-corner air to help combat that weird flush.
Thankfully, this worked.
He stopped well down the pavement, standing against the glossy black exterior of the skyscraper where the Pink and Black Club took most of the lower floor (save the lobby). It was also rumored Prince Aleksei not only owned the building but had a penthouse at the top of it.
"First time?" the doormale queried.
Before Catla could pretend we were regulars (something she would do), Gayliliel piped up, "Yes."
He nodded. "You'll go in. To the left, check your units with the bot on duty. You'll walk through a scanning tube. Any weapons, send, receive or

recording units will be identified in the tube, so check them before you enter. If you don't, you'll be ejected from the club and banned from returning."

We all nodded, unsurprised that rich people protected their safety and privacy at all costs.

He put his palm to the shiny black façade of the building and an until-then invisible panel shifted inward before it slid to the side.

Nifty.

"Enjoy your evenings, ladies," he murmured as we trooped in.

I noticed, as Gayle moved at my side, he had his eyes aimed at her behind. This meant I further noticed he was fae, and he was hot.

Hmm.

The door sealed behind us in a manner that was mildly alarming, but Cat was already handing over her Palm to a bot standing behind a counter in an alcove to the side. I dug mine out of my shimmery pink evening bag, surprised that the bot on duty was not one of the more expensive humanoid ones.

Then again, the polished black metal that made up the body of the machine couldn't be on theme if it looked like a human.

It took our Palms, scanning our left retinas for pickup purposes, then we headed into the tube, the blue and green lighting circling the five or so feet of it being the only lighting in the narrow space.

"One at a time," the bot's mechanical voice came at us as we moved as a group to the tube.

Cat, as ever, went first.

Gayle pushed me in next.

I lifted an already achy foot (these shoes were fabulous, but they were also torture devices) to step into the tube.

And I froze.

I did because a feeling made itself known in my chest. Like a feather fluttering. Almost imperceptible. But I felt it.

I felt it.

And I knew what that feeling was.

Longing and melancholy assailed me.

Gods.

After I got home from the hospital, I'd looked it up and learned there could be phantom sensations of your beast, even after it was gone. There'd also been reports of a beast communicating with you, when that could no longer happen. This occurred especially if you elected not to have its essence surgically removed after death, which I absolutely elected not to do.

She was lost to me, but I couldn't let her go. Even after the staff at the hospital, regardless of my fragile state of mind, pressed very strongly for me to make the opposite decision, I refused.

Very few shifters made this choice, so truly, I was surprised how hard my doctor and nurse pushed it.

"Laura?" Gayle asked, concern in her voice.

Okay, I was freaking about being out in the world. I'd successfully avoided this by having food delivered and avoiding the Subterra and Monorails, instead springing for private crafts to take me when I hung out with Cat, Gayle, Monique (or any combo of the three).

Sometimes I'd have to hit a work meeting, but since the current gig I was on hadn't started production yet, and wouldn't for at least a few more weeks, I hadn't had to worry too much about that.

I'd hit the corner shop, of course, but Mr. Tanugu was more of a father to me than my own, so that didn't seem like a big adventure or any threat, but instead like going to my pop's, having a gab at the same time buying bananas.

Therefore, this reaction was not a shocker. I should have planned for it. The last time I was out in the world, truly out in the world, I'd been brutally assaulted. So brutally, defying my control, my beast had torn out to defend me.

And she had died for me.

So of course, this wouldn't be easy.

"You all right?" Catla inquired.

"Do not walk back through the tube," the bot ordered. "Forward only, into the club."

"Just go," I whispered to Catla. "I've got this."

Cat scanned my face. Then, wearing a worried expression, she glanced over my shoulder at Gayle.

"Go. Let's get her a drink," Gayle urged.

Cat nodded, and with one last study of me, she turned and moved through the tube.

I stepped into it and slowly did the same, that feather-flutter coming back, and getting stronger.

I loved it and hated it because I missed it with all that was me, but I knew it wasn't back. It was just panic and an illusion.

By Lilith, this was torture.

The flush had also returned to my skin, and by the time I made the end of the tube, I felt short of breath.

Right.

What was wrong with me?

I was stronger than this, surely.

Yes, I was.

I squared my shoulders.

The club lay before me, and I wanted to take it in, but instinctively, I stepped aside so Gayliliel could join us, and my eyes went directly to a half-circle booth, the one dead center of a line of them that covered the back wall.

The lighting was dim, but I noted five people sitting in that booth. The ones around the edges of the group were illuminated (two females, two males). But the being at the back, I could only make out he was male (not to mention the well-cut suit on his obviously well-honed body), but I couldn't make out his face. He was obscured by shadow.

I strained to see him, I just couldn't.

However, I could make out the fact that his head was turned in my direction, and I could swear he was looking at me.

Actually, it felt like we'd locked eyes, and he couldn't only see me, he could see *inside* me.

That was when every inch of my body started tingling.

By the gods, I was totally losing it.

I had to pull myself together.

With effort I wrenched my attention from that booth in order to scan the club.

This section of the P&B couldn't be more different than the loud, lively, energetic vibe of the Pink Room.

In Pink, there was always a crush of people. There was a dance floor that was constantly heaving. The music was deafening and physical, thumping into your skin with each beat. Drinks were expensive and mostly came in lurid colors and deadly concoctions.

Here, the music was a vague, sensual throb. Everything was black. The elegant but comfortable furniture that made up the many seating areas in the center space, like it was one gigantic living room; the bar stools that lined the bar; even the shelves of booze and mirrors behind the bottles of liquor. Small, onyx-shaded lamp drones hovered over tables and above thoroughfares, genius in their placement and illumination. Just enough to see, not enough to expose.

Most every seat was filled, the hum of conversation subdued, as if the entirety of the company was talking in whispers, but it wasn't crowded.

It was elegant, refined, minimal yet sumptuous.

For a person with my disposition, it was so much better than the Pink

Club, it was startling. If it didn't cost a fortune, I'd happily be here on the regular, chatting with my chicks, drinking fun drinks, and hoping Cat ran into someone she could love with all her heart, who loved her that way in return.

"I spy a couple of stools, let's hit it," Cat said, and forged along the plush soot carpeting under our feet, her trajectory: the bar.

I tried not to look to the booths as we moved, which probably cost more to reserve, which meant there were likely very rich, very famous, very aristocratic or (maybe!) very royal people sitting in them.

I was an avid people watcher and had a job where I was frequently around celebrities, so I'd honed my skills to such a point I'd take it as a personal fail if it came off as gawking.

Mostly, the sensation I felt when entering the club, more precisely from seeing that male at the back of it, had unnerved me, and I didn't think it was a good idea to revisit that feeling.

Therefore, I focused on the fact that there were really no other shoes I could wear with this dress, but I still lamented wearing them. I'd barely been standing for fifteen minutes, and I wanted to unstrap them and donate them to the nearest resale pane.

Thus, when we hit the two open barstools, I eyed there being only two with a very unsisterlike intensity, because neither Cat nor Gayle were wearing footwear that was comfortable, and at that point, I might engage in physical combat to claim one.

"Take mine," a deep voice said as a male slid off the stool next to one of the empty ones.

I looked up at an exceptionally handsome black-haired, black-eyed demon.

He smiled at me, and that was exceptionally handsome too.

On this thought, my stomach twisted so brutally, I nearly bent double with the pain.

"Lord of hellfire, you okay?" the male demon asked me, bending from his tall height to look into my face and reaching out, possibly to guide me to the stool he vacated, but before his hand even touched me, he murmured, "Shit, the heat coming off you is mately."

The pain had subsided, so I looked at him, bemused at his words. "Sorry?"

"Is your mate here?" he asked while glancing around.

My attention immediately went to the booth, now directly across from where I was standing. I vaguely noticed the people in it were sliding out, all but that one male who was sitting dead center at the back.

I still couldn't see his face in the shadows, but I could see the breadth of his shoulders, which were astonishingly wide, and considering my vocation, I noted again the cut of his suit, which was superb.

I could also feel his pull.

Whoever he was, he was somebody. Somebody important. Somebody magnetic.

Gods, maybe he was even the prince.

The prince was tall. He had very wide shoulders. He'd have reason, even in an exclusive club, to hide himself in the shadows.

And he always wore impeccably tailored suits.

"She doesn't have a mate," Gayle said, helping me hike my rear on the stool.

Once settled, I gazed up at the demon, who'd had a fae friend, with thick, leonine hair and lilac eyes, join him to stand in front of us. "Just to make you being kind enough to give me your seat even more awkward, I haven't been out in a while because of some…life stuff. And I'm not really a going-out type of person anyway. So I think my body's just having some difficulty getting into the swing of things again. That's some TMI when I don't even know your name, but I'd rather TMI than you thinking I'm weird."

Okay, so, maybe I'd rather him think I was weird than blurting semi-personal stuff two minutes into not quite meeting the guy.

Ugly side effect of being shy number one: you often blathered stupid things that made you seem weird.

Side effect of blathering stupid things that made you seem weird: in order not to put yourself in this excruciating position, you became a homebody.

He grinned again, my stomach reacted with a pinch again, but fortunately not as strong this time, and he said, "Honesty is never too much. And we'll rectify part of that. I'm Bash." He gestured to his friend. "This is Tay."

Cat inserted herself into the conversation, thank the gods.

"That's Laura, this is Gayle, and I'm Cat."

"Ladies," Tay's deep voice rumbled over us.

"Drinks?" a bartender asked.

We all twisted to order, and of course I asked for my one of my usuals, a pink fizz.

"On my line," Bash said to the bartender, putting our drinks on his credit line.

"That was kind, but not necessary," I said softly.

"I disagree," Bash replied, matching my tone.

Right, this male seemed kinda lovely.

"So what do you all do?" Tay asked.

I wasn't in the zone for a hookup, and Bash seemed nice, and he was very easy to look at, so I announced, "Cat manages the Tempera Gallery downtown."

Both Bash and Tay turned right to her.

"Seriously?" Tay asked.

Cat executed a move that was something else in her repertoire I envied, preening without looking like she was preening.

"Yeah," she confirmed.

"So you're the one who cornered Terrinton for the first-ever showing he's attended that's happening next week," Bash noted, not hiding his interest.

Cat shrugged with faux humility. "Guilty."

"Impressive," Tay said.

Cat sent him a dazzling smile (in case you're keeping track, yup, I was also covetous of her dazzling smile).

I watched under my lashes to see if Bash was dazzled.

It was as if he felt my gaze, and he looked right at me.

"And what do you do?" he queried.

Damn, not dazzled by Cat.

But maybe, against all that was right in the world, dazzled by me.

I struggled for words that would make what I did sound a lot less interesting than it was, when Gayle, having a different goal entirely, answered for me.

"Have you seen *Sheets* or *The Sunny Glade* or *Rumors and Tremors*?" Gayle asked him.

"All three," Bash answered her while watching me.

Gayle hooked a thumb my way. "Laura was the lead costume designer of all those vids. She also did all four seasons of *Rain and Pavements*. Got nominated for an award for that. And she got another nod for *The Sunny Glade*."

"I lost," I said swiftly. "Both times." I then leaned forward to look around Gayle, who was sitting next to me, to Cat. "It seems these guys are interested, so maybe you have a couple more invites for the Terrinton showing?"

"We have room. I can certainly add a few names," Cat purred.

"That'd be fantastic," Tay said.

"Are you going?" Bash asked me.

"Actually,"—shit!—"yes."

Tay seemed into Cat, when Bash needed to be into Cat, and Tay should be into Gayle, not because they were both fae, but because, clearly, I could barely handle a night out at a club. I didn't need to be flirting or fielding requests for dates or actually *making* dates.

If I couldn't walk into a bar without nearly fainting, what would happen if I had to go out to dinner with a male?

I'd been looking forward to the Terrinton exhibit. His art was wild, but I loved it. As such, my personal goal in coming out tonight had been an attempt at cutting my teeth so next week I wouldn't do something foolish, like bow out of the hottest ticket in town (outside the Midnight Masque at the Palace that was, which I would never get an invitation to, though Cat was going), vomit on a hot male's shoes or pass out at the feet of the great and mysterious Terrinton.

"Digi-post?" Bash called to the bartender.

The bartender slid a digital memo card on the bar between Gayle and me. Apparently, without being allowed our 'tronics, that was how you shared deets when you met someone you wanted to meet again outside the club. A nice little bonus, since those cards didn't come cheap.

Bash reached for it, and as he did, his fingers brushed my upper arm.

I jumped when he jerked his hand back, hissed sinisterly, and his black eyes glowed red.

"Are you okay?" I whispered.

His eyes remained red as he scowled at me and accused, "You've got a mate."

Was he crazy? Why on earth would he say that?

"I—" I began to deny it.

"I don't know what game you're playing, but it isn't fucking cool," he growled.

"I—" I started again.

I got no further that time because we heard an officious, "Gentlemales. Ladies."

Tay and Bash stepped aside, and a human male with dark, thinning hair, a slim mustache across his upper lip, a slightly shorter than average stature, and a barrel chest, wearing a splendidly cut suit locked his attention on me.

"You are Laura Makepeace, shifter," he declared, like I didn't know that.

"Yes," I confirmed.

"The prince requests your presence at his table."

Ummmmmmmm...

Every molecule in my body stopped moving and my throat got tight, both of these things good as, because of the first, my gaze didn't dart to the booth at the back, and the second, I didn't release a scream.

After a very long, very heavy moment of pure shock, I had to force the word "What?" out.

"Prince Aleksei requests your presence at his table." He paused, glanced through my company, and came back to me. "Now."

"Go," Gayle wheezed, clearly having the same difficulty I did with this stunning turn of events.

She added shoving me off the stool.

Bash swiftly sidestepped me touching him in any way, but I noted this only distractedly as the barrel-chested man had begun sauntering through the seating area toward the booths, doing this like he owned the place.

Precisely—yep, you guessed it—he was heading for the center booth where now only one male sat, his wide shoulders seeming impossibly wider, his attention, even if his face was still hidden in shadow, I knew was on me.

There was no feathery flutter in my chest as I moved behind the human.

No.

Instead, it felt like my beast was there, alive, real, tugging me forward like a happy puppy on a leash, yearning to tear out of my chest and gallop across the space to the prince.

Okay.

Okay.

Okay.

What was happening?

CHAPTER 3

UNEXPECTED

The booths were elevated from the rest of the club by three steps, the better to look down on the little people, who were big people to the other 99% of the population.

I navigated these steps like my life depended on it, even as I battled with everything that was going on in my brain and body.

Feet hurting. Phantom beast rearing her head for the first time since I lost her. Dream come true of meeting Prince Aleksei and doing it in a posh club when I was in a pretty frock with sexy shoes and really good hair.

I mean, how was this even real?

The human stopped just to the side of the low table sitting before the prince, and I stopped right in front of it. I barely caught myself from crying out, "I did it!" when I made it there with no incident.

I then stared at the long, powerful body folded into the plush booth, his face still in shadows, and I did this thinking it was good I couldn't see his face, for after besting the effort of appearing before him without incident, I didn't want to pass out at witnessing his sheer male beauty, live and in person.

I said nothing.

He said nothing.

The human said nothing.

I said more nothing.

The prince remained silent.

The human made an annoyed noise, got close, and hissed, "It's customary to curtsy."

Such was my surprise at his statement, my head jerked to the side (and slightly down) to take in the human. "What?"

"This is the True Heir of the realm. You curtsy," he snapped imperiously.

He could not be serious.

"In a club?" I asked.

"*Anywhere*," he spat.

Holy Beelzebub.

I turned back to the prince, and it was then I felt a chill sluice over my skin, the phantom in my chest subsided as my stomach curled into itself.

I felt this because he was sitting there, silent, expecting me to curtsy.

By the gods, it was the Year of the Dragon 2118. I'd seen people genuflecting to Aleksei, his father, King Fillion, his mother, Queen Calisa, brothers, Princes Timothee and Errol, and his sister, Aleece, but this was at ceremonial events where the royals were wearing crowns or troll skins or royal battle armor.

Not out at a (very elegant, but nevertheless just a...) *bar*.

I'd never curtsied. I didn't really know how.

What I knew was I could feel the attention of everyone in the club, they were expecting me to do something, and I feared what they were expecting me to do was curtsy.

So I did.

It was awkward. It was frightening due to having to balance all my weight on a slender heel in an unnatural way that made me worry I'd fall face first into the table in front of the prince. It was terrifying considering I knew I had attention, and that always made me uncomfortable, but the fact I had everyone's was excruciating.

And last, it was humiliating.

"Rise and then you can sit to his highness's right side," the human ordered.

I rose and moved to sit as told, doing this stiltedly, and that had nothing to do with the ache in my feet. I sat primly in the curve to his side, not close to him, thighs, knees and calves pressed together, and I tucked my handbag in my lap with the fingers of both hands curled tightly around it.

"Drink, madam?" the human asked.

My eyes jolted to him, and I told him something he knew, but I did it with a purpose.

I wasn't "madam."

I lived in the real world.

I was Laura.

"My name is Laura."

His head bowed, but his attention shifted to the prince, so mine did too.

Almost imperceptibly, his face still in shadow, the prince nodded.

"May I bring you a drink, Mistress Laura?" the human queried.

Mistress Laura was even worse.

I opened my mouth.

"Champagne," the prince drawled.

I closed my mouth.

Ah, so it was all coming clear.

I was summoned and expected to appear...*now*. I didn't get to sit without genuflecting. I didn't get an introduction, even if I knew who he was, he didn't know who I was, and truly, neither of us knew each other at all outside of names. And I didn't get to order my own drink.

I liked champagne (who didn't?).

But I liked more ordering the beverage I would myself be consuming.

Since I could string two thoughts together as a wee child, I'd thought Prince Aleksei was everything a boy, then a man, then a prince who would be king should be.

He was exquisitely beautiful even when he was far younger, and it only grew bolder with age. He didn't court the limelight. He didn't do stupid stuff (like both his younger brothers did, and on occasion, his baby sister).

Sure, when he came of age, he was often seen out with a very beautiful female on his arm, and they had an alarming tendency to cycle in and out of that position frequently.

But it was known widely he had a head for business, and he spent a goodly amount of time amassing a vast fortune to coincide with the colossal fortune the Starknight Dynasty already owned. It was also known he gave freely to charitable endeavors. However, in doing so, he didn't put himself front and center. He just gave funds that they were so grateful to have, they were vocal about him giving them.

He wasn't picced on a horse playing polo or participating in a laser joust (like Timothee). He wasn't snapped frolicking on a sky yacht, or a sea one either (like Timothee...and Errol). He wasn't caught on digital drunkenly lurching out of an ice casino in Sky's Edge after losing a veritable mint at a gaming table (again, like Errol).

In fact, I didn't know what he did as hobbies or in his downtime, outside date gorgeous females and any private activities my active imagination speculated might come with that.

I had built him up in my mind as being so unattainable, and so extraordinary, I'd never even bothered to dream about what meeting him might be like.

However, if I had, this would not be it.

Further to this not being it, I'd had all these many thoughts, sitting stiffly in his presence, his whatever that human was to him off to get me a drink, and he'd not said a word. Not even hello. And I didn't know if I was allowed to do so without his permission.

I did know he was watching me, his head turned my way, and there was something I didn't like about that either, since the way the booth was illuminated, I knew he could see all of me, but I couldn't see his face, and as such, his expression.

This went on so long, unusually for a quiet person like me, I couldn't take it any longer.

"Am I allowed to speak?" I asked.

"Why would you not be?" he asked in return.

I'd heard his voice. He made speeches every once in a while. He spoke for the Dynasty, and occasionally, for the king. He was a succinct speaker and had a smooth, deep, delicious voice.

Live and in person, the deep, rich, posh silk of it was staggering.

And for some reason, it made me mad.

I pried my fingers off my bag to flick a hand to where I'd curtsied. "Obviously, I'm unaware of royal protocol."

"Obviously," he replied.

"I feel like I need to apologize for that," I said, not sounding apologetic at all.

"Accepted," he said, sounding scrumptiously, but infuriatingly haughty and like he deserved the apology he very well knew I didn't want to give him.

And this, for reasons that didn't escape me, made me even madder.

"For future reference, considering I'm stunned to my absolute *core* that I'm privileged enough to be in your presence, say, if I ran into you at Captain Jacques's Fish and Chips, and you were incognito, enjoying a tri-filet boat, should I curtsy to you then?"

There was droll amusement that I couldn't be sure wasn't aimed at me, rather than shared with me, when his remarkable voice queried, "I've never had a tri-filet boat at Captain Jacques's. Is that the meal you suggest?"

Of course he hadn't eaten at Captain Jacques's fast food fish emporium.

"No. Totally go for the chicken schooner. Less greasy," I advised.

"I'll file that for future reference," he murmured, even though we both knew he'd never be caught dead in a Captain Jacques's.

And mm-hmm.

I was amusing him, and not in a good way, or at least, not in a good way for me.

Was it the pink dress?

Everyone was wearing dark. Sleek. Sophisticated.

It wasn't that mine was gauche, or even inexpensive. I was a costume designer. I didn't *do* gauche (though, I did inexpensive, but that had more to do with budget than choice). I'd designed period pieces and curated elaborate contemporary wardrobes. I knew clothes down to the last stitch over the last three hundred decades (this was not an exaggeration). Some of my dearest friends were well-known artists in the fashion world (this why my current frock was not inexpensive, friends gave discounts).

But my dress was light and airy. It was soft and girlie.

It was me.

Was it so boring being a prince that you had to call over a strange woman and get your kicks by making fun of her?

I noticed his long, attractive fingers were wrapped around a squat glass filled with amber liquid. He had this resting on the knee of his very long crossed leg. And I noticed it because he lifted it to his lips.

This movement brought him into the evasive light, and for the first time, close up and personal, I saw in profile the sublime beauty of Prince Aleksei, the True Heir of Night's Fall.

The elegance of his brow, the enticing hollow under his high cheekbone, the strength of his square jaw, the allure of his full lips, the shine to his thick black hair.

I watched him sip the amber liquid, a sensation I'd never felt when she was alive happening in my chest, like my beast had turned over to her back and exposed her belly, and yeah.

Oh yeah.

I got even angrier.

Fortunately, before I said anything that might send me to the guillotine (not that we had a guillotine, it'd been retired a couple hundred years before, but I'd gone sarcastic with the Captain Jacques's business, and that was already pushing it with a male who expected you to curtsy to him in a bar, so I figured I'd best be on good behavior from here on out), the human returned with my champagne.

I took the coupé glass he offered with a murmured, "Thank you," and brought it to my mouth.

Even before I tasted it, I knew it was liquid heaven by the delicate, flirtatious way the bubbles teased the tip of my nose, the heady fragrance I scented, but when it exploded across my tongue with graceful flavor, I had to press my thighs more tightly together, because I had a sexual response to it.

And considering how unexpected that was, once I swallowed, I gaped at the human and said, "Holy wow."

He dipped his chin.

"Chateau LeBrand," the prince put in.

I turned my head and blinked at him back in his shadow.

Chateau LeBrand?

The Chateau LeBrand?

I'd never had it (obviously), primarily because I knew the glass in my hand cost over two thousand marks. An entire bottle would be considered a bargain at twelve.

"You have good taste," the prince decreed.

"I—"

"I've seen dukes sip that, set it aside, and get themselves a beer," he went on.

I made a face.

"Precisely," he drawled.

I lifted the glass his way. "Well, thank you for allowing me to experience it."

"My pleasure," he murmured.

Okay, that murmur and him saying the word "pleasure" made me press my thighs more tightly together again.

I never in my life thought I'd think this, but now that I'd met him, I needed to know how fast I could get away from him.

"Are you here for a celebration?" he inquired.

Of course he would assume I wasn't a regular and this was a special night out.

Then again, it would be easy for him to assume if he was and had never seen me there.

"Of a sort," I mumbled and took another sip of the amazing champagne.

"What are you celebrating?" he asked.

I couldn't tell him I was celebrating releasing myself from the confines of my own home where I'd barred myself due to loss, fear and grieving. I'd gone the TMI route that night already, and anyway, it wasn't any of his business.

"My friend finding a male to love," I replied.

"Which friend would that be, and which of those males is she falling in love with?"

I turned my head to look across to the bar.

Bash and Tay had changed positions, thank goodness, with Bash talking to Cat, and Tay to Gayle.

However, both my gals were not paying a lick of attention to the handsome males chatting them up. They were failing miserably at surreptitiously watching the prince and me.

I needed to give them lessons.

"Catla, I hope," I said, and took another sip of champagne.

"And she's the half demon, or the half fae?"

"Demon," I said shortly.

"She looks familiar. She also looks to have Truelock blood."

"That's because she's Mammon Truelock's daughter," I told the table in front of me.

"I know Mammon well, I've yet to meet his daughter."

"I could arrange that pretty easily," I offered the table.

"I could as well."

"I'm sure," I muttered and took another sip.

"Is there a reason you're avoiding looking at me?" he asked.

I turned to him. "Not really. Though, even if I did, I can't actually *see* you."

He shifted so he was turned more fully toward me, and his entire magnificent face, not just the profile, was exposed to me.

At being confronted with it, I tried not to gasp and ended up making a mew I was pretty sure he heard, seeing as, unlike me, he did still have his beast, and they helped you do things like that.

What made me surer was the way his full, perfect lips tipped up in a sexy, smirky smile.

"Better?" he asked smugly, and he was smug because he knew it so much was, and absolutely was not.

"Yes, thank you," I answered prudishly.

"I never answered you," he stated.

"Answered me?"

"About curtsying to me at Captain Jacques's."

I didn't catch my lip curling fast enough, which made his smug, smirky, sexy smile come back.

"Yes," he carried on. "It's in public, and any time you're in public, you must adhere to protocol."

"I see."

"However," he purred, his voice going low and changing from silk to velvet, "say you were walking into my bedroom, and it was just you and me, it would be entirely unnecessary."

Hang on...

What?

Oh.

My.

Gods.

I was wishing for the shadows back when I watched his eyes make their lazy way down my body to my shoes before he said, "In fact, it's highly likely I'd find myself bowing to you."

My nipples peaked and I was pretty sure I made another mew.

He gaze locked on mine when he finished, "Though, we'll have to see."

Again...

What was happening?

He leaned toward me.

I didn't know what to do, throw myself at him, recoil, or run.

But by heaven and hellfire, seeing him even closer, he was downright *poetic.*

"Laura, when I rise, you rise," he said softly.

"Oh-okay."

"Allain will arrange for your protocol instruction."

"I...my..." I started blinking again. "Wait, what?"

His eyes moved over my face, and the way the light and shadows played with them, I couldn't see their famous color.

"You aren't what I expected," he murmured musingly.

Before I could ask after that, he stood.

I'd learned my lesson, so I instantly set my glass to the table and stood with him.

Once I gained my feet, he swept up my hand and brushed my knuckles with his lips in a move so old-fashioned and gallant, mine parted. I stared at his glorious head bent over my hand, my phantom beast nestled and cooed, and my legs threatened to cease holding me up.

Then without another word, or even a scant glance, Prince Aleksei dropped my hand and walked away.

CHAPTER 4
HERE

She had the male in her maw, shaking him viciously before she tossed him to the side, his body breaking grotesquely against the bricks of the wall of the alley.
She whipped her head toward the other one.
While she'd been dealing with the first, he'd produced a weapon.
It was aimed at her.
She went to attack...
No.
To defend.
To defend me.
I saw the look in his eye.
He wasn't afraid.
He wasn't fleeing.
The other one was a sacrifice.
This one...
He was here to do just this.
"No!" I shrieked, tucked protectively in her broad breast, powerless to stop her.
The weapon fired.
And all turned black.

I jerked awake, feeling hot, sweaty, scared.
All familiar.
Too familiar.

My bedroom was not dark. With the half-wall, continuous slant of windows that connected to the roof allowing the city lights to drift in, it was never dark, unless I activated the privacy shields.

I didn't like to do that.

Not anymore.

The alley they'd dragged me in had been dark. Dank. Reeking.

I used to set privacy at sixty percent when I slept, so I'd have the city, but I'd still have that cocoon of night.

Not after the incident.

Not after she was gone.

I needed the light.

I fell to my back and rubbed my chest with my hand.

The phantom wasn't there with me. It hadn't made itself known since we left the club.

As bittersweet as it was, alone in the dark of night with memories assaulting me, I could use her.

The nightmares came too often. I was beginning to worry it wasn't healthy.

My gals were worried too.

Gayliliel had suggested I speak to a counselor.

Catla had suggested a visit to a clinic for a memory scrub and went so far as to talk to Mr. Truelock about it, whereupon he agreed to pay for it (he really did like me...and Gayle).

I couldn't scrub that memory though. As hideous as it was, it was the last moment we had together.

It was her doing what she did for me.

It was her taking care of me.

To her dying breath.

My own breath hitched, and I sent three cats flying as I pulled the covers off me.

I shuffled out of my bedroom into the living area.

My place was the top floor of a Pre-Unification warehouse. Spacious, with the whole back wall being that slant of windows that started at about four feet up. Occupying the entire floor under it was my studio. The floor under that, the one at ground level, was divided into two. It housed a pizzeria and a mystic sanctum run by a witch named Alchemy, who I suspected was just a human, but I didn't think she was a scammer. Instead, she wanted to have magic so much she convinced herself she did and was able to convince other people of the same.

Bottom line with Alchemy, her sanctum rocked. There might not be any actual mystical healing happening, but I'd used her before, and she gave great vibe.

Maybe it was time for another visit.

I went to the open kitchen and got myself a glass of water.

I stood at the counter looking out the windows, where, across the road there was a broken block that contained a row of six Pre-Unification, three-story brownstones, and next to those, a Post-Crash, personality-less, five-story cube filled with micro-flats.

Over the last few years, my neighborhood had begun shifting.

Island living off the coast had almost always been out of everyone's but the elite of the elite's price range, this being the reason it was populated by castles, villas, mansions and a gamut of really exclusive (but excellent) shopping and eateries.

Now uptown was becoming too expensive for most as well.

So downtown they went, buying up old brownstones or blocks of micro-flats and renovating them.

I didn't pay attention, but I suspected, instead of fifty units in that cube, there were now maybe ten, because there were always noisy construction crafts and rubbish tips lining the road, workers inside undoubtedly tearing down walls and making micro, macro.

Human, fae, demon, witch, conjurer, we seemed to always be searching for more space.

As I sipped my water, it wasn't hard to turn my attention from the nightmare to the night.

I rested a hip against the counter and glanced behind me at the seating area where I'd left the two empty bottles of wine and three glasses, the detritus of Gayle, Cat and I dissecting and re-dissecting every second I spent with Prince Aleksei (and incidentally, not coming up with any answers to his and my short, bizarre tête-à-tête).

We'd left the club almost immediately after Prince Aleksei left me because we had a ton of dissecting to do, and we didn't want anyone to hear it.

Although we came up with no answers, I did learn from Cat that royal etiquette was expected to be observed, no matter where you were.

"King Fillion, but more, Queen Calisa are really into that shit," she said.

She would know. She'd actually met King Fillion and had been presented to Queen Calisa and served two seasons at court in her seventeenth and eighteenth years. She'd also been at a weekend house party at Capice Point with Princess Aleece and had been propositioned by Prince Timothee in an ante-tent during a laser joust (she had declined, but only because he was more than mildly inebriated at the time, and if she went there with him, she wanted him to remember it).

I still thought all of that protocol nonsense was archaic.

Yes, I (along with everyone else) had seen Prince Aleksei's beast soaring over the midnight waters around Celestial Palace, and his beast was as handsome, huge and powerful as Prince Aleksei, with his gleaming blue-black scales, purple-hued webbed wings and abundance of cruel spikes.

Anyone with an imagination could hark back centuries and see that beast laying claim to Night's Fall in a manner no one would challenge him, and if they did, they'd be reduced to ash in purple fire.

But it wasn't that way anymore.

Constant war, death, intrigue, broken accords and treachery had given way to the establishment of the Four Realms, the slender strip of a neutral Center and diplomacy.

So sure, sometimes that diplomacy was tenuous and other times heated.

But there had been peace among the realms for decades.

And at this juncture, each realm had stood solid under their royal claims for centuries.

The Center, where nearly everyone who lived there was involved in governance and inter-realm relations, was where ambassadors debated, trade deals were forged, and compromises were sought for grievances. Onward from that, each realm had its own government, both realm-wide and locally.

On the other hand, in the lands of Night's Fall, Dawn's Break, Sky's Edge and Land's End, kings and queens held state dinners, hosted elaborate balls and provided pomp, circumstance and militantly guarded tradition.

Not in generations had anyone in the Celestial Palace shed blood or sacrificed anything for the glory of Night's Fall. And although the king, all three princes and the princess were delegates to the Center, and the king's word held great weight, each province, parish or county of each realm had an elected official at the Center, so the royal family was not our only representation.

No.

They were merely born royals; they hadn't done anything to earn their status or the respect they thought it demanded.

I didn't argue this with Catla. She was a royalist, through to the bone.

Gayliliel didn't really care one way or the other, but if forced to lean in a direction, I knew she'd lean toward the royals because she adored pageantry...and gossip.

I would have done the same, until I was forced to curtsy to a male who was just a male, doing this with the attention of a room full of rich people, and then made to feel like a fool by him.

A shadowy streak jumped up to the counter from the floor, and my flame-point Comet asked, "Meow?"

"No, it's not time for breakfast."

"Meow," he disagreed.

"I think you've well learned these last few months, just because I'm awake, it doesn't mean you get food."

"Meow!"

I set the glass aside and took hold of my cat, tucking him under my arm.

Comet wasn't a fan of being held (because usually, me carting his heft around induced me to telling him he was too chonky), and therefore his next, "*Meow!*" was filled with insult.

As usual, I ignored it, and we went to bed. The minute we were ensconced, he shared he was still nursing his affront by jumping away.

Nova, my cuddle muffin, took his place, already purring.

I rolled into her, stroking.

She made biscuits on the duvet.

I sighed and forced my eyes closed.

I had Gayle. Cat. Monique. Lancet (the designer who'd made my pink dress). Other friends. Comet and Nova and their brother, Jupiter.

I was not alone.

And yet, I so very much was in a way I always would be.

Forever.

At the pain of that thought, I opened my eyes, Nova's affectionate drone humming in my ears.

"Just tonight, baby," I whispered to my cat. "But this is the last time. I can feel sorry for myself tonight. Tomorrow will be the day after I met the True Heir to the realm. Sure, it had been annoying, and weird, but he's even better looking in person than in digital, and it's a story I can tell for the rest of my life. And tomorrow will be the day after I pulled myself together and got back out into the world, which meant I had the opportunity to meet the True Heir, even if it was in an annoying and weird way."

I cuddled Nova closer, and my voice dipped lower.

"They took her, they didn't take me," I mumbled. "She made it so I'm still here. I owe it to her to be *here*, not back there, when she sacrificed herself for me."

Nova head butted my chin.

"Yeah," I murmured. "We miss her. But we're here." I drew in a breath to steady my emotions and repeated, "We're here."

Nova continued to knead and purr.

I continued to feel sorry for myself and listen to her.

Eventually I fell asleep.

It wouldn't be long before someone woke me up.

CHAPTER 5
NO CONTACT

My space might have been Pre-Uni, but it had still been modernized. There was a welcome kiosk in the vestibule. And someone was in it, ringing up to my flat.

I turned to the bed display on my nightstand and saw it was before seven in the morning.

Okay.

I could see one of my friends hearing about my chat with Prince Aleksei and showing up to get all the hot deets, but I wished they'd waited another five hours…or just sent an excited text comm.

Not wanting to give whoever it was a visual of me lying in bed, I didn't answer the ring on my nightstand display.

I shoved the covers aside, feeling foggy and vaguely nauseous from lack of sleep.

I shambled to the door, calling, "Okay, okay, I'm coming!" even though another part of the warehouse's modernization had been sound and scent proofing, and whoever was visiting was two floors down. I waved a hand in front of the display beside the door, and ordered, "Activate camera."

The blank window shifted to a digital of Allain, the prince's whatever he was.

I stared at the display.

"Meow!" Comet demanded his breakfast.

Allain moved and the ringer went again.

Through stiff lips, I ordered, "Engage welcome." I then said, "Can I help you?"

Allain tipped his head back so I received his full face in the camera.

"I come at behest of the prince."

Behest?

Who talked like that?

Yeesh. This dude was a trip.

"It's early. I'm in my pajamas," I told him.

"It's seven in the morning, most of the Realm is either at school, at work or on their way to work."

"Lucky me, I work from home and make my own hours."

Sometimes.

"We can carry on this conversation with me in the vestibule, or you can allow me up," he parried. "Your apparel is of no consequence to me. However, the prince does wish for me to leave you with something." A pause before, "I won't be long."

Could I get out of this?

If I refused him entry, would royal guards come storming in to force me to talk to this guy and accept whatever the prince wanted to leave me?

I didn't suspect they'd go that far.

No, what I said next was all about my infernal curiosity.

"Allow entry." I watched Allain move into the stairway after my command gave him access. "Open door," I finished.

The locks could be heard disengaging and my door slid into its side panel.

Not long later, Allain marched in, his gaze moving swiftly, taking in his surroundings, before he turned to me.

"Mistress Laura," he greeted.

Not that crap again.

"Really, you can call me—"

While I spoke, even if I hadn't had the opportunity to say many words, he opened the leather satchel that rested against his hip and pulled out a tablet.

And he interrupted me when he shoved it toward me.

Automatically, my hands moved to take it, but I nearly bobbled it, for the instant my hands were close, he let go, so I had to catch it.

I stared, knowing it was DY5000XX, the most expensive tablet on the market and one I'd been wanting to buy, even if I knew I could never afford it.

The resolution of the display was second to none. The computing was warp speed. The memory capacity was astronomical. Every design I drew could be stored on one of those tablets, even in 3-D and with motion simulation, regardless of how memory-heavy they were, without slowing its processing.

It also had send, receive, pic, vid, magnifying, telescopic, holo, tracing and tracking capabilities.

Yes, I said *holo* capabilities!

"The password for that tablet is 'pink,'" Allain informed me. "You can change it to what you wish after you gain entry. Your schedule is in the calendar. It took some doing, but you'll be with Madam Garwah for training. She's by far the best, knows centuries of royal etiquette, and she trained Queen Calisa herself."

I said nothing, just stood in my jammies staring at him.

He continued speaking.

"Considering you have employment, classes will be in the evenings. They will, of course, be interrupted by any engagements made with you by His Royal Highness."

I felt my brows wing up, but I still could find no words.

Allain pulled out another tablet. It wasn't a DY5000XX, but it wasn't shabby either (if you're curious, it was a DS3500Pro).

"Now, I have a few things that need to be sorted," he declared.

I opened my mouth, to say what, I had no idea, but it would be something regarding asking after what the heck he was on about.

He got there before me.

"It's established you have no dealings with your parents."

My middle swayed back like I'd been hit by a wave.

How did he know that?

He looked from his tablet to me. "However, you haven't officially filed for no contact. Do you wish to do so?"

I didn't even have a chance to open my mouth (not that I would, I was still stunned), before he went on.

"And before you answer, it's recommended by the Palace that you do. Your sires have no offences on record, outside your father being flagged by His Majesty's Revenue Department for underpayment of taxes. Your father fought this. He lost. He filed his official displeasure, which is, obviously, on record, but he was refused reevaluation. He then missed the three initial payments, until incarceration was threatened, and then he began paying. This isn't good, but it isn't dire. However, we're operating under the assumption that, since you have not logged time with them, and they have also not logged time with you, there's some issue that's lasted at least thirteen years. Rather than there being an attempt at reconciliation, considering what's to come, which makes you vulnerable to emotional manipulation due to lofty connections, we recommend an official filing."

Logged time?

Boy, I was seeing I might need to message my province rep to share my displeasure about the Trace and Log Law which allowed the government to collect data on where your crafts went, as well as any Palm, tablet and portable comp units registered to you, because really...it was none of their danged business.

Sure, when the whole thing went down, they'd said they'd only use this data during criminal investigations, and then only after a magistrate provided a warrant after receiving probable cause.

But obviously, that was not the case.

Allain turned his tablet toward me and carried on. "You can do that by signing here, and it will be filed, retroactive to the date of your seventeenth birthday, so they, or anyone who might dredge up the order, can be under no mistaken impression about how you regard them."

"What's going on?" I finally asked.

His dark brows formed a heavy V between his eyes, and he repeated, "What's going on?"

"Yes. Why are you here? Why are you invading my privacy, physically and otherwise?"

The V got even heavier, but it was added to an expression on his face that did not hide he thought I was a moron.

"Why? Obviously because the prince intends to court you."

What?

Whoa!

My mouth dropped open, and such was my shock, I didn't close it.

"Naturally, as that's the case, you'd be vetted," Allain continued.

The words were squeaky when I asked, "The prince intends to court me?"

Allain crossed his arms on his broad chest, still holding the tablet, and declared, "He made that clear last night."

"He did not."

"He most certainly did."

"When?"

Now he appeared like he didn't think I was a moron, but instead, maybe touched.

"The moment you walked into the club."

Oh my gods.

Prince Aleksei had been staring at me from the moment I walked in.

Shit, the heat coming off you is mately.

And he'd marked me!

I hadn't even met the male *and he'd marked me*!

My voice sounded choked when I noted, "He's very decisive."

Allain uncrossed his arms from his chest and proffered his tablet to me again, muttering, "Get used to that."

"I will assert the fact he did not make it clear he intended to court me," I stated.

"He did."

"Did not."

"He very much did."

"No, he did not!" I snapped.

Definitely he thought I was touched with the way he was regarding me, and the manner in which he asked, "Do you...not want him to court you?"

Of course I did. It had been my heart's desire from when I was six years old. By all the levels of hell, it was every girl's heart's desire.

And...I didn't know.

He was arrogant and elitist.

And what could come of it?

Not much.

Though, the champagne was pretty awesome.

And, of course, the small fact the prince was ludicrously gorgeous.

"Well?" Allain prompted impatiently.

I threw up my hands. "I don't know. It never occurred to me this was in the cards. Our conversation was strange, at best."

Though, the bedroom comment was not at all veiled.

I just thought he was playing games with me.

"It was short," I went on. "And then it was over very abruptly."

Allain sniffed. "He does not relay his innermost thoughts and feelings to me, but one can assume he did not expect to meet you last night, and he had other plans he couldn't avoid. So he made his intentions known, and now I'm here to move things forward."

What an astronomical trip, sending your lackey to "move things forward" with a female you intended to court.

"What if I don't want things to move forward?" I queried.

He gaped at me.

Honestly?

I could see that reaction.

I drew breath into my nose and straightened my spine. "I can't make this decision on the fly. I need time to think about it."

He dropped his gaze blankly down to his tablet, mumbling, "We have other things to go over."

"You can share all about how you invaded my privacy when I've made my decision," I announced.

His attention returned to me, and his eyes narrowed. "You do know I'm talking about Prince Aleksei, don't you?"

"Of course I know that," I replied curtly.

"This makes an odd kind of sense," he said like he was talking to himself. "It would, of course, be an unusual female."

"I'm not an unusual female," I retorted. "I'm actually a very usual one. I'm just not used to people digging into my life, waking me up in the wee hours of the morning for unexpected visits and telling me what to do. Nor am I used to princes of any realm sending their...no offense, but whatever you are to share with me they want to court me." I decided to drive one of my points home. "Again, in the wee hours of the morning."

All of a sudden, his demeanor changed from churlish and perplexed to the dawn of understanding, a light twinkling in his eyes.

"I will inform the prince that you need time to consider his suit. When shall I tell him he'll have his response? Twenty-four hours? Forty-eight?"

I shook my head.

I wasn't even sure I was fully awake. I definitely hadn't had enough sleep.

And I absolutely was in no state to make a decision like this.

Seriously, me and the gals would need a lot more than two bottles of wine to get through this mess.

Though, truthfully, I knew their answers.

Catla, an unqualified *YES!*

Gayliliel, a less loud, but still unqualified *yes*.

Monique, a definitive, *yes*, with the addition of, *why in all the realms did you take even a second to answer affirmatively*?

But, with regard to the pursuit of Prince Aleksei—I never thought I'd think this, and if I did, I would expect when I thought it my brain would catch fire—I wasn't so sure.

"I'll know when I know," I replied. "Is there some way to get word to you?"

"My contact information is on your tablet."

"Great."

"As is His Royal Highness's. Direct access, office and Palm. His assistant's information is also provided, and if you can't get to him directly, she'll get him for you. Her name is Muriel."

She'll get him for you.

Like, I was important.

Like, all I had to do was reach out, and he'd drop everything and take my comm.

The tablet in my hand suddenly felt like it was too hot to hold.

"Really?" I breathed.

"You *will* need to talk to get to know one another," he remarked.

My gaze drifted down to the tech in my hand.

Allain tucked his tablet back into his satchel and made his way to the door.

Woodenly, I shifted to watch him go.

He stopped at the still open door and turned back to me. "One warning. Prince Aleksei is not a man to wait on anyone's whim."

I wondered if Princess Anna found that out the hard way.

I nodded.

"This is most interesting," he murmured.

He could say that again.

With that, he disappeared.

CHAPTER 6

FIVE HOURS

I sat on my couch surrounded by fabric swatches and five old-world paper sketchpads (they didn't come cheap, but they were how I preferred to start with preliminary designs), three of which were being used as post-breakfast nap beds by one flame-point, one cream-point and one blue-point ball of fluff (though, Comet's ball was a lot bigger than the other two).

It was lunchtime, and I was debating whether or not to use the gals' lunch hours for a conference comm to discuss Allain's visit.

However, as much as I needed to hash this out (and I needed that badly), I didn't want to interrupt them at work.

With the showing coming up fast, Cat would be super busy. Gayle was up to her neck in an upcoming rollout of a huge ad campaign her company had dumped a ton of money into. And Monique, one of the top aestheticians in the city of Nocturn, was on a mission to do some renovations to her flat (this being why she wasn't with us last night—she had a late client and then would be "In my bath pod for two hours" (her words)), and as such, would be covered in clients.

No, it was better to do the conference comm after work when we had plenty of time to suss it all out.

Though, it was killing me to wait.

I sipped coffee (my fourth cup, I'd decided hyper-caffeination was the best way to go after my sleepless night and inexplicable morning) and tipped my head down to the new tablet sitting nestled on the crossed legs of my lap.

"Screen engage," I murmured.

The screen came up to where I left it (obviously, I'd set up voice acknowledgement, but for some reason, I hadn't changed the password).

It was the contact list.

At the top, it said HRH Prince Aleksei, and then there were two sequences, one labeled Office, one labeled Palm, with a subcategory of Muriel, Personal Assistant to HRH Prince Aleksei and again with Office and Palm. Under that was Allain, Royal Aide to HRH Prince Aleksei (so that was what he was). And he had three sequences: Office, Palm and Urgent.

I couldn't imagine what would ever be urgent, but I was sensing that Allain was a thorough kind of human.

"Holo conference," I mumbled my decision about what to do with the girls that evening, moving to reach to my Palm so I could sync it with the tablet, which, among other things, would enter my friends' sequences. Then, I could send them a text comm to set it up.

While doing this, my ringer from the vestibule went again.

Ugh!

Well, that twenty-four to forty-eight hours didn't last long.

It didn't surprise me that Prince Aleksei might be impatient (or even insulted), and he'd send his aide to speed things up (or tell me off).

But it did annoy me.

I set the tablet aside, snatched up my Palm and snapped, "Engage vestibule," then immediately continued, "Forty-eight hours isn't what it used..."

I trailed off.

Because on the screen I saw HRH Prince Aleksei himself standing in the vestibule, staring right at the camera.

And if that wasn't enough to strike me mute, the silken cords of his voice drifted around me as he stated, "I was hoping to convince you only to take five."

By the gods.

The True Heir was in my vestibule.

The prince was *here*.

"I—"

The one syllable came out strangled, so it was fortunate he interrupted me by commanding, "Laura, let me in."

"Allow entry," I pushed out.

He disappeared off camera and I sat frozen.

Then I leaped off the couch, sending three cats flying, and raced to the bathroom.

I looked in the mirror.

My blonde hair was pulled back in a haphazard ponytail, the haphazard part being tendrils falling around my face and neck.

I tried to tell myself it looked sexy-messy-cute, but I wasn't quite able to convince myself of that.

I also didn't have that first swipe of cosmetics on.

I was one of those gals who swung both ways.

I could go cosmetics-free (say, if I was nipping out to get a croissant and coffee from Mr. Tanugu), or I could go hog wild (I'd splurged on one of the best cosme-masks on the market, but I also had the brushes, sponges, pots, bottles and palettes, because sometimes, I liked to paint my own face).

Thus, a clean face didn't bother me (much).

I still would prefer to be made up for a visit from the prince.

And I was wearing an ivory lounge outfit with a cropped, heavy-knit top that wasn't much to look at from the front but had peekaboo overlapping panels at the back that made it kind of sexy. On my bottom half were drawstring joggers in matching material that were just not much (though I liked to think they did nice things for my behind).

The outfit had been a gift from Ernesta Transcendica after I'd used several pieces of hers in *Rain and Pavements* (and put her on the map, if I did say so myself, but whoever said it, it would be true, Princess Aleece herself (oh, and Princess Anna too) had attended Ernesta's last three runway shows, so there was that). In other words, it was a great set.

But it wasn't what you'd want to entertain a prince in.

I didn't have time to slap on my cosme-mask, even on a setting of "natural, casual, at home," which only took five minutes. I definitely didn't have time to don my mane-mate to do something with my hair.

The door ringer sounded.

Shit, I forgot to open the door.

Okay, okay, okay.

I would have to do this as just me.

I raced out of the bathroom, calling, "Open door."

It did its thing, and Prince Aleksei sauntered in.

I rocked to a halt, having no choice but to allow my brain and body to respond to his presence in my space. It did this by bolting through me, sparking a myriad of pleasant, terrifying and stunned embers that burned, shook and soothed every inch of me.

His suit was black, his shirt blue-black, both attractive, both clearly tailored for him, both in material I might weep if I ever had the opportunity to work with it.

His thick black hair was brushing his collar and curving around his ear in a way my finger itched to trace that delectable lock.

No. It wasn't an itch.

It was a longing.

His head turned my way, and my breath caught.

It was the first time I'd truly seen his famous eyes, no shadow obscuring their direct hit, which was what it felt like.

Like I'd been struck by a laser stream.

They were what identified him as the first True Heir of the realm in two centuries.

I remembered when the change had happened for him (he'd been thirteen, so I'd been nine). I also remembered the exhilarated announcement from the Palace. And I remembered the week of celebrations it had brought on for the entire realm.

Right now, they were a cloudy sky-blue.

The exact color of the sky outside.

They would change to whatever the color of the sky was, that being the magic that denoted a True Heir.

The current color seemed stark in his tanned face, and by Beelzebub, it was *astonishing*.

That was laser hit one.

Laser hit two was his sheer size.

I knew he was tall and built, you couldn't miss it in his public appearances, how he often dwarfed anyone around him.

But last night, I'd been so muddled by all that was happening, it hadn't struck me just how much of him there was.

And how delicious was every inch.

It was then, the smell permeated the tumbles of my brain.

My gaze jolted down to his hands.

In one, his fingers were wrapped around the handle of a drink carrier that held two beverages.

In the other was a bag printed in well-known blue and yellow stripes.

He lifted the bag, turning it my way, exposing the illustration on the broad side of the peg-legged, wild-haired, patch-eyed, maniacally grinning Captain Jacques of Captain Jacques's Fish and Chips.

As my stupefied gaze took in Captain Jacques, Prince Aleksei's silk wove around me. "I thought we'd share lunch."

I forced my eyes to his. "You...you bought me Captain Jacques's?"

"You piqued my curiosity."

Right.

Well.

Dang.

That was...

Holy Lilith.

It was sweet, and...and...

Actually *cute*.

Uh...

Wow.

Prince Aleksei could be *cute*.

He glanced around my space, and more embers sparked, these tense and anxious.

My loft was large, seeing as it took up the whole floor.

And it was every inch *me*.

What it was not, was elegant or palatial.

Along the left side of the loft was my bathroom, which had doors to the main space and to my closet, something that separated it from my bedroom.

In front of that wall was my dining room table, an oval of glass over curved lines of wood slashing in various ways to support it. It hosted eight comfortable, upholstered chairs, those also a study of curves, in cream. Over this, three crystal-covered lamp drones hovered, currently unlit.

To the back was a long bar with four mismatched stools on the outside, a variety of cookware hanging from a rack above it. Opposite, there was a long counter and the uninterrupted slant of windows (which I now saw, with a sinking stomach, needed to be cleaned, inside and out). All of this made up my kitchen.

The middle of the space was taken up with my wide, deep couch and four armchairs arranged around a circular table.

At the corner back right, facing the kitchen (and the windows) was a big, old-fashioned drafting desk for use when I wanted to sit at one and work, but not go down to my studio. The wings to its sides and the trays stationed under it were cluttered with a disorganized rainbow of colored pencils and pens.

At the corner right front windows, there was a chaise longue that had an elaborate gold hook lamp drone drifting above it, a colorful silk, tasseled shawl thrown over it, and an antique, tri-legged table at its side.

There were various rugs of differing sizes and styles under these furniture arrangements or simply scattered about willy-nilly, these covering the wood-planked floors.

And the right-side wall had its entire lower half covered in built-in shelves, where I stored my small (but growing, and very precious) collection of real books (the ones made of paper), along with bits and pieces I'd found that intrigued me or I thought were pretty.

Sitting on top of these, between the windows, were two large shadow-boxes, one displaying the famous, slinky dress the character Reeva wore in *Rain and Pavements*, a garment of my own design that had become iconic to that show. The other held the vintage-inspired undergarments the character Porcelain wore in the famous sex scene in *Sheets* (something I'd also designed).

Across from this, adorning the wall by the dining room table, also in a shadow box, was the massive gown I'd created for *The Sunny Glade*. The intricate embroidery, tiny lace ruffles, satin bows, delicate piping, slender velvet belt with its oval diamanté fastener and extraordinary seam work, draping and ruching were what earned my first award nomination.

This dress, in the colors of a peach, from fresh to ripe, was displayed with the intricate, creamy-peach gossamer bow that had been tied around the actress's neck pinned above it, and the blushing-peach satin and grosgrain tri-cornered cap with its bruised-peach feather situated in the frame at the top.

Mr. Truelock called it a work of art, and I tended to agree. I was super proud of it.

But it wasn't a sculpture by LeMond or a watercolor by Arrivi.

"Considering the content of our repast, shall we adjourn to the couch?" Prince Aleksei suggested.

Fabulous.

I wore no cosmetics, my hair was in a ponytail, my outfit was on the lower scale of cute (until you saw the back, which he had not) *and* I was being a bad hostess.

Well, at least he didn't seem put off by my eclectic space.

"Of course," I replied, swinging an arm toward the couch in a belated invitation.

He moved that way and sat, saying, "I didn't know your preference, so I called the club and requested the manager ask the bartender who served you. He said you ordered a pink fizz. So I deduced you enjoyed sweet and tart, and brought you a grape sparkle."

Grape sparkle sodas were *my favorite*.

And the effort he put behind that wasn't cute, it was just sweet.

But...wait.

"You went *yourself* to Captain Jacques's?" I asked.

"I hovered through their flyby," he murmured, pulling one of the beverages out and setting it on the table in front of the empty side of the couch, all while I tried to wrap my mind around the idea of Prince Aleksei piloting his craft through a fast-food flyby.

He then started to unearth the food.

So, of course, Comet joined him.

And by joining him, I meant that Comet hefted his great cat weight up, perched all four paws on the prince's thigh and aimed his meddlesome, sunken nose toward the food.

"Who's this creature?" the prince asked, his attention on Comet, as it would of course be. When Comet didn't want to be ignored, he wasn't.

I headed toward the couch, offering, "You can push him off. He won't like it. But he'll eventually get over it."

He turned to me. "That's not an answer to my question."

Well then.

I sat and shared, "He's Comet. And no, as you can tell, I do not starve him, no matter what he says. And he's not allowed treats, or Dr. T will yell at us again during his annual. He's had his morning kibble. Later, he'll laze on his back while Nova and Jupiter play with the kitty-light drone, instead of joining in and getting his doctor-mandated exercise. As such, I fear I'll go into the annals of Bad Cat Moms when he gets arthritis at age four."

I was sitting as far from him as I could get, but I was close enough to see clearly as the prince wrapped his long fingers around the back of Comet's neck, and I noted through the thick, creamy fur, his thumb stroking.

Watching this, I got a melty feeling in two places. One, around the left side of my chest. The other, parts south.

Comet looked from the bag of food to the prince and stated, "Meow."

"That's not what your mother says," Prince Aleksei replied.

Terrific.

He spoke Comet.

"Meow!" Comet dissented.

"I would give you fried chicken formed in logs. But it isn't my choice. You need to talk to your mother."

Totally spoke Comet.

Comet's baby-blue eyes glared at him, then he moved them to me.

Prince Aleksei curved his hand under Comet's belly, lifted him and gently dropped him to his golden paws on the floor.

Comet tipped his grouchy face toward the prince and griped, "Meow!"

"Sorry, buddy," the prince mumbled.

Okay.

Um.

Who was this guy?

Comet decided to circle the prince's ankles in a last-ditch attempt at changing his mind while Nova decided to say hi, jumping into the space between us and peering up at him with her trusting round blue eyes and adorable scrunchy face.

"Hello there," Prince Aleksei greeted her.

It took her a second, but she was female, so that wasn't a very long second before she placed one paw on his thigh as her invitation to show some love.

He accepted and stroked her spine while he asked, "How many of these do you have?"

"Three, but don't worry. Jupiter is timid. He barely comes out even for me."

The sky of his eyes came to mine, and I felt a lazy lurch in my chest.

Oh my. Was my phantom beast back?

"Do you intend to get number four?" he inquired.

"I'd absolutely get another kitty." Or two. "But I worry Comet would eat them."

A deep, velvety chuckle rolled from his chest, and no, the phantom wasn't back. Because that lurched in my belly (okay, no, not there...full disclosure: it throbbed in regions south).

He stopped stroking Nova (who didn't mind, she never did, but then again, she was a cat and could curl into a ball and lick her paw at his hip, which was what she decided to do next). The food was exhumed, one blue-and-yellow-striped parcel for me, the other he set aside before upending the bag and a variety of sauces rained on the table.

"I didn't know what you liked, so I told them to give us two of everything," he explained.

Seriously.

He could have saved me and my gals a lot of intense dissection last night if he'd been even slightly like this guy at the club.

I tore my attention from him and looked to the sauces. Spoiled for choice, I was my usual indecisive.

But who was I kidding?

For Captain Jacques's chicken oars, it was always herbed cream sauce, and for the fries, it was garlic aioli.

I grabbed my packets, split them open, perched them in my schooner and nabbed an oar.

I was munching when the prince queried, "The fish is greasier than this?"

My gaze flew to his face to see his handsome features fixed in a picture of sheer disbelief.

I wanted to laugh, but I was horrified.

I mean, he probably frequently ate foie gras (diabolical), which wasn't that healthy.

But if he had a hankering for strawberries, they'd jet them in supersonic, fresh from Land's End.

"I could..."

I faltered as my mind mentally scanned the contents of my integrated Chill-Cupboard/Cook-Companion as to what I could program up for him.

When was the last time I'd sent in a food supply order?

"Calm, Laura," Prince Aleksei said in a low, soothing voice. "They're very good, as food like this tends to be. But they're also greasy."

"Okay," I whispered.

His eyes dropped to my mouth (and yep, more sensation in those regions south).

Fortunately, his attention slid over the seating area, and before he took another bite of his oar, he noted, "You're working."

"Yes," I said, though I wasn't working as such. I was *trying* to work. But he'd long since interrupted me before he even showed up.

He chewed, swallowed, I watched his corded throat introduce the food into his stomach, I worried his beast's sense of smell would share precisely what was happening in my regions south, and he asked, "Did I interrupt you?"

I shook my head, shaking some sense into it (I hoped) while I did.

This was just a male.

A rich one. A handsome one. And recent evidence suggested possibly even a sweet and thoughtful one.

But just a male.

"No, I'm kind of stymied."

"Not that I can help, but I'm interested. How are you stymied?"

I squinted my eyes at him. "I take it you know I'm a costume designer."

He nodded once, his gaze sharp, and I knew he was studying me closely, missing nothing. "Yes. I've had a limited brief on you."

Mm-hmm.

I decided to set that aside, for now.

"Well, I'm doing a period piece. It's early days, so I have time. A lot of pre-production stuff is going on. But part of that pre-production stuff is me giving them ideas of where I'd like to head with the design so they can sign off, and then I can get stuck in designing. And I'm not sure where to take it."

"What's the period?"

"The Troll Invasion."

He nodded again, this time more than once, "Year of the Dragon, thirteen twenty-four. Art was interesting then, most of it rough, due to the rudimentary implements and materials they had to use. I never noticed it, but I can imagine the artists didn't tend to spend a good deal of time documenting what people were wearing."

"No, I can get a sense of that," I told him. "It's the troll skin that's throwing me."

As my work had wont to do, and since we were talking about it, I got into it. I set my schooner on the table and reached for some swatches I'd been trying, and failing to make work.

I fanned out the leathery, scaly, spiky pieces in my fingers and flapped them at him.

"I've seen you and your brothers wearing the troll skins, but only in pics. The hero appears in one in the final scene, the big climax that shares he was victorious, and he has the skin to prove it. Not to mention, the SFX people need a direction to go with building the creatures. I want to get it right, but I can't get the feel of it. I just know none of these are it."

I tossed the swatches onto the table and kept blathering.

"Troll skin is so valuable, none of it's on display. I've been to the Musée de Vêtements I don't know how many times. Millions?" I asked with maybe a slight exaggeration, but I didn't expect him to answer.

I was on a roll.

"They have garments from the thirteen hundreds, even before. I'm a member, and friend of a few of the curators. They allow me to get close, touch, examine, look at the stitching, the fabric weaving, the fastenings, etcetera. But the limited troll skin they have is kept under lock and key. They never take it out. I've magnified some of the pics of you and your brothers wearing them, but, it might sound weird, I need to see it up close. Feel it, not only to feel the design I'm going to make, but how I'm going to create the textile to make it."

"Laura."

My name was not only human, but old-fashioned. I'd never really liked it. I thought it was feminine, but plain.

Sliding along Prince Aleksei's silk to my ears, it was the most beautiful name I ever heard.

I looked from the swatches to him.

He said nothing.

I said nothing.

He tipped his head to the side, but still said nothing.

"What?" I asked.

"I know someone who could not only allow you access to a troll skin, but also allow you to touch it."

Was he...?

Holy Hecate!

"Would you...you would *do that*?"

His beautiful full lips curved upward. "Of course."

"That would be...it'd be...I can't..." Pull yourself together, Laura! "That would be amazing, your, uh...highness. I would sign something if you need me to. I won't take pics, obviously. I would never do anything to harm—"

"Aleksei."

"Sorry?"

"My name is Aleksei, Laura."

Why was he telling me that?

"I know."

"You called me your highness."

"Yes, because you're that too."

"We're alone, in your home. There are no formalities here, so that isn't necessary."

"Oh. Right," I mumbled.

Now, his full lips twitched. "Like, you didn't curtsy to me when I walked in."

Whoops!

"That was more about me being surprised you were here," I explained.

"The element of surprise is often a useful tool."

I'd never used it, but his recent use of it certainly worked for him.

"I understand," he said softly, so softly, his silk became velvet again and lured me in so completely, I was riveted to everything about him.

"You understand what?" I whispered for fear I'd break his spell.

"You're frightened."

I was?

"Obviously, I don't understand from a place of actual understanding, since it's all I've ever known, but instead, from a place of empathy," he clarified. "I garner a great deal of attention. It's rare I can go anywhere without it being digitized within instants in all Four Realms. And myself, or anyone I'm with, is scrutinized and commented on with alacrity and swift judgement. This alone would give any female with even a modicum of sense, pause. One with a good deal of it would need time to consider if she wants it to be a part of her life. Along with that, there have been..."—he dipped his head to the side with a self-deprecating slant to his lips—"numerous females before you. Not to mention, I ended a highly publicized engagement not long ago."

Oh.

Okay then.

And...well, *yeah*.

That was all pretty scary.

"It's..." he seemed to be struggling, then he stated, "*difficult* for me to make this admission, but much of that, I can't protect you from. It's a large part of my duty as a royal to be seen, to be available, to be present. The extent of it is maddening, and I don't agree the media deserve every pound of my flesh, like they think they do. Nor do the beings, as loyal as I am to Night's Fall and its citizens. But I've learned in my time to find ways to keep my private life private and protect those in it. And that would, most especially, be extended to you. That said, I cannot protect you from all of it. It is their due."

It was their due?

Whose due?

Before I could ask, he said, "So, I suggest, in our beginning, we have times like this, where you can get used to me. And times, like tomorrow evening, when I take you to the Catalogues of the Palace so you can see the troll skins. In other words, times when I can be who I will be to you. Simply Aleksei."

Who I will be to you.

Simply Aleksei.

"Why did you mark me last night?" I asked quietly.

His brow furrowed in open bewilderment. "Because you're mine."

An enchanting shiver glided over me.

Because you're mine.

I wasn't.

It was well-known the royals didn't marry their mates. They didn't even seek them.

In days gone by, they married for alliances, for power, money.

More recently, it might be cynical (but the fact Queen Calisa was the top vid star of her generation, and ridiculously beautiful to boot, before she became queen (and the beautiful part held true to this day), offered evidence of this), they married for the media.

I was certain this wasn't that.

But maybe this was just a male, who was attracted to a female, and he wanted to court her.

The male just happened to be Prince Aleksei, the True Heir.

And the female, against all the odds, seemed to be me.

Perhaps it wasn't so strange, if you really thought about it.

I mean, did models, vid stars, clinically enhanced debutantes, equally clinically enhanced aristocrats and royal princesses get boring?

Maybe.

Maybe they did.

And maybe the female in a pink dress living at the top of an old warehouse with three fluffy cats was a new adventure.

Maybe, at least for a while, he wanted Captain Jacques's and to be able to be simply Aleksei.

Bottom line, he should be able to date whoever he wanted.

And I should be able to date him.

Right?

So okay, there would be no strings. No ties. No future. I had nothing to offer the Royal Family.

But he brought me a Captain Jacques's chicken schooner, for goodness' sake.

And he was Prince Aleksei, my deepest crush, right here, on my couch... with me.

So yeah.

Okay.

I could be his, for a time.

"Laura?" he called.

I pulled myself back to the place I was with him, here, in my flat, eating greasy fast food, and I reached for my schooner.

After I dipped a fry in the aioli, I said, "I guess five hours did it."

Hearing that, he smiled fully for the first time, and let me tell you, it was so glamorous, it was heart-stopping.

I doubted mine was either, but that didn't stop me from smiling back.

CHAPTER 7
DREAM

I was in my closet, and, as holograms beamed through my fabulous new tablet, so were Gayle, Cat and Monique.

"I cannot believe this is happening," Cat breathed. "I mean, Madam Garwah!" she cried. "Dad tried to get her to train me before my presentation, but her waiting list is years...*years*."

"I still cannot believe we're in holo. This is so freaking cool. I am one hundred percent asking for a DY5000 from Mom and Dad for Dead Winter," Gayle put in.

"I cannot believe I haven't taught you, no matter what, slap your cosme-mask on for a natural, day look the minute you finish brushing your teeth," Monique groused, taking us back over old territory, seeing as this was her refrain last night. "You never know what's going to happen. If you need to pop down to Mr. Tanugu's and you run into your mate. Or, I don't know, say, the *True Heir of Night's Fall shows up at your door with chicken oars*."

Monique, by the by, was a human, though she had some witch blood in her, along with some fae. This made her a wee bit magical and was one of the reasons why she was such a sought-after aesthetician.

She was also mocha-skinned, willowy, had a Nubian nose, round violet eyes that denoted the bit o' fae in her, and a head of thick, wild black curls.

And yes, I envied all of that about her.

Mon, too, came from money, but again, those humans expected their young to make their own way. And Monique, like Gayle, was all over it.

"Tell us again about how interested he was in your books," Cat urged. "I'd heard that about him. He's a collector of vintage things. It is *so mega* you two share that in common."

"Right?" Monique asked. "And the cooking thing." She turned back to me. "Who cooks anymore? You do. And I cannot *believe* the prince does too. *And* he suggested you do it together."

"What I like, outside the Captain Jacques's sitch," Gayle began, "was how into the *Glade* gown he was. I mean, he probably didn't care, but he asked about it, at length. How many males give that first crap about what your passion is? They'll go on and on about some pit ball game or ring ice match, and how fab it was they landed that huge account they'd worked so hard to get, but do they care about what you're into? *No.*"

It was the next evening, and obviously, the one before, I'd filled in the gals about my lunch with Aleksei, which did not end with the consumption of our chicken oars, but with him asking to take a tour of my loft.

And yes, he seemed really interested in all of it.

But in a little under half an hour, a craft was being sent to take me to meet Madam Garwah so I could attend my first royal protocol lesson.

In other words, I had other things on my mind.

Yeah.

I'd decided to go with this.

In for a credit, in for the entire line.

They were supposed to be helping me pick an outfit, because, after I spent an hour with Madam Garwah teaching me how to curtsy, Aleksei was picking me up to take me to dinner and then the Royal Catalogues (as per the comm I got from Allain confirming the plans Aleksei suggested).

As such, important matters were at hand.

Thus, I whirled on their 'grams and reminded them, "Stay on target, females. This is a critical decision."

"Go back to the mask, program it to cleanse your natural, night, semi-casual in pinks and have it change it to night, semi-drama, in browns and wear that chocolate jumpsuit," Monique advised.

I made a face.

Cat explained my face. "Jumpsuits are super out, Mon."

"The cleavage that one gives will never be out, Catla," Mon retorted.

Cat shook her head. "Change the face to blacks and grays, and go with the silver, faux leather pencil skirt and gray mesh top with your shiny chrome high-heeled boots."

"She doesn't want to look like a bot," Monique retorted.

Cat scowled at Monique.

Gayle chimed in. "The sheer blushy top with the medallions sewn in, and that flirty, flowery skirt that hugs your ass and thighs but has that little flippy thing at the hem. The strappy red sandals. And the pink satin trench coat. It's girlie, like you. The top is long sleeved, so it works for coming autumn, but we're still in summer, so it works for that too. And it goes with your face's current color palette and your hair being down, which looks awesome by the way. What setting did you use for that?"

"Night, casual, elegant, windswept, sophisticated, stylish, dinner date," I shared, poking the control panel with my finger, trying to find my sheer blushy top, because I was thinking Gayle was onto something.

"Holy Lilith. And the mane-mate didn't short circuit? I never put that many settings in," Cat remarked.

"Oh, queen, you have to load 'em up," Monique educated. "The more challenges you give them, the more the algorithm works for you, if you don't put it back on and change it right away."

"Really?" Cat asked.

"Totally," Monique replied.

I put the top and the skirt on up and down valet rails, setting the red sandals on the floor under them, stepped back, took one look, and shrieked, "*Eureka! Perfection!*"

Nova slunk to the shoes, sniffed one, then, starting with her ear, rubbed most of her body along it before she collapsed on both.

Nova approved too.

"I cannot believe you're going out on a date with Prince Aleksei," Monique said.

"I can't believe he brought you Captain Jacques's," Gayle said.

"I can totally believe both, because, look at her," Cat demanded.

The three holograms looked at me.

"Mm-hmm, he read you like a book," Monique declared. "That Captain Jacques move was so smooth, CJ should make it a sauce. Their flybys would be jammed, north to south, east to west, sea to sea."

"I'm still recovering from it, and it didn't even happen to me," Gayle put in.

But I had my eyes on Cat. "What do you mean, look at me?"

I got three identical eyerolls.

"Here we go again," Gayle mumbled to Cat.

"Totally not going there," Cat replied.

I turned fully to them. "I'm learning how to curtsy then going to see troll skin, something I never thought I'd touch in my life. It's the enchanted moonstone of the textile world. *And* I'm eating dinner with a guy who doesn't have an M and R in front of his name, but an *HRH. And* he might kiss me."

Gods, I hoped he kissed me.

And Gods, I was terrified of the same thing.

"So humor me," I finished. "What did you mean?"

Cat stood.

Gayle reached out to her, even if she couldn't touch her 'gram.

Cat shook her head. "Nope. No. Not gonna do it," she said irately, then bent her head, stabbed at her Palm, kept stabbing at her Palm, Monique, Gayle and I exchanged a variety of glances, and then Mr. Truelock's tall, straight body blinked into my closet.

Eek!

Well, good thing I'd put on my robe.

"Hello, my lovely," he said to me. Then he turned to Monique and Gayle. "And my other lovelies."

Lilith, but I loved this male.

"Hey, Mr. Truelock," Gayle and Monique singsonged in unison.

He smiled at them and came back to me. "Cat shared last night, and I'm absolutely delighted, but in no way surprised you turned the True Heir's eye."

Oh boy.

"Mr. Truelock—" I began.

"Quiet, darling," he said gently.

I shut up.

He moved to me and lifted his slightly-brighter-than-normal, just-that-teeniest-bit-see-through hand as if he would cup my jaw.

He couldn't, but I felt the warmth anyway.

"I would ruin them, if you'd just say the word," he whispered.

I knew who he was referring to, so I turned my head away.

But I took note, because, man, could Catla stab at a Palm, summoning Mammon Truelock like that.

"Your heart is too kind, but they deserve it," he continued.

I pulled breath into my nose and looked back at him.

"You're the best, Mr. Truelock."

"I'm actually not. I'm just a male. And a father. I know what they did to you...*here*." He moved as if he was touching my forehead, and then he dropped his hand. "It isn't real, Laura. You are beautiful. You are kind. You are immensely talented. You're not my daughter by blood, but I claim you by right, and I'm immensely proud of you. Set aside what they left you, and know, Aleksei is no fool. He sees what I see." He swept an arm out to indicate the females behind him. "What we all see, it's only you who doesn't see it."

"I think he just needs a break from all the super-celebrities," I shared.

"No one on this planet ever needs a break from basking in the best there is to have, and as such, he is *not* doing that."

Oh. My. *Gods.*

I dug Mr. Truelock *so much*.

But I couldn't do this now. He was going to make me lose it.

"Don't make me cry," I warned. "My mask gave me the perfect look."

He shot me a fatherly smile, something he did a lot, and something that never failed to move me, and then he pulled his Palm out his pocket, said, "Enjoy tonight, Laura," and he turned to the gals, "Ladies."

"Bye, Mr. Truelock," Gayle said.

"Always good to see you, Mr. Truelock," Monique said.

"See you later, Daddy," Cat said. "And thank you, you're mega."

Mr. Truelock winked at his daughter.

"Disengage," he said, and blinked out.

"That was dirty dealing," I told Cat the instant he was gone.

"You know, you have a mirror," Cat returned.

"I know I'm not...hard on the eyes," I forced out.

"Gods, she can't even say it," Gayle muttered.

Monique sighed.

"Who says, 'I'm gorgeous'? That's gross," I sniped.

"Do you know you're gorgeous?" Cat asked.

Ulk.

I decided not to reply.

Cat did not share my silence. "You're thirty years old, already lead costume designer for some big gigs, and have also already been nominated for two, I'll repeat, *two* awards. And they aren't some rinky-dink awards from some obscure digi-pane. One was the Golden Screen, and the other was the damned Edgy. Everyone watches those ceremonies on display. *Everyone.* There are parties across all Four Realms when those awards shows are on."

"Well—" I tried.

"How many jobs did you turn down to pick this one you're currently on?" Cat demanded.

"Okay, so I'm good at my job too," I snapped. "But I already know that as well."

"So what gives?" Gayle asked.

"What gives is that you all"—I circled my finger at them—"get totally weird when stuff like this comes up."

"Stuff like, something good happens to you, and we're not as surprised about it as you are?" Monique queried.

"Mon, *I'm going out on a date with the future king of Night's Fall.* Tell me that's not something to be surprised about," I retorted.

"She has me there," she mumbled to Gayle.

I looked to the ceiling and requested, "Deliver me, Beelzebub."

"He's not up there," Cat joked.

I set my glower on her.

"You deserve good things happening to you, Laura," Cat pressed.

"Yes, if beings are nice beings, everyone does," I returned.

Cat spoke on like I didn't. "And you deserve it without fighting, scratching and breaking your back working for it. Like a hot guy, prince or not, giving you an expensive glass of champagne and taking you to touch troll skin."

"I didn't say I didn't," I retorted.

"No, you didn't, but you don't believe it," Cat shot back.

"Mm-hmm," Monique hummed.

"Can we not do this now?" I requested. "I need to change. I need to accessorize. I need to program a bag switch." I shook my head. "This isn't that big of a deal. It's not like he's going to marry me. It's just a date."

"And there it is," Gayle mumbled.

"What?" I snapped.

"Who says he's not going to marry you?"

I loved them all.

I really, really did.

But they were crazy.

I threw up my hands. "By the gods! It's just a date."

"But you've already decided that's all it's going to be," Cat returned.

"He's courting me. I don't think it's all it's going to be. He's got me going to this Garwah female, so obviously, for whatever reasons he has, he wants to get to know me."

"And then what?" Monique asked.

"I don't know. I'm not thinking about that. But I'm also not dreaming up some impossible dream that I'll be wearing an extravagant Celestina gown and floating up the steps of the Star Cathedral toward a midnight mass to marry the True Heir."

"And why wouldn't you do that?" Gayle asked quietly.

Gods!

They needed to let this go!

"I don't know, Gayle, because it hurts when you don't get what you want really, really badly. It hurts a fuck of a lot," I bit.

"Oo, damn," Monique whispered. "She's cussing."

"Everybody has to dream," Gayle replied, still going quietly.

"You can. Cat can. Mon can. But I learned the hard way that if shit happens, it will. Like parents hating you only slightly less than they hate each other…and the whole world. Like you can be walking home after getting yourself a whirly-whip, be dragged into an alley and—"

"Okay, shh, okay," Cat soothed. "Don't go there, honey."

I snapped my spine straight and turned to the valet rails. "I need to change."

"We really fucked this up," Monique muttered.

They grew mercifully silent as I shrugged off my robe and headed to my plethora of bottles of perfume (yes, I was old-fashioned there too, I didn't even have any scent loaded into my bath pod).

I was perfumed, dressed, accessorized, had the bag switch programmed and was seated on my lilac velvet poof, buckling the thin straps on my shoes when Cat broke the silence.

"I just want you to think about the idea that, if this was just a date, if this was just the prince wanting a break from the monotony of his fabulous life, why he's arranged for you to go through instruction with Madam Garwah."

My head snapped up to look at her as my lungs compressed all the air out of me.

"I can guaran-damn-tee you, his aide does not call on Garwah for every female he dates," Cat continued.

"They taught you not to dream," Gayle said.

"We're just saying, maybe, just maybe, they were wrong," Cat finished it.

"Mm-hmm," Monique hummed.

And I knew, while I was getting dressed, they'd conspired their coordinated exit to punctuate this last point because, completely synchronized, once they delivered it, they all blinked out.

CHAPTER 8
SOMETHING

Shocker: Royal protocol was actually kind of interesting.

I learned this as I sat alone in a room (alone save Madam Garwah) at the middle of five desks arranged in front of a step, up on which a female who appeared a well-cared-for age of two hundred and seventy-five paced the "stage" slamming her intricately carved cane down with every other step so hard, it seemed she used it to punctuate the importance of her words.

She had silvery hair pulled back into a bun at her nape. She was wearing a dress that was very stylish...in the Year of the Dragon 2002. Her eyes were beady. Her nose hawk-like. She was excruciatingly thin and very tall. She had not bothered to visit any clinics to deal with the wrinkles that lined her face and hands. And Catla had shared the rumor that she had troll blood in her ancestry.

A lot of people claimed they had troll blood, but I'd never seen anyone who actually looked like a troll.

Including Madam Garwah.

No, she was a shifter. I couldn't get a lock on her beast, but if I had to guess, I'd say it was a snake.

So far in our session, I'd learned there were different curtsies.

During formal occasions, a very deep one for the king and queen, with your arm thrown out to the side and your head bowed (when she made me practice (over and over) I found the arm thing was good, because it helped you balance).

A less deep, but still deep one (no arm), for the princes and princess, and during less formal occasions, the same for the king and queen.

But for everyone else, you could just sort of...*bob*.

You had to wait for the king or queen to tell you to rise. But all the rest, you just did your thing and got straight again.

I'd also learned the manners of address.

His (or her) Royal Majesty for the king and queen. Your majesty would suffice.

His (or her) Royal Highness for the princes and princess. Your highness would suffice.

Your grace, for dukes, duchesses, marquesses and marchionesses.

My lord or lady for anyone else, except knights and dames. They were sir or dame.

"But those last are old school," Madam Garwah had barked, but then, she barked everything. Her manner of address had been alarming at first, until I realized that was simply how she talked. "If there's a count or baron who expects you to refer to him as 'milord,' rest assured, he's a pompous poppycock. Simply refer this matter to the prince, and he'll see to putting the male in his place straightaway."

I was kind of hoping some pompous poppycock made me call him "milord" just so I could see how Aleksei handled it.

We'd moved on to how you entered a room or sat at a table (entering a room: in order of succession, but she informed me I didn't really need to worry about this, for I'd be on Aleksei's arm; sitting a table: once the king, queen and True Heir were seated, it was free for all).

You didn't eat or drink until the king imbibed (or the queen if the king wasn't around). And you were finished when they were if you were taking a meal with them ("But never you mind, both King Fillion and Queen Calisa have made an art of lingering over meals so their guests can get their fill.")

It was all ridiculous, of course, but still fascinating.

"So, it's like a constant reminder that you're in the presence of your leader," I stated. "Something, way back when, they had to do, because if someone questioned the leader, things got real, as in assassination attempts, coups and wars breaking out. All of this was an effort to control even the subconscious, so in every way, from entering a room to how you addressed them to when you had to stop eating, you knew who the boss was."

Madam Garwah stopped pacing and banging her cane and whirled toward me.

Once she did, her piercing eyes took their time examining me, and I couldn't be sure, but it seemed like she was a good deal more interested than she had been for the last forty-five minutes.

"Precisely," she decreed.

"And now it serves what purpose?" I queried.

She squinted her eyes. "I beg your pardon?"

I tossed up a hand. "Well, we vote for our representatives at Central. And in our parishes. Every realm has a monarchy, but we're all democracies. The vast majority of people will never meet a royal, or even an aristocrat."

She rocked back, situated her cane dead center in front of her and placed both hands one on top of the other on the carved dragon head at the pinnacle. "Ah, the world is more civilized, so we no longer need to adhere to the civilities."

"Is it a civility to expect someone to bow to you?"

"Is it not true that Night's Fall and Sky's Edge were locked in brutal war for four centuries?" she retorted. "And even during the period of Great Peace, those of the Edge picked at our borders constantly, to the point they eventually broke that Great Peace."

"Our last war ended in 1932," I replied. "Nearly two hundred years ago."

"And do you not think the True Heir annihilating their king and much of his castle to end that constant conflict is not something that still burrs under the skin of those that live in the Edge?"

Was she for real?

"Are you saying you think there's a possibility that some lunatic has designs on harming the Royal Family because those of the Edge are still smarting after we ultimately spanked their behinds because they reneged on an agreement after they used our dragons to conquer the trolls who had all but vanquished them nearly eight hundred years ago?"

"I'm saying *they* don't believe they reneged on anything at all, hence six hundred years of war and skirmishes between our realms," she shot back.

"And curtsying keeps that in check?"

"Regardless of our modern weaponry, the dragons would fly if anything happened to King Fillion."

They absolutely would.

"And again, curtsying keeps that in check?"

"It is not the male," she barked more sharply this time. "It is *the throne*. It is the history. It is the idea. It's the blood, shed and drawn. It is the males and females who shaped this realm, their bravery, their sacrifice, their ambition, their foibles, their failures, their corrections. A weaker throne might mean what we know as Night's Fall would not even exist. We've had good rulers, and bad. It is not one male, or female, who made us what we are. It is all of them, their actions, their decisions, their loyalty. And as a collection, *that* is the throne. *That* is what you curtsy to. And *that* show of respect is how those of the Edge know the citizens of the Fall are loyal."

"Which makes others hesitate to pull anything, because we'd all go batcrap crazy if they did."

"Indeed," she sniffed. "Our king, our queen, our True Heir, all of them are the personification of the totality of our realm. As such, they are elevated as representations of Night's Fall. No. They *are* Night's Fall. So, they are untouchable. As such, if someone would wish to enrage the entirety of a nation, draw them into conflict, inflict the gravest insult, who would they select to bring low? A citizen would anger us, but taking aim at the *Fall* would be setting your sights on *the throne*."

Oh yeah.

This protocol stuff was totally interesting.

It was also super scary, because obviously, in the grand scheme of the general crazies that roamed around and foreign policy's tendency to get iffy, you understand in a vague way that there were threats to the Royal Family.

But now that I knew one personally, and was coming to like him, I wasn't a big fan of this at all.

Suddenly, her ramrod-straight back went ramrod straighter, doing this before I heard most of her bones crackling as she dropped into a curtsy.

I got up from my desk, turned, and saw Aleksei leaning on the open doorjamb.

Gods, he sure was hot standing in that doorjamb. He looked like he could hold up the entire building.

Nevertheless, I sighed and dropped into a curtsy too.

When I rose, I noted his eyes dancing and one side of his lips was hitched up as he strolled into the room.

"As ever, an honor, your highness," Madam Garwah said (and yes, it was still a bark, a quieter one, but one nonetheless).

"Is my female causing you problems with her disrespect for tradition?" he asked, the smooth of his voice rippling with amusement as he approached the stage.

"Not at all, Prince Aleksei," she responded, and she sounded like it wasn't a lie.

He offered his hand.

She put hers in his.

He squeezed it and dropped his head in a modified bow.

She preened.

Again, he could be sweet and cute.

He let her go and came to me.

And then he was not cute, instead he was just...*everything*.

His eyes were now night blue.

Seriously, that was so *amazing*.

He offered his hand.

I put mine in it.

He didn't take his eyes off me as he raised it to his lips and brushed them against my knuckles.

I wobbled on my heels and bit my lip.

"Good evening, Laura," he murmured, causing another wobble.

"Hey," I choked out.

That earned me his eyes dancing again, another lip hitch, then he moved to my side and curled my fingers in the crook of his arm.

Annnnnd...

Yup!

I was right. Touching the sumptuous material of his suit was life-altering.

"I know I'm stealing her early, but we have a busy night," he said to Madam Garwah.

"And I have a brandy and book to get to," she replied, flapping a bony-fingered, swollen-jointed hand at us. "Shoo, young people." Her eyes focused on me. "Tomorrow night, Laura. Five thirty sharp."

"See you then, Madam Garwah."

At this point, I didn't collect my bag and coat. Ever the gentlemale (I was beginning to see the lure of all this etiquette), Aleksei did.

He handed me the first and helped me on with the latter.

After I tied the belt, he put my hand in his elbow again and we headed out to the lift.

But I stutter-stepped in the hall when I saw the tall, built, bald demon standing outside the lift, his gaze on us.

And it was glowing red.

"That's Set," Aleksei told me when he felt me balk. "One of my bodyguards. He remains always at the ready when he's on duty."

That explained the glowing eyes.

And this made sense, considering a demon's speed and senses were significantly heightened when they were, as Aleksei put it, "at the ready."

Not to mention, I was glad he was around, especially after my recent conversation with Madam Garwah.

"Set, this is Laura Makepeace," he introduced when we came abreast of the male.

No unnecessary courtesies, Set dipped his chin and grunted, "Laura."

"Nice to meet you, Set," I replied.

He nodded to me, to Aleksei, and we got in the lift.

Set stood at alert facing the doors.

Aleksei and I lingered at the back.

"Was your entire session a history discussion or did Garwah teach you anything?" Aleksei asked.

Hmmm...

Seemed like someone eavesdropped for a while.

I looked up at him. "I learned to eat fast when I'm around your dad."

He chuckled.

Oh yeah, I liked that sound. I'd jump through hoops to get that sound. I could see a time in my life where I might not be able to live without that sound.

"I thought it would be silly," I told him as the lift doors opened and we remained where we were as Set walked out, scanned the space, and only when he turned back and jutted his chin did we walk out. "But it was really interesting."

"I believe it was interesting for Garwah too," Aleksei replied as we followed Set to the doors of the building. "I don't know Garwah very well, though she's always invited to events and celebrations at the Palace. However, I doubt she engages very often in historical debates, and it appeared she enjoyed it."

"I was probably being impertinent," I mumbled, then I blinked because, as we strode over the pavement, the doors to a sleek, black JetPanther 570 boosted up with a sultry purr.

I knew about the JetPanther because everyone knew about the JetPanther, considering it was the pinnacle of land-sky craft in all the realms. Every inch of it was handmade (unheard of), and it was so highly engineered, and as such, high performance, you could actually pilot one to a satellite resort.

I wasn't all about crafts, so I didn't pay attention, thus I couldn't be sure, but if I remembered correctly, I heard it took so much time to make one, not to mention, very few could afford them once they were made, they only built five a year.

Aleksei stopped us at the passenger door that perched high like a wing and turned me to face him, which successfully tore my attention from his elite craft.

"I suspect she deals mostly with the social-climbing daughters of social-climbing mothers who salivate over royal etiquette and twist themselves into knots to be the best at it in hopes of catching the eye of a duke."

"Or a prince," I put in, realizing in that moment that he'd been a sort of prey all his adult life.

Also realizing how much that had to suck.

He conceded my point with a tilt of his head. "Or a prince. In other words, you were probably a breath of fresh air."

It was unexpected, but I sensed I was. "I hope so."

"I've little doubt," he murmured as he helped me into the low-slung craft hovering at the curb.

I settled in, unsurprised at the luxury, but surprised at how roomy it was. It was small, a two-seater, but it had great leg room.

He settled in beside me, the doors descended, and he commanded, "Stained Glass. Brush Island. Manual."

The dash lit blue and replied, "Assessing clear route, your highness."

Stained Glass?

He was taking me to the finest restaurant in all of Nocturn and its islands? Maybe even all of Night's Fall?

Were we ready for that?

I thought we were doing private things to get to know each other.

As if he knew my thoughts, Aleksei shared, "We'll enter from the back. No one will see us. We'll have our own room and be attended by bots programmed to confidential. The only being who knows we're coming is the chef, who's a friend of mine. I would have liked to take you to my flat and cook for you, but there isn't time to do that and go to the Catalogues, because I have a meeting off-planet in the morning, and I need to leave early."

"Why didn't you leave tonight?" I asked stupidly, seeing as I was in his JetPanther and he was taking me out to dinner.

He shot me a glance confirming he didn't because I was beside him in his JetPanther and we were off to dinner.

"Clear route accessed and loaded. Manual engaged," the dash said.

When Aleksei put his hand on the control, the display in front of him showed the elevation we were to attain, my body vibrated in a delightful way as the thrusters under us lit, and up we went, high, higher, until we could clear the tallest skyscraper.

Whoa.

That was a damned fine rush.

The display changed to knots, he flipped some switches, entered some data, the boosters at the rear of the craft engaged, and off we flew, fast and incredibly smooth.

And that was a rush too.

Land crafts used stacked routes accessed above the old grid of streets that used to be traversed by horses, carts, then cars and hovers.

It was a thrill to take to the open sky.

Even so, I had other things on my mind.

I didn't get to broach them because Aleksei spoke before me.

"I failed to explain, but I will now, though I suspect you already know I always travel with a security detail."

Yeah, I already knew that, or at least expected it.

"Of course."

"It depends on where I'm going and who I'm with how big that detail is. Tonight, because I'm with you, its four males and two females."

"Right."

"Once we go public, you'll have your own detail."

Oh boy.

"Uh...okay."

"I'll select them for you personally."

"Um...all right," I replied.

"They're very good at being circumspect and giving me privacy. You'll get to the point you won't even know they're there."

I doubted that immensely.

Though, this discussion gave me pause to return to something I'd resolutely put out of my mind from the moment Cat lowered the boom on me.

That being, did he assign a detail to every female he courted?

I wasn't sure it was time to get into that.

But it was time to get into something else.

"Did you change your plans for me?" I asked.

"Pardon?"

"Tomorrow, you needing to be off-planet for a morning meeting. Did you change your plans so you could be with me tonight?"

"Yes."

Wow.

I shifted my attention from the lights of Brush Island getting closer to watch him navigating the craft, his gaze set to the skyscreen in front of us, his long fingers curled casually around the control, the trajectory we needed to follow so we wouldn't crash with another craft illuminated on the dash in front of him.

"You didn't have to do that," I said softly.

"You're unable to move forward with your designs without seeing troll skin," he pointed out.

"I could wait."

"Or you could see the skin and not wait."

"Can Allain get access to the Catalogues?"

"At my command, yes."

"So he could have shown them to me. Or some other admin person at the Palace. You have a gazillion of them."

He glanced at me, a lazy (thus phenomenal) grin on his face. "We have just a few less than a gazillion, Laura. And Allain travels with me."

Of course he did.

I shook off the effects of that grin.

"What I'm saying is, this means a lot, but I feel badly you had to change your plans."

"It isn't that big of a deal."

"What time is your meeting?"

"Nine."

I gaped at him. "*Nine?*"

"Yes."

"In the morning?"

His voice was rustling velvet with his humor when he repeated, "Yes."

"What satellite are you going to?"

"Thoth."

Holy Hecate!

"That's six hours away."

"I can sleep on the ship, *bissi*," he said gently. "Your concern is heartening but...*relax*."

I snapped my mouth shut and looked forward.

I did this because his gentle voice did a number on me.

I did this because his change of plans was a pain in the behind for him, but he did it anyway, to be with me, and that took sweet to a new level.

I did this because he called me "*bissi*," which was old-world language, a term of endearment for females only, used for all ages and all relationships, but it was definitely affectionate. Now, even more so, because it wasn't used that often, so it was usually used only for those who meant a good deal to you.

And it meant "my little love."

No one had ever called me that. My mom, dad, even Mr. Truelock.

So yes.

Oh yes, I needed to take a big, long pause and think about what was happening here.

I wasn't seeing a midnight mass marriage in the future. Not at all.

But this was...*something*.

I just had no clue what it was.

And on our first date, it wasn't the time to ask, "Hey, what *is* this?"

I knew one thing. It was without a doubt he was going that extra mile, even if he barely knew me. So to him, it was definitely...*something*.

Still, no female in her right mind would press a male she liked very much, and liked more every time she was with him, to share his intentions for the future on the first date.

It would have to wait for the second.

Or maybe the third.

(Or perhaps the fourth.)

I just knew it wasn't going to happen now.

We were going to eat at Stained Glass. He was going to show me something very few beings ever got to see. And we were going to get to know each other better.

When it came to all of that, it was definitely enough to deal with.

For now.

CHAPTER 9

PLEASED?

After dinner, I sat beside Aleksei in the JetPanther and watched the Sceptred Isle get closer, as well as the expansive gardens, spires, turrets, flags and majesty of the Celestial Palace gracing the sweeping slope of the highest peak on the island.

One could say, I was now in deep need to take that pause I already deeply needed to take to figure out where I was in regard to what was going on with the prince.

Because dinner was fantastic.

Not just the food.

No.

Mostly it was the company.

At first, Aleksei spent a lot of time telling me what was in the Catalogues and offering to show me other stuff if I wanted to see it (and I was all over that, asking to see the royal jewels, and he'd told me security measures around those were tighter, thus it would take more arranging, but we'd go back later so I could pore over them).

I also learned (what I already knew, considering I'd have seen pics of it everywhere if he had) he didn't laser joust, "Because the possibility of serious injury is sheer stupidity to court just for the five-second thrill of riding a robotic horse and aiming a laser lance at a shield."

I was relieved he thought this, because I agreed.

I never understood the lure of the joust. It seemed like long stretches of boredom punctuated by mere moments of superfluous violence.

Aleksei also wasn't a fan of pit ball, but did like ring ice, and (this was news) played it himself.

"We have a secret league. Some friends and acquaintances of mine throughout the Four Realms. We keep it secret so we can play and concentrate on that without the media taking the enjoyment from it."

I had visions of Aleksei on the ice, and then I had to force those visions out of my head so I didn't ruin my outfit by throwing myself over the used dishes on the table at him.

I further learned his favorite style of cooking was Land's Endian. "It's hearty, so people underestimate it. They think it's simplistic. But they program their Cook-Companions to make it. They don't know how many steps there are or the importance of the perfect blend of spices."

In fact, he pretty much let me grill him the entire dinner.

So I also knew he did own the Pink and Black Club, the entire building it was in, and further rumor proved true, sharing he lived in the penthouse at the top when he wasn't in his suite of rooms at the Palace (he also shared he wasn't often in his suite of rooms at the Palace since he'd moved out three years ago).

I learned his hobbies were not only ring ice and cooking, but also reading and target shooting, both on legs and in craft, but he didn't often have time to partake in any of these, save the reading (and yes, he too, collected real books, he told me his collection was (unsurprisingly) bigger than mine, and he promised to show me that too).

He further disclosed he did not gamble, though some of his ring ice friends pulled together a friendly poker game every once in a while.

And he traveled often, mostly for business, rarely for royal appearances, which fell to King Fillion, Queen Calisa and Princess Aleece, "Because Timothee and Errol have their brains in their balls, and until they're surgically removed and relocated, they're one step above useless, and sadly, too often, two steps below it."

Yes!

He talked smack about his brothers.

Right to me!

As delicately as I could, I shut down his gentle probing about my parents (no way I was ready to go there, at least not over beautiful food with a handsome man in a private room).

Truth: I'd prefer never to talk about them.

But although he backed off with grace, I saw the way his eyes darkened, the tiny pinpricks of stars that came out in the irises, and while this was fascinating, and beautiful, it was also more than a little scary.

To show my gratitude, I didn't ask about Princess Anna.

At dessert, Sirk Parrin, Stained Glass's famous chef, showed personally.

This was my favorite part of the night, not only because Sirk was a big, brown-haired, friendly, burly bear shifter, but because there was no bowing and scraping or your royal highnesses.

Aleksei and Sirk were, indeed, friends (Sirk was in their ring ice league). Good ones.

While I looked on in astonishment, they did a male hug, bumping chests and slapping backs. Sirk even lightly smacked Aleksei's face affectionately a couple of times after the hug and before he turned to me.

"Ah, look at this female! The fates have always shined on you," he announced grandly before he pulled me into, yes, a bear hug.

When he let go, he asked, "Enjoy the meal?"

"Aleksei introduced me to Chateau LeBrand a few days ago. Your food was better," I replied with total honesty.

After I said that, he swooped me into the side of his bulky body with his arm around my shoulders, turned to Aleksei and declared, "You can't have her, seeing as I'm in love with her."

Aleksei just made a point to stare at his arm around my shoulders, which meant Sirk chuckled good-naturedly and let me go.

He sat down and ate dessert with us, whereupon Aleksei—continuing to exhibit his prevailing tendencies of being a gentlemale and oftentimes sweet—pulled me into the conversation by talking about the vids I'd worked on.

Sirk wasn't a screen or display kind of male, but he had seen *Sheets*, because pretty much everyone of majority age had seen it. And he commended me on my ability to design great underwear.

The food was amazing. Sirk was gregarious and hilarious and welcoming. The famous stained glass in the windows was a work of art. And being one of a select few people in four realms to experience a ride in a JetPanther was a thrill.

But the dinner had been a male and female getting to know each other (okay, it was the female getting to know the male more than the other way around, but I hadn't had a brief about *him*).

It was tremendously enjoyable. Aleksei was approachable, forthcoming, attentive.

But it was normal.

Which made it exceptional.

I wasn't out to dinner with Prince Aleksei, the True Heir.

I was out with Aleksei, who had friends he let smack his face teasingly, brothers who annoyed him because they were no longer young, but they seemed dedicated to acting like bros for eternity, and opinions he didn't mind voicing.

He flew wide around the Palace, and I straight up pressed my nose to the skyscreen at my side in order not to lose sight of its graceful lines, heart-skipping size and architectural beauty, all of it lit, so Nocturn could always see the entirety of its stately grace, sitting high on its hill, day or night.

I'd just never seen it that close.

Far away, it was striking.

Up close, it was stunning.

He aimed us toward some buildings on the east side of the island, down the hill from the Palace. Buildings that were also old and attractive, but it was clear they had a more utilitarian purpose.

After we landed, as he did when we arrived at the restaurant, Aleksei contained me in the craft until he could help me out of it (and truly, I needed his help, my heels were high, and the JetPanther slung *low*) by keeping my door closed until he was out and around the craft at my door.

I'd noticed the female standing in the light coming out of an opened door on a building when we landed. As I alighted, I also noticed Aleksei lift his chin to acknowledge her.

But as he would tuck me at his side with my hand in his elbow again, I stopped him by curling toward his front and putting my other one to his chest.

I slid my teeth over my lower lip when I encountered the hard muscle under his light-blue, custom-made button down, but when I lifted my gaze to his, I saw his head bent, his attention aimed at my hand.

I quickly took it away.

Even more quickly, he caught it and brought it back, opening his hand over the back of mine to spread it across his shirt, and finally, his gaze captured mine.

"I am not a priceless work of art," he said low.

"I know, but—"

"You may touch me."

My skin started to tingle. "Thank you, but—"

"You seem hesitant with me. I'm a prince of this realm, Laura, but I'll not ever simply be that to you."

Gods, he was so sweet.

"You don't have to use deference with me," he continued. "Even when you must show it to others, we'll know what we have between us."

So. Danged. *Sweet.*

And he was right. I'd been distant. Maybe even...

Dear Hecate...

Testing him.

I felt badly he'd noticed, and it obviously bothered him.

But I didn't trust this.

Who could blame me? I'd never had anything so amazing.

That wasn't something to share on the first date either.

"Don't worry," I joked. "I'll get used to being courted by a mega-hot shifter and eventually stop thinking you'll go up in a puff of smoke if I touch you."

His lips twitched, his face softened, both special Aleksei-style gifts he gave me before he stated, "I'll be off-planet for three days. This annoys me because I'll be quite busy, and I won't have much time to connect with you. Your friend Catla's showing is during that time, and I won't be here to escort you."

Oh man, Cat would be bummed at that. Having the prince there would be a huge coup for her.

I thought this so I wouldn't think about how upset I was that he wouldn't be there to escort me. I was a little scared about us going public (okay, full disclosure, *a lot* scared), and the timing of the showing seemed really soon.

But we'd been in each other's presence for mere hours, and the level of how dismayed I was not only that we wouldn't be going to the showing together, but that he'd be gone for three days, was, well...seriously *dismaying*.

"That's okay," I lied. "I'm used to going to things alone. But I wanted to say—"

"I would ask you to come with me on my trip, but as I'll be busy, I fear it'd be boring for you."

I'd been off-planet once. During a shoot for a vid titled *The Other Side of the Sun*. It was a sappy romance couched in an action-adventure. The hero died. The audience was incensed.

But my costumes got good reviews.

When I was there, I didn't have a lot of time to explore, and I'd always wished I had. Off-planet travel was expensive, and I didn't know when I'd get another chance.

Still.

"I don't get bored easily. The thing is—"

His brows shot up. "Would you like to come?"

I started laughing as I reached high to press my fingers to his mouth.

Those weren't hard like his chest; they were soft and lovely.

"Can I finish a sentence?" I requested playfully.

He took hold of my wrist, kissed my fingers, then pulled my hand back to his chest.

Mmmmm.

Nice move.

"Continue," he urged.

"I just wanted to say..."

Dang.

How to say what I wanted to say?

A breeze ruffled his hair and picked up mine, so he pressed my hand to his chest as indication he wanted me to keep it there, then he reached out and gently tucked my hair behind my ear.

I felt his touch shiver down my neck in a tender way that settled right in my heart.

Okay then.

I knew how to say it.

"Thank you."

"Pardon?" he asked.

"Thank you," I repeated. "Thank you for being normal. Thank you for letting me grill you at dinner. Thank you for taking me somewhere fabulous, but not making a big deal out of it. It was an exceptional dinner, but it wasn't an *event*. It wasn't, look! Prince Aleksei is out on the town, squiring his latest squeeze. Thank you for making it just...us."

"That *is* what we agreed, Laura," he reminded me.

I shook my head. "Maybe you don't understand. What I'm saying is, you could do that by just being you. Instead, what you did was you gave me *you*, the real you. That's what you gave me tonight. And I really enjoyed having it. So...thank you."

When I stopped speaking, he made a rough noise deep in his throat.

I felt that noise drive deep between my legs.

And then his hand was sliding along my jaw, back into my hair, and I could feel the heat from his body beating into mine.

I thought he was going to kiss me.

He didn't.

"Come with me," he murmured.

"To see the troll skin?" I breathed, so caught up in him, I was no longer following.

"To Thoth."

Oh dear.

"I want that," I whispered.

"Then it's done," he growled.

Growled!

That drove between my legs too.

Focus, Laura!

"Aleksei—"

"I'll comm Allain to make arrangements."

He shifted to move away, it seemed in order to pull out his Palm, but I caught his wrist this time, keeping it where it was and him where he was.

"Something to know about me," I started quietly, and I had to admit, a little worried (right, more than a little worried) about what I had to say.

"Yes?"

I took in a deep breath and gave it to him.

"You're going to show me that troll skin, and I'm going to get inspired. Then I'm going to descend into a place where it's all about the script, the characters, the possibilities. By the time you get back from Thoth, I'll have several options to present the director, with a full complement of sketches to back them up, because I'll become obsessed." I squeezed his wrist. "This is not about you. It doesn't reflect on me wanting to spend more time with you and get to know you. It's just how I am. It's how my process works. And part of that will be frenzied trips to half a dozen fabric stores to pull swatches, and I'm not sure they'll have what I need on Thoth. I could design while you go to your meetings, or whatever. But it'd be incredibly frustrating not to have access to a plethora of textiles to feed the obsession, the vision, and see what it'd be in execution."

Aleksei said nothing.

I said nothing.

This was becoming familiar.

He spoke first. "Then you won't go, and I'll rearrange the meetings so I can be back in time for your friend's showing."

Oh, this sweet beast.

"That's really thoughtful," I whispered. "But unnecessary."

"This showing is concerning me greatly, Laura."

It was?

My question must have shown on my face because he answered, "It will be very difficult for me to know you're among unattached males without me in your presence so I can mark you."

Hunh?

"Why?"

"Why?" he repeated after me.

"Yes. Why?"

"Because you're mine."

"You've said that before, but not counting Captain Jacques's, which maybe I should," I shot a tentative smile to his attentive (Lilith save me from a male who was genuinely attentive when I spoke), handsome face, "we've only had one date, and it isn't even over yet."

His brows drew down.

Heavily.

It showed severe confusion.

But still, it was ominous.

"I could understand your hesitance to move forward with this because of all the baggage I carry, but I have to confess, your apparent confusion about what we have is...odd."

Uh-oh.

Maybe we *were* going to talk about what this was on the first date.

He assumed a suspicious expression. "Did you not feel the connection at the club?"

"You'd marked me."

"I felt you before you even entered the room. Did that not happen to you?"

I thought about the hot flashes. My phantom beast. The fact I looked right his way the minute I exited the scanning tube.

"You're my mate, Laura," he declared.

Ummmmmmmmmmmmmm!!!!!

Holy Hecate!

Shock jolted through me physically, I let his wrist go and tried to step away.

Alas, his hand was still in my hair and it tensed, keeping me where I was, and if that didn't do it (which it would have), he curled an arm around my waist so my breasts brushed his chest.

Uh-oh!

"Did that not happen to you?" he pressed.

"It...was that...is that how...?" My voice pitched higher. "*We're mates?*"

"You're very lovely to look at. And you have a definitive style and bearing that's insanely attractive. I've also never had anyone be so honest with me within seconds of being in my presence as you were with openly showing how pissed you were at having to curtsy to me, and then going into your Captain Jacques's diatribe."

I felt heat hit my cheeks and mumbled, "It was hardly a diatribe."

He smiled. "You're right. It wasn't. What it was, was hilarious.

Instantly, I couldn't believe my luck. At once, I had a mate who was shy and strong, knew herself but could be adorably awkward, spoke her mind, didn't hide her reactions, had a sense of humor, good taste, and bonus, she had gorgeous legs, fantastic hair, a beautiful face, and pardon my vulgarity, but also a tremendous ass and a great pair of tits."

"So...this is..." I couldn't bring myself to say it.

"This is us getting to know one another before we let the world know we've found each other, something that will throw you into a unique form of hell before I can sort it out for you, which will mean me mostly helping you get used to it. And then we'll do what mates do. Get married. And have babies."

By Lilith!

My breath came so fast, I was pretty sure I was hyperventilating.

"You didn't know what you were experiencing," he noted softly.

"No!" I cried.

"Didn't your mother—?"

He cut himself off as I jerked my gaze to his broad shoulder.

"Look at me, *bissi*," he whispered gently.

I forced my eyes to his.

"We'll have to discuss them," he remarked.

I nodded stiltedly.

Then I shook my head vehemently.

"We will," he asserted.

Drat!

"Right," I forced out.

"I thought you knew."

Royal protocol lessons. Getting my own detail. The strength of my feelings, the connection between us being so intense, my psyche formed a phantom beast to accompany me through its first moments. One of his close friends greeting me like I was his long-lost sister.

It is their due.

Because you're mine.

I should have known.

"I didn't know. And no, I'm not an idiot. I just didn't...put it all together."

"I don't think you're an idiot."

"Are we going to have a midnight mass wedding?" I asked.

He drew me closer so my breasts were in full contact with his chest.

Gods!

"That is the tradition, though I'd like to strategize it with you. Guard our time together as we come to know one another. It'll give me the opportunity to do what I can to help you understand what's to come, and ease you into a public life, so the onslaught of the media won't make you run very far away from me."

He'd kissed my fingertips after I shushed him with them.

It was our first date (or, arguably, second), but I wasn't sure anything could make me run far away from him, even if he wasn't my mate.

But he was.

Prince Aleksei was my mate!

How in any level of hells did this happen?

"So that mass will be some time from now," he concluded.

"That's...um, good. No offense," I said the last quickly.

Another smile and, "None taken. I can imagine this is a lot to digest."

"Mm-hmm," I mumbled my understatement.

His smile turned into one of his devastating grins and he said, "You'll have to design your own wedding gown."

Oh my gods.

That devastating grin turned roguish. "But I'll state my preference now for what's under it being akin to what you have pinned in that frame on your wall."

He wanted sexy, vintage-style, lacy, practically see-through, corseted, be-ribboned underwear.

I shuddered.

He pulled me even closer.

Oh gods, please kiss me.

No, don't.

Yes, do.

No, don't.

(Please do.)

"Calm, *bissi*," he murmured to my mouth, which, incidentally, did not one thing to assist in calming me. "You've processed a good deal just now. I'm not going to give you our first kiss in the midst of that."

Okay, good.

And that totally sucked.

His eyes lifted to mine. "I'll want you to remember every second of it."

Argh!

He was killing me!

"Maybe you should let me go," I suggested.

"That is physically, mentally and spiritually impossible."

Gah!

Totally killing me.

"Aleksei—"

He wrapped his hand around mine still at his chest and pulled it to the base of his throat. I felt the strength of the corded muscle there, the heat of his skin, the pulse of his heart, but I couldn't focus on any of them with the look that was in his eyes.

"Are you pleased?"

Was I pleased...about him being my mate?

Was he really asking me that?

Was he...?

I looked deep into his searching night eyes.

To my shock, I got it.

He had everything. He *was* everything.

And when you didn't have it, you thought it would be awesome.

But when you had it, everything was far too much.

He was about to give me everything.

And he, Prince Aleksei, True Heir to Night's Fall, was worried I didn't want it.

"I've had a crush on you since I was six," I admitted.

His face started to shut down, and I understood.

He had that already from practically every female in four realms, possibly all twenty of them.

It wasn't what he needed.

"But I had no idea until I had normal Aleksei tonight how much there actually was to crush on, because you are very correct. Laser jousts are stupid. So, well, I guess I have an even bigger crush on you now."

He changed his mind about kissing me, obviously.

Because I barely got out the word "now" before I was plastered to his long, hard body, up on the very tips of my toes, and his mouth crushed on mine.

So, yes.

I was in for a credit, in for the whole line.

I parted my lips.

I got that rough noise again, this time it filled my mouth, which made my knees fully buckle. His arm tightened to hold me close, he cocked his head, and his tongue swept inside.

He tasted like cognac and Sirk's pastry chef's chocolate, almond, cherry soufflé, and he felt like warmth, safety and protection.

Naturally, receiving all those gifts from him, I leaned all the way in, because I'd always wanted all of that, and here he was, offering it to me in one delicious kiss.

He lifted his head, breaking our intimate contact far too soon, sliding his hand out of my hair and swiping a thumb along my lower lip.

Another smooth move.

And one could say I was moved, down to my soul.

His sleek voice was husked with velvet when he said, "You have sketches to draw. I have meetings to attend. We'll continue that thought when we have plenty of time to enjoy it. Now, let's go look at troll skin."

I wanted to laugh. And cry. And immediately comm all my gals to let them know that maybe they weren't crazy to get in my face about daring to dream.

I did the first, tucking my own hand in his elbow and shifting to his side.

And together, we walked to the entry to the Catalogues.

CHAPTER 10
HE KNEW

My head was in the clouds.
    I'd never experienced that sensation, but I knew exactly what it was as I walked at Aleksei's side toward the door to the Catalogues, feeling his arm brush against mine, the heat of his body, the strength of his biceps under my fingers.

I was his.

And that meant he was mine.

By all the gods...

He was mine.

I was in such a daze, my greeting to the female who'd been waiting for us was vague, perfunctory, and therefore rude, but for once, I didn't have it in me to care.

I was all about Aleksei and what just happened, even though I'd been looking forward to this. Very few were allowed access to the Royal Catalogues. Just staff, curators, historians and researchers (those last two, only if they jumped through hoops and cut through a ton of red tape). So I'd wanted to take it all in.

We'd entered, walked to the lifts, the lift doors had opened, we stood in them, and hearing Aleksei's silken voice switch to steel was the only thing that clicked me back in.

"Precautions will be taken, Nata," he bit. "It's unnecessary for you to accompany us. As you know, this isn't my first time here, and Mistress

Laura has made comprehensive study of a variety of garments. She knows to take care."

Mental note: I needed to ask Madam Garwah about that "Mistress Laura" business.

The tall, cool, slender, attractive blonde human began, "Your highness, it would be—"

"You're dismissed," Aleksei cut her off with uncharacteristic (as far as I could tell in our short acquaintance) impatience and authority. "I'll comm you when we leave so you can engage the lockdown sequence. Therefore, I'll thank you now for staying late to allow us entry."

To my surprise, her mouth tightened in open annoyance, she bobbed a curtsy, then, without even a glance at me, she turned on her sleek pump and swanned away.

Aleksei drew me into the lift.

"What was that about?" I asked when the doors closed.

"My guess, Timothee or Errol slept with her, making promises they didn't keep, and now she's compromised. And since she works in a sensitive area, she'll need to be reassigned," he clipped, his anger sharp, but I couldn't tell if he was angry at his brothers, having to reassign a female when that shouldn't have to happen, or both.

Hmm.

Timothee or Errol got their jollies, and it was the female who had to uproot her life because of it.

I was beginning really not to like his brothers, and I hadn't even met them.

He ordered the lift. "Sublevel five."

Hang on.

Sublevel?

Five?

There were five sublevels to his joint?

I didn't know there was even one.

"Erm...how big is this place?" I asked.

He looked down to me, and the instant his gaze fell on my face, the irritability left behind by the blonde visibly melted away.

Really, he was just *so lovely*.

"There are two buildings devoted to the Catalogue. Three levels in both above ground, where there are vaults but also administrative offices, extensive records and databases and conservation labs. This building has six sublevels. The other, which was an add-on when an overflow became necessary, has seven. Quite a bit of that is empty, but it was built proactively to be filled at a future date."

I wished I had a better response than I did, but there really wasn't more to say but, "Wow."

He grinned, the lift doors opened, and, outside of the light coming from the lift, utter darkness greeted us.

"There's twelve hundred years' worth of history to preserve, some of it even older," he remarked. "And that takes space." He then ordered, "Lights on, seventy percent. Display cases full illumination."

Immediately, the vast room lit, and at the wonder that met my eyes, I gasped.

Loudly.

"Oh my..." I drifted forward as if walking on air. "Oh my..." I repeated as I approached the first large, glass display box. "Oh my *gods*," I whispered, staring at what was in the box.

I felt Aleksei come up beside me, his hand lighting on the small of my back, but my eyes swept the long line of glass vaults, and I was transfixed by the bounty that was before me. And that didn't even take into consideration whatever treasures were hidden in the plethora of cabinets meticulously positioned to stand at attention, ready for perusal.

"My mother's wedding gown, my father's wedding suit," Aleksei informed me of what was on show before us.

Though I already knew. I'd seen the pics thousands of times.

But to see it, live and in person...

Divine.

His hand glided to the side of my waist, his fingers pressing in, and he moved us to the next box.

"My grandmother and grandfather's. And then there's my great grandmother and grandfather's. I think you can take it from there."

I stared at the extraordinary garments fastidiously exhibited on custom-made, headless mannequins.

And I knew he knew.

He knew before he brought me here, he was giving me this remarkable gift.

He knew.

My eyes started to tingle as he murmured, "Come."

I would have gone anywhere with him at that juncture.

He took my hand and led me down the line of wedding apparel that ranged from YoD 2080s to...

He stopped us at a glass case.

"Princess Mathilde. Married to Prince Atlas. Year of the Dragon 1319, five years before the trolls invaded," he said. "Our clan was Starknight then, and that was the name of the land we ruled."

Oh yes.

He knew.

I tore my gaze from the flame-red velvet gown with its cameo neckline, stunning gold silk-braid edging, pearls and ambers stitched into intricate gold embroidery, the deep fall of the bell sleeves that nearly brushed the floor, the intricate gold lace of the undersleeve embellishment and the sumptuous sable cape that flooded down the back of the gown and flowed across the dais the mannequins were standing on.

And I looked up at him.

A million words filled my mouth, but before a single one could escape, he tugged my hand again.

He guided me from the display cases into the long rows of cabinets sporting wide, shallow drawers. Along the way, he nabbed a pair of white gloves from one of the many cannisters of the same that were readily available.

We stopped in front of some drawers that started at ground level and went up to my neck.

Aleksei called, "Open DR dash SK thirteen, twenty-five dash seventy-eight M."

He pulled me back as a drawer around calf height slid out and up to hover at waist height in front of us, whereupon the top slid away, folding into the back panel.

I expected to see troll skin.

It wasn't troll skin.

It was a gold gown with a gossamer white tucked shawl at the square bodice. The fall of the bell sleeves were prettily scalloped. It was folded over itself precisely to fit in the flat, wide drawer, but still in a manner that exhibited the features of the garment.

And it was so painstakingly conserved, it looked brand new.

I'd never seen a garment of this age so well presented.

"You can touch this one," Aleksei said. "With the gloves."

I tipped my head back to look at him in surprise.

"It's also Queen Mathilde's," he shared. "From 1325. The trolls had invaded. As I'm sure you learned in history class, on our continent, there were nine realms then. They often clashed, disputing territory, boundaries, the legitimacy of kings or queens. Any event could be twisted into a grievance. Case in point, infamously, the King of Cliff's Mountain once declared war due to a thunderstorm he swore was cast on his realm by neighboring Day's Rise."

"But the Troll Invasion stopped these petty skirmishes," I put in.

He inclined his head. "For a time. They had to band together to defeat a common foe."

"And in the end, the four monarchs who were credited with vanquishing the trolls, sending what was left of them back to their boats, divvied up the land and created Night's Fall, Sky's Edge, Land's End and Dawn's Break," I concluded our shared history recitation.

But I loved that he started talking about it, drawing me in.

It was giving me all sorts of ideas about what the feel of the costumes should be for the vid.

He nodded, moved us down the line and ordered up another drawer.

It opened, and there it was.

Troll skin.

Right before me.

Troll skin.

"Not our suits, I'll show you those in a minute," Aleksei said. "But these are strips and samples that I thought might help you build your textiles."

He thought right.

"Can I have the gloves?" I asked eagerly.

"You don't need the gloves, darling," he murmured, reaching into the drawer and selecting a largish strip of greenish-gray scaly hide.

He offered it to me.

"I shouldn't—" I began.

"It's virtually indestructible."

I knew that.

However.

"That's why it's so valuable, along with its scarcity," he went on. "Why it was so difficult to defeat them, even if it's since been estimated their capacity for thought and logic was so low, strategy for them was impossible. Their invasion wasn't tactical. It was instinctual. It was about the survival of their race. Multitudes of scientists have gone back to the isle they abandoned, and they speculate that the trolls had raped the resources of their land to such an extent, they'd go extinct if they remained. In order to survive, they needed new horizons. Their boats were decidedly elementary. It's projected that at least three quarters of their population drowned before they even reached the shores of the Four Realms."

"It was also why their invasion was so terrifying," I put in. "There was no reason to it. It was widespread kill, rape, burn." I made a face. "And eat."

His lips tipped up at my expression. "Definitely a common enemy when they considered babies, breasts and male genitalia delicacies."

I made an even bigger face.

He chuckled and shook the skin at me.

Hesitantly, holding my breath, I took it.

It was heavier than I expected. Thicker. Rougher. It seemed, when looking at pics of it, like the scales of a fish, one overlapping the other. This wasn't the case. It was unbroken and rippled, but the ripples weren't random. They had a pattern.

"Considering it doesn't even decompose, it's impossible to wrap my mind around the stupidity of finding ways to destroy most of the supply culled from the cadavers," I mumbled.

"Well, once the trolls were gone, the rest of us started fighting again. It was only the Starknight House that had the bright idea to stitch the skin into armor. The rest of them experimented on it, tried to use it in rituals and spells, thinking it was magic, but they only managed to weaken it, which eventually meant it was destroyed." A wicked grin hit his lips. "Which of course sent my ancestors scouring the realms to grab as much of it as they could."

"Something that bought us the name of Starthieves."

"A moniker we were quite proud of, and still are."

This was true. Those of the Fall thought we were very clever doing that. Then again, we were. Between our dragons and that armor, it made us nearly undefeatable in future conflicts.

"Do you believe the rest of them perished in the Dolphin Sea?" I asked.

"Yes," he stated, sweeping away centuries of conspiracy theories that some realms (especially ours) held live trolls, experimented on them and bred them for future military use. "For centuries, anthropologists, beastiologists, marine biologists and well-funded fortune hunters have scoured the seabed for thousands of miles around the Four Realms. And they've found multitudes of troll bones and pieces of their weapons on the sea floor. Both to the east of us, which gives credence to the theory many were lost on their journey here, and to the west, which was the direction they took when they retreated. It's a long voyage to the Six Realms. They didn't make it."

Dipping my head to watch my thumb rub along the ripples, I then peered up at him.

"How many suits of armor are there?" I asked.

He called out to the room, "Database, access number of troll skin armor."

"Troll skin armor," the computer's mechanical tone droned through the cavernous space. "Seventy-eight full sets. Sixteen partial sets. One-hundred-and-twelve individual pieces. These include twenty torso shirts. Eighteen trousers. Thirty individual gauntlets. Eleven gauntlet sets. Seven individual boots. Four boot sets. Seven codpieces."

I giggled at "codpieces."

For your information, Aleksei and his brothers didn't don that part of the armor for the ceremonies.

Though, to be historically accurate, I would probably have to incorporate them in my designs, because the armor and clothing from that day often included them.

The computer continued, "Two kings and one prince buried in troll armor. Inventoried, but inaccessible. Sixty-two strips and swatches unincorporated in any garment. Request further information on the number of other garments with troll skin integrated in the design and their location in the vestment vault. Troll armor inventory list complete."

"There had been tens of thousands of them," I whispered. "And that's all that's left."

"Not quite," Aleksei told me. "There are many aristocrats and nobles, not to mention citizens with a long history in Night's Fall, who have everything from full sets of troll armor to pieces of skin used for armoring purposes for garments from that era. They come up for auction occasionally, but not often due to its ever-increasing value."

I should have guessed that.

"Experts disagree," he carried on, "but there are some who contend there were upwards of two hundred thousand trolls that invaded at random points all along the eastern shore, with some drifting north, others south. Regardless, their numbers were vast, as was their size."

"I've seen some of the skeletons at the Musée Histoire Bestiale. They're over seven feet." I smiled at him. "Even taller than you."

He tipped his head to acknowledge my words, but said, "And they weren't very attractive."

We only had artists' depictions, even so, all of them distinctly resembled each other, and Aleksei was correct, though he underrated their grotesqueness.

With flat faces, bulging eyes, non-existent noses that were just slits in their faces, flabby lips on overwide mouths, two rows of razor-sharp teeth inside, sparse, coarse hair on their heads, this atop gigantic bodies with gangling, overlong arms and torsos, long claws curving from the tips of their four fingers and short, bowed legs, they were walking horrors.

I scrunched my nose. "I can't imagine what it would be like to one day be milking your cows or weaving on your loom, taking care of the day's business, and you look out the doors of your barn or your cottage window and see a band of trolls bearing down on you. Then to find your arrows bounced off and your sword glanced away. It would feel like the end of the world."

"I sense you've been inspired," he murmured, his night-sky gaze intent, interested and locked on me.

I grinned. "Totally."

"Would you like to see the armor now, or inspect Mathilde's gown before we head that way?"

I wanted both at the same time.

And then he said, "The trolls, both male and female, wore what we would conceive as loincloths. The females did not cover their breasts. We have a few intact, a few pieces. Would you like to see those as well?"

Seriously?

Okay, I had to know.

"Had you been to this room before you offered to show me the skin?" I asked.

"No. The armor is brought to us."

Oh.

I deflated.

"However, after I offered you a visit, I accessed the databases, saw how much was in the same vault, so I came down to see what might be available to you and decided, instead of having the skin brought up to one of the conservation rooms for you to inspect, to bring you to it so you could have access to all the rest."

So I could have access to all the rest.

So he could give me this enormous, precious, unprecedented gift.

Oh yes.

He took time out of his life to come here.

So *he knew*.

"Is there a moratorium on kissing until we can explore it to its fullest, or can I throw myself at you right now?"

He emitted a sharp bark of surprised laughter before he replied, "It's early days, darling, but I suspect there will never be a time you can't throw yourself at me."

With the path clear, I took it.

I'd dropped the troll skin in favor of diving my hands into his thick, silken hair. I was pressed to him, and although I got a taste of the hot, musky depths of the inside of his mouth, in short order, Aleksei assumed control, and he took a thorough exploration of mine before he again broke our kiss way too soon.

"I have a ship to catch in five hours, *bissi*," he murmured. "And you have a room to play in. Your gratitude is enthusiastically accepted, and I promise to bring you back however many times you like. But regrettably, this time, we don't have much of it."

I sighed but didn't unpeel my body from his or untangle my fingers from his hair when I shared, "No one has ever given me anything this huge."

Even if what he had to give was unheard of, his eyes darkened, those pinprick stars reappearing, both reactions showing he understood part of that statement had to do with the lack I received from my parents.

"Not true," I amended swiftly. "Mr. Truelock owns the building my flat and studio are in, he went all out on bathroom and kitchen upgrades before I moved in, and I know he charges me bargain basement rent." I paused as if to consider. "But this is better. And anyway, he's my dad not really being my dad, so I guess that's part of his job. At least he thinks so."

"I always admired Mammon, now I very much like him."

"He's pretty mega."

Aleksei smiled, and oh my, but I loved watching him do that.

"Now I must ask a question I never thought would pass my lips," he said. "Gown, skin or loincloths?"

I burst out laughing.

And then, just to tease, I answered, "Totally loincloths."

His amazing chuckle sounded, we replaced the troll skin to the drawer, but left them open so we could come back.

He then wrapped his arm around my shoulders, and he took me to the loincloths.

CHAPTER 11

THE ZONE

My eyes were bleary. My sketchpads were scattered. Pages torn from them were tangled in the mess.

Nova was asleep in a front window. Comet was also asleep, flat on his back on the floor, his pudge spreading, his paws dangling in the air. And Jupiter was batting around one of the many scrunched up rejects of paper I'd tossed aside.

This was in my studio, which was populated with a host of dressmaker dummies, deep shelves stuffed full of bolts of fabrics, a wall of painstakingly organized bins, cannisters, drawers, pots and binders filled with tokens, trimmings, pencils and past sketches.

There were large tables for pinning and cutting.

Tucked by the shelves there was a used mid-level Pro Seam-Stitch I bought that had been malfunctioning, but Mr. Tanugu's brother fixed it for me.

There was a cozy corner where I had another drafting desk.

In another corner was a counter, a Bev-Buddy and small-size Cook-Companion.

Yet another corner held a curtained dressing area, and in the last, a walled-off bathroom.

But I was ensconced in the center of the room in a loveseat sitting atop a thick, circular rug and flanked by tables where I could put drinks, plates, pencils, pens and swatches.

This was where I was when the display on my Palm lit, and the tinkle of bells (my tone to tell me I had an incoming vid comm) sounded.

I grouchily turned my attention to the display, annoyed I'd been interrupted.

The grouch exited the building, and maybe even the planet, when I saw HRH Prince Aleksei on the display (of course I programmed in the HRH and the Prince, because...*duh*, it was hilarious *and* hot).

I snatched it up, saying, "Engage video comm."

His glorious face filled my screen, and he didn't look bleary-eyed at all.

"Hey," I greeted.

"Bloody hell, have you been up all night?" he asked.

I should be concerned about the state of my face.

I was not concerned about the state of my face.

"Look!" I cried, grabbing at the pad I'd set beside my chair.

I showed him the sketch.

"That's the heroine's wedding gown," I announced. I flipped the page. "That's the gown she'll wear when she meets the hero." I tossed the pad aside, seized another one and showed him that. "Hero's costume for when he battles his first troll. And this!" I exclaimed, flipping the page. "Troll in loincloth!"

His chuckle sounded, and I dropped the pad to see his face soft with humor.

Maybe my favorite look on him, though, it had stiff competition.

"So the answer to my question is...yes. You were up all night," he remarked.

Again, I should probably worry about looking a fright, but I didn't. I was far too jazzed, far too hyped, far too caffeinated, and far too happy to be chatting with him.

I also didn't confirm, because I figured he got the gist.

"Are you on Thoth?" I asked.

"Just finished my first meeting. I have a few minutes before we need to head to lunch for another one."

He'd finished his first meeting?

He'd already arrived?

I glanced around distractedly. "What time is it?"

"Eleven forty."

Whoa.

I probably should lay off the coffee, wind down and crash. At least for a few hours. Then I could hit it again.

"Listen, darling, I had a brainstorm," Aleksei declared. "I've asked Sirk to take you to the showing. He's agreed. Muriel is juggling my schedule in hopes I can get back in time, even if we won't be at the place to appear in public together yet. But Sirk can take you, and I can trust him with you. My beast considers him a member of my clan, even if we're different species of shifter. He won't come off as a threat."

My stomach twisted at the mention of his beast, something I didn't have.

Though, I suspected, through his vetting—which at this juncture probably was no longer preliminary, but instead very thorough—he knew that.

And I liked him even more because he hadn't brought it up.

He, specifically, knew how much it would hurt. Far worse than talking about my parents, and it meant a lot that so far, he'd let it lie.

Maybe one day he'd go there (alas, it was unavoidable), but I loved the fact he didn't broach the subject or even allude to it now.

"I'll attend on my own," he continued. "That way, we can spend time together, because no one would question Sirk and I doing so. But I'll warn you, there'll be hawks who note your presence, and when we do go public, they'll think that was where we met. This has ramifications for Sirk, who it will be assumed is romantically interested in you. But there's no one else close who I can trust you with, save one of my brothers. And sadly, that trust excludes my brothers. No one but Aleece knows I've found my mate, but even if I told them, only Lilith knows what those two would get up to, even with my mate."

I was feeling all happy squidgy that he'd thought up a way to keep us private, but we could still be out in public, spending time together…not to mention how much of a hit it would be for Cat if he attended.

But something else took precedence.

"Princess Aleece knows?"

He nodded. "She commed me this morning. She'd heard I brought a female to the Catalogues, and she was curious. I'm considering bringing her to the showing, but I don't want there to be too much pressure on you."

I weighed the pressure that would put on me (which would be a lot) versus the cachet Aleece's additional presence would bring to Cat (which would also be a lot).

"If you, Sirk and Princess Aleece show, that would be huge for Cat," I noted.

"I'm sure," he agreed. "But it would be tough on you."

"I'm going to meet her someday, right?"

His eyes warmed (they were back to night, then again, he was on a space station, which was constant night).

"I'll consider it," he murmured.

"Is Sirk going to be okay with beings thinking you stole his date out from under him?"

"Sirk gives a shit about food, his restaurant allowing him the means to travel to learn about and eat more food, ring ice, the members of his ring ice team, and last, finding females who will put up with these obsessions, at least long enough so he can bed them. He wouldn't give two fucks about beings thinking I stole his female."

"Well then, this sounds like a plan."

His lips curved up. "Excellent. Do you need me to ask Allain to postpone your instruction with Madam Garwah while you're in this zone?"

He was so sweet.

"No. I'll need reasons to hit the bath pod and go out into the world, or I'll become a vampire."

"Vampire females are very sexy," he teased.

"Yes, but they burn to a cinder under the sun, and I like wearing sundresses."

He chuckled, I enjoyed it, then he said, "I'll let you get back to it, but I'll do it suggesting you carve an hour out to get a nap."

I rubbed my eyes, which were itchy with fatigue, unknowingly flaking off and smearing what was left of the mascara I hadn't cleaned off.

"I think I'll throw back a sleep smoothie and crash so I don't lapse into unconsciousness at my desk at Madam Garwah's. I don't think she'd like that."

"Probably not," he agreed.

The screen flashed, telling me I had an incoming text comm.

It also reminded me I'd sent some myself the night before, telling my gals we were having a holo conference during their lunch hour (Aleksei brought me home so late, even if the news was huge, I didn't have the heart to wake them to share it, but also, I was raring to get to my sketchpads, so I flew off some texts, and then got down to it).

But that time was nigh, thus, I'd have to do that before my smoothie.

However, while I had him...

"Quick question," I said to Aleksei.

"Hit me," he invited.

And again, he could be cute.

"Madam Garwah explained about the 'my lords' and 'your graces,' but she didn't share about this madam and mistress business."

He smirked.

It was sexy.

And then he explained his smirk when he asked, "Madam and mistress?"

Mm.

He was thinking of other uses of both.

"Be a good boy," I ordered.

"I'll do my best," he purred.

"You're failing," I warned.

His lips quirked before he got serious and stated, "You aren't titled, neither is she, but you both have status. It's an informal, but important form of address to be certain others know where you stand." His expression grew even more serious. "Especially for you, darling. At this juncture, even not having a title, you outrank everyone but me and my parents. This is the case even over my brothers and sister."

Wow.

This was news.

"I do?"

"You're the future queen, Laura."

Oh boy.

"Okay, we need to stop talking about this," I said quickly.

"It's a good deal to get used to, I understand that. But eventually, you'll have to," he cautioned.

"Can I get used to it tomorrow?"

He smiled. "I'll give you that."

Another flash happened on my screen.

"I'm getting comms, Aleksei," I told him. "I set up a holo conference with my girls to tell them about our mate thing." Saying that, it hit me, maybe I shouldn't, so I asked, "Is that okay?"

"They've been vetted, along with you. There are no concerns. Though, please advise them to keep it to themselves until we've decided to go public."

"Will do."

"I'll let you go."

I experienced something I rarely did when I was in my creative zone. That being I didn't want him to let me go.

But he had meetings.

And I had good news to share and a nap to take so I could do some more work.

So I said, "Okay. Hope you get done what you need to do."

"Hope you get some rest."

"I will."

His smile at that was soft and lovely. "Until later, *bissi*."

"Until then, Aleksei."

We disconnected.

I ran to get a glass of water before I grabbed the fab tablet my *mate* gave me so I could program the holo conference.

Two minutes later, all three of my gals popped into my studio.

I told them about troll skin and loincloths.

I told them about delicious kisses.

And I told them I'd found my mate.

They were holograms, but still...

After I imparted that news, the decibel level of their screams nearly shattered the windows.

❖ ❖ ❖

It was late, I was in bed with my tablet and stylus, fiddling with a design I'd scanned in from a sketch, when the screen flashed green with an incoming vid comm.

The words HRH Prince Aleksei showed and faded across the top, and I immediately said, "Engage video comm."

His face came on the screen.

"Excellent news, *drahko*," I shared. "I know what a shrimp fork is."

At me calling him *drahko*, another old-world endearment, exclusively masculine, which meant "my little dragon," the warmth that infused his expression caused the same through my body.

At my announcement regarding the shrimp fork, he burst out laughing.

"I cannot express how relieved I am you won't embarrass me during the fish course at a state dinner," he drawled.

Before I could respond, Nova crawled onto my chest, leaned forward and sniffed the tablet.

"Hello, love," Aleksei greeted her.

And again, warmth flooded my body.

I mean...

Was this male for real?

She marked the tablet with her ear before she lay down on my chest and started purring.

"You're in bed," he noted.

"Just finishing one last 3D of a design before I call it a night," I told him.

"I won't keep you, I just wanted to say goodnight."

I wanted him to keep me.

To that end, I asked, "How'd your day go?"

"Darling, you need to sleep," he replied.

"Are you tired?" I inquired.

"Aren't you?"

I was, but with him on display, I also was not.

"I'm more curious about what you're doing on Thoth, if you want to tell me."

"You can know anything about me, Laura."

Totally.

This male was not for real.

"Then tell me, how'd your day go?" I urged.

He gave me what I wished for, telling me about the state-of-the-art loading dock one of his construction companies was in the midst of building, a major coup for the aging satellite.

Tech had advanced so much, and so many other space stations had been built since, the beings that lived on Thoth were experiencing lower tourism, faltering trade and the resultant heightening of the cost of living, which wasn't awesome, considering there were a lot of beings out of work.

If newer ships found it easier to dock and offload, more supplies and materials could be brought in, upgrades could be done. But since Aleksei was already exclusively using labor sourced from those who lived there, he was already infusing much-needed capital into the local economy.

There were issues, however, because a rival construction company saw the merits of having the offloading permits, and they were playing games using the local council, which was stalling construction.

Not to mention, the Space Junkies, an outspoken protest group whose mission it was to dismantle all of what they called "space debris." This included industrial, botanical and resort stations, but also unmanned tech and energy satellites, which were essential to planetary and off-planet infrastructure and the mustering and storing of solar power to fuel it.

They were working hard to stymie the progress of Aleksi's construction of the docks, saying Thoth was outdated and therefore should be decommissioned and demolished.

"The locals aren't happy about the Junkies flying in and sharing loudly their home should be struck, returned to the planet and melted for reuse. It's not a good situation, and the council isn't helping by waffling between bribes from my rivals, what it would mean if they pissed me off, and pressure from Junkie supporters," he said.

"It sounds like a mess," I stated the obvious.

"Fortunately, I'm the only one paying salaries, which have been halted because the work has been. Because of this, there's an increasingly loud call for a general election to replace some of the council members. They tend to enjoy their positions. We're committed to the project, but we can't pay beings not to work, and it isn't us that's halting progress due to bureaucratical bullshit and implied demands to best the bribes my competitors are offering to delay the approval of permits. This kind of thing does get messy and protracted, but in the end, the beings hold the power."

"Well, I hope whenever that end might be doesn't make those beings suffer any more than they already are."

"Several of my meetings have been with union leaders," he shared. "We're forming a united front. I'm hoping by the time I leave, enough members of the council will buckle, and they can be back at work before I step on my ship."

I hoped that too.

However...

"This is important, Aleksei," I told him something he knew. "If you haven't done all you need to do, Cat's opening will survive. And I'll be with Sirk, so you won't have to worry about me."

"I've never been certain I could make it, darling. But I'm delighted you'll understand if I can't."

"Of course."

"It's late, but since we're discussing this, it's an opportunity I can't let slide."

I was confused.

"Sorry?"

"First, I knew you were concerned about telling me how deeply you descend into your creative process. But at the time, considering you didn't know you were my mate, and I had loincloths to show you..."—I grinned, he reciprocated—"I didn't get into it. But I find it immensely attractive you have a passion, you allow yourself to sink into it and warn those in your life you need that."

I found it immensely attractive that he found it the same.

"I'm glad," I whispered by way of sharing that, but even if they were quiet, there was a lot of feeling in those two words.

"Further, it means a great deal to me you give as good as you get."

I was confused again.

"What do you mean?"

"I mean, we'll discuss her to whatever extent you need me to explain. But at this point, since it's apropos, I'll share that one of the various reasons I could not carry through my promise to Anna was that she refused to understand my life was not simply about being a prince to the realm, visiting hospitals, shaking hands, wearing tuxedos and existing solely to rub the little beings' noses in the fact they will always be the little beings."

I didn't know how to process the clear evidence there was some bitterness behind his break with Princess Anna.

This wasn't a surprise, as such. A break was a break, and they weren't ever fun.

But although their break was not long ago, no new female in a male's life wanted to think there was any feeling lingering, outside vague fondness, or alternately, annoyance, or something of the like.

I also couldn't process the unexpected knowledge Princess Anna, the fair and ethereal, was, at least according to Aleksei, a classist bitch.

As he remained silent, it was clear some response was expected of me, however, all I could come up with was, "Um."

"We've known each other since we were children," he said quietly. "And we've been friends since we first met. As adults, a romance sparked from that, and I'm not proud of how easily she deceived me, but she did. In retrospect, I see this mostly extended from the foundation of our many years being friends, and the fact we had a lot in common, both of us being the children of royals. It was still a long con on her part."

He paused.

I wasn't sure if he was waiting for me to say something, but since what he'd already told me had me mildly reeling, and I didn't, he continued.

"I was not expecting ever to meet my mate, *bissi*. The last fated ones of my line were my great-great grandfather and grandmother. My parents were delighted with the match with Anna. There are...things happening with Sky's Edge, and the alliance would have positive political outcomes. But Anna had no patience with the pleasure I derived from the work I do outside my royal duties. She had even less with my desire to keep as much of my life private as I can manage. And she required far more attention than any female I've been connected with. It was all immensely draining, then frustrating, annoying, and finally, intolerable. It was clear she wasn't the female for me, even if I'd never met you. But I've now met you. And the point I'm trying very poorly to make is, it's coming clear the many reasons why you are."

"Okay," I whispered.

He released a heavy sigh and stated, "I hesitate to share this, but I hope you come to understand, in my position, this isn't expected, and is sometimes actively discouraged. I wasn't in love with her. I cared for her, had affection for her, was attracted to her, but I didn't love her."

"Okay," I repeated.

"Bloody hell, I fucked this," he muttered.

"No, it's all right," I assured. "We would have to talk about it. And I get you. I'm relieved you understand what I do for work isn't a job, it's part of who I am, and if I wasn't able to do it how I have to do it, I don't know how I'd react. I don't think I could live with that. So yeah. I get you."

"I'm glad."

"But, since you two broke it off, are there political ramifications? And since we're, well...what we are, and that will eventually be known, will that cause more problems?"

"Anna will be pissed. Although how she gives it, and expects to get it, is unhealthy, the bottom line is, she was in love with me."

Fabulous.

"Queen Delanta isn't my biggest fan," he went on.

Queen Delanta of Dawn's Break *was* a classist bitch, that was well-known, so screw her.

"King Dagsbrun is very well aware his daughter is a pain in the ass and that I'm not a man to be leashed, so it was obvious he was expecting it. And Prince Bainan was surprised we ever got together in the first place."

That was a relief.

"So that's good."

"It is, but it doesn't matter. It's over and fate has decided my queen. Fortunately for me, fate has excellent taste."

Even if his words made me feel gushy, I gave him the side eye. "You're very smooth."

"Yes, darling," he drawled. "I very much am."

My legs grew restless at his promise.

Nova lifted her head.

Jupiter, who lay close to my feet, jumped off the bed to share his aversion to me reminding him I existed.

"And now, I'll let you finish your 3D so you can sleep," he finished.

"All right."

"Just so you know, you can comm anytime. If I can't take it, I'll reach out when I can."

I smiled at him. "All right."

"Sleep well, Laura."

"You too, Aleksei. 'Night."

"'Night, darling."

We disconnected.

I didn't finish my design.

I set the tablet aside, stroked Nova, then stroked Comet when he joined us, settling down my side facing away, his indication he wanted booty scratches (something he got).

And I processed through all Aleksei had told me.

What was left unsaid: he was bitter, and maybe hurt, that in what had happened with Anna, he'd lost a friend.

But she was then.

And I was now.

I was also the future.

So I could live with that.

The only problem was, Aleksei was honest, forthcoming, committed to sharing, allowing me to get to know him, doing it easily, quickly and deeply.

This meant, eventually, I'd have to give that back.

And I dreaded that eventuality...for two reasons.

But eventually wasn't now.

Now was about Aleksei saying, *Bloody hell, I fucked this*, in a tone where the silk of his voice snagged, because it meant so much to him *not* to fuck it because he didn't want to upset me.

And I could very happily live in a now like that.

So I would.

"Lights off," I called.

My room went dark.

And in the middle of kitty strokes and booty scratches, without that first issue, I fell fast asleep.

I did it deeply.

And I didn't dream, not good ones, but better, not bad.

CHAPTER 12

CANCER

I was running between bathroom, closet and bedroom in a tizzy.

I should have cancelled my instruction with Madam Garwah that night. Attending it didn't give me enough time to get ready for the showing without rushing, and I hated to rush.

But if I had cancelled, how would I have moved from what fork, spoon, wineglass (etc.) to use and what topics of conversation were acceptable with my dinner companion, depending on if he was an aristocrat, a peer or a statesman, to acceptable behavior in a receiving line, of which (it had become clear Madam Garwah knew my future before I did), I would eventually be the one receiving, rarely the one shuffling through the line?

I needed to be ready for what was to come, and I couldn't miss a day.

Although I'd heard nothing from Aleksei since his return comm after I'd left him an audio message that morning (during which he'd shared it was still iffy he'd be able to attend the showing), there was a small chance I not only would be attending him as a royal that night, but also his sister.

Though, I'd also heard from him the day before. He'd given me a good morning comm, which was short since he had to make a meeting, and a goodnight one, which was much longer and fortunately just flirty and chatty. We didn't get in to anything deep.

Not that I didn't want to know him deeply, but it had been intense, and it was clear we both could use a break.

And anyway, flirting with him was all kinds of fun. Aleksei was an excellent flirt in a manner that was very Aleksei.

Hot and sweet.

But a possibly imminent audience with two royals was on my mind.

The fact I'd buzzed Sirk up and he was currently heading toward the door I'd opened was on my mind.

The fact Allain had gotten in touch earlier that day to press about me signing the no contact order against my parents (this he'd sent, and I'd signed, and I'd subsequently received a notice from the Royal Ministry of Law and Justice that it had been filed), and I wondered if my parents received the same notice, was also on my mind.

The fact I couldn't find one of my two silver strappy high-heeled sandals was on my mind.

And the fact that Cat was on my Palm display, freaking out about champagne, was on my mind.

"Everyone's coming, Laura. *Everyone!*" she all but shouted. "I mean, I knew Terrinton was a draw, but Bash and Tay are seriously connected."

Cat, being Cat, tapped into those connections and, good news!—even though she was working, Bash was her date that night.

"So it's going to be a crush," she continued. "Royal Fire and Safety will be all over my ass if I don't put out a velvet rope, something I've done. I had to hire a door attendant who can let in the VIPs, and cycle people in when others leave. It's become a nightmare. And I know, I just *know*, because free booze makes beings deranged, I'm going to run out of champagne. I put an emergency order into food supply, but they're backed up, and estimated delivery time is between three and four hours from now. The doors open in twenty minutes, so I don't have three hours. I'm sunk! This is a disaster!"

"Laura?" Sirk called from the other room.

Dang it!

I limped, one sandal on, one sandal off, toward my bedroom door, assuring Catla, "Sirk and I'll stop by an off-license on the way there. What do you need? A case? Two?"

"Oh my gods, I'd love you forever. Two. Can you make sure it's chilled?"

I hit the door saying, "We'll do what we—"

I looked toward the entry and saw Sirk standing inside, looking fabulous in a brown suit, light-blue shirt and burgundy tie.

And standing with him, holding Nova to his chest, giving her a neck rub, was my mate.

Therefore, I shrieked, "*Aleksei!*" hobble-ran like an idiot across my loft, and he had to quickly drop Nova, because I threw myself in his arms.

He lifted me up his chest and tucked his face in my neck.

"You made it," I whispered into his ear.

"Indeed," he whispered against my skin.

I shivered.

He set me on my mismatched feet and pulled his face out of my neck, but as he did, he ran the edge of his teeth along it.

Oh...

My.

My nipples beaded and my head tipped back.

"I don't wish to mess up your lip stain," he explained the sultry scrape.

I couldn't care less about my lip stain.

"Or devour you in front of Sirk," he went on.

Okay, that would be awkward.

I smiled at him, pressed my hands into his chest and then frowned at said chest.

"You have Nova fluff all over you."

And he did, her fur marring the miraculousness of his royal-blue three-piece suit, which he'd coupled with a crisp white shirt, a navy blue-and-white diagonally striped tie and matching pocket square.

He looked confident, stylish and good enough to eat (even with the fluff).

"Not the end of the world, especially when my female's a celebrated costume designer. I suspect you can help me with that."

He suspected correctly.

I beamed at him, got up on tiptoe, kissed the underside of his jaw and turned to Sirk.

I shambled to him, gave and received a big hug.

"Hello! Hello!" I heard Cat's voice. "I'm delighted the prince has arrived, but *I need champagne!*"

I lifted the Palm I'd forgotten I held as Sirk asked, "What's this?"

I gave her my face even if I was answering Sirk. "Cat, my friend and the director of the gallery we're going to tonight, is having a champagne supply problem."

With no warning, he plucked the Palm out of my hand and peered at the display.

"You need champagne?" he asked.

"Oh my gods, you're fucking gorgeous," I heard Cat breathe.

When she did, I took in Sirk and realized she was right.

Sure, Sirk was so handsome, I didn't miss this, but it only registered in my mind in a vague way, considering Aleksei's looks were god-like, thus he outshone every male around him.

Now it was registering in a not-vague way.

Aleksei still looked like a god.

I glanced over my shoulder to smile at my mate.

He wasn't paying attention to the conversation.

He was staring at my behind, and the expression on his face put goosebumps on my flesh.

I didn't know if he would make it, but I was me, thus, I would have worn something like what I had on regardless.

But right then, with his expression, I was glad I was wearing my flamingo-pink satin, to-the-toes gown that was cut on the bias, had a halter-neck, zero back, clung to my curves and showed side boob.

I wore nothing else but the little diamond studs I'd bought myself after my first lead costume designer gig, and the diamond bracelet Mr. and Mrs. Truelock bought me when I graduated from the Royal College of Art and Design.

Oh, and a single silver sandal.

My mane-mate had put my hair into a messy, side pony.

I sensed (mightily) that Aleksei approved.

"I'll have my suppliers propel three cases, chilled," Sirk was saying, so I turned back to him. "You'll have them in less than an hour."

"Oh my gods," Cat repeated. "I love you."

Sirk grunted and tossed my Palm to me.

I caught it and aimed the display at my face. "You good?"

"Get here, I need you. I'm glad the prince made it. I can already tell you look amazing. And I love you. Byeeeeeeee."

My display went blank.

I pivoted my head between the two gorgeous males in my presence and stated, "We best get going."

"I think you best find your other shoe first, *bissi*," Aleksei suggested on an amused half-grin.

"Oh! Farg!" I exclaimed, and totter-ran to my closet.

I eventually had to run through a third of my shoe display program before I found, for some unhinged reason, I'd shoved the other sandal in with a pair of foam kicks that I'd bought because I thought I could pull them off, but I wasn't a foam (or a kicks) type of female.

And after successfully rejoining the males, fully shod, I had to dash back to the closet to grab a handheld lint vac.

But I finally got Nova's fur off Aleksei, and I was on his arm as he escorted me down in the lift.

He went out first and got in his JetPanther.

Sirk and I exited five minutes later, and he situated me beside him in his awesome, sporty bright red BratShot 250.

And off we went for Aleksei and my first officially unofficial appearance in the same public space being mates.

Color me crazy, me, Ms. Homebody, was looking forward to it.

But mostly, I was glad he was back.

✦ ✦ ✦

"Okay," I whispered, sitting beside Sirk, five crafts back on hover over the street, waiting for our turn for the VIP valet to let us onto the deep-purple carpet outside Cat's gallery, Tempera.

I was watching Aleksei stride purposefully through the lightning storm of the flashing cams to the front doors.

"That was terrifying," I finished when he disappeared inside.

Sirk had told me Aleece wasn't coming, and I was kind of glad, because the frenzy I just witnessed had me inwardly quailing, and she might have made it worse.

I'd seen it happen to him and other famous people.

But knowing him, him meaning something to me, and witnessing it in person, I was struggling with a mixture of outrage, revulsion and fear.

The first two I felt for him because this was his life, and I knew he didn't like it.

The last was for me.

"It's all he knows," Sirk replied. "Sure, sometimes he finds it mildly annoying, but he's learned to play the game, and when he needs his space, he knows how to get it."

"Right," I mumbled.

"Laura, this is his life," Sirk said low what I'd just thought.

Left unsaid, *And it's going to be yours too, so buck up, buttercup.*

I turned his way. "There could be a half a dozen crazies on that pavement."

"Considering no one knew he'd be here, if they were Lex's personal crazies, they're slavering over social tape, hoping for a lock on his position. But his team is second to none. The king made the decision to shift the brightest in Royal Service to Aleksei when his general popularity outdistanced the king's. Part of that team has been here, scouring every inch of this block for the last few hours. He's covered. And I know you are too."

"But no one knows who I am."

"It won't matter to him. We have someone following us. And you'll have someone with eyes on you outside as we go in, and someone waiting on you to arrive inside. He or she will then shadow you, doing it without anyone knowing they are. These will be different beings than those assigned to Aleksei." His tone changed to guarded. "Hasn't he shared this with you?"

"He did, I just…I've never seen the frenzy in action, and I have to admit, it spooked me."

He touched my forearm so briefly, I wondered if Aleksei already marked me, or if that was just a show of respect to a male of his clan.

"Just know, the vast majority…and you know this, Laura, that vast is *vast*…utterly adore him. They wouldn't harm him in any way, and some would lay down their lives at just the threat that someone else might. And when they find out you two are fated, they're gonna lose their minds at the romance and destiny of it all, and they'll love you too. That's all good. And if I know Lex, he'll break his back to keep your focus on the good. He'll deal with the bad."

I didn't find that as reassuring as he thought I would, considering that was not fair at all.

But I didn't have a chance to enter into a discussion with him.

My door was swinging open, and a valet was helping me out.

Sirk met me on the carpet, put a hand to my back and guided me in. He got his share of flashes, definitely. But nothing like the blitz Aleksei received.

We were barely two steps in before Gayliliel was on us.

She grabbed my arms, kissed both my cheeks, leaned back and gave me a top to toe, announcing, "Oh my gods, you look fucking phenomenal."

"So do you," I replied, thinking her bronze, one-shoulder gown was perfect.

She glanced over and up, blinked and whispered in Sirk's direction, "Oh my gods, you're just plain phenomenal."

"I already know I like your friends a whole fuckin' lot," Sirk declared.

I laughed and introduced, "Gayle, Sirk Parrin. Sirk, Gayle Vinestrong."

He swept up her hand and held it to his chest. "It is my utmost pleasure."

She just blinked at him, mouth open, and I mentally inventoried my evening bag in an effort to remember if I had a handkerchief should she drool.

I had one, of course.

I didn't need it, because Cat descended, I got cheek brushes, and then she pointed in Gayle's face.

"Don't even think about it. I saw him first. I have dibs," she warned.

"He just got here, so I saw him first," Gayle returned. "And you're on a date."

"I saw him on vid on Laura's Palm," Cat informed her. "And I'm on a *working* date, where I'm working and I have a date. But I always keep my options open."

I glanced around to make sure Bash wasn't close and didn't hear that.

He wasn't, so at least that was all good.

It was also indicative of why Cat hadn't made a true connection. I didn't know if she was always on the lookout for something better, or she was scared who she found might disappoint her father, or if she was terrified of giving her heart to someone like Dagon.

But whoever she was with, it was Cat who held herself distant.

"Palm vids don't count," Gayle shot back.

"They *so* do," Cat retorted, and turned to Sirk and me. "Get champagne." She gave Sirk a narrow look and suggested, "Avoid the hors d'oeuvres. My caterers are excellent, but I've been to Stained Glass, and they're about fifty pegs down from what you're used to. Now I need to sell paintings, sculptures and what Terrinton calls 'experiences.' Must dash. *Amusez-vous bien!*"

And she was off.

Gayle got close, huddling with Sirk and me.

"Okay, this place is a mad crush, but we need to pretend to care about what this obviously somewhat unhinged, no offense to the somewhat unhinged, artist calls art so we can"—she paused to give me two exaggerated winks—"*run into* a certain someone."

"You'd suck at subterfuge," I said out of the side of my mouth. "And I know this because you're using subterfuge, and you suck at it."

Sirk snickered as he pulled Gayle to his left side, curling her fingers around his arm, his opposite hand returned to my back, and with the three off us attached, he led us into the crush.

"Then it's good I'm a marketing director and not a spy," she rejoined while we moved.

We navigated the space, during which Sirk expertly nabbed three glasses of champagne off a tray, handing two to Gayle and me.

As we walked, I saw all around me what I expected to see, since I was a fan (if you will) of Terrinton's.

He didn't create beauty.

He created chaos.

But there was something beautiful about it.

At least I thought so.

Though, nothing was more beautiful than the tall, black-haired man in his royal-blue suit, who was in a back corner talking to the artist himself, his attention on me, but his chin jutted toward Sirk.

Sirk guided us directly there.

He gave a casual bow, and Gayle and I dropped into curtsies (mine was much more fluid, since Madam Garwah started every class with ten minutes of thigh-burning curtsy practice, which I doubted I needed, she just got a kick out of me collapsing into my desk chair after it was over).

Aleksei and Sirk then did the whole alpha male handshake that started with hands, then moved to grip forearms, before Sirk turned to Gayle and me.

"Your highness..."

Dang, he even made that sound friendly and not fussed.

"...may I present Laura Makepeace and Gayle Vinestrong."

"I've had the pleasure of meeting Laura," Aleksei replied, his deep voice sharing volumes by dipping straight to velvet as he took my hand and brushed his lips across my knuckles. He let me go to take Gayle's. "And I'm honored."

"Me too, *totally*," she whispered, her eyes—oh boy—were bright with unshed tears and a wonky, happy, tremulous smile was on her face.

I bumped her with my hip to tell her to get it together.

She cleared her throat and added a sniff.

Aleksei let her go, skated an affectionate glance across mine, and turned to Terrinton.

"And allow me to present the man of the hour. Terrinton, this is a good friend of mine, Sirk Parrin, and as you heard, Laura Makepeace and Gayle Vinestrong."

"Both like sisters to Catla Truelock," Sirk added.

Terrinton, who was human, short of stature, had a shock of gray-white hair that had been haphazardly slicked back at the top and sides, but was dry, unruly and fluffing out around his neck and the frayed collar of a much-worn shirt. His eyes were faded blue. His skin was lined. The top of his head barely came to Aleksei's shoulder. And he appeared to be a man who enjoyed the peaceful countryside with a hobby of whittling, not one who created controversial masterpieces of color, shape and form, who'd been the darling and devil of the art world for the last five decades.

In fact, he appeared to be a man who wanted more than anything to be absolutely anywhere but here.

He dipped his chin to both of us, then his gaze skittered away, caught on something, and he shrunk into himself.

I glanced to where his eyes skittered, saw someone on the approach, no...on a *determined* approach, and I immediately forged toward him.

He recoiled from me as well, but I ignored that, linked arms, and announced, "If you'll excuse us, I'm dying for an explanation of a certain piece."

I caught Aleksei's thoughtful expression aimed at me before I drew the elderly man away.

I tipped my head toward his as I semi-dragged, semi-walked him toward a piece installed on a wall opposite Aleksei. "I think you may know how to do this, but just in case it's been a while. Conference in with me, like we're engrossed in something immensely important, and hopefully no one will be rude enough to interrupt."

We stopped in front of what appeared to be a gazillion old-fashioned smoked cigarette butts, all of them scrunched dead at their filters. These were nestled in a bed of gray ash and pressed between matte and glass.

It was ugly, horrid.

And amazing.

But my mind was mostly on how Cat didn't realize this guy needed a minder.

"Do you have someone who—?"

"She needed to use the toilet," he said in a quiet, timid voice. "Catla summoned the prince, thinking he'd keep the wolves at bay."

"Something he did, until we showed up, opening the seal," I deduced.

He shrugged uncomfortably.

"Sorry about that," I muttered.

"You're mates. If you didn't come to him, he would have left me where I stood and prowled the room until he could get to you."

I jolted before I turned to stare down at him.

"You know?" I whispered.

His faded eyes came to mine. "I'm an artist, Ms. Makepeace. I feel everything."

"Of course," I murmured.

"He tensed, I suspect the minute you entered the gallery. He only relaxed after you rounded the first installation and came into view."

Although this both moved and staggered me, I went to release Terrinton's arm. "Oh gods, am I burning you?"

He laughed shortly, finally seeming to relax.

"My dear, I am no threat to that beast." I realized his eyes might be faded, but the intelligence behind them wasn't. "I expect you're a much better minder. His mark is so strong, no one will get near you, male or female, unless they were someone like me, or your friends. I take it your acquaintance is new?"

I nodded to confirm this.

"I would take heed and settle quickly," he advised. "The prince is not the kind of male to allow this intensity to falter. You two will be facing your final days decades from now, and the heat of his possession would burn through legions."

I felt my heart roll over at his words but admitted, "I didn't even realize we were mates. He had to tell me."

He patted my hand on his arm. "Well done, Ms. Makepeace. Fate may have decided you belong to each other, but he's a male who doesn't respect something unless he earns it...or wins it. If you were to fall at his feet, he would accept you as his fate, it would make him happy, but it wouldn't fulfill his needs."

This was not good news.

"It didn't take me long to fall at his feet," I shared.

"Nor did it take you long to snatch me and leave his presence. I'd say that's happened to him very few times in his life. Perhaps...*none*," he returned.

"I wasn't—"

He patted my hand again. "Your heart is kind. He won't have missed that either. You still left him. Turned your back and walked away." He smiled, exposing very big, very healthy, very white teeth in his tanned, leathered face. "I would suggest you keep him on his toes, but I believe you'll do that anyway." He tipped his head to the cigarette piece. "Now, is there a reason you brought me to this one?"

I looked at it, seeing the small digi-sign at the bottom left side named it *Cancer*, it cost one point three million, and it was sold.

"It's hideous," I stated bluntly.

He chortled.

I turned back to him. "And I love it."

"Before my time, definitely yours, this world was practically covered in what they referred to as 'butts.' *Butts* that killed beings. Demons and shifters couldn't get cancer, but fae could, though their superior immune systems could beat it. Before the vaccine was created, it was an epidemic for humans. A killer in a *butt*."

He chortled again and I couldn't stop myself from doing it with him, but I had a mind to the fact we could only do that because that epidemic, and its long-lived, tragic results, had long since been eradicated from our planet.

He leaned toward me and rolled up on his toes to confide, "I'm told I have an odd sense of humor."

"Doesn't seem odd to me."

"Wanna know what's even more hilarious?" he asked.

"Absolutely," I answered.

"It took me all of an hour to smash those *butts* into a frame. An hour!" he crowed. "And some poor chump shelled one point three mil for it. Now *that's* hilarious."

We both busted out laughing.

I swallowed mine and gasped, "Gods, I hope the prince didn't buy it."

"No. I can tell he has excellent taste. I noted he had a particular interest in *Marie*. That, I labored over for months. She was my muse, 2072 through 2078. She passed last year."

My head listed to the side at this news.

"I'm so sorry," I whispered.

He nodded curtly. "She was beautiful. The painting I honored her with is beautiful. And she had the most delicious cunt I've ever tasted."

I huffed out a shocked breath, caught his cheeky, reminiscing grin, and started laughing again.

While I was doing it, something snagged my attention at the corner of my eye.

Or perhaps I felt it because I knew the feel.

I knew it down to my bones.

I peered over Terrinton's head.

And froze solid.

No.

It couldn't be.

But it was.

The male from the alley.

The male who shot my beast.

The male who murdered half of me.

"My dear?" Terrinton called.

"Danger," I forced through stiff lips.

"I'm sorry?" he asked.

"Danger," I said.

He was dressed as a caterer.

His eyes were locked on Aleksei.

He began to set his tray aside at the same time reach inside his jacket.

"*Danger!*" I shrieked, garnering the attention of those around us, pulling my hand from Terrinton, dropping my champagne to the floor where the sound of it shattering barely pierced the din of conversation, and planting my foot to race toward Aleksei.

But I didn't have to.

Set and some female were on the threat. Set flying from out of nowhere, tackling him at his back.

The tray he was still carrying went flying, some cheese puff type things strewed, the female was right there, at the ready, legs planted, her weapon trained on him. Set popped to his feet, and she zapped him. The villain's body jumped then went inert with the stun.

They both moved in unison to put restraints on him.

The hum around us rose sharply as people made their alarm vocal, shifting away from the ruckus, a few shrill noises of shock sounded, and I felt Terrinton's surprisingly strong fingers circle my wrist.

"I think I should take you to—" he began.

Sacrifice, I thought.

Diversion.

Back in that alley, there had been one.

And he was easily neutralized.

Giving the other time to—

I whirled, distractedly noting Aleksei was fighting the press of what was clearly his security detail—and I didn't pause to count, but there were at least six of them—trying to push him to a door at the rear of the space...and safety.

But he was struggling against them in his effort to get to me.

His eyes were blazing purple.

But I didn't have time for that.

I kept searching and I didn't see him.

I felt him.

"*Weapon! Weapon! Weapon!*" I screeched before I even saw one.

I had to warn them all because I knew it was there.

At my words, panic ensued, shouts, screams, running feet.

The assassin didn't panic or run.

He stood true.

His gaze, too, was locked on Aleksei.

I raced toward the space between him and my mate, my gaze never leaving the traitor.

He whipped out his firearm.

I stopped between the two males, throwing my arms out and screaming, "*No!*"

As my scream echoed, the assassin lurched (and I did too) because the earth under our feet shook. The walls trembled. *Cancer* dropped, its glass shattered and butts littered the floor.

And my blood turned cold as the air split with the sound of an enraged dragon's roar.

CHAPTER 13

ASLEEP

The beam released from the weapon half a second after the amethyst-hued, black-spined, webbed wing of the dragon gently knocked me into Sirk's arms.

Regardless, the aim was too high, and the stream burned a dark hole close to the ceiling into the wall beyond, luckily striking nothing.

I felt pandemonium around us but could do nothing but stare as the long, strong, entrancingly scaled silver and black neck slithered menacingly across the space, the be-horned head both elegant and terrible, the slit eyes glowing purple, the multi-fanged mouth opening.

The horrified, panicked shriek of a man was cut short as the blaze of amethyst fire bellowed from the dragon's mouth, starting and stopping in the blink of an eye. The strike so swift and sure, it left the would-be assassin to stand as he was, with arms bent and raised before him in a paltry effort to shield himself from certain death, but the form was now black ash.

And I swallowed hard as I watched it filter to pool on the floor, the calcified weapon clattering into the mess, diffusing a poof of black dust.

I'd barely finished doing this before I was caught between a claw and a crook of Aleksei's beast's wing.

"Oh, fuck," Sirk grunted as I was pulled from his arms.

I had no time to react.

I was lifted and deposited behind the line of lethal spikes that slanted backward and ruled his long neck.

"Stay low!" Sirk shouted up at me. "And for fuck's sake, *hold on*!"

I just had time to hike up my skirt so I could straddle his neck and grip tight with my legs, grab the spike in front of me and bend low, before Aleksei took one step, two, and then we were gliding, his bulk so huge, his wingspan covered the large gallery, wall to wall, knocking people off their feet, paintings off their moorings, upending sculptures and scattering installations.

He destroyed everything in his path, including—I tucked my chin in my neck before he hit—the plate glass windows and doors at the front that he burst through headfirst, his impenetrable scales taking the brunt of the shattered glass.

I heard the screams, saw people throwing themselves to the ground to avoid his wings, his flight and his massive, clawed feet, and when we got outside and I raised my head, I saw others running for dear life.

But we were lifting up, up, and *up*, the wind beating against the satin of my dress, whipping the ponytail out of my hair and chilling my skin to ice.

He was soaring.

I was panting and gripping him with everything I had, whimpering with every powerful flap of the wide span of wings that jostled me.

Fortunately, our flight didn't last long.

He hit uptown, coasted, circled and landed on a landing pad at the top of his building that was designed for heli-crafts such as JetPanthers, not dragons. But it made do.

When he stopped, he bent his neck low, which I took as him telling me to hop off.

I did, nearly turning my ankle, not only at having to jump off and land, doing it in my high heels, but because my legs were frozen, and I was jittery as all heck because, let us not forget, I just barebacked a freaking *dragon*.

"Have you lost your mind?" I shrieked at the enormous, ferocious creature before me.

He shook his body, wings and scales like a dog would shake off water.

And then Aleksei stood before me in human form, naked as sin (and, no matter the current craziness of my sitch, his body was such, sin was all I could think about when confronted with what seemed like acres of bulky, defined muscle, not to mention, one particular well-endowed part of his anatomy).

Before I could get my wits about me, he stalked toward me, swung me up into his arms, and prowled toward a door.

"Alek—" I began.

"Shut it," he growled, no silk or velvet in his tone now.

It was rough, commanding.

Incensed.

"Doors open," he barked.

The door in front of us opened, he jogged down some steps, jostling me again with this new flight I was taking under his control, that being, this time, in his arms. He strode through another door and into a dark space that had dim light I knew was created by the city.

I heard the door whoosh closed behind us.

And latch.

"Lights, forty percent," he ordered and dropped me to my feet with a jarring thud.

I barely stopped swaying when I went dead still because his long finger was a hair's breadth from my nose, and his handsome face transformed to horrible beauty carrying its sheer wrath was right behind it.

His eyes still glowed amethyst.

"You move a fucking *muscle*, Laura, I'll gods-damn chain you to my fucking bed for a fucking *year*."

With that, he stalked off, leaving me so stunned, I couldn't even begin to process the new knowledge that the sight of him nude from the back was almost as good as the front.

I took a breath.

Another one.

I got myself together enough to notice I was on a long, wide landing that appeared to be a continuous slab of perfect, gleaming black marble.

There was a sunken living room to my right, which led to a low ledge that rose about three feet, giving way to all windows. It had a splendorous view of the city of Nocturn, the Dolphin Sea and the various off-coast islands connected by old-world, still maintained, rarely used (except for cyclists, walkers and runners), pretty bridges.

And last, a direct view to Sceptred Isle featuring the prominent, illuminated, graceful fortress of the Celestial Palace.

To my left was a kitchen with what seemed like miles of glossy black cupboards and monochrome countertops.

Everything, as far as I could tell, was decorated in black, grays, matte silver and polished chrome with accents of amethyst.

This was all I took in before Aleksei was back, stunning me immobile again because he was in a long-sleeved dark-gray T-shirt that hugged his pecs and biceps, faded jeans, and Sky-Trek running shoes.

Not once, in all my life, had I seen him in casual gear, and as noted, I paid attention to him.

He stopped four feet in front of me, like he didn't trust himself to get any closer, and I saw immediately his temper had not cooled even a little bit, even if his eyes were now dark as night.

"Now...explain," he bit off.

"E-explain what?"

"Explain..."

He drew a sharp breath into his nose.

"Explain..." He tried again.

And failed again.

"Explain...what the fuck..."—his torso spiked toward me—"*you were thinking, putting yourself in the path of a PR60!*"

A PR60?

What on earth was that?

"I think maybe we both need to take a brea—" I began to suggest.

"Answer me," he gritted.

"Perhaps—"

"*Fucking answer me!*" he roared.

Oh no.

No, no, no, no...

NO!

I lived with this *shit* my whole fucking *life* before I left my parents' home.

I would not have my mate speak to me this way.

No.

Fucking.

Way.

"Calm down," I snapped.

"I'll calm down when you answer my fucking question," he fired back.

"And I'll answer your question when you can speak to me rationally."

"And I'd be speaking to you rationally if you'd been behaving rationally and hadn't walked right in the path of a fucking PR60," he clipped, not even slightly doing what I asked.

So I lost it and yelled, "I don't even know what a PR60 is!"

"It's the weapon he trained on you. Prison issue, in case an inmate manages to escape the benzos they pump into everything and is able to shift. It's got humanoid settings, demon settings, fae, bot, and the strongest, *beast settings*. And it's powerful enough even to ring *my* beast's bell. Which was what that fucker was set at, and you stepped right in godsdamned *front of it* in fucking *human form*."

That was the same weapon that killed my beast.

"I wasn't thinking," I whispered, my mind tumbling over itself.

"No shit?" he bit.

My mind stopped tumbling, and my head ticked. "I would appreciate, considering *you know*, a little bit of compassion here, Aleksei."

"A little bit of compassion for you doing something so motherfucking stupid?" he demanded, just like he thought I was motherfucking stupid.

"It was instinct." I threw up both hands and guessed at why I did what I did, "You're my mate."

"And that venue had twelve RS agents crawling all over it, one two feet behind him, weapon trained. He'd have been neutralized, except you stepped in front of the gods-damned stream, so he couldn't stun the fucker, because if he did, and it triggered his finger to stream, you would have been caught in that fire."

Well...

Whoops.

"Okay, you have to cut me some slack. I'm new to this," I said.

"Cut you some slack," he whispered, and I did not take his change in tone as a good thing.

Oh no.

I could tell it was a bad thing.

Very bad.

I opened my mouth, but he lifted an imperious hand for me to keep quiet, which rankled in a major way, and he shifted his attention over my shoulder.

I turned.

The doors to a lift situated behind me opened. Set and the female agent strode out, and it was only then I noticed the female was dark fae.

"Scene is locked down. The team is already there. Truelock and Vinestrong are being transferred to interrogation, District Three Constabulary. Constables from there as well as Districts Two, Four and Five are corralling witnesses and gathering evidence, but the RMI is sending agents in to take over," Set reported.

"Wait, what?" I whispered.

"The assailant is being transported to the Hold. And RS, RIC and RMI are already squabbling about who's going to have the first go at him," Set finished reporting to Aleksei.

He didn't even spare a glance at me.

I whirled on Aleksei. "Why are Cat and Gayle being interrogated?"

"Because no one knew I might be there, except Cat and Gayle," Aleksei all but spat.

"They wouldn't—"

He dismissed me by ordering Set, "Mammon and Freya Truelock need to be picked up too."

"No!" I cried.

"Already ordered," Set told him.

"My father been informed?" Aleksei asked Set.

Set nodded. "Allain is doing it. Then he'll be here to assist you."

"There is absolutely no way Cat, Gayle or Mr. and Mrs. Truelock are involved in this," I announced.

No one paid me any mind as Set informed Aleksei, "I clocked him when he came in. At first, he had eyes only for Laura."

"Same," the female said. "She's pretty, but it wasn't that. He was locked on."

I turned on her. "Of course he was," I snapped furiously. "But there's nothing left for him to take from me. He's already killed my beast."

At my announcement, the air in the room turned completely static.

This highly uncomfortable feeling didn't alter one bit when Aleksei asked sinisterly, "I beg your pardon?"

I whirled on him again. "He was one of the ones who attacked me in that alley three months ago. Obviously, the police didn't find him. And now I think..." I shook my head. "I don't know what to think. Because from the instant I saw him, he was looking at you."

Aleksei stared at me.

I stared at him.

He stared at me.

Before I started screaming, because we were doing this again, he said with clearly forced calm, "Your beast isn't dead, Laura."

My stomach twisted, the pain so excruciating, the bitter dripping off my words was barbed.

"Then you didn't read your briefings on me very closely, your highness."

"Your beast isn't dead," he repeated.

I opened my mouth.

"I feel her right now."

I closed my mouth, and a bolt of fire shafted through my internal organs.

"She's been very quiet," he said, his voice exceptionally low, like he was talking to a being clinging to the edge of a tall building, hoping to convince them not to jump. "She was highly communicative the night we met, but since then, nothing. I've thought it curious. But my creature communicated to me she's small, vulnerable, and he suspects she's been taught to hide, and seek your shelter, my guess was, because what your parents thought of you…and her."

I felt my eyes begin to sting, because he was touching too many raw chords with his words, but I slanted my chin to the side in an effort to control my emotion and kept my gaze steady on his.

"She's not quiet, Aleksei. She's there, because I refused to allow them to cut her out. But she's still gone."

I was feeling something come off him. Something dangerous and scary.

But his voice remained calm and painfully reassuring when he asked, "Someone wanted to cut her out?"

"At the hospital, after the attack."

"The attack three months ago," he said.

"Yes. It had to have been in my brief. I made a statement to the detective inspector. He's even commed me since. Not often, but he's been in touch to share where he is with the investigation. Which isn't far, something that became very obvious tonight. Cat and Gayle were there when I reported it. They were also there when the doctor and his nurse tried to encourage me to surgically let her go. My gals got pissed, particularly Cat, because they were badgering me about it, I didn't want it, they wouldn't let it go, and eventually Cat lost her shit, demanding they leave the room and eventually chasing them out. Then she called Mr. Truelock, and he had me transferred home and had a home healthcare nurse look after me the next couple of days."

"This detective inspector's name?" Aleksei asked.

"Farlay."

"District?"

"Seven."

"The hospital?"

"Mercy Royal."

"The doctor and nurse?"

I'd started shivering.

Something was wrong here.

Really wrong.

"The doctor's name was Buildlore," I told him shakily. "Shifter. The nurse, she was human. I think her first name was Carmen. Last was… Fitzgerald?" I asked like he could confirm.

His gaze shafted over my shoulder, and he growled, "Get on this. And send a team to Laura's warehouse. Someone's filtering benzos into her water supply."

"On it," Set grunted, and he and the female turned back to the elevator.

The doors closed on them and slowly, carefully, like my body would shatter if I moved too fast, I turned to my mate.

"What's going on?" I asked, my words trembling as much as my body was.

"Come here, *bissi*," he urged tenderly.

"No, tell me what's going on," I demanded lamely, because, yes, my voice was now even shakier.

"Do you know what benzos are?"

I shook my head but said, "Sedatives."

"There are two types. Benzodypenes are sedatives. Colloquially, they're referred to as dypes. There are also Benzobytines. Those are referred to as benzos."

"I'm not understanding why you're sharing this information with me."

"I'm sharing it with you because Benzodypenes are used widely, as prescribed by a physician, as sedatives, and in lower doses, to combat anxiety. Benzobytines are also sedatives, but they have different results. They're used strictly and solely for two purposes. In fact, there's a law that if they're used outside of these purposes, it's a felony, with a mandatory prison sentence starting at two years."

"O-okay," I stammered, rolled my shoulders to pull myself together, and asked, "What are the two purposes?"

"In healthcare for the mentally deranged, they're used on shifters to make certain they cannot shift. And in the prison system, so inmate shifters will be arrested in the same."

Okay.

All right.

Okay.

Was he saying...?

I wrapped my arms around my stomach tightly and protectively, doing this instead of putting a hand hopefully to my chest.

"All inmates get it," Aleksei continued. "It has no effect on demons, fae and humans. It's filtered into the water, so they receive it even through their skin in the shower pods, which means everything they consume constantly delivers a low-level dose that keeps their beasts alive inside them, but unconscious and thus not a threat."

"Oh my gods," I breathed.

He came to me then, but I didn't move, even when he got in my space, cupped my jaw in both hands, and dipped his face to mine.

"Your beast is not dead, darling. She's in there. Except for the night we met, which undoubtedly sparked her waking because, for the first time, you were in the presence of your mate, and so was she, she's been asleep for three months."

My legs gave way.

Aleksei caught me.

Swinging me up in his arms, he walked me down into his living room, sat on something, set me in his lap and held me close.

I felt none of this.

Because I'd rounded his shoulders with my arms, held on for everything I was...

And *sobbed*.

"Who would...who-who w-would do that to me?" I moaned.

"I don't know, *bissi*," he whispered, and the sinister was back. "But I'm sure as fuck going to find out."

CHAPTER 14

SPIN

One could assume the aftermath of an assassination attempt was a chaotic time.
I could confirm this was correct.
But at first, it was just Aleksei and me.
My mate let me weep into his skin for a while, but this was interrupted when the sounds of the blades of a heli-craft could be heard overhead.
Rattled, I pulled away from him.
"Shh, love," he murmured, cupping the side of my head and tucking my face back into his throat. "The RS will have mobilized a unit. Agents on the roof. More in the lobby. Others on the street. The Constabulary won't want to be left out, and they'll position a heavy presence around the building. Regardless, I was involved in the design of my security system, and it rivals the Palace. No one can get up here unless I wish them to."
"Okay," I mumbled, sniffed, then said, "I think I'm done crying."
The gentle pressure of his hand lessened and I lifted my head.
He placed both hands on either side and swept my cheeks with his thumbs, his eyes watching them go.
I wasn't over our fight, or how much of a dick he acted during it. I also wanted my family released from interrogation immediately.
But even so, I couldn't deny his touch was sweet.
His gaze captured mine. "I'd like to call a doctor to have you looked over."
Panic filled me, he sensed it and continued swiftly.

"She's there, Laura. I feel her. But I'm certain you've been drugged for months without your knowledge. It's my understanding this doesn't have lasting effects. But I want you checked out."

I wasn't a big fan of doctors (anymore).

But give a little, get a little.

Right?

"Okay," I agreed. "And I want Gayle, Cat and the Truelocks released."

"Darling—"

I pulled from his hold and planted my hands firm on his chest. "No, Aleksei. They would never, ever hurt me. Not a one of them."

"I'm afraid this has to be ascertained without a doubt."

"You said you vetted them."

"Beings manage to hide a variety of things in order to get into a number of mischiefs."

"Not *my* beings."

"This has to be done."

"It's a waste of time. I don't want them frightened, or—"

That purple glow started to seep into his irises, and the sleek of his voice abraded when he stated, "You almost died tonight. And someone has been fucking with you for an unknown purpose, but whatever that purpose is, it's nefarious and has to have caused you no small amount of pain. We are who we are, and it cannot be cast aside you are the future queen of this realm, which means you're the future mother to a monarch, and as such, what's been happening to you is high treason. But to me, that's beside the point. You...are...*my mate*. And I will be *without a doubt* as to those who are in your life who might, no matter the outside chance, wish you harm."

Without a doubt.

Oh gods.

He couldn't be considering...

My voice had pitched high when I asked, "Are you going to give them truth serum?"

Gayle probably wouldn't care (I hoped). Neither would Mrs. Truelock (and she simply wouldn't, she was just as lovely with me as her husband).

But Mr. Truelock would think it was the height of indignity, and Cat, who hated to be out of control in any situation, would be pissed as all heck.

"It's illegal to administer truth serum without a being's consent," Aleksei said.

I relaxed.

"However, if they refuse the injection, this will be taken into account and not in a positive way," he concluded.

I tensed again, and was about to say something, but he beat me to it.

"If they love you, they won't blink at taking it."

"I can't lose them, Aleksei," I told him, sounding just as panicked as I was, which was to say, a whole lot of panic. "They're all I have."

The purple glow was not as fierce as it was when I was in danger, and after he'd transformed back to human, and he was ticked.

But that glow lit in his eyes now, and it was both wonderous and frightening.

"We will discuss your parents later, not as late as you'd like, far from it, Laura. I'm warning you. I will know how they scarred you."

With that glow in his eyes, I had no choice but to placate him.

"All right."

"And your friends are no longer all you have," he bit off.

Oh dear.

He was right.

Crap.

"I didn't mean to offend you," I promised.

He ignored that and declared, "If they love you, not one of them will balk at the injection after what happened to you tonight. They'll be eager to be cleared, so they can be done with it and get to you."

He was right again (I hoped).

I just hated that they had to be put through it.

He returned his hands to the sides of my head, pulled me in to kiss one cheek, the other, and then my nose (I was finding there were times where his sweet could be inconvenient, this being one of them, when I was still smarting from our fight, and I'd just lost in an important discussion).

He released me and said, "Go. Up the stairs, my room is the only room on the upper level. Hit the bathroom. Clean up. It's going to be a long night, and I have comms to make."

"I should probably get back to my cats," I told him.

He did a slow blink, ending it studying me like I'd grown a third eye.

"If you send a team to my place, it's going to freak them out," I explained.

"I'll handle it."

"You can't handle it. Jupiter is—"

"Darling," he sighed. Massively. "Please, go clean up."

I huffed, slid off his lap and decided to revisit this discussion after he had time to make a few comms. He had to have a ton on his mind, so he needed to check on things and probably issue a bunch of orders.

I found the floating tread, switchback staircase next to a long dining room table that seated twelve and sat perpendicular to the kitchen.

The stairs led to a large landing and enormous double doors, both open, that led to his bedroom.

I got the sense the lower level of his penthouse took up the entire floor of the building, but the upper level was half of that (the other half was the landing bay).

Which meant his bedroom was colossal.

Therefore, obviously, I was impressed with its sheer size, but downright stunned at how ginormous his hover bed was.

And the nuanced change in décor (this was silvers, with hints of black, gray, purple topaz and some sky blue) was masculine, attractive, yet somehow inviting and even...*homey.*

I could design in this room.

I could laze here for weeks, reading, watching vids...

Cuddling with and making love to my mate.

Ahem.

Moving on.

There were a number of doors that led from the sleeping space, and it took to door number three to find the bathroom.

(For your information: the first door led to a library/small office stuffed full of books that I would absolutely explore at a time when my world hadn't just exploded; the second, a deeply masculine closet that smelled like leather, pepper and cinders, Aleksei's scent that was so a part of him, I hadn't noticed it until I scented it without him there.)

His bathroom was mammoth as well (yep, matte black tile abounded, with silver towels and chrome fixtures) and gave more credence to the fact he was into vintage, because he not only had a bath pod, he also had an actual bathtub and a real shower that could easily fit two, and it sported a dizzying array of shower heads.

I squeaked just a little when I saw myself in the mirror.

The brilliant cosme-mask setting I'd selected of cocktail party, nighttime, drama, playful, sophisticated was now a disaster.

My mascara coated my eyelids, and there were a few smears at the sides of my eyes, but Aleksei had cleaned some of the mess of that. My cheeks were high pink, and my eyes were already swelling from crying.

I should have gone waterproof, but how was I to know all that would befall me that night?

I doubted he had a cosme-mask or a spa-visor to help me out, so I did what I could with an old-fashioned washcloth.

Once I wrapped the cloth over the edge of the sink, I took in a huge breath and returned to the mirror.

I lifted a hand to my chest.

Tears threatened again, so I closed my eyes and pressed into my own flesh.

"You're not gone," I whispered.

Nothing from my beast.

I wondered how long it would take for the sedative to wear off and was tardily thrilled Aleksei had thought to call a doctor.

Maybe there was a reversal.

I opened my eyes and stared in the mirror, feeling the warmth of my skin under my hand, and such gratitude, such profound gratitude, it was unreal. I had to tamp it down, or I'd be overwhelmed and unable to function.

"I'm so fucking glad you're not gone," I whispered.

Still nothing from my beast, but she was there.

Praise Hecate, *she was there.*

Another deep breath while I pulled back my shoulders, then I ran my fingers through my hair to bring some semblance of order to the windswept mess.

With that, I decided I was ready for whatever else was going to happen that night.

Or at least as ready as I would get.

I headed out to the landing.

I stopped there when I heard voices.

And at what those voices were saying, I rested a shoulder against the wall of the alcove around the double doors, and I listened (okay, eavesdropped).

"Son, you *incinerated* a man in an *art gallery* for Beelzebub's sake," a man stated hotly, and I could tell it was over a comm. "We have due process in this realm!" he nearly shouted. "This is a PR *disaster.*"

"We need to spin it. Immediately. I'm calling Germaine." That was a woman's voice.

"And then you destroyed said art gallery and flew over the city with an untethered female on your neck." The man's voice was back and going at Aleksei like the woman hadn't spoken. "The safety issues you ignored with that alone are going to dog my reign, and yours, until our deaths. I can't even begin to imagine what got into you."

I jumped guiltily when Aleksei appeared on the lower level, just beyond the edge of the upper landing, where I could see him, but more to the point, he could see me. He was holding a tablet, but his attention was on me.

He lifted a hand, crooked a finger, and I had no choice but to leave my eavesdropping spot and join him.

"Are you listening to us?" the man demanded from the tablet.

Aleksei met me at the bottom of the stairs, guided me back to the freestanding kitchen bar, slid an arm around my shoulders and turned us both to the display.

I gasped and then immediately dropped into a clumsy half-curtsy that was hindered by Aleksei's arm around me when I saw King Fillion and Queen Calisa scrunched together on display.

Her famed burnished-brown tresses were arranged in an elaborate updo, and she was dripping in jewels at ears and throat. His black hair was swept back, and I could see the ends of an untied bowtie dangling at the sides of the opened collar of his pristine white shirt.

Unlike any time I'd ever seen them before, when they were always collected and completely put together, now, they both appeared wildly harassed.

Then again, their son's life had been threatened, and he did indeed commit a number of rather alarming felonies that night.

Aleksei sounded amused when he told me, "You don't have to curtsy over a comm."

I straightened.

"As delighted as we are in this time of strife to know you are not alone," Queen Calisa began crisply, "perhaps we can speak to you without your female present."

At this juncture, with no warning (to me!), Aleksei landed it on them.

"Mother, Father, it is with great pleasure I introduce Laura Makepeace. My mate," Aleksei announced.

Oh boy.

Both the king and queen froze so completely, I thought there was a glitch in the comm.

And then Queen Calisa crowed, "Dear Lilith, this is *brilliant*! Germaine will make a meal of this. All is saved! It's *perfect*."

"Your mate?" the king asked.

"My mate," Aleksei confirmed.

The king's eyes narrowed. "How long have you known you had a mate?"

"I believe we met five days ago."

The queen focused in on the important matter at hand (or, the other one).

"And you were going to share this with us...when?" she queried.

"When we got to know each other better."

The queen studied the ceiling like it could deliver her from her independent-thinking and living son.

"Excuse me...but let me get this straight. The assassin took aim at my son's mate?" the king inquired.

"Strictly speaking, she put herself in the line of the stream to protect me," Aleksei drawled.

Red instantly infused the king's face to the point I grew concerned he was going to have a stroke. It wasn't common in shifters, but it wasn't unheard of.

"Where is this cretin?" King Fillion demanded in a tone I could only describe as kingly.

The queen looked at her husband. "Fillion, calm yourself."

He snapped his head around to face her. "He's found his mate, Caly. *And she was in the line of fire*," the king retorted, looked beyond his display and asked someone in the room with them, "What's that? The Hold? I'm going there promptly."

And then he began his journey to go there promptly, because he disappeared, and Queen Calisa danced on our display until she got control of their tablet.

"Dad is only going to get in the way of the RS's investigation," Aleksei noted.

She waved a hand in front of her display. "Let him do what he has to do. He's a male. All that 'protect my female' rubbish." She rolled her eyes.

"Laura is not his female," Aleksei pointed out.

"Ah, say that should your son find *his* fated mate," she returned. "It is as if she's his, but in the daughter-type way."

It was?

Really?

Mega!

Her eyes shifted to me. "You're lovely dear."

"Thanks," I replied shyly.

"The vids are already flooding the social tapes," she informed me. "You looked quite stunning in that satin gown astride my son's beast."

Aleksei cleared his throat.

I kicked his ankle.

He broke out in a broad smile.

"Mind out of the gutter, son. My goodness. *Males*," Queen Calisa griped. It was her turn to look beyond her display and she called, "Excellent, Germaine. You're here."

"I wish to speak to her," Aleksei requested, though no one was under any impression it was anything other than a demand.

"Always needing control," Queen Calisa mumbled irritably. The visual showed her lovely, beaded dress as she said off display, "Comm from the prince. Good news, the female is his mate."

"No kidding? That's *exceptional*," a female replied, then she appeared, platinum and honey hair pulled back in a bun, her lavender fae eyes staring at me through the display. "And you're fabulous. Even better." Her attention shifted to Aleksei. "Hello, your royal highness.'

"Release a statement," he ordered. "Along with agents of the Royal Service, His Royal Highness, Prince Aleksei, thwarted an assassination attempt this evening at the art gallery, Tempera. One suspect is in custody. The other lost his life during the attack."

She dropped all pretense and exposed the relationship she really had with my mate by retorting, "This is not going to fly, Lex, and you know it. Yes, there was drama and danger, but no one, not even you, is allowed to lose control of their creature, no matter what the circumstances." She took a dramatic pause and made her point by slanting her gaze to me then back to Aleksei. "Except one."

"This is not true, and you know it, Maine," Aleksei shot back. "If a beast is defending his being's life, it is absolutely considered lawful."

"You had twelve RS agents defending your life," Germaine pointed out. Before Aleksei could retort, she said quietly, "I get you. You know I do. But you're going to have to let her out, my prince."

Aleksei made a ferocious noise in his throat.

"The socials are eating this up. There's vid from every direction," she told us. "And yes, you are definitely getting positive commentary for saving the life of some beautiful, random female who stepped in the way of danger to defend our True Heir. But you are also getting a lot of very negative commentary about privilege and acting as judge and executioner by immolating a suspect holding a PR60, which is not known to do much but stun a beast unconscious. And *your* beast? It would only daze you."

"However, on the setting he had it, it would have burned a hole through Laura's body," Alexei gritted. "Or anyone he might have mistakenly hit."

"Yes," she agreed. "And the courts would have decided his punishment for that." She hurried on again before Aleksei could. "There is not a single being, be they shifter, fae, demon, vampire, witch, conjurer or human who would even begin to question a shifter changing to his beast to defend, protect and even annihilate a threat to his mate. There is no question this is what you did. It's on vid from at least two dozen directions. You did what any species would do, and in doing it, it is not only lawful, it's championed. You know that, Lex. We have to use her. She has to be outed."

"*Her* name is Laura Makepeace," Queen Calisa chimed in from off display.

"*Fuck*," Aleksei clipped right beside me and looked down at me.

I understood his unspoken question and shrugged, because unfortunately, this Germaine chick was right.

"Do it," he grunted to the display.

Germaine excelled at not openly appearing victorious, but her eyes did light with excitement.

"I need her brief," she said.

"Get it from Allain," Aleksei replied.

"Any skeletons?" she asked me.

Aleksei answered, "Her parents are pieces of shit."

Sucky.

But accurate.

Her brows shot up. "Are they going to be a problem?"

I got a few words in. "I haven't seen them in thirteen years, but if I had to guess...yes."

"Don't look so downhearted," she assured. "If they're the only problem, then they're the problem and everyone loves the story of a plucky heroine plugging away at life against all the odds and eventually finding her prince."

I was realizing why this female was the royal spin doctor.

Her gaze shifted back to Aleksei. "We need to plan her introduction."

"We have other things going on at the moment, Maine," Aleksei drawled sardonically.

"A week," she haggled.

"A month," he stated.

"That is not going to fly either, my prince. If you make them wait, you both will be hounded, even if you escaped to the Clan Caves," she returned.

"We're going to be hounded anyway," Aleksei pointed out.

This was sucky too.

But indisputably accurate.

Germaine suddenly disappeared from the display and Queen Calisa filled it. "Two weeks. That's all you have, son. Two. And she's getting the purple topaz ring. There's a matching coronet that will work perfectly for the wedding, and she can make it her signature."

At what the queen was referring to, I stopped breathing.

"Perhaps you'd allow me to select my own engagement ring for my mate?" It was sheer sarcasm from Aleksei that time.

And yep.

That was what I knew the queen was referring to.

"Like males can pick jewelry," she muttered.

And seriously.

The queen really had a thing about males.

"Fine," Aleksei grunted. "Two weeks."

"We'll chat," Germaine's voice was heard.

"And we'll have tea, dear," Queen Calisa said to me.

Fabulous.

Eek!

"*Au revoir*, you two," Queen Calisa finished it, and the display turned blank.

I looked up at Aleksei. "Did I just have a vid comm with the queen of our realm, also the king of our realm, and a master PR guru?"

Aleksei didn't bother confirming I did since he didn't have to.

He asked, "How are you doing?"

"About what?" I asked in return. "The assassination attempt? The knowledge all those I hold most dear are right now sweating under the heat of a lamp aimed two inches from their faces as royal agents fire questions at them? Or about the fact someone out there wants to torture me, and not only that, they succeeded, and they're very good at it?"

What I did not add was how I was not real thrilled to learn, when he got angry, Aleksei was more than a little bit of an ass.

"Any of that," he answered quietly. "All of it."

My answer was planting my face in his chest.

He wrapped his arms around me.

In the top of my hair, he murmured, "The doctor is on his way. Allain and Muriel are dealing with Nova, Comet and Jupiter, bringing them, along with other things you'll need, here, so we can settle in and start to process all that's going on."

"Right." My word was muffled by his chest.

"Before my parents commed me, I made the decision the RS will interrogate the male in custody about the plot tonight, because it happened on their watch. However, the RIC and RMI will collaborate, cooperate and communicate fully, because I've tasked the RMI with taking over the investigation of your earlier attack and what happened subsequent to that. Obviously, they overlap."

"Obviously," I mumbled.

By the by, the RS was the Royal Service. They were responsible for the security of the royal family, royal lands and properties, and sacred relics, artifacts and other things of historical significance and value, including the Catalogues and jewels.

They were known as the best of the best of the best.

The RIC was the Royal Intelligence Commission.

They were spies.

The RMI was the Royal Ministry of Investigations.

They were cops who operated on a realm-wide level and held higher authority than local constabularies.

Aleksei kept speaking.

"I want that investigation closed with no delay."

It was safe to say, I did too.

I just nodded.

"Allain has checked the brief, and he has a comm into the investigators who compiled it. There's no mention of your assault, the police report or the stay at the hospital. He's going to get down to the reason why there wasn't."

That was interesting.

And scary as all heck.

I didn't have the energy to think about it.

I tipped my head back. "You got a lot done while I was swiping at my makeup."

His lips curved up. "It's important to know how to multitask and communicate succinctly."

Mm.

Moving on.

"Is your mom sort of..." How to put it? "Anti-male?"

"She gets like that when my brothers are up to something, and when she and my father are arguing. When they're not, all that disappears. They're not overtly affectionate. Their marriage, it probably won't surprise you, was strategized by someone like Germaine. But they did grow to love one another. And just to say, my father is a decent male, but he can be spoiled, thoughtless and obtuse. My mother is none of those things. She worked hard to get where she was before their marriage, and she considers her role as the of Queen of Night's Fall being the second most important occupation in this realm, and as such, Dad's position as king is the first. So when Dad acts like an idiot, it gets on her nerves, and I don't blame her."

Hmm.

Moving on again.

"Jupiter is not going to be happy in a new space," I told him.

"Jupiter would prefer to be here with his momma than be alone in your flat without you. Jupiter would also be happier his momma continues breathing while agents work to uncover whatever plot is unfolding than having to be rehomed because you are no longer of this earth. I cannot claim to understand the feline mind, but my guess would be, he wants you safe, like I do, and is content to do what he must to make that so."

The ultimate in sucky.

But definitely accurate.

I asked the question that was most important last.

"Do you know how soon benzos wear off?"

His face softened, his eyes twinkled with pinprick stars, and he whispered warmly, "No. But we'll ask Dr. Fearsome. However, I must warn you, what I do know is that, after long-term dosage, it does take a while for the sedatives to fully leave the system."

"A while as in a day or an hour?" I pressed.

"Several days, *bissi*. Maybe even a week," he told me, making it clear he wished he didn't have to share that bad news.

"I miss her," I whispered my colossal understatement.

Those pinprick stars shone brighter as his affection for me was taken over by his anger on my behalf. "I can't even imagine. I don't want to. And we will get down to why that was done to you, Laura. I vow it. And those who did it will be punished to the farthest extent the law will allow. I vow that too."

I believed him.

With that look on his face, I believed him.

He cupped my head and pulled my cheek to his chest, tightening his other arm around me.

There was a whole bunch up in the air, but even so, this felt good.

It felt very good.

He heard something I didn't and murmured, "The doctor is here."

Excellent.

Answers.

And...

Hope.

At last.

CHAPTER 15
TARGET

I lay on my back on Aleksei's bed.
Aleksei stood beside it, arms crossed on his massive chest, watching everything Dr. Fearsome was doing in a manner, if the half-demon, half-fae doc did something he didn't like, he'd tear his head off.

Dr. Fearsome—young, midnight skin, fae-built tall, solid body, demon-crafted elegant features—was someone I might have to introduce Catla to (if she was still speaking to me after tonight, that was).

Totally unaffected by Aleksei's menacing glower, he just got on with it.

He'd taken my blood first and entered it into a machine he'd set on one of Aleksei's nightstands. The vial instantly unloaded so I could see my red blood flowing to what appeared to be eighteen separate sections. I heard the unit lock down and a soft whir as it got on doing whatever it was it did.

That was when Dr. Fearsome instructed me to tell him everything that happened.

I didn't get too deep into the assault part, because Aleksei's energy was growing more and more stifling as I spoke, and if I got into certain bits of it (the parts where they threatened to rape me), I knew he'd go batcrap crazy.

So I gave the doc an abbreviated version that included all I thought he'd need to know.

I didn't miss the hardening of his features, the red glow that heated the depth of his eyes, or the furious glance he exchanged with Aleksei when I told them about Dr. Buildlore and Nurse Fitzgerald pushing me to allow them to cut my beast out of me.

But, weirdly, it felt nice to be under the care of a doctor who would never do such an ugly thing to a shifter.

He then pulled out his long, narrow, porta-ano-scanner and switched it on.

The blue light shone down on me, causing some heat, some tingles, as, starting from my now-bare feet, he very slowly floated it over my body, his attention riveted to whatever was showing on the monitor at the top of the scanner as it moved.

I got a little freaked when he went back over my torso three times, before he finalized the exam by moving it over my head.

He shut it off and looked down at me.

"You can sit up, Mistress Laura."

I didn't sit up.

Like I was an invalid, Aleksei moved in and helped me up.

Then he went further by arranging me with my bottom half curled on a hip, whereupon he threw a silvery cashmere throw around me, tucked it tight and sat next to me, tugging me deep into his side by clamping an arm around me.

Okay.

I was losing the will to be pissed at him for being such a dick earlier.

At that time, he didn't know I'd been attacked and I thought my beast was dead.

And I had to admit, it *was* kind of unhinged I'd throw myself in front of a weapon to save the life of the fiercest dragon in the realm.

"I'm sorry, your highness," the doctor said diffidently to Aleksei. "Patient confidentiality demands I—"

"He knows everything," I told the doc.

"You're all right with my reporting with him present?" Dr. Fearsome asked me in order to confirm.

Stupidly, since Aleksei actually didn't know everything, I repeated, "He knows everything."

The unit on the nightstand beeped, taking the doctor's attention, and while he scrutinized the readout of results, Aleksei tightened his arm around me.

I rested my weight into his side, and it felt inordinately good to do that.

The doctor's attention returned to us.

"As you suspected," he said to me, even if it was Aleksei's supposition, "long-term benzo dosing. However, the dose was elevated from what's used in sanatoriums and penitentiaries. Either they didn't know what they were doing, or you consumed more water-based beverages than they expected, or they were very intent to make sure your beast did not awaken."

I clenched my teeth.

A low rumble sounded from Aleksei's chest.

"It's caused you no harm," Dr. Fearsome assured. "But it does mean recovery of your creature will take longer."

"So, she's okay?" I asked.

He smiled kindly at me. "She is very okay, Mistress Laura. She will be well rested when she wakes, and very likely feeling rambunctious."

Feeling rambunctious.

It took everything not to weep again.

"Is there any way recovery can be expedited?" Aleksei queried.

The doctor nodded and my heart leaped. "IV fluids every other day"—he glanced at me with a good-natured grin—"and your B vitamins are low, so it'd be good to add those to the first IV drip." When I nodded, he finished, "This will help flush the system. I still estimate it'll take seven days, maybe a day more, perhaps if we're lucky, a day less."

"What can she expect?" Aleksei pressed for more details. "Will her creature simply just suddenly awaken? Or will there be a process?"

"I would expect, if Mistress Laura does the IV therapy, in two to three days, her beast will give indications it's emerging from its unconscious state. It's been described as flutters or quivers. Some warmth. Eventually stronger movement. But it's rare for there to be any communication. It's like taking a very long time to emerge from a deep sleep. The beast will be fidgety, she'll eventually become restless, but the creature will still be unconscious."

Flutters. Quivers. Warmth. Movement.

I wanted it all, ASAP.

"Do you have the IV stuff now?" I asked impatiently.

"I can have it delivered and administer it before I leave," he offered.

"Please do that," Aleksei said.

The doctor pulled out his tablet where the results of the scan had been transferred, and while looking at it, he said, "All other systems are a go. Very healthy. The remodeling of your ribs is strong. However, your wrist was not well set, which is causing a ten percent loss in strength in that hand."

Ah…

Heck.

I'd gone solid.

Aleksei's vibe had gone hot.

The doctor looked at me. "You can visit my clinic, and we'll see to that. We'll rebreak it and remodeling will take two days. Physical therapy for a week, and you'll have full function in that hand again. Through all this, there will be no pain."

"Um," I hummed.

"These breaks happened during the assault?" Aleksei asked tersely, as he would since I'd been significantly beaten, but they'd concentrated on my face, hadn't broken any bones, and Aleksei had heard me explain all of that earlier.

The doctor appeared confused. "No. These breaks are—" His attention darted to me.

"They're what?" Aleksei pushed.

"Aleksei," I whispered.

He ignored me and demanded of the doctor, "They're what?"

"Mistress Laura?" the doctor asked.

I bit my lip, but there was nothing for it. I'd have to tell Aleksei one day.

I guessed today was that day, and it wouldn't be me telling him, but Dr. Fearsome.

I nodded to the doc.

Gods, I was such a coward.

Dr. Fearsome studied my face, then he turned to Aleksei. "They're from her childhood."

"Are you done?" Aleksei suddenly barked, and I jumped against his side.

His response was to tighten his hold on me.

"I'll arrange the IV," the doctor murmured.

Definitely getting the gist of what was going down, he left his stuff and us alone in the room.

When he was gone, I turned to my mate. "Aleksei."

He didn't look at me when he stated, "We're not talking about it now."

That was fine by me.

"Which one?" he asked the wall beyond us.

"Sorry?" I asked back.

He turned to me, and it was unfortunate I was attached to him when I saw his amethyst was back.

In full glow.

"Which one of your two fucking parents broke your bones?"

Okay, so we were talking about it now.

"Mom, my wrist. Dad, my ribs," I whispered.

"Right," he grunted.

"Let me just explain—" I started.

"No. Oh, hell no, *bissi*. For now, that's all we're going to say. We narrowly escaped an epic shitstorm tonight. We don't need to court another one."

I thought about my mother and father standing as statues made of ash before they filtered to piles of nothing, and mumbled, "Probably wise."

His head ticked to the side, and he announced, "Allain is here."

And again, like I was an invalid, he took his feet and lifted me out of the bed and put me on mine.

The cashmere throw felt good against my skin, and I had to admit, I was a little bit shivery with all that was going on, so I held it closed tightly at my front, not realizing at first that Aleksei wasn't moving, and further, he was barring my path to the door.

I tipped my head back.

And my heart squeezed with the expression on his face.

He was in agony, and I felt that for him. I felt it for him and for me.

I felt it blaze deep.

It wasn't as if I didn't know how it felt when people cared about me.

I'd known Cat since I was eight, we'd been bestest gals since practically the minute we set eyes on each other. We both met Gayle when we were nine, and same. And with them came the Truelocks and Vinestrongs, who, it did not escape me, did everything in their power to be the parents they noticed I didn't have. Especially the Truelocks.

Monique came later, but I was in no doubt how deep a place I had in her heart, and I hoped she felt the same.

But this was different.

This was magic. Destiny. History. Future.

Forever.

This was a male who wouldn't even let me sit up straight without helping me after an ano-scan when I was perfectly healthy.

This was something I should have had from birth in the undying depths of parental love.

But I had it now, in the undying depths of feeling between fated mates.

And it was everything.

"One more question," he said gently. "How old were you?"

"Please, later?" I pushed out, coming to terms with so many things (so many!), I couldn't take more. "When you learn about all of it, I need time to see to you."

"How old, *bissi tressa*?"

Oh heck.

Bissi was bad enough.

Bissi tressa meant my beloved little treasured one.

In other words, he'd pulled out the big guns.

"Maybe six, my wrist. I think nine, my ribs."

His chest expanded with the huge breath he took.

He took his time letting it out.

"Okay," he whispered, nabbed my hand and guided us out of the room.

We were halfway down the stairs when two matte-steel bots of the same model as the shiny black one that manned the tech check at the Pink and Black Club entered at the bottom, wrangling before them my three-piece set of hover luggage, and five other pieces I'd never seen.

"The female closet is empty, unpack her there," Aleksei ordered as we passed them.

"As you wish, your highness," both bots mechanical voices answered in unison.

"Erm...how much of my stuff are they bringing over?" I asked.

Aleksei didn't look down at me, which was a strategically brilliant move I should have read to its fullest (but alas, I didn't), when he said, "Enough to suffice."

Eight suitcases surely had to be more than enough to suffice.

We made the foot of the stairs, and there stood Allain with a lovely, curvy blonde human female who had decided middle age with mild enhancements worked great for her, and she was right.

The kitty hover-carriers floated off to their side.

Comet got one look at me and howled.

"For fuck's sake, let them out," Aleksei commanded.

The woman clicked a control in her hand, the cages drifted to the ground, and then she clicked the control again, and the doors opened.

All of this in the time I said, "No...wait."

Jupiter darted out like a shot and disappeared.

As expected.

I wouldn't see him until I put wet food out in the morning.

Comet came out, sat on his fat, furry behind and howled again.

Nova trotted our way, bypassed me entirely and meowed up at Aleksei.

He bent instantly and lifted her to cradle her in his arms.

She marked his T-shirt with her ear and started purring.

Brazen little flirt.

"Are you all right?" the woman asked Aleksei, not hiding her worry as she examined him so thoroughly, it was a surprise scan rays didn't shoot from her eyes.

"I'm fine, Muriel," he replied affectionately. Then he (with Nova) guided me to the woman. "And I'm delighted to introduce you to Laura."

Her warm brown eyes turned to me, and she smiled. That smile was shaky, but she gave it her all.

"So very lovely to meet you," she greeted.

"Same to you, though I wish we didn't have to mess up your night with all of this."

She nodded but didn't reply to that.

"I'll go see that the bots are taking care of everything," Muriel announced to no one. "Excuse me."

With that, she rushed to the stairs.

I started to go after her, because after all, it was my stuff, but Aleksei waylaid me.

"She needs some space."

I was a hint confused as to why she'd need space with my stuff, but replied, "All right."

"She's been with me for seven years," he explained. "About a year into her tenure, she lost her son in a craft collision. Some drunk asshole overrode course approval and hit Paul going two-hundred-and-seventy-five knots."

"Good gods," I breathed.

"He was her only child. Now I'm her only child. Tonight would trigger her, and it has. Therefore, she needs space."

I bet she did.

I nodded. "Okay, honey."

He (Nova) and I turned to Allain.

"Any status updates?" Aleksei asked.

"There was a fatality."

"Outside the one I killed?" Aleksei inquired, not hiding his surprise.

"Yes. A female," Allain answered.

What?

Oh no!

How?

The only shot fired had gone wild.

"A half and half, demon/human female was found blasted in the face by a PR60 on full-beast stun," Allain reported. "Cat Truelock hired her as an assistant associate about six weeks ago. Her job tonight was to mind the artist."

"Oh my gods," I said, horrified.

I hadn't even thought to wonder where she went for all the time she'd left Terrinton. Certainly, it was plenty to be able to take care of bathroom business and return.

But she didn't return, because she was dead.

"Don't feel too badly for her, Mistress," Allain stated sourly. "She's been cohabitating with the deceased assassin for nine weeks. Her résumé was deep-faked. Cat Truelock said in interrogation, the only thing she seemed good for was being a minder, and in the end, she wasn't good at that either. She had several discussions with her, had given her warnings, was deeply suspicious her education and experience were fabrications, but couldn't prove it. Regardless, after the showing, she was going to let her go. Whoever is behind this placed her there. They didn't bother wiping security cams. They clearly show she let them in. And when she was no longer useful, they killed her. And that's on vid too."

I would think on how Cat hadn't shared with me she was having trouble with an employee later.

Now...

"In other words, she overheard Cat talking about the prince attending the showing, and she told her boyfriend," I surmised.

"Darling," Aleksei murmured in a tone I'd never heard before, but unlike most of his other ones, I didn't like it.

I peered up at him and braced, because I didn't like his expression either.

"What?" I asked.

"She'd been working for Cat for six weeks," he said carefully.

"Okay."

"We haven't known each other for a week," he continued.

In a flash, it all came together.

Set and his partner saying the first assailant only had eyes for me.

My attack, months before I ever stepped foot in the Pink and Black Club.

No one knowing Aleksei would be there, but I for certain was on the guest list.

This was...

I was...

"You were a surprise. I was the target," I blurted.

All Aleksei could say in reply was...

"*Bissi.*"

I was right.

I was the target.

Shit and *dang*.

CHAPTER 16

SPOILED

"Sire."

I jerked awake because the mountain of muscled flesh I was sprawled on also jerked awake.

Aleksei's arms circled me before he performed a heroic ab crunch, taking me with him, and we both stared at Allain who was loitering at the door.

For my part, I was bleary-eyed and confused.

Aleksei was feeling something different.

"I know I'm not seeing you standing in my doorway while I'm in bed with my female," Aleksei growled.

"My apologies, your highness." Allain bowed his head, looking and sounding wildly uncomfortable. "But you set all tech to mute and there are some...situations brewing."

"Fucking hell," Aleksei muttered. "And those would be?"

"Your parents are here. Your brothers are here. Mistress Laura's friends are all here. The constables have had to cordon off the street due to the number of press and well-wishers outside. So, that is to say, the Palace issued their statement and, well...the good news is, the realm is rejoicing that you've found your mate."

It was striking me that Allain might be master of the understatement, because that wasn't what I'd describe as "situations brewing."

More like all the proper ingredients for a coming Armageddon.

"Fuck me," Aleksei grumbled, clearly feeling the same as me.

I was beginning to be less bleary-eyed and confused.

And a lot more freaked out.

"Oh, and the orange and white cat keeps making a racket," Allain added. "I think there's something wrong with it."

Naturally, Comet would throw in his lot with potential Armageddon.

"Have you fed him?" Aleksei asked.

Allain's chin went into his neck in open affront. "Fed...*the cat*?"

"Don't worry, Allain," I said, pulling from Aleksei's hold and reaching to throw back the covers, doing this wondering if Aleksei had Madam Garwah's sequence so I could comm and ask her the royal etiquette around feeding your cat in front of a king and queen. "I'll do it."

I got nowhere because Aleksei hooked an arm around my stomach to keep me where I was.

"We'll be down in a minute," he told Allain.

Not hiding his relief, Allain escaped.

Right.

The last thing I remembered, post-IV therapy, was sitting on a couch in the living area, and my head was nodding because we'd gone through a stiff-backed report delivered directly from the Chief of District Three, a more concise one from the Deputy Head Minister of the RMI, security briefs from the Chief of District Ten and a Lieutenant of the RS. And finally Set and Antheme (his fae partner) were the only ones left, and they were giving Aleksei and me (and Allain, Muriel had gone) the real skinny, during which, clearly I conked out.

On the couch.

In the living room.

I turned to my mate.

"So we've jumped from taking time to get to know each other in a chill way to surviving assassination attempts to your staff and bots stealing all my clothes, shoes, bags, accessories and toiletries and kidnapping my cats to us *sleeping together*?"

He grinned, slightly sleepy, still a little grouchy, totally sexy, and all of a sudden, I was sprawled on a mountain of muscle again.

Regardless of how great this felt (and make no mistake, it felt *great*), I pushed up.

He rolled, and I was trapped under a mountain of muscle.

Wow.

That didn't feel great.

It felt *spectacular*.

However...

"Aleksei!" I snapped.

"While Set and Antheme were briefing me last night, you crashed on the couch," he reminded me about what I'd just reminded myself about.

New discoveries (and all I let filter into my exhaustion before passing out): Set was the commander of Aleksei's personal detail. Antheme was his second.

"Yes, I did," I confirmed.

"The future Queen of Night's Fall doesn't sleep on a couch."

"I was perfectly comfortable." Or, at least, comfortable enough to pass out.

"We could ask Madam Garwah, but I'm relatively certain it isn't the done thing, darling," he teased.

I was not seeing good things for my future, learning how he could whip out the sweet and cute to muddle my brain and get his way.

"Stop being cute when I'm taking you to task for taking liberties. Did you carry me here?"

"Guilty," he said like he didn't feel any vestige of that word at all.

"How many bedrooms are in this penthouse?"

"Five."

"Including this one?"

"Yes."

"So you had four other rooms you could take me to?"

"Why would I do something as bloody stupid as that?"

"I don't know. Maybe because we've known each other less than *a week*."

"I can't be certain, but it *feels* like surviving an assassination attempt together is akin to about two months of courting."

Honestly?

I couldn't really argue that.

Even so, I slapped his bare shoulder, and although I didn't do it hard, the way my hand bounced off his muscle was sobering.

"Laura, *bissi*." His gentle tone pulled my attention from his sinewy shoulder to his face. "After last night, you can't ask me to be apart from you. It just...won't work."

What was this?

"Seriously?"

"We can hope this overwhelming...*drive* to see you safe settles down, but for now..." He shook his head. "For now, Laura, it's on the edge of my consciousness every waking second, you standing with your arms thrown wide between me, an enemy and a weapon. My beast is riled. He can't settle either. The only moments of peace he and I have had since it happened was when I stretched out beside you, felt your body against mine, healthy and alive, but unconscious, and I fell asleep."

That was awful.

And one must pause to consider if this was behind him being such a jerk last night.

Being the one who needed to pause, with a monarch in my midst, I'd have to consider that later.

"But you're awake and it's back?" I asked.

"It isn't as fundamental, pervasive, but it's still definitely there."

It seemed like the males definitely got the short end of the stick with this mate business.

"Well, we'll just have to...play that by ear," I mumbled.

His big hands moved on me.

Oo.

Nice.

"Would you like to take this time to explore other avenues of getting to know each other?" he suggested throatily, moving to run his nose along my jaw.

Lovely.

I could totally take this time to explore other avenues. His hands felt nice, his weight arguably better, his playful mood was hot, even his seriousness.

In other words, the answer to that was a resounding *yes*.

But...

Was he mad?

"The king and queen are out there."

He lifted his head. "Doesn't count. They're in my house. They're only parents in my house."

I puffed out a breath as his hands kept moving...and feeling much too good doing it.

I squirmed underneath him.

His gaze went hooded...and wicked.

Oh my.

His head started descending.

My body was melting.

But annoyingly, rational thought spiked into my brain.

"People I love are out there too. They all took truth serum last night... *for me*. And now I have to face the music for that," I whispered.

I had him there, lamentably.

He sighed so heavily, it felt like my body depressed three more inches into his amazing mattress and the entire hover bed swayed full feet.

But then he dipped in and kissed the hinge of my jaw, rolled off me and out of bed.

The moment he did, I was rethinking ignoring royalty, familial sacrifice and assassination plots, and instead diving deep into exploring getting to know each other better.

And seeing as I was in a much clearer state of mind to process how much I enjoyed the view of the muscles of his back moving as he did, even if he was wearing sleep pants on the bottom, which hid his perfectly formed behind (kind of, the material was deliciously clingy)...

And I was very much enjoying this view...

This made me totally rethink my earlier decision.

Then he said, "I'll feed the cats."

I sat straight up and called, "Aleksei, wait."

He turned to me.

Oh yeah.

The front was better.

"They have custom daily food parcels. They're in the Chill-Cabinet," I informed him.

"I don't have Chill-Cabinet, Laura. It's called a refrigerator."

He was so totally old school.

And it was so totally mega.

"Okay, in the refrigerator," I amended. "Their names are on them. Jupiter gets his on the counter or Comet will bully him out of the way and eat it. Nova can defend her own meal, but I still feed them as far away from each other as possible. I know it doesn't make sense, but the food is designed for all their specific tastes, so he'll make a play for the others, but he's willing to wait for his, and as such, Jupiter goes first, then Nova, so they can get a head start, and Comet last. That said, he'll follow you through the whole process and complain about it."

He stared at me.

I stared at him.

He stared at me.

I heaved a sigh.

He spoke. "Custom-made cat food?"

"Yes."

"To their taste?"

"I had them profiled."

"You had your cats profiled?"

"Yes."

"To ascertain their favorite flavors so you can have food created specifically to satisfy their individual palates."

"I'm not certain why you need this deep of an explanation on this subject."

"Because you're to be the mother of our children."

Oh.

Right.

Erm.

"Are you as fond of children as you are of cats?" he asked.

I stretched out my lips and lifted my shoulders to my ears but decided against a verbal answer.

Even so, he didn't miss my answer.

"While we continue, in a far faster, deeper and more intense way, to get to know each other, I'll share about how I feel about spoiled children."

This sounded vaguely like a threat.

It wasn't fair, but we were here, and I had to stick with him here, because he also sounded really serious.

"And I'll share mine about how a child feels when their mother snaps her wrist."

His eyes grew dark as night, his jaw bulged, veins in his arms, neck, and rising up his flat stomach from his groin came out in stark relief.

Okay then.

As insanely sexy as all that was, perhaps I should have tempered what I'd said.

"That was dirty, darling," he warned low.

"We'll find a compromise, Aleksei," I promised.

He sauntered back to me, his powerful hips swaying almost hypnotically, and I'd be hypnotized if the vibe he was giving off wasn't so concerning.

He dropped to his fists in the bed on either side of my hips so his face was in mine.

"I want to know. I need to know. I also know I'm going to hate knowing. But what I already know, you had it far worse than I did, Laura. That said, shitty parents can come in all forms. Abuse. Neglect. And just being pompous, enabling morons."

I blinked, because for some reason, his words felt like a punch in the throat, not delivered by him, one I experienced *with* him.

Sadly, he continued speaking.

"And how a pompous, enabling moron can create two far worse, those who are even more spoiled than he is, and as such, they become unrelenting fuckwits. Not as bad as what befell you, I know it without knowing it all. But it's still bloody fucked up."

On that, before I could utter that first word, he pushed up and strode out.

I was sensing I understood there were more reasons than the obvious why he wanted to delay attending our families, seeing as what he just said was about his father and brothers.

And now I wished with my whole heart I'd let him.

"Well...dang," I said to the empty room.

CHAPTER 17

CIRCUS

On my ever-lengthening mental *Discuss with Aleksei as We Get to Know One Another* list, I added sharing how I felt about him changing me from my satin gown into one of his T-shirts while I was dead out of it.

Of course, it was far more comfortable than sleeping in a halter-neck gown.

But still.

I really wanted to take a bath in his tub, or a shower. I hadn't had either since I stayed in that old hotel during the filming of *Sheets*, and they were both way better than any bath pod.

But a bath pod could have you clean and dry in five minutes, top to toe.

And we had exalted company.

So I needed to get my rear in gear.

After I lay for those five minutes, letting the light diodes cleanse my skin and hair, I pulled myself out of the pod.

I slapped the cosme-mask on for a natural day look that took two minutes. The mane-mate I programed for casual at home, and that took another three. And I had to block out huge portions of the "female closet" (door four off his bedroom) as I programmed in the outfit I wanted to wear, because the closet was just that awesome, and if I paid too much attention to it, I could be lost in it for hours.

I might not be sure about how I felt about the fact that, for all intents and purposes, I'd been moved into Aleksei's penthouse without a word exchanged between us before this happened.

But I was sure I'd move into that closet.

All said and done, I had soft, wide-leg, silvery-cream, drawstring pants on the bottom, a horizontal stripe semi-oversized shirt up top (stripes in silver and cream). My hair was half up and half down, the down part having bouncy waves. And a pair of silver, flat mules were on my feet. They had notched-side uppers featuring intricate embroidery in greens, pinks, silvers and blues.

It wasn't a meet-the-king-and-queen outfit, as such.

But they were just his parents here.

Right?

I hit the living area feeling vaguely nauseous because I was not so vaguely nervous and was greeted not only by a loud meow from Comet, even if he was still licking his chops after consuming breakfast, I was also greeted with the knowledge that Allain had not lied.

King Fillion, Queen Calisa, Princes Timothee and Errol were there. As were Gayle, Cat and Mr. and Mrs Truelock.

And Sirk.

They were all assembled in the luxurious built-in couches and freestanding armchairs that were positioned with a talented designer's eye in the sunken living room.

Good news: none of my beings looked like they wanted to launch themselves at me in order to throttle me.

They didn't appear entirely comfortable (save Mr. Truelock), but they also didn't seem homicidal.

I further noted, somewhere along the line, Aleksei had donned a white, long-sleeved T-shirt and another pair of jeans, these less faded than the ones he wore last night.

Last, Germaine was in attendance, pacing the landing close to the bottom of the steps.

And the instant she saw me, she took all my attention, because she announced, "Oh my gods, she is just so perfect...I could *die*."

"Uh...hey," I said to her.

"Stunning, natural, casually stylish, relatable. Dead Winter came early to me this year," Germaine went on rhapsodizing about me.

What she didn't do was greet me.

I wasn't sure about this female.

She was making me uncomfortable, and I was already feeling mightily uncomfortable, so I turned my attention to the seating area and began to do my thing for the king and queen.

"If you curtsy, I'm throwing their asses out," Aleksei warned.

Seemed the grouch was back.

"Over here, with me," he ordered.

Since he was holding a coffee mug, I went over there, to him.

He poured me a cup, manually, from a glass carafe that was set inside some kind of shiny, black electronic unit.

He then dolloped cream in it from a little pitcher (likewise shiny black), doing this also manually.

He stirred it (manually).

And he handed it to me.

"Um..." I said.

"I don't have a Bev-Buddy either," he replied to my unasked question.

Righty ho.

I sipped and found it was better than Bev-Buddy coffee, or at least the brand I supplied my Bev-Buddy with.

By a lot.

He positioned me at his side and made sure I knew to stay there by wrapping his arm around my waist.

I didn't want to catch certain eyes.

But I had to catch certain eyes.

Sweeping through my beings, I took in the fact that Mr. Truelock looked cool as usual, lounged casually in an armchair like he owned this penthouse, his long legs crossed.

Mrs. Truelock sat in a chair next to him wearing one of her signature elegantly feminine dresses, her coppery-blonde hair perfectly coifed, and Jupiter was in her lap (she was the only one Jupiter liked, which told you all you needed to know about the lovely Mrs. Truelock).

Gayle and Cat shared a couch, and they, unsurprisingly, considering where we all were and who we were with, appeared alert, but also surprisingly rested considering the night they'd had.

Time to face the music, so I asked quietly, "Are you all mad at me?"

"Hells no," Gayle answered, then said to the king and queen. "No disrespect."

"Be yourself in *my home*," Aleksei put in before the king or queen could say anything.

Oh dear.

I wasn't having good thoughts about this unplanned, post-assassination-attempt, inter-family mingling, and I was already not having good thoughts.

"Anyway, truth serum is a trip, sister," Gayle told me. "A killer one. I'm feeling a whole lot better about law and order in our realm after dealing with those RMI guys. They're like...*whoa*. Totally *on it*."

Sirk grunted unhappily.

Gayle darted a glance at him and then her face flushed prettily.

"He almost got arrested when the constables took Gayle into custody," Cat educated me.

Gayle's cheeks got even pinker.

Sirk's pecs popped when he crossed his arms irritably over his chest.

Interesting.

I filed that in my *Make Cat and/or Gayle Tell Me the Story Later* folder.

Not catching the vibe, someone rudely wanted the story now.

"What did you do?" Prince Errol asked Sirk.

"Nothing smart," Sirk replied sharply.

Denied the goods on a misadventure by Sirk, who was adult enough to know whatever it was, it was a misadventure and not be proud of it, Errol sneered at Sirk.

I studied another prince of my realm.

Aleksei's youngest brother was the picture of a morph of his mother and father, except he got the more feminine traits of his mother, including her hair, and the weaker traits of his father.

In other words, he wasn't unattractive, but he wasn't handsome.

He was pretty.

I returned to Cat. "Is Terrinton okay?"

"He's ecstatic," she shockingly shared. "He said all the pieces were better after Aleksei was done demolishing them. He wants to refund all the money, hike up the prices, and sell them all again."

From what little I knew of the old guy, that tracked.

"And before you worry," Cat went on. "Aleksei's people have already been hard at work. Everything's boarded up. Terrinton could sell a sandcastle he kicked over for a million marks and pretty much any being would buy something the True Heir wrecked. So once we get the front repaired, which insurance covers." She shot a look at Aleksei. "In other words, your offer to pay is declined." She came back to me. "We'll do what Terrinton says. Double our take. And right now, I'm sitting on the hottest gallery in all Four Realms." She returned to Aleksei. "So thanks for the drama, my prince. I feel a big, fat bonus coming on."

That was a weird way for all that to work out.

But it was good to know it all worked out.

"Although your concern for us is not surprising, as you are our Laura," Mr. Truelock's dry voice cut in. "I believe we're all more interested in how you're doing, my lovely."

Aleksei pulled me closer to his side.

"I've been really worried about you," I admitted.

"Again, unsurprising," Mr. Truelock replied. "But something like what happened would mean I'd be disappointed if any stone went unturned in discovering what was behind it. It was a minor inconvenience, and expeditious in moving on to discovering what's really going on."

It wasn't a minor inconvenience.

It was just how much they cared about me.

Aleksei had been right about how they'd react to interrogation under truth serum.

In my instruction, Madam Garwah also hadn't gotten into whether you could burst out crying in front of the king and queen, even if you were in your mate's house.

I was saved this possible breach of etiquette by the intervention of another royal.

"Are we going to be introduced to your mate?" Timothee cut in to demand of Aleksei.

I turned my attention to him.

Conversely, Timothee looked a lot like Aleksei, just a shorter, thinner, watered-down version.

And I felt upon laying eyes on him there was just something...*off*.

"Tim, Rol, this is my mate, Laura. Laura, Tim and Rol," Aleksei said in an offhand and insulting manner.

Hearing that, I shot Cat a look. She returned it and then shot Gayle a look. Gayle aimed one at her then at me.

Annnnnnnd...yeah.

There was perhaps more dysfunction here than I thought, and I was thinking there was some serious dysfunction here.

King Fillion rose, and obviously, I wasn't the only one to get Aleksei's memo, because everyone remained seated when he did.

"We're all here to form a united front after what happened last night, and to indicate our support of the match of Aleksei and his mate," he declared. "As such, in a few minutes, we'll appear at the front of the building for a photo op and a short speech from the king."

Oh, gods, no.

I tensed.

When I did, the pads of Aleksei's fingers dug into my waist and the heat of his displeasure beat into my side.

"I wouldn't have picked that outfit," Germaine put in, studying my clothing critically. "But I'm feeling it. It says, *casual stay at home with my hunky mate, the True Heir, after drama and intrigue filled our night.*"

"It would have been nice if you checked with Laura and I first to ascertain we were at one with this plan," Aleksei said to his dad.

"Your tech was muted," King Fillion returned.

"It's nine thirty, Father. The day is hardly wasting," Aleksei shot back.

"We were curious to meet her," Timothee put in.

"As she'll be by my side the rest of my life, you'd have plenty of opportunity," Aleksei retorted.

"Perhaps there's somewhere my wife, my girls and I can…relax while you all…discuss," Mr. Truelock suggested haltingly, but diplomatically.

Aleksei turned his attention to him. "You asked for the injection before they even mentioned it."

Wait.

He did?

That was news.

My gaze shot to Mr. Truelock as my heart skipped contentedly.

"So did Freya," Aleksei continued. "Cat and Gayle agreed the minute it was suggested."

Ah.

My queens.

I sent a grateful smile their way.

Aleksei kept talking.

"Therefore, I'm glad you're here so I can thank you personally for your sacrifice on behalf of my mate, your show of loyalty and solidarity, and your willingness to go to extremes to prove I can trust you with her. I'm also glad you're here because she fretted about all of you last night. It's important you know, we disagreed that you should be interrogated. Laura argued against it. She vehemently didn't want to put you through it, but more, she knew in her heart it was unnecessary. Further, she worried what it would say that you had to endure it. As such, it heartens her to see you here and know you hold no ill-will against her."

"Never," Mrs. Truelock whispered. "And those shoes are lovely with that outfit, sweetheart. You always have the perfect eye."

Geez, Mrs. Truelock was the best.

"Thanks, Mrs. Truelock," I replied.

"No heartfelt speech for your blood family?" Timothee sniped.

"Did it occur to you that, after what happened, we'd be up most the night and therefore would need to rest this morning?" Aleksei clapped back. "But no matter when we woke, it wouldn't erase the fact that someone nearly killed Laura last night, I was put in the position of having to take his life, so maybe we didn't want a living room full of bodies Laura feels like she has to curtsy to in what will be, and now is acting as, her own fucking home?"

Oh yeah.

Way more dysfunction than I expected.

I put my hand on his back.

Aleksei seared his angry gaze from his brother to Germaine.

"And for the three years I've lived in this penthouse, I took pains... *pains*, Germaine, to keep my city address private. And you guided every fucking citizen right to my fucking door. Even the cops took steps to keep that on the downlow."

Oh boy.

I forgot about that.

And now such a big crowd had gathered, they'd had to close down the street.

"I know you hate it, Lex, but this situation is PR gold," she replied. "We can't miss the opportunity it affords us."

"The opportunity it affords who?" Aleksei inquired dangerously.

"The royal family. *Your* family," she replied.

"Considering the statement you made thoroughly explains my beast's actions of last night, and the crowd gathered in the street right this very moment is indicative of the joy the realm is apparently experiencing because of it, what opportunity now needs an even bigger statement that includes most of my family appearing before the public in front of my home to make it?" he pushed.

"No opportunity this good should be squandered, your highness."

Dang.

She was hedging.

And Aleksei knew it.

"What'd they do? Or alternately, which one did something?" Aleksei demanded.

Germaine's expression turned openly cagey.

"What'd they do?" he pressed.

She cast her eyes toward the queen.

Queen Calisa sighed delicately before she spoke.

"It's unsurprising he figured it out. He's far from dim. Therefore, admit it, Timothee."

Oh dear.

This was my first time in her presence. I didn't realize how tense and angry she was.

But regardless of that delicate sigh, I wasn't missing it now.

"I'm not a child," Timothee bit back.

"Lilith, even though he's been on this earth thirty-one years, grant me the day when that's actually true," the queen prayed.

"Quiet, Caly, you're too hard on him," the king, who'd seated himself again, murmured.

"And you, sir, are not hard enough," she rejoined.

"We have company," the king retorted.

"As I understand, they're not that, but instead, they're Laura's family, and she is now ours," the queen returned.

His chest puffed out. "But they are not mine, nor are they Tim's. He doesn't have to confess in front of strangers just because of some masculine peccadillo he got up to. He's a male! He's a prince! He's young. Males have oats to sew."

"If I hear one more metaphor that absolutely does *not* in any way excuse bad behavior, but instead, is an indictment of it, because a male who is a *male* should know better, I'll scream," the queen declared.

"Bloody hell, enough!" Aleksei clipped loudly. "What the fuck did he do?"

It was Errol who told on his brother, and he did this gleefully.

"He got a human female pregnant, and when she refused to get rid of it, he doused her drink." He grinned slyly. "And that sure did the trick. But it made her sick. She hit a clinic. They ran tests. And she knows what he did."

The entire room grew preternaturally still.

For my part, I thought it would be me who got sick at hearing Aleksei's brother was capable of this level of vileness.

"Get out."

The skin all over my body got cold at the terrifyingly murderous tone of Aleksei's voice.

And this was aimed at Timothee.

I shifted closer to him and started to stroke his back, hopefully soothingly. But at the feel of how tense his muscles were, I knew I was doomed at offering any solace.

Then again, regrettably, I was seeing where he was coming from when it came to his brothers.

And it was a very dark place.

I was also seeing why the queen had been so anti-male last night.

So seeing it.

"Lex—" Germaine started.

He swung his fury at her.

"Do not 'Lex,' me, Maine. And mark this. Laura, nor I, are available for you to trot out to cover for his juvenile, and now *criminal* bullshit."

"Says the male who murdered another male last night," Timothee said under his breath.

Aleksei swung back to Timothee.

"The PR60s those assholes were carrying were modified. If he'd hit me with the beam, even with me as my creature, there's a very good chance he would have stopped my heart."

I gasped.

That was news too!

Boy, it had been a really bad idea to conk out during the briefing last night, that much was certain.

But this wasn't really a surprise, considering I thought the same weapon had killed my beast.

I told him that last night, but once I learned she was with me, it didn't occur to me to discuss how that same weapon actually would have been able not only to kill my beast, but to kill *his*.

Which made me wonder, did they not have that same laserpower when they attacked me? Or did they not intend to kill my beast?

"He was there to kill Laura, and/or me, but I killed him first," Aleksei clipped. "So do not equate what befell my mate and I last night with dipping your wick into yet another female who you conned into bed with bullshit promises and total lies, did so wrong by her, you didn't protect her from pregnancy, and then you drugged her without her knowledge. All your shit descends to worse shit every time we have a family meeting, and I'm not covering for you anymore, Tim. Find a gods-damned moral compass, for all of our sakes, but mostly the beings whose lives you tear through, so you'll stop tearing through them. If you don't, there will be nothing Germaine can do for you. The beings of the Fall will call for your head. And these days, that means being stripped of your titles, your accommodation, and your allowance. Dad might throw you a few marks, but the life you know will be gone. Take this as the final wakeup call. And grow. The fuck. *Up*."

Back to Germaine, and with just an intake of breath, he carried on.

"You are very good at what you do. Release a statement. Get them to back off. Explain that the prince and his mate need time to recover from their ordeal. We thank everyone for their well-wishes, and to assuage their concerns about us, we'll appear what?" He looked down at me. "Tomorrow? The next day?"

"Whichever you feel comfortable with, *drahko*," I said gently.

"Tomorrow," he decided, aiming that Germaine's way. "No questions. Photo op only. West garden at the Palace. Fifteen minutes. And find someone you trust to do an interview for next week. Just me. Not Laura. I'll speak very briefly on what happened at the gallery last night. Book it. Then book another photo op for the unveiling of the engagement ring the week after, and one interview, the both of us. If they don't back off from my door today, none of that is happening, and the media freezeout that will ensue will be very fucking cold for a very fucking long time."

"Seems he's covering your ass anyway, bro," Errol noted toward Timothee.

"This isn't for Tim," Aleksei bit. "This is because you threw Laura right under the bus this morning, and now I have to pull her out. Last night, she faced a threat, and I took a male's life because of it. Right now, you sit in the shelter I provide for her, and you guided an onslaught right to *our door*. This is about *my mate*. Get used to this, all of you. From here on, it's going to be all about my mate. Unless you find yours, you won't understand, but that's the only way it can be. But even if it wasn't, I'm done with this bloody fucking circus."

And with that, he disengaged from me and stormed out of the room.

There was complete silence after his exit.

No one said anything for a long time.

So I did.

I looked to Germaine and suggested, "I'm so sorry. But I think it would be best to carry through with his requests. I don't think he's going to change his mind."

"Would you—?" she started.

"I would very much consider," Mr. Truelock cut in coldly, "what you're about to ask next."

Germaine rubbed her lips together.

She then said, "I'll just head back to the office."

She hit the elevator and was gone.

Timothee stood. "Well, now that my high and mighty brother humiliated me in front of my new sister and all her gang just because I got my rocks off with a bitch who isn't smart enough to cover her shit, I'll go self-flagellate or whatever."

"*Timothee!*" the queen snapped.

Timothee looked at me. "Don't fool yourself he hasn't dipped his wick in a fair few honeypots himself. His saint act is pure bullshit. Ask Anna. She'll tell you all about it."

Queen Calisa stood. "You have my sincere apologies, Laura. And I haven't apologized for a damned thing since a crown was put on my head."

"Ah, Mom, the glamorous screen star who landed herself a throne. Always so humble," Timothee sniped so viciously, it took my breath away, before he turned, sauntered to the door to the landing pad, ordered it opened, and I watched him jog up the steps before the door closed behind him.

"Errol, call the craft and have them stop circling and pick us up," the queen ordered.

"I'm an aide now?" Errol asked.

She whirled on him, squared her shoulders, took a breath, but hissed (albeit elegantly), "*Just do it.*"

He stared at her in shock, clearly never having been spoken to like that, and then he pulled out his Palm.

It hit me then that one of her sons was, lamentably, what Aleksei called him.

A fuckwit.

The other one seemed to lean that way too.

But her first son had been the target for murder the night before.

I knew how it felt being intimately involved in the sitch. It was zero fun.

So I could just imagine she was worried as all heck, and the antics of her other boys were exacerbating an already very bad situation.

At a quick glance, I saw a king who was embarrassed, sulking and furious.

No help there.

"I have Aleksei's glorious kitchen, and I'm really good at eggs and toast. Why don't you all stay while I make breakfast?" I offered.

Queen Calisa pulled her dignity around her and replied, "You are kind, but my schedule today is packed. I'll just freshen up before I meet the craft upstairs. I look forward to our tea. Excuse me."

She swept out of the room.

"I'll just head to the landing bay," the king said. "Errol," he called him like he was a dog, and like a dog, Errol jumped up and followed his father to the stairs.

They didn't bother to aim their gaze, or a farewell, to that first person before they disappeared.

We all remained painstakingly quiet until Queen Calisa rounded the corner, offered smiles, head bobs, and a "So lovely to meet you, dear. My aide will be in touch about tea," to me, before she disappeared too.

When the door whooshed closed behind her, Gayle and Cat jumped out of their seats and practically raced to the kitchen bar.

"One could say, never look behind the magician's curtain. Holy Hecate," Gayle whispered.

She was very right.

"I think I need to find my mate," I replied.

"Yes, honey, you do," Mrs. Truelock called from living room.

I swallowed, nodded to my gals, caught Sirk's gaze as I walked toward the hall, taking encouragement from his chin lift, then went in search of my mate.

The place was so big, with so many rooms, it took a while to find him.

He was in what was obviously his office, a way more official one than the one off his bedroom. He was seated behind a big desk, a display in front of him, and he was obviously on a business comm.

I wandered to his desk, and his gaze came up to me.

You okay? I mouthed.

"One moment, please. Video and audio mute," he said to the screen, then came back to me. "That's my question."

"That wasn't my family."

"Yes, darling, it was."

Eek!

"You were really angry," I noted.

"I will be angry again. And again. And definitely again."

My poor Aleksei.

"Quiet night in tonight to talk about family dynamics. This will, obviously, be accompanied by a great supply of alcoholic beverages," I suggested.

He gave me a soft smile. "I'll cook."

"It's a plan."

"The team has removed the Benzobytine delivery system and otherwise has done a full sweep of both of your spaces. Your loft and studio are safe. You should feel free to go to your studio to work if need be. But I'll need to call Antheme to put your detail together so she can check things out, transport and secure you if you need to work. She's rather good at secreting people away. She can get you there without anyone knowing you're there."

"Are you okay with me being that far away?"

"Will you be home later?"

"Yes."

"Then I'll try to be okay with you being gone."

"If things get, well…too intense, just comm and I'll come home."

"I'd appreciate that."

"I'm really…" Gods, this was hard. "Dang, *drahko*, I'm really sorry all that happened this morning. We should have just stayed in bed."

"Although I sense it will be rare I ever decline such an offer, I'm not sorry. They could paint a veneer over it, but it would chip, crack and fade eventually. That is the family you get from me. You need to know it. The family you bring to this union needs to know it. Now, you all know it. It's out there, unvarnished. And we move on."

His matter-of-fact attitude about this was a tad bit alarming.

"You're right," I whispered. "I'm still sorry."

"A quick kiss before you go," he dismissed me sweetly.

I really wanted to take some time with him, make sure he was okay.

I also wanted to ask about the PR60 business, just in case he hadn't processed I'd mentioned they'd used one on me during the attack. I felt the investigators needed to consider this.

But he was indicating he needed space, needed to retreat to doing something he enjoyed, like work, and my instinct told me I needed to let him make that play.

Thus, I rounded the desk and knew how upset and distracted he was because that was all we did.

A quick kiss.

And then I went.

CHAPTER 18
CANDLELIGHT

Insider RS knowledge (or maybe just Antheme's): the way she was able to "secret" people was using some of her dark fae magic to throw a glamour over me.

Strictly speaking, this was highly illegal. You had to register the use of a glamour so the authorities could trace any appearance you might assume back to you.

It was awesome magic, but if people could change their appearance whenever they wanted, they could rob a thousand banks (and get up to other bad stuff), and maybe never get caught.

But I guessed it was okay for the RS to use it whenever they wanted.

This meant, that evening, even if the street had been cleared, there were still quite a number of people loitering outside the front door (and they weren't lining up to go to the Pink and Black Club), we were able to nip in her craft to the back door in the alley without a cavalcade of paparazzi chasing us.

And although there were others who were skulking in the alley to catch me or Aleksei out, they didn't recognize me or Antheme (she'd glamoured herself too), as we ducked into a back-alley door.

As an aside: I wasn't having pleasant thoughts about all this attention. Although Aleksei and I talked about it, and I'd watched him run the gauntlet to the door to the gallery, being in the thick of it (or, more accurately, taking such care in trying not to be), was an altogether different, and alarming, thing.

Once we were in a lift that was tucked into a private vestibule that had stunning gothic damask, black and silver wallpaper and an impressive chandelier dripping with crystals (oh, and an RS agent at the entry to it), she dropped both our glamours.

"He's programmed you in, but he wants us to test it," she said after the doors closed. "Put your hand on the print pad. You'll feel a slight prick. It reads print, but it also tests DNA."

And this would explain why we didn't hit the landing pad and came in at the back alley. Aleksei wanted to test to make sure I could get up to his penthouse without delay.

I glanced at the silver plate gleaming against the matte black of the lift interior.

"Are you serious?" I asked.

She nodded shortly, all business, which was what I'd learned that day was Antheme.

"Also blood oxygen and adrenaline levels so if someone cut off your hand, dragged your dead body in here or forced your hand to the plate under duress, it'd know you weren't actually the one operating the lift."

I'd never heard of tech like that. I was impressed.

And boy, one could say *that* was thorough.

I put my hand on the pad, felt a minor prick, and almost instantly, my stomach dropped due to the speed with which the lift started racing up.

"Nifty," I muttered.

"Secure," she replied.

Mm-hmm.

All business.

"Thanks for looking after me today," I said.

"I'd say you're welcome, but I get paid a lot to do it. I've been made head of your detail, so now, I get paid a lot more than I used to. This means, if you keep thanking me, you're going to be saying that to me every day."

"Right," I mumbled.

"I'm not unfriendly," she stated in a straightforward, unemotional, thus mildly unfriendly way. "I'm a cool chick. But you're my responsibility. I take it seriously. It's my job to die for you. So we are never going to be that."

"Right," I repeated.

Message received.

The doors opened.

I knew the drill and waited while she stepped off.

However, a heavenly smell wafted in, so giving her the three seconds it took for her to return to the lift and jerk her head at me to tell me it was safe to exit was a test of willpower I couldn't believe I bested.

But then I hit Aleksei's penthouse.

And my whole world fell away.

I learned the low ledge in the living room wasn't dead space.

Oh no.

The entire length of it was a fireplace, which was now lit with cozily dancing purple flames.

Thousands of pinprick drone lights floated randomly in the air all over the living and dining areas making it look like Aleksei had welcomed the night into his penthouse. The rest of the lights in that area had been set, at best, to ten percent. The effect was soft, peaceful, welcoming, but sophisticated.

Oh, and romantic.

Very, very romantic.

There was full lighting over the kitchen, however, which was an absolute disaster, sharing the intel that Aleksei was a messy cook.

There was also a cluster of white tapers in crystal candlesticks, lit and glowing around a squat oval bowl stuffed bloom to bloom with perfect, creamy-white roses. This adorned corner seating at the kitchen bar set with black plates, placemats, napkins, shining cutlery and sparkling wineglasses.

Mellow classical music filled the air.

My cats had taken to their luxurious new digs with the haughty entitlement only cats could make work.

I knew this because Comet was sitting on a stool at the kitchen bar, just his eyes tall enough to see over it to the food. He was quiet for once, openly content, his fluffy tail sweeping along the side of the seat (which made me wonder if Aleksei had been feeding him scraps).

Nova was curled asleep in an armchair.

And Jupiter was fully visible, enjoying the heat from the fireplace and his spectacular view, lying hunkered down on his belly on the ledge by the window, his attention to the craft traffic and city lights.

And from Aleksei's oven came the mouthwatering scent of roasting meat.

More mouthwatering, the amazing male standing among all of this, the lights gleaming blue on his jet-black hair, his shoulders strong and wide enough to hold up an entire realm, his eyes, twin nights, aimed at me.

Suddenly and inexplicably, at this reminder I was being courted by the

True Heir, who happened to be my fated mate, and just how much effort he was putting into that, I was struck shy.

And moved deep to my soul.

To hide that, I quipped, "Why, your royal highness, I sense you intend to seduce me."

Standing at the kitchen counter, building a salad, he ordered, "Come here."

I went right there.

I mean, what would you do?

I set my bag on the kitchen counter.

Aleksei pulled a dishtowel off his shoulder, wiped his hands, tossed it aside, and was at the ready to cup my face in both hands and dip right in for a lip touch when I made it to him.

He didn't lift his head far nor take his hands from my face, when he asked, his voice straight to rich velvet, "How was your day?"

"Bodi, that's my director, told me I don't have to bother with offering another direction for the costumes. He's all in with where we are. Casting is almost complete. We'll start fittings in a few weeks. Oh, and he congratulates both of us on our mating."

"Mm," he hummed, and he could have been doing that right between my legs, such was that area's response to the sound.

So, when I continued, it was breathy. "And I figured out how to make troll skin."

His brows rose with heartwarming interest in my work. "How's that?"

"I was trying overlapping. When that failed, gathering. But I should have been scoring. It's perfect."

"Excellent."

"How are you?"

"Better, now that you're home."

Gods, this male, this *amazing* male, was *my* male.

For sure, I could stand there, my face in his hands, his face all I could see, and I suspected I could do that for a long time.

Maybe years.

And definitely, that timidity I felt was still there, low level, partly because I couldn't believe my luck. Mostly because he was just so magnificent.

But farg this noise.

I threw my arms around his neck, got up to the tips of my toes and kissed him.

My tongue darted inside to taste his heat and musk, but his forced it out to feast on mine. Together, they danced delightfully as his hands slid from my face, one going into my hair, the other trailing a delicious line of fire down my back.

I pressed closer, feeling his heat, his hardness, his strength, his immense energy, and when he nipped my lower lip between deep kisses, I whimpered.

At the sound, his head shot back.

Losing him, I whimpered again and dazedly opened my eyes.

It was then, he *growled*.

And that was when I learned he'd been keeping it light.

The kiss he came back with was greedy, hungry, *devouring*.

I'd never been kissed so thoroughly.

I'd never had any lover demand so much of me, while giving the world in return.

I pressed all the closer, practically burrowing into him, and moaned into his mouth.

He hauled me up his chest then smacked my behind, causing a ripple of decadent sensation to tingle over my entire body, and I knew instantly what he was demanding.

I wrapped my legs around his waist.

He turned, and all the while kissing, up the steps we went, into his room.

He lifted a knee, and then we were down on his bed.

Yes, good call.

This was so much better.

I wanted to flip him to get more of him, but there was none of that happening.

Oh no.

Aleksei kept me firmly under him as he plundered my mouth. He pillaged my neck. He invaded the shells of my ears.

All the while his hands moved, dragging, gripping, claiming.

I was able to get mine up his shirt and another whimper escaped at encountering the silken heat and hardness, skin to skin, of his back.

My hands were removed, though, when he arched away, and my shirt was up, so my arms were too, then my shirt was gone, my hair flying all over his bedclothes.

His darkened gaze raked over my face, my body, a soft, amethyst light mingling with the night in his eyes, and then I watched his head drop down.

With a scrape of teeth against my skin, and a deft flick of his tongue, the front fastener of my bra released.

Holy Hecate.

Smooth.

Released, the cups popped aside, my breast (swollen), my nipples (beaded and aching) were exposed to his gaze, and my hips drove up, feeling the hard, promising line of his cock pressing into my thigh as his head dropped again.

He blew on one nipple while his hand curved over my other breast. And then he took it hungrily into his mouth just as his fingers pinched the opposite one.

By the gods.

"Aleksei," I moaned, plunging my hands into his hair.

He sucked, licked, scraped his teeth on one and squeezed, twisted and pulled with the other.

So good.

So, so good.

And then he switched.

Gods.

Beautiful torture.

I was mindless, squirming, my fingers fisted in his thick, soft hair, my other hand seeking, demanding, tugging at clothing.

Begging.

He pulled away and I gasped audaciously at his loss.

Then I watched as he stood at the side of the bed, yanked off his shirt, pulled down his jeans, exposing the total fullness of his beauty, leaving me quivering. He reached in and dragged my pants down my legs, taking my panties with them.

He tossed them aside, dipped low while his big hands ran up the backs of my thighs, lifting them, spreading them.

And then his mouth was on me.

Oh yes.

So good.

So, so good.

I arched fully, driving myself into Aleksei's lapping, gorging mouth.

"Yes, by the gods, *yes*," I breathed, coming up to my elbows and nearly climaxing at seeing his dark head working between my thighs, his big tan hands curled around the pale skin at the juncture of my hips, pulsing me into his hunger.

I reached out and clutched his hair to claim him, hold him to me, and he kept working me even as he tipped back and the deep-violet topaz that had taken over his eyes fired through me.

Our gazes locked as I gripped his hair, he gripped my hips and fed from me, brazenly, downright pornographically, like we were daring the other to look away.

And then with all he was doing, giving, demanding, I couldn't. The climax was speeding toward me.

My eyes drifted half-mast, my head was about to fall back.

"Don't you fucking dare," he grunted into my flesh. "Look at me."

With effort, I focused on him.

"Honey," I begged.

He lapped agonizingly, gloriously, back to front while I watched.

Oh my gods.

"Watch me eat you," he ordered.

My entire body trembled.

He kept at me. "You don't come until my cock is driving inside you."

His hands seized my hips like a marauder seizing his loot, pulsing me into his mouth.

"Watch me," he growled into my wet.

I watched.

His eyes locked to mine, he ate.

I watched.

He tongue fucked me.

I watched, whimpering, and quivering.

He scraped my clit with his teeth.

I gasped and shuddered.

He surged up, clamping his hands behind my knees, rolling them back, positioning, and with our eyes still secured, I felt the head of his cock search, stretch, probe.

I caught my lip between my teeth.

A predatory sound rumbled out of his chest and settled over me like chains.

I was his.

He was mine.

But right now, *I was his.*

He thrust, filling me.

Oh yes.

I was his.

I cried out, my eyes fluttering closed, my entire body arching, my pussy accommodating, taking all of him.

"Laura," he clipped, my name harsh, guttural.

Magic.

I righted my head, opened my eyes and saw the most cruelly beautiful sight I had ever seen.

And then it got better as I watched Aleksei fuck me.

I panted, clutched the sheets, rocked with his thrusts.

He hiked my knees higher, spread them wider.

"Feel us," he grunted.

Oh, I felt us.

Even so, I reached out, scraping my nails along his ridged abs, watching him grit his teeth, the muscle jump in his jaw, feeling the power I had over him, clutching his cock with my pussy as it drove into me. I sifted through the curls at its base and felt the wet, hot, silken steel shaft brand me inside.

And it was...

It was...

Why I'd been born.

"Yes, *bissi tressa*," he encouraged gently.

Given permission (thankfully), I finally let go, cried out, drove down onto his cock and exploded.

Reaching the stars.

And they were all mine.

Aleksei gave me the stars.

"*Fuck yes*," he groaned, dropping his weight to mine, clasping a hand at the back of my neck and one at my hip to hold me steady as he rode me, drilled me, and then he planted himself deep, and for the second time in my life, I heard a dragon roar.

His big body shuddered powerfully and then collapsed on mine.

His weight was great, but I could do nothing but accept it gladly.

I wound my limbs around him.

Coming back to myself, I felt how big he was, how much I had to stretch to accommodate his size. I throbbed between my legs, feeling used, even abused.

And I fucking *treasured* it.

"Um, thanks for the flowers and candlelight," I mumbled.

Aleksei huffed a laugh against my neck, then nuzzled there and shifted some of his weight to a forearm.

I stroked his hair.

Because I could.

I played with a curl at the end.

Also because I could.

With my other hand, I traced the tips of my fingers down the hollow of his spine.

Ditto on the because I could.

His lips came to my ear.

"I fuck hard, darling," he whispered.

"I didn't miss that, *drahko*," I replied.

He lifted his head and looked down at me.

Lilith, he was beautiful.

And mine, mine, *mine*.

I moved my hand to his jaw, ran a thumb through the hollow below his cheekbone, across his luscious lower lip.

Yes, because I could.

"*Bissi.*"

I gazed into his eyes.

The violet was gone.

I missed it.

"But I've never fucked that hard. Are you okay?" he asked.

"Dandy."

"Certain?"

"What about me in the melted pile of female you've made of me indicates I'm not one hundred percent preening that I landed a mate who fucks like a rocket."

Aleksei started chuckling.

Way, way, *way* the best way to hear and feel him do *that*.

"You're remaining hard," I whispered with no small amount of surprise.

"That's new too," he whispered back. "I could fuck you again right now."

Oh *my*.

"Seems this mate thing might ultimately have some bonuses," I noted.

"Seems like," he teased.

"Are we going to do that?"

"Are you going to be honest with me and tell me the actual state I've left of your pretty pink cunt?"

I darted my eyes side to side.

His hand still curled around my neck squeezed. "Laura."

I looked at him. "Okay, she might need a wee break."

Instantly, but gently, slowly, and mind-bogglingly sweetly, he slid out.

He then fell to his back, but he pulled me around and tucked me to his side.

This very much worked.

New terrain.

I trailed my fingertips over the swells, peaks and valleys of his chest.

"You're very easily seduced," he told the ceiling.

I tipped my head back to look at him.

He dipped his jaw down to catch my eyes.

He looked satisfied, even arrogant.

It was hot.

"Don't annoy me," I warned. "It might mess with my enjoyment of the pot roast you made me."

He immediately assumed an offended expression that wasn't entirely playful.

"Prime rib roast, darling," he corrected.

I smiled at him. "But of course."

He drifted his hand to the cheek of my bottom, but he simply cupped it before he said with a warning tone, "We have plans tonight, Laura."

Of course, he'd steer us back to that.

I sighed. "We do."

He narrowed his eyes. "You didn't throw yourself at me to avoid them, did you?"

I made a mental note to load that in my arsenal for the future.

He squeezed my behind. "I saw that."

I focused on him. "Saw what?"

"You filing that away for future use."

"I would never play those kind of games," I sniffed (and lied).

He pulled me fully onto his chest and then tucked my hair behind my ears.

A lot of it still fell to curtain our faces anyway, but it was sweet how he did that.

"One thing that's good to know. My creature and I are both a lot less tense, not only now that you're home, but now that I've had you."

Not seemingly able to get enough of him, my fingertips trailed his jaw, then his neck, the column of his throat, his collarbone.

They did that as I said, "That's good."

He wrapped his arms around me, gave me a squeeze, and said, "All right, darling. Let's go eat."

And part two of me wishing we could stay in bed.

But this was us.

Now and forever.

I needed to know his.

He needed to know mine.
Once it was done, it could be done.
And we could get on with it.
So might as well get it done.
Even if it was going to suck.
Though, luckily, once it was done, we could go back to bed.

CHAPTER 19
UNIQUE

Cozy night at home, post-coital, with my ridiculously handsome mate meant Aleksei put the white long-sleeved T-shirt back on, with some charcoal-gray sleep pants.

I donned a pair of soft-knit, ballet-pink lounge pants, a matching shelf-bra cami, and a slightly darker, lightweight, shawl-neck cashmere cardigan.

And together, holding hands (he was so totally cute), barefoot, we walked down to the kitchen.

Fortunately, our bed frolics didn't burn the roast.

Also fortunately, Aleksei had a fully stocked wine room (of course he would, he sure had the room for it), and the red he selected might not be as good as Chateau LeBrand, but it was smooth, rich and tasty.

And we both discovered (at least I hoped it was both of us) that tinkering around, putting the finishing touches on a meal together was relaxing and kind of fun.

Aleksei didn't mess with courses.

So the salad, rolls, meat (with *jus* and delicious homemade horseradish sauce), buttered asparagus and fondant potatoes he served all at once.

And I knew, once we settled, and after I'd only had one bite of the crisp lettuce tossed in a creamy, peppery, garlicky dressing, he wasn't leaving anything to chance.

Because he didn't hesitate to start it.

"Should you go first, or shall I?"

I cut across the top of the squibs of the asparagus to save them for last, saying, "How about we wait for in front of the firelight, over cognac."

"Laura." He used my name as a warning.

I looked at him even as I placed a bite of potato in my mouth.

I bit down.

Annnnnd...

Yowza!

Yum.

I chewed, swallowed and said, "This food is too good to waste, eating it while discussing that."

"You're evading."

"Only until we're finished eating."

He stared at me.

I kept eating (because seriously, my mate had a way in a kitchen) but did it staring at him.

As usual, he went first.

"I don't know this as fact, but I can guess that my mother was selected not only because of her popularity as a screen actress, her beauty, her style, her unimpeachable reputation, but also, her ambition and her ability to play to the public. My father was born with blood that meant he wanted for nothing his entire life. So although he understands duty, and on a certain level, hard work, he has never experienced a time where all of his needs weren't met. From someone else making his bed, to dealing with the laundering of his clothes, to arranging for him to get from one place to another."

"Okay," I said softly, and added, "And can I just say, this meat is cooked to perfection."

"You can say that, darling," he replied just as softly. "And thank you."

I smiled at him. "Right, I'm listening. Go on."

He nodded.

"Obviously, even before it became apparent I was the True Heir, I would be the next king. And Mother made it clear, even if she wasn't born royal, it was her who would be molding me into that position. I was too young when it started, but reflecting on it, I believe she also made it abundantly clear she was going to be absolutely certain I did not grow up with what she considers certain weaknesses that are abhorrent to a man who holds the throne."

It wasn't hard to read between those lines.

"Oh boy," I whispered.

"Yes," he agreed.

"And those would be?" I asked.

"For starters, from the time I was eight to the time I was sent to boarding school, and then of course at boarding school, I made my bed."

Actually, for a boy born to a palace, that said a lot.

"Right."

"And I went to a military school. Not one aristocrats send their children to, the ones that started centuries ago in order for them to buy officer's commissions for their second and third born sons so those males would have something to do with their lives, and a salary to come with it. Schools that are now just boarding schools where the students wear uniforms and march sometimes, but they aren't much more that. I went to Red Lair where, for millennia, boys were trained to be warriors."

"I know," I said, because everyone knew about Red Lair, and they knew Aleksei went there.

"It is not for the faint of heart."

I'd heard that too.

However, at his words, my heart lurched. "Did you hate it?"

"I loved it."

I was back to staring.

"My mother took hold of me, and being so focused on that, and then she had a girl, and she was beside herself she did, she lost sight of her middle two children. And my father got hold of them."

"Uh-oh."

He nodded glumly. "Maybe they wanted her attention. Maybe they were jealous of me because I had it or that I would be king. Maybe they were always just assholes. But they fucked with me. All the time."

I knew I didn't like those guys.

"How did they do that?"

He shrugged. "You name it, they did it. Throwing ice water on me in the middle of the night when I was dead asleep. When we were standing as royals during a public appearance, pinching the skin on the back of my arms, which hurts like fuck, but I couldn't make a face or do anything. Stealing my homework. Telling girls I liked them when I didn't. When I was still quite young, getting into luggage the staff had packed when we'd go on trips and taking out my underwear so I didn't have any, and then I'd have to admit it to someone, which was embarrassing at that age."

Oh yeah.

Really didn't like them.

Aleksei kept sharing.

"Being at Red Lair was an escape from them. Being at Red Lair, they've had over a thousand years of finding ways to uncover what boys will turn into men, and what boys will always be boys, and then cultivating all manner of exercises to cull the wheat from the chaff."

"You were the wheat," I stated firmly.

He tipped his head to the side, his eyes warming at my words, and he shared, "Both Tim and Rol went to Red Lair at Mom's insistence. Tim was kicked out within six months, no matter he was a prince of this realm. Rol lasted a year and a half before he was booted."

"But you thrived."

He shrugged again and ate a piece of succulent beef. "I found my place. Perhaps it was Mom's influence, perhaps it was because I knew from the moment I could form coherent thought I was destined for the throne, but I was always serious. There are two things that happen at Red Lair. One is that they have ways to be certain who remains is supposed to remain. The other is the boys find ways to get out if they don't want to be there. I've known some who were smart enough to best the studies, physically and mentally capable enough to excel at the drills and exercises. And they still found ways to get expelled. The challenge of an advanced curriculum coupled with the physical challenge spoke to me. It was something I understood integrally. I was in my place. My brothers were just not Red Lair males."

"But I sense your brothers were culled, they didn't find ways to get expelled," I noted.

"Tim was culled. Rol tried, but he just wasn't smart enough and couldn't endure the physicality of it."

"So...what? They just never grew up?"

"I haven't yet explained about our beasts."

Ah.

"I've seen Aleece's," I told him. "She's fierce, but so beautiful."

And she was. Pearly-white scales with gold horns and claws, feathered rather than webbed wings and blue topaz eyes.

Stunning.

Unusually, though I'd never thought about it before, since the royal family occasionally featured their dragons during special events, I had not seen either of the princes transformed.

I wasn't very interested in them, so I didn't think about it much. I'd just always thought, through some trick of genetics (Queen Calisa's beast, it was known, was a red fox), meant their beasts weren't dragons.

"They aren't what you'd think, considering their personalities. We are all the blood of the first True Heir. I'm not sure there's been a royal dragon that could not do its part in defending the throne."

So they *were* dragons.

"Okay, so I don't get it."

"When did yours first come out?" he asked.

"When I was five."

He nodded. "Between four and seven, usually. Tim's didn't come out until he was nine. Rol's came out at seven. Tim had a complex about his late transformation, and I think that was why he transformed all the time once his beast appeared. But our creatures used to tussle. Play."

"And yours always won," I presumed.

He shook his head, but said, "As you know, we don't always have complete control over them, especially when we're younger. So yes, mine bested theirs. It was bigger, always. And I was older, also always. And mine was with me when they'd fuck with me, and he didn't like that, so perhaps he took it too far occasionally."

I tried not to smile, but I had a feeling I failed.

"Not sure they didn't deserve that, Aleksei."

"I'm not saying they didn't, but it was easy, and everyone has pride. Tim, too much. Rol, it was too easily bruised. Although they have strong, handsome creatures, Rol's is quite small. And Tim's is smaller than mine, larger than Rol's, and mean. It plays dirty. This is something that might get you ahead in schoolyard bullying, in a street fight, but in battle, there's only so far you can get using nasty little shortcuts. You need to think on your feet. Be able to pivot. If a strategy you're using isn't working, you have to have dozens more you can try. There are only so many tricks you can roll out. Eventually, it comes down to strength and intelligence. Someone has to win. I always won. And they're very poor losers."

"So in all things, you bested them, and rather than finding their niche, their vocation, some mission, something that set them apart from you and could give them a calling, they decided to be fuckboys."

"It's arrogant to assume it's all about me."

"But they didn't have to make their beds."

He seemed relieved that I got it.

"Mom tried, but Dad wasn't happy she did it with me. He put his foot down with them."

"And as such, they never learned inner accountability," I deduced, then carried it forward. "And since you have, and due to your position in your family and your popularity, you're used to covering their foibles and missteps, which puts more pressure on you to be perfect. To perform. To put yourself out there when you prefer privacy."

I just knew this was going to spoil my appetite.

And it did, as I harked back and put together times when Aleksei would show up at a youth ring ice match after Timothee stole some pit ball player's girlfriend then promptly dumped her, making her cry prettily on social tape while he squired around another pit ball player's girlfriend he also stole.

Or when Aleksei was walking a street during some village's septuacentennial, accepting flower bouquets from little girls and smiling at crowds waving handheld Night's Fall flags with its purple dragon on black, doing this after the Palace allegedly paid off some males who got in a back-alley shifter fight with Errol and some of his bros.

"I love them."

When Aleksei said this, my eyes shot to his.

"They can be funny," he went on. "They dote on Aleece. And they're just my brothers."

"Okay," I replied, not having any siblings, so not really getting it.

"That's why it's so disappointing, *bissi*, especially what I learned today."

"Because they can be better?"

"No, because they never will."

Oh gods.

"Also, they just get worse," he carried on. "Today, with what we learned, the worst of all. I can't even wrap my head around doing that to anyone. He should be facing charges, but instead, Dad will pay the female off, and it'll all go away. And learning that after finding you'd been drugged against your will was bad timing, but even if that hadn't happened to you, I'd be livid. Making it worse, it won't stop. They never learn, and they're not stupid. They can. They simply refuse to. And since Dad makes it so there are no consequences to their actions, they have no reason to try."

I had to bury how I felt that Timothee would get away with what he'd done. I just had to hope that the payoff was worthwhile for the female.

And I didn't have time to think too long on it.

I had to stay here with Aleksei.

"I'm sorry, honey," I whispered.

"I am too."

"With the bullying when you were younger, didn't your parents intervene?" I queried.

"At first, Mom didn't because she thought it built character. The length of time it went on, and how unrelenting it was, she eventually tried to put a stop to it. Dad was adamant she not get involved, saying, 'Boys will be boys, we have to let them be boys.'"

King Fillion seemed to be a dab hand at platitudes.

"Are you close with Aleece?" I asked.

A fond smile hit his beautiful mouth. "Yes."

I was glad he had that.

And Sirk.

And now…me.

"What about your parents? Are you close with them?" I asked.

"There's love, it's remote. Duty is in the way."

I nodded.

"My father is proud of me, and he shows it. My mother's expectations are high, and she has no problem voicing them."

Hmm.

Not sure what to think of that.

"We're not a normal family," he finished.

"Who is?" I asked in an effort to make him feel better.

"I suppose that's a good question." He bit off the tip of a stalk of asparagus, chewed it, swallowed it, and asked, "And yours?"

Blast.

It was my turn.

Okay.

We were here.

Get it done and over with.

"They're just…"

I looked down at my plate.

Forked into my potato.

Ate the bite (really, so yum, even in the middle of discussing all this garbage).

Pulled in a deep breath.

And looked to Aleksei.

"Bitter. Dad found his mate. I don't know how it happened, but he didn't have her long before she died. He married Mom, who…again, I don't know. I think maybe she was too lazy to quest for her mate. Whatever the reason, she took him on, but I have no idea why. She didn't want him either. There was no love in our house. Not them for each other. Not them for me."

"And this translated to physical abuse?"

I pulled my shoulders forward, then released them. "Dad's just mad at the world. Maybe it's because he found and lost his mate so young. But for him, it's everything. Taxes are too high. His boss is too demanding. Mom doesn't fold his underwear right."

"He could fold it himself," Aleksei remarked.

I ate an asparagus crown. Fortunately, it too was yummy enough to cut through the ash in my mouth.

"Yeah," I replied. "She's told him that. Repeatedly. Shouted it even."

"Darling."

I looked from my plate to him and got into the tough stuff.

"The wrist thing, she was just being rough with me. Impatient. It wasn't good it happened, but it was an accident. She was actually kinda horrified she did it, though she was more horrified what people would think about it than upset at the fact she broke her child's bone. The ribs. Well, that was something else. Truly, he didn't often get physical. Mostly it was an icy-coldness, disinterest. But even though the times were rare, it would get physical. And that time, with the ribs, obviously, it was really bad."

"This seems very..." He struggled for a word for so long, he didn't find one.

But I had it for him.

"Matter of fact. Like you were this morning, when we talked after our so-not-fun, inter-family mingling."

"What I'm dealing with is a scar left from my family's dynamic far less deep than what you have."

I shook my head. "It isn't about comparing scars. Deciding who had it worse. Doing that diminishes the fact you didn't have it that great either."

"Agreed," he returned. "With the caveat that not recognizing how much worse you had it is a form of diminishing how bad it was for you. And that can hinder finding effective ways of healing from it."

He had me there.

"It was all you knew," I stated. "It was all I knew. They were never affectionate. They mostly were so wrapped up in their...whatever was wrong with them, they spent a lot of time stoking it, encouraging it to sour, fester, infect them deeper. The physical abuse didn't last long," I told him hurriedly when it appeared he was getting annoyed I was blowing all of this off. "They took me to an uncredited clinic for my wrist. The ones people go to so records won't be filed. I think they did that because Mom was embarrassed. When the ribs things happened, they took me to a hospital. It was flagged. They got a visit from the RVPB. It was then, that part ended."

"The Royal Vulnerable Persons Bureau visited them?"

I nodded.

"And left you?"

I nodded again.

His mouth got tight.

Okay.

Finish it.

Fast.

"It started when she appeared."

His expression cleared, almost as if he was excited, no, *eager* to learn more about her.

"Your creature," he said quietly.

I turned to him. "*I* think she's beautiful."

"I'm sure she is," he murmured.

"She's just not...*normal*."

He tipped his head to the side with open curiosity. "Do you have a pic of her?"

I swallowed but didn't answer him.

Because I did. Several.

But I'd buried them in a folder in my Palm, thinking one day I'd be glad I hadn't deleted them, but not about to run across one so soon after I thought I'd lost her.

"Did they ever talk to you, at all, about what makes mates, *mates*?" he asked.

"No. But I've read about it."

"So you know it's you and me. But just as importantly, it's them."

Gods.

This was huge.

Gods.

The fact she was there, asleep, instead of gone, like I thought, made me have to think about it.

I'd seen his creature. His beast.

His dragon.

He was massive, mighty, fierce, terrifying.

And so, so handsome.

But she...

"He is just as clicked into her as I am to you, Laura," Aleksei said. "I'll find her beautiful, because she's his mate."

I knew that.

I knew it.

But...

I fiddled with my roll.

"Show me, *bissi*," he urged.

Ugh!

Okay, he'd see eventually.

And anyway, my father was wrong. My mother was ignorant.

She *was* beautiful.

I slid off my stool, went to my bag and got my Palm.

Head bent to it, heart hammering, I dug out the pic folder and found a pic of her.

Seeing it, my stomach rolled over, because...yes.

She was beautiful, I missed her so dang bad, and I couldn't wait to have her back.

I slid back on my stool and handed him my Palm.

He took it, his gorgeous eyes already cast down, like he couldn't wait to see.

I watched.

His eyes widened.

I braced.

"Fucking hell," he said gruffly.

Gods!

"I've never seen the likes of her. She's very unique," I said primly.

And she was.

Gayle said she could be in commercials.

Cat said she knew artists who would wish to paint her, and sculptors who would wish to mold her.

Mr. Truelock said he was glad she surfaced in our time, for if she'd been born years ago, wars would be fought over her.

I just loved her.

I sawed off a piece of meat that was so tender, it needed no sawing (I did that anyway) and shoved it in my mouth.

"Laura," Aleksei called.

"She's small," I said, aiming the words across the room, my mouth still full. I snatched up my wine and took a sip, struggling to swallow because my meat needed more chewing, but by damn, I managed it. "Not dainty or anything. She's like the size difference from me to you in terms of her and your creature."

"Laura."

"And yes, she's shy. She was terrified of my father." I continued talking to the lift. "She came out once when he was..." I shook my head. "Anyway. He shifted and beat the crap out of her too."

"Darling, look at me."

I turned to him.

He had her pic on my Palm aimed my way.

"She has your eyes."

"Yes," I whispered.

"They look like aquamarines."

My throat suddenly felt very scratchy.

"She's the most extraordinary thing I've ever seen," he whispered.

Uh-oh.

"Aleksei," I said soothingly.

"Someone tried to cut her out of you. A creature can't survive an excision."

His eyes had shifted straight from a starry night and were glowing, and the veins were standing out in his neck.

And his forehead.

"Honey," I whispered.

"Your father made her hide. Made her shy. Made her scared."

I wrapped my fingers around his wrist and reached my other hand for my Palm.

"You need to chill, baby," I said carefully, slipping my Palm from his fingers since he didn't give it to me.

"Someone tried to cut her out of you."

Truth?

I'd wanted to get through this whole family dynamics chat so we could move on to any news he had about all that had been going down. And he had to have news. Every agency in the realm it seemed had a hand in investigating it, and all of them paraded through his penthouse last night, reporting directly to him.

But I was sensing that would be a bad idea.

"I love it that you think she's pretty," I said.

"She isn't pretty, like you aren't pretty. She's stunning, like you."

He was just the best.

"You wanna have sex again?" I tried.

"Absolutely, but we aren't going to."

"Why not?"

"Because it's taking everything I have not to shift, explode out my windows and incinerate a few beings."

"Let's not do that again, at least not tonight."

"Agreed."

"And Jupiter likes your view. I wouldn't let him hang out by the window if there was no actual window."

"Mm."

"I seriously, seriously love it that you like her," I whispered.

"*Bissi*," he whispered back, caught me behind my neck and brought me to him for a hard kiss.

When we broke, he kept me close, and I was relieved to see the night taking over the amethyst of his eyes.

No incinerations.

That was good.

"There are those who know they're not much," he stated. "So they don't try for much. They don't do anything but give up and let the world prove to them how hard life is and how little joy there is to find. The one thing they can easily identify is the thing that infuriates them the most. Something...or someone...special. Someone who is more than they are, just breathing. Someone who will be more than they'll ever be, and they can't stand it. So they'll do everything to cut her down. They'll do everything to convince her she's not special, so she'll give up and wallow right along with them in their mental filth. They knew who you were. They knew who your creature was. And they couldn't stand it."

I loved that he thought that.

However.

"I'm not sure it's about me. It's just them. Honestly, a lot of the time, it seemed like they forgot I was around."

"No, darling. They didn't. Because they've been in touch with the Palace. And they've demanded an audience with the king...and me."

I went perfectly still.

Oh.

My.

Farging.

Gods!

CHAPTER 20

PLOT

Even totally still groggy, my eyes opened, and I rolled, vaguely (but contentedly) feeling the deep lethargy in every muscle in my body and the light ache between my legs.

The sun was high.

Morning was here.

I reached across the bed, already knowing he wasn't there.

And I was so fuzzy, it didn't hit me as strange that I also knew precisely where he was.

Instead of processing it, I just made moves to get there.

The hover bed rocked like a cradle as I found the edge of it, threw my legs over the side, and got up. I groped for my panties, tugged them on, found my cami, pulled that on too, and listed across the room to Aleksei's upstairs office.

He was behind the desk, his eyes on me as I entered, like he knew I was coming even if I hadn't made a sound with my bare feet on his plush carpet. His beast senses were good, I knew this, but that was really good.

He rolled back in his chair, and I accepted his invitation.

I slid onto his lap.

He hooked his arm behind my knees, pulled them up to my chest and tucked me into a ball, wrapping both arms around me and holding me tight.

Okay.

Wow.

Gods, this felt *good*.

I nestled my forehead into the side of his neck.

"Sleep okay?" he murmured.

"Mm," I hummed because it was all I had in me.

He gave me a squeeze. "Good."

I rested in the safety of his arms, and he held me like he'd do it all day as I let the sleep drift away.

As I did, our night before floated through my head.

Our amazing first time, as well as the second, the third, the fourth (for your information, this mate business meant Aleksei *could* stay hard all night, we'd tested it, and both of us had passed out before we found the end of his stamina—it...was...*awesome*).

Regrettably, the conclusion of our conversation about my parents also sifted into my head.

It went like this:

Aleksei: "I'm going to grant them an audience."

Me: "Are you crazy?"

Aleksei: "No. I want them to look me in the eyes when they say what they feel entitled to say after they treated their daughter, and my mate, so abominably."

Me: "Who cares!"

Aleksei: "I do. Know your enemy, Laura. Them even asking for an audience tells me something. They'll tell me more when I lay eyes on them. And more when they say what they have to say. In the end, I'll know what I'm dealing with in regard to those two vipers. And if they're stupid enough to give me the opportunity to discover what I can use to control them, or what will destroy them, I'll let them."

I was seeing his time at Red Lair might have ramifications for me.

"They didn't even wait a day," I mumbled into his throat as I sat in the cocoon of his big, strong body in his office.

"Pardon?"

I blew out a sigh, shook off the rest of my bleariness, and lifted my head to look at him.

"My parents. They didn't even wait a day after learning we were mates before they reached out to try to get...whatever it is they think they'll get. Thirteen years, I haven't seen or heard from them. But they didn't reach out to me. They contacted the Palace."

"Are we surprised they're giving indications of what we already know, they're pieces of shit?" he asked, watching me carefully.

"No," I huffed and then collapsed against him again. "It's just sucky."

"They're suspects, Laura."

My head shot up again. "What?"

"In whatever is going on with someone trying to harm you. It's another reason I'm granting them an audience."

"You think they're behind drugging me?" Dear Lilith! It wasn't just that. "And *attacking me?*"

"No. They aren't high up on the suspect list. I've had a briefing on them as well. A detailed one. They both make decent money, but they aren't in a position to hire goons to attack you. And the male we have in custody isn't talking. But what we do know is, he's not some average street tough. He's a skilled mercenary. And they cost money."

Holy Hecate.

"Really?" I asked.

"Yes," he answered. "I'm simply telling you because you should know they're being investigated."

"What else should I know?"

He pulled me closer and sighed.

I felt that with him.

Our cozy night in, sex-fest and cuddle time was over.

Back to the real world.

"The investigators are operating on two theories. That one. The one where your parents dislike your creature so much, are embarrassed by her or whatever their fucked-up mindset about that is, they put a hit out on her. The reason that seems unlikely is, first, it's thin because it's deranged. They're pieces of shit but have given no indication they're twisted, homicidal pieces of shit. Also, the time that's passed with no contact between you since you left their home. If this bothered them that much, it would be expected they'd do something in the last thirteen years. And last, it doesn't explain why they shifted targets and aimed at me."

"No, it doesn't," I agreed. "What's the other theory?"

"That someone took pains to discover you were my mate. And they targeted you first, in order to dispose of her, so we would be less likely to find one another."

Oh boy.

I couldn't say I knew a whole bunch about this mate business, not ever having one before, and not having parents who explained it to me.

That said, it was exceptionally rare a shifter would lose their beast without losing their lives as well, as in, the human side died, and when that happened, the shifter died with them.

A shifter's beast was always something strong, cunning, wily or swift.

They healed quickly when wounded. And their senses were heightened. So heightened, they normally heightened the human side as well when they were dormant. Thus, they were hard to kill (why the scientists hypothesized we'd advanced from humans to shifters, because they'd appear to protect us when we were in danger). There were some who were weaker than others (like mine), and some were nearly impossible to kill (like Aleksei's).

But they had evolved to keep their human alive by fighting, outwitting or escaping to stay alive.

On the other hand, part of the protection of a beast was that, if they died, the human part of them didn't. In other words, if you killed a creature, in order to kill the being it inhabited, you then had to kill that being. As such, once a beast was dead, it would immediately transform back to its being.

However, again, this was very rare.

Therefore, I didn't know what might happen when one ran across their mate without their beast alive within them. They didn't write that scenario in romance novels.

Mates were mates, the human part of us, and the creature. But clearly, the creatures called to each other, like mine did, even being roused from a drugged state to do it.

I didn't know what would have happened if I didn't have her.

But I sensed I might have missed it altogether, since, when she went back to her unconscious state, I did just that.

"Is that possible?" I asked about identifying someone's mate before they knew of their mate.

He nodded. "Yes. There are witches who have the power to pinpoint a being's fate. They cost a good deal of money. There aren't many of them, but they exist."

"Okay. But why would someone do that?"

"Well, if that someone was Anna, she'd have the means and the motive to make certain I didn't find the being who was meant to be mine since she considers me hers."

"Oh my gods," I breathed.

"However, their switching targets to me does not seem like something Anna would wish. That said, she was not happy I broke things off with her, so it's highly doubtful, but it isn't entirely out of the realm of possibility."

I was thinking we had more to talk about when it came to Princess Anna.

Aleksei kept sharing, but not about her.

"The same with means and motive for Timothee, or less likely, Errol, just to fuck with me."

"Oh my gods," I said a whole lot louder.

"However, considering they turned their weapons on me when they had the chance, an order I cannot begin to think either of my brothers would be behind, it hints at something deeper, more sinister and more concerning."

Uh-oh.

"That would be?" I asked, even if I wasn't sure I wanted to know.

"I introduced a bill in the UCR that would make it illegal, and punishable by prison time, to have sexual relations with or marry, even with parental consent, a minor under the age of fifteen."

The UCR was the United Council of Realms, the governing body that oversaw all Four Realms in matters that could supersede the laws a realm made for itself.

It also had other functions that carried on after Unification crashed. There was a central bank, so we all used the same money. There was open trade and open borders. And some taxes went their way, so they could allocate resources, say should there be a natural disaster where humanitarian efforts and rebuilding were needed.

"I heard about that," I said. "But it isn't controversial. Each realm has a law in place that forbids it anyway. Except the parental consent thing. Even so, they say it'll breeze through passage."

"It has some opposition."

Yuck. From who?

Aleksei answered my unasked question. "Sky's Edge."

I wanted to roll my eyes.

I didn't roll my eyes.

Sky's Edge was always stirring up trouble.

"King Arnaud," I guessed.

"Apparently, he's in love."

"He's in love a lot," I replied.

And he was, usually with very young females. It was gross when he was in his thirties.

But they were all majority (that said, they were all only seventeen or eighteen).

"She's twelve," Aleksei shared.

Lilith and all her fiery friends!

"Ulk!" I gagged.

"And unofficially, they haven't announced it yet, they're engaged."

"She's just a child," I snapped.

"He says it's their religion."

"It *was* their religion, hundreds of years ago. Oh, and that included sacrificing these poor virgin brides to their gods after they violated them. Are they going to resurrect that too?" I shook my head in disgust. "Those of the Edge always gave demons a bad name."

"King Arnaud is feeling a shift to the fundamentals of their faith. And if he asserts that the bill is discriminatory on the grounds of religion, he has the basis to defeat it."

"King Arnaud isn't actually the king," I shared my opinion on the matter. "He's a pretender. He was second born. It was just that his father was a douche canoe, scraped off his first family and disavowed them when he fell for the wiles of Queen Tatra, and changed succession so Arnaud would have the crown. But that isn't their law. He couldn't do that. I still don't know how he got away with it."

"As such, things have been precarious in Sky's Edge the last couple of years since King Riland died. A great many of the Edge feel the same way. Prince Tanyn, the true king, has a lot of support. And although they're battling this out in the courts, if for some reason that shouldn't go his way, there are rumors he's planning a coup. Not everyone is feeling Arnaud's shift to fundamentalism. And the rumor of his engagement to this girl is not popular with many, even if it's very popular with some."

"How have I not heard of this?"

"Do you keep up with current events?"

I couldn't say I did. Social tapes gave me a headache. Everyone had an opinion, and most of them weren't very informed, and those that were, were seriously skewed. Others were just plain boring.

And the news was usually depressing.

Case in point, what we were currently discussing.

"This sounds like a mess," I said. "But I don't understand why he'd target you."

"Because something is wrong with Arnaud. Even if he wasn't a pedophile, there's always been something off about him. And I've always been clear I thought so. I also haven't made it a secret that I support Tanyn in his claim to the throne. However, this is the first bill I've introduced that's directed at him and his off behavior, and part of his being off is that he is completely incapable of dealing with someone who doesn't agree with him."

"An attack on you would mean war between our realms, and Dawn's

Break and Land's End might have to get involved because they're our allies."

"Yes. As I mentioned, this could be far more sinister and concerning. The reason nothing about your assault was in the brief compiled on you is because there are no records of it. Farlay *was* a detective inspector at District Seven. He hasn't reported to work since the gallery incident, and no one can find him. And before he vanished, he did not file your report and there's no evidence he was investigating it."

This was *not* good.

Aleksei continued sharing. "Both Dr. Buildlore and Nurse Fitzgerald were on staff at Mercy, but they too have disappeared. The same with them keeping your stay and care out of hospital files. And Dr. Buildlore is in the middle of two inquiries. One, a complaint lodged by another nurse that he was taking inappropriate liberties with yet another nurse, not Nurse Fitzgerald, and showing her favoritism. The second, he performed a procedure that his patient didn't consent to."

Oh no!

"Removing a beast?"

"No, removing a shifter's entire uterus when she was supposed to be having a routine D and C."

This had started out terrible, and it wasn't getting any better.

"I feel it important to note that I recognized that weapon, because it was used on me," I told him.

He nodded. "I didn't miss when you said that. I've informed the task force."

"But if those were the same weapons, it's clear they didn't want to kill my beast, because they definitely could have if it's powerful enough to maybe end yours."

He held me closer and said, "This has been discussed. Since the male we have in custody isn't talking, we can't know if they were the same weapons, or if they've been modified since. However, we're operating on the theory that their firearms had not yet been upgraded, because it appears they were turning to medical science to be rid of your creature."

Oh.

Of course.

I should have put that together.

"But ultimately," Aleksei continued, "at this time, we don't know what their plans were or are. But I can assure you, every effort is being made to find out."

I wanted to be assured.

Regrettably, I wasn't.

"Okay, it's safe to say I was freaked by this before, Aleksei, but I'm totally freaked now."

He gathered me even closer and stated, "You are safe, Laura. And there's been an inter-agency task force set up with the best investigators we have looking into this. I knew many of the beings before they were assigned to it, and I trust and respect them. They'll get the job done."

That made me feel better.

"I'm afraid you'll need to tune into current events a lot more closely, darling," he warned.

Ugh.

Probably important for the future king's mate to stay abreast of important stuff.

"All right," I agreed.

"You'll have an aide to help you filter through it, though."

I would?

"But for now," he continued, "if you catch any news, the story that's being put out is that these two assailants acted alone and were members of a fringe group. So, for the general public, they'll think it was just a couple of disenfranchised loners who took their best shot, were thwarted and all is well in Night's Fall again."

"Is it...you mean...we're lying to people?"

"Best case scenario, we'll figure out what's going on and quietly handle it so no one will know your parents, my brothers, my ex, or the sovereign of a foreign realm had mal intent, which would cause my brothers to be run out on a rail, or a serious inter-realm incident with either Dawn's Break or Sky's Edge. Worst case scenario, it actually is Anna or Arnaud, word gets out, beings will lose their gods-damned minds, call for blood, someone will surely get up to some stupid shit, and dragons will have to fly."

"So, in other words, we're lying to prevent the possibility of all-out war."

"Precisely."

"It's really good I now know you cook great and can go all night, or this mate business might not be a lot of fun," I quipped.

"I could probably go all morning too."

I didn't just see the shift in his mood on his face and hear it in his voice, I felt it against my hip.

My mood shifted instantly too.

"Could you now?" I whispered.

"Panties off, darling," he whispered in return.

His arms loosened and I wheeled those babies off as fast as I could get rid of them.

The moment they were gone, Aleksei gripped my waist, lifted me up and positioned me with my knees in the seat on either side of him.

His gaze holding mine, I felt him work between us, releasing his cock.

His hands went back to my hips, and he bore me down.

My head fell back at taking him, but I brought it forward again so I could see the lazy heat of sex flicker in his eyes as I started to ride him.

"Yeah, this part makes it fun," I gasped.

"Indeed," he grunted. "Faster, Laura."

I didn't go faster.

His eyes narrowed.

And then he said, "You'll go faster, darling, or you'll be bent over my desk, and I'll decide the pace."

Spoiled for choice.

"*Bissi*," he warned.

I went faster.

He pulled my cami down to expose my breasts and multitasked.

So I went a whole lot faster.

He shifted a thumb to my clit.

And I went even faster.

Aleksei had to grasp my ribs in order to prevent me from tumbling back as I arched violently into my stellar orgasm.

And then he used his grip on me to drive me onto his cock to find his own.

I fell forward and nuzzled his neck through my aftermath.

He wrapped his arms around me in his.

"Can we do this all day?" I requested.

His chuckle was delicious.

But he said, "No. We have a royal photo op at two."

Oh dang.

I forgot.

Ugh.

"You'll be fine," he assured. "Just smile. They'll call out questions. Say nothing. Keep smiling. Wave. Change your position frequently. Look at different ones, but don't actually make eye contact. Fifteen minutes. Then we'll be done."

"I suppose I can do that."

He smoothed both hands over the cheeks of my behind then again crossed his arms around my back to hold me.

And then he said, "You'll be perfect."

CHAPTER 21

SMILE

I got to make us breakfast (totally a "got to" situation, Aleksei's kitchen was *insane*), and we were back at our corner of the kitchen bar, cats fed, breakfast consumed, dirty dishes pushed aside, lingering over coffee.

Aleksei had a tablet on a stand propped in front of him, and as far as I could tell with the letters and numbers that were scrolling across the display, some of which he tapped notes about on his tablet, it was some business-type stuff that seemed to me like it was written in another language.

I was scrolling the tapes on my Palm and processing my second freakout that morning, because I was all over them.

Sure, if I were in charge of costuming the scene of the heroine astride the mighty dragon's neck soaring above the city of Nocturn, I would *so* put her in that fabulous flamingo-pink gown.

But...

Dang.

I was everywhere.

Everywhere.

During breakfast, at the beginning of my freakout (around the time I started making choking noises), Aleksei told me Germaine had released details about me, and she wasn't stingy. They included my name, age, education, occupation, the shows I'd worked on, the awards I'd been nominated for, and my no contact with my parents (though, no details on that).

My close relations with Catla and Gayliliel had also been included in the release.

When I'd asked him why, he'd said, "The Truelocks were some of the first demons to leave the Edge after the Demon Rift of 1637. They came to Night's Fall and swore fealty to a True Heir. They're one, and there's some debate, but they might be *the* First Family of Demons in the Fall. And a Vinestrong was the general who commanded the legions who defeated a rogue faction of the dark fae in the Dark War in Land's End in 1278. That was a long time ago, but they still have celebrations where they put a mug of mead on their stoop in honor of that day. When Vinestrong marched his troops home, the fae put out the mead as a show of gratitude to him and his males. So that ritual, even today, celebrates one of Gayle's ancestors."

I didn't know this about Gayle. I didn't even know if Gayle knew about Gayle's family legacy.

But I did know about the Truelocks.

"When it comes to blood, crowns and thrones, it's about lineage and how strong or elite your pedigree or connections are," Aleksei finished.

"And do you know about my people?" I asked.

He inclined his head. "The Makepeaces have been middle-class shifters for the last few hundred years. Before that, there were merchants. Some publicans. Some military males. Not landed, but not servant class."

"So nothing special," I muttered.

He grinned. "Until now."

Dang, but I really liked this male.

Just a note: even before the continent condensed into the Four Realms, and definitely when it did, there was a division of who was welcome where.

The continent was very long, but somewhat narrow.

The western coast was where the shifters stayed.

The northern lands were the haunt of the demons.

The eastern coast was where the witches practiced.

The southern shores were the land of the fae.

And the humans huddled in the mountains in the middle.

This had all integrated, and mixed, even before they tried (and failed) the Unification.

But even now, the majority of species in each realm held true to the old populations.

Now, I had to deal with the fact that, overnight, I'd become famous, fodder for chatter, speculation and outright lies.

And I had to get over it, because I had no choice.

A sound chimed from Aleksei's tablet, and he took the comm.

"Your highness, Germaine Newleaf and Madam Garwah are here. They'd like to come up," the agent on his display reported.

"Fuck, I should have expected this," Aleksei muttered. "One moment. Audio and video mute."

Aleksei turned to me.

"I'll be needing to have a chat with Maine about her ambush tactics and when they aren't necessary. Like now. But this is good. She and Madam Garwah can guide you through what's expected at the photo op a lot better than I can. I've lived it my whole life, I can't see it from where you'll be approaching it."

Actually, this sounded good to me. I suspected I'd need all the help I could get. And due to reasons no need to explain, I'd missed my instruction with Madam Garwah last night (though, of course, I'd commed her to let her know I would).

"Are you okay for them to come up?" Aleksei asked.

"Full disclosure, I don't know how to feel about Germaine," I admitted.

"Which shows you have excellent instincts. Allow me to assist. She's brilliant at what she does, but her loyalty comes from her salary, which I'm sure you can imagine, is considerable. If she got a better deal, and if she hadn't signed an NDA that would mean we'd take everything even her grandchildren might earn, she'd turn and share every detail she knows about us if it benefited herself or her client. She's a master at weaving tales, telling lies and harnessing the art of manipulation."

Well then.

There you go.

"That said," he carried on, "I genuinely think she cares deeply for my mother. I wouldn't say she'd take a stream for her, but she'd shed an actual tear if something happened to her."

"And how does she feel about you?"

"We have mutual respect, as it were. I don't like that we need her, but I know we do, and she excels in her role. She knows I don't like that we need her or what she does, but she knows I understand the game needs to be played. And I trust her to do right by my family, and now you."

"So, cautious acceptance?" I asked.

He smiled with approval. "Another good instinct, darling."

I smiled back.

"Allow them up?" he inquired.

"Sure."

He turned back to the tablet. "Resume video and audio." Pause and, "Send them up."

"Yes sir."

The agent blinked out.

Aleksei sipped coffee.

I gratefully closed down my Palm.

The lift didn't open, but I heard a rustling from the back of the flat.

"Freight lift," Aleksei murmured, and I saw his brows had titched together in surprise.

The need for a freight lift was explained when Germaine and Madam Garwah emerged from the back hall where the door to the landing pad was, and they had a long, stuffed-full clothing rack floating with them.

I wasn't thinking good thoughts, because I was who I was, I did what I did, and even at just a glance, I could tell the clothes on that rack were terrifying.

"Of note," Madam Garwah barked. "Attempts on your life are the only excuse to miss my class."

"I'll be there tonight, Madam," I promised.

"See that you are," she said, and then she dropped into a curtsy. "Your royal highness."

"Always good to see you, Madam Garwah," he said. Then he turned his attention to Germaine. "Have you lost your Palm? Or Allain's sequence?"

"You weren't very happy with me the last time I was here," she pointed out. "And this needs to be done."

"I didn't ban you from my penthouse, Maine."

"Good to know," she said as she put a box on the kitchen bar and slid it down to us.

Aleksei threw out a hand and stopped it from crashing into his breakfast plate.

I gasped in delight.

It was an Ultra-Paint 5000, the enchanted moonstone of cosme-masks.

It had twenty more settings than the closest top model. It had a scanner so you could scan your outfit, and it would take that into account when it manifested your look. It administered the premier serums, moisturizers, primers and dews, had advanced cleansing that gave it spa-visor functionality, and its cost was astronomical (but it came with its first year of reloading free, though I'd heard the yearly subscription after that was super steep).

I nearly knocked the coffee cup out of Aleksei's hand when I reached beyond him to snatch it up.

And I held it to my chest like the beloved treasure it was.

"Is this for me?" I breathed.

"Of course," Germaine replied. "Now we need to talk wardrobe."

My delight turned to horror as she touched a button on a remote in her hand, and an outfit Madam Garwah would wear cycled out from the others on the rack.

I fought retching.

I was now very worried that this visit would not help me to face what was to come that day at all.

"I'll just go get some work done," Aleksei, ever the male, murmured, sliding off his stool to escape what was to come next.

Instead of grabbing his arm and begging verbally, I gave him *don't leave me alone with them* eyes.

He bent, kissed the top of my head, straightened, turned to Germaine and reminded her, "My mate knows clothes."

"And I know that sixty-seven percent of the population of Night's Fall value their royal family due to nostalgia, historical protections, the inherent wealth, status and glamor of it all, and you remind them of esteemed traditions," Germaine retorted. "And you can't have traditions without being traditional."

I was not traditional.

I had not a traditional bone in my body.

I kept begging my mate with my eyes.

He winked at me, and although that was hot, he followed it by sauntering away with his coffee mug.

I watched him go, and then I watched Nova scurrying after him like a fluffy badger.

Traitor!

"No!" Madam Garwah barked, bringing my attention back to the matter at hand. "Next!"

"This green is—" Germaine began.

"Putrescent," Madam Garwah finished. "I said next."

Germaine cycled to the next.

"No," Madam Garwah said before I could. The next. "No." The next. "Lilith, no. Who picked these? They're *dire*."

I was stunned I had an ally in Madam Garwah and was kind of enjoying how red Germaine's face was getting.

"No," Madam said again. "No," to the next. "Balls, no. What on earth?"

Germaine cycled, and out came a deep rose, skim-body-fitting, to-the-knee, lightweight wool dress with long sleeves and a simple crew neck. It was plain, but classic, and clearly exceptional quality.

"That one!" both Madam Garwah and I exclaimed at the same time.

My mind accessorized it.

Diamond stud earrings. My oversize, pale pink, organza gardenia Celestina broach. My chocolate-brown pumps.

Simple, but with a hint of flair from the broach and a hint of sexy from the pumps.

Perfect.

"This one?" Germaine asked me.

I nodded.

She pulled it off its holder and tossed it over the back of a stool, then sent the rack back down the hall on its own.

Another rack came trundling in.

"Smile," Madam Garwah barked at me.

"Sorry?" I asked her.

"Smile," she repeated.

I smiled.

"Too much, smile less," she ordered.

"We need to go through shoes and accessories," Germaine said.

Through less of a smile, I told Germaine, "I've got that covered."

"I want approval," she returned.

I stopped smiling and looked right into her eyes. "Aleksei is my mate. I would do nothing to embarrass him. But I am me, and today, the people are going to get their first real look at me, and it's going to be *real*. Classic. Traditional. Stylish. Royal. But *real*. We're going to have to learn to trust each other, and for you, that starts now."

Germaine gave me a look that was clearly taking my measure.

"Smile!" Madam Garwah demanded.

I smiled, a whole lot less this time.

"More," she instructed. "Less...no, a bit more...a bit more. Perfect!"

I tried to memorize the curve of my lips and knew I probably failed.

"Now, wave," Madam Garwah ordered.

I waved.

"Close your fingers," she said. "Less movement. All in the wrist. There you go. That's it."

"They're going to hurtle questions at you," Germaine warned. "No responses. At all. Smile. And then smile more. Don't even dip your head or tip it. It can be taken as a response."

"You may hold his hand. You may lean into his arm. But that is all," Madam Garwah put in. "He may touch you. Guide you. If he puts his arm around your waist, you may reciprocate. Stand close. Walk close. You're communicating connection. Solidarity."

I nodded.

"You're also communicating romance. Happily ever after," Germaine added. "You're living every girl's dream. Act like it."

"But with modesty. Decorum," Madam Garwah said.

"They'll tell you to kiss. Don't," Germaine said. "That has to happen with the engagement op."

The idea of a ton of photographers snapping pics of me kissing my male did not sit well with me.

But this was my life.

Again, I had to get used to it. I had no choice.

"Lex will probably speak. They'll ask about the assassination attempt, and since they deserve an answer, he'll assure them you're both fine. When he does, whatever he says, gaze at him as if every word out of his mouth is a drop of nectar," Germaine ordered.

That was probably the only thing I could manage to do authentically.

"Move, shift, adjust, give them different angles, different shots," Germaine instructed. "They have fifteen minutes. They'll beg for more as you walk away. Just keep smiling, waving and walking. Lex will know how to work it. Follow his lead."

"Right," I said.

"Set the Ultra at clean, day, timeless, bright, healthy, fresh. Nothing heavy. Nothing smoky," Germaine demanded. "You're young. You're falling in love with the male who's destined for you. You're starting a fairy-tale life by assuming a role that's millennia old. Females need to like you, trust you, relate to you, envy you. Males need to want to fuck you."

"I say!" Madam Garwah barked at her. "Manners!"

"I'm not wrong," Germaine told her.

"You are not, indeed. However, there are many words you could have used and did not. We are in the presence of the future Queen of Night's Fall. It is now where *you* must learn never to forget that."

Germaine visibly clenched her teeth.

I was stuck back on *you're falling in love with the male who's destined for you*, because, bottom line...

I was.

And that was a lot.

But as Germaine seemed to be gearing up to have a throwdown with Madam Garwah, I had to wade in.

"She can be herself with me," I told Madam.

Germaine sent me another measuring look.

"You don't expect respect, Mistress Laura, you demand it," Madam Garwah retorted.

"I'd rather earn it," I said.

Both of them gave me a measuring look then.

Madam Garwah's eyes lit before Germaine's did. But I got approval from Germaine too.

Phew!

"Lex will land right on the west lawn in his JetPanther, or better, his OpuStar. It's less flashy, more luxurious," Germaine said. "You wait. He'll help you out. He'll walk you to the delphinium field. That will be your backdrop. There's a gravel trail to it, and it's been dry, so your heels shouldn't sink in. Even so, watch your step. He'll then guide you back to the craft, and you'll take off. Be aware, they'll be snapping pics before you even land. So control your facial expression in the craft, coming and going. There's a blockade on airspace above the Sceptred Isle, so no crafts can get close to you there. But other airspace isn't blocked, even if it's regulated. So if they manage to get an approved course anywhere near you or within a long-range lens, they'll snap you. Be aware."

I nodded again.

"Smile," Madam Garwah barked.

I painted on what I hoped was the approved smile.

Madam Garwah nodded smartly and declared, "She's got it. We're done."

I hoped I did.

Gods.

✦ ✦ ✦

Several hours later...

Aleksei held my hand as we walked down the stairs from the landing pad to his penthouse, leaving his lavish OpuStar next to the JetPanther up top.

When we got in, he let my hand go and went directly to the glassed-in wine room that sat opposite the dining room table beyond the stairs.

He came out with a bottle of red and two glasses.

He lifted the bottle my way.

It was barely three o'clock.

I nodded.

He uncorked, poured, handed me one and grabbed the other.

Then he caught my gaze.

"Want to run far away from me yet?" he asked softly.

Oh, my sweet male.

It could not be denied that photo op was nerve wracking. Just the shouting at us set the hairs on my neck to raising. But then there was the jostling of the throng of paparazzi and reporters. The pushing. Worrying if my smile was too big. If I was waving from the wrist. If I leaned too far into Aleksei when he wrapped his arm around my waist. If I could get back to the craft without tripping on a stone.

It was a feeding frenzy, and we were the buffet.

But through it all, he was at my side, and in one way or another, his hand was always on me, wrapped around mine, around my waist, at the small of my back.

Tall, straight, protective, and so, so very handsome.

This was my happily ever after.

No one ever claimed they were perfect.

Just that the hero would be.

And mine, for me, absolutely was.

"Not even close," I replied.

He didn't drink his wine.

He swept an arm around me and pulled me to his body.

Then he kissed me.

Oh yes.

Not even close.

CHAPTER 22

WE

I felt the flutter.

My eyes popped open, and instantly, I tossed the covers aside and hurtled myself out of bed.

I nearly dashed to where I felt Aleksei, but then I realized I was only wearing panties.

I snatched up the shirt he'd worn with his suit at the photo op, shrugged it on and had started to race out of the room, when Aleksei burst into it and swayed to a stop.

I stared at him.

He stared at me.

Then I tore across the space and threw myself at him.

He caught me.

My arms were around his neck, my legs around his waist. He had one arm slanted at my back, the other tight around my waist.

"She fluttered," I whispered into his ear.

"I know, my creature felt her and hauled my ass up here."

I lifted my head to stare down at him in wonder.

I felt another flutter.

And then I felt something else.

I knew Aleksei did too when our mouths crashed into each other's.

The kiss was heated but not long, before he broke it, took two steps toward the bed and threw me the rest of the way so I'd land on it.

My sex drenched as I bounced once before he pinned me with his weight.

Ready, raring, I heaved, successfully flipping him to his back.

Before he could take over, I forced myself into position between his legs and tugged his sleep pants down (and one could say, when I did that, he didn't try too hard to take over). I grabbed hold of his thick cock, leaned in and drew him deeply into my mouth.

I cast my gaze up and saw nothing but miles of muscled chest, the arched column of his throat and the underside of his square jaw, but I heard his low, long groan.

Oh yes.

I worked him, pumping with my fist, sucking with my mouth.

His gaze came to me, burning amethyst.

I worked him harder, faster.

He reached, grabbed me under my arms and dragged me up his chest.

Then he tore my panties off me.

Heck yes!

I took hold of his cock again, positioned him, sat up and took him deep.

He grunted.

I moaned.

And then I rode, and rode, and *rode*.

Until he threw me off, on my belly, tugged up my hips and drove in again.

He fucked me. I reared back to get more of him.

Close.

I was getting so close.

He pulled out and rolled me to my back, pushing his hips between my legs, and I had him back.

As he fucked me, I took everything from him I could get, nipping, biting, scratching, licking, sucking.

It was animal.

Rapacious.

Carnal.

Aleksei captured my wrists and pulled them over my head, pinning them to the pillow in one hand. The other one, he hooked behind my knee and held it high, capturing me, containing me, controlling me.

I gazed in his eyes, my whimpers mingling with his grunts as he thrust and I rocked my hips to meet him, our flesh slapping in a primal tattoo.

"Go," he growled.

I went, arching, aching, reaching for the stars he was offering and finding them.

I was coming down when I watched his head snap back and heard and felt his deep groan as he buried himself to the root, filling me with him and his seed.

His large body bucked off the aftermath deliciously, before he collapsed on me, only to immediately pull out and roll to his back at my side.

I was panting.

He was panting.

We kept doing that.

Eventually, he said, "Right, evidence suggests when your creature fully awakes, sex is going to kill us."

I giggled and rolled to press myself against his side, lifting up on my elbow.

When I caught his eyes, he concluded, "That's not a complaint."

I giggled again and dropped my face to his chest, nuzzling it before I kissed it and lifted my head again.

"Your beast felt her?" I asked.

"I was making coffee and then I was sprinting up the stairs."

It hit me then.

"I'm feeling you."

His grin was roguish. "I hope so. I put a fair amount of effort into it."

I lightly slapped his chest and said, "No. I mean, it started yesterday. I didn't really notice it. When I woke up, I knew you weren't with me, but I knew exactly where you were."

His expression grew contemplative. "You didn't feel that before?"

"You feel me?"

His brows drew down. "How much did you read about mates?"

"Well, I haven't read about them, as in, did research or anything. I learned what I know from romance novels."

"Novels," he said.

"Yes," I said.

"Fiction," he said.

"Yes, that's what novels are," I replied.

He reached to tuck some of my hair behind my ear.

I loved it when he did that.

"Yes, *bissi*, I feel you. When you're in close proximity, I don't see you or know what you're doing, but I always know where you are."

Knowing that made me feel warm all over.

And that had happened to me yesterday too, I was just so into him, and we'd become deeply intimate, I didn't process it.

When I was in class with Madam Garwah, no.

But when we were together in the penthouse, yes.

Oh my gods.

This was mega!

"What else is going to happen when she wakes?" I asked.

He turned into me, tucked his hands under his shirt at my back, drew me into his arms and tangled our legs together.

"Well, obviously, sex is going to be cataclysmic," he remarked.

I smiled. "It kind of already was. So I'd say apocalyptic."

He assumed a smug look.

I rolled my eyes.

Males.

"What else?" I pushed. "Can they communicate?"

"Yes."

Whoa!

How awesome!

"It isn't the same for everyone," he continued. "What's always the same, beasts will recognize their mates, maybe even before the human side will consciously do so. This happened to us. I wasn't sure what I was feeling, but he knew you were there before you even entered the building. I caught on when you did."

I nodded, eager for him to continue.

"And they're tuned in to each other. Like we can sense each other when we're near."

"Can they do it from afar?"

"I've heard tell of mated beasts tracking from a distance."

More awesome!

"When they communicate, will we know what they say?" I asked.

"My creature is tuned to me. We talk as you would, say, to your cats. It's more like we understand each other. The same for you?"

I nodded.

He continued. "He's also tuned to you. He's cognizant of what goes on between us, the feelings we share, if not the things we say to each other. He's tuned to her, though he didn't know she was sleeping or drugged, because as an animal, he doesn't understand those concepts. He sensed her as timid, shy, hiding, vulnerable, because he could feel her alive. And in their way, they'll talk to each other. If we'll understand what they're saying, or to put it better, conveying, we'll have to find out."

"But when she fluttered, he felt her."

"It's been probably two decades since he's taken that kind of control of me when I'm in human form. But as an example of how he talks to me, I knew exactly what happened and why he was keen to get to you…or more to the point, her."

"Is he communicating to her now?"

He smoothed his hands over my back. "No, love. She's with us, but not quite *with* us."

"Oh." I pouted.

"But this is progress. Today, Dr. Fearsome is sending a nurse to administer your—"

Even held in his arms, in his bed, after having sex, at his words, my body chilled over.

"*No*," I whispered fiercely.

He pressed me closer to him. "Laura, you can trust her. She's Fearsome's sister."

"I'd rather go to his clinic. I'd rather see them take the IV bag directly from supply."

"I can have a machine delivered to test the contents before it's administered if you like."

"You can?"

"Absolutely."

"I don't want to offend her, but I'd like you to do that."

"I think if you tell her what happened to you, she'd understand your hesitance around healthcare workers."

Hesitant was understating it, and I blamed Buildmore and Fitzgerald for leaving me with that damage, because if you needed to trust anyone, you needed to trust doctors and nurses.

"It'll probably go away," I muttered.

"You endured something traumatic, *bissi*. Your reaction is understandable."

I took in a big breath and let it go.

He tucked me close to him. "I'll comm Allain. Get him to source a unit to test the solution."

"Thanks, *drahko*," I whispered.

"As you know, I have meetings today, and you're going to your studio and to Madam Garwah's this evening, but you need to carve some time in the next couple of days to interview aides. Allain is sorting through resumes. He'll have a shortlist for you by the end of today. And he'll sit on the interviews with you, for another ear and an informed opinion."

I scrunched my face. "Do I actually need an aide?"

"So far, you've had one hundred and eighty-nine invitations to everything from coffee mornings, dinner parties, and the opening of plays to visits to pediatric units, with an abundance of schools across the realm wanting you to come to their art and theater departments to give speeches."

I blinked.

One hundred and eight-nine invitations?

Aleksei kept going.

"You have your own detail now, and someone will have to have intimate knowledge of your schedule, so they can share it with your team in order that they can scout locations, send agents ahead of time to assess safety, decide personnel numbers, arrange travel and coordinate arrival and departure. And they'll need to know these things with as much notice as possible. I'd like to say you could go to the local patisserie to buy a treat on a whim, and if you did, they would scramble to arrange for you to do that. But it's a hassle for them, adds stress to their jobs, and hobbles them in being able to do it well."

"In other words, I need an aide."

"Yes, darling," he murmured, pulling us both up and arranging the pillow so he was resting his back on them, and arranging me so I was resting on him.

He slid his fingers through my hair tenderly, and I should have taken that for the warning it was, when he asked, "I sense you'll wish to remain working after we become officially engaged."

Oh gods.

I was supposed to start royal duties upon our engagement?

That was less than two weeks away!

And I was in the middle of a job.

"Yes," I said. "Is that a problem?"

"If you ask my mother, yes. If you ask me, we'll make it work."

"Aleksei—"

"The only raised-voice row I ever got into with my mother, and my father was right at her side when it was happening, was after years of hoarding chunks of my allowance, and I bought my first company."

I tried to imagine Queen Calisa yelling.

I couldn't do it.

"Raised voices? You mean shouting?" I queried.

"Yes, them to me and me to them. They were incensed that I not only wished, but fully intended to have a life and my own pursuits away from the Palace. My brothers and sister still live there. That was another row, without shouting, when I moved here."

"Will they expect us to move back there when we get married?"

"No. They'll expect us to move into Spikeback Castle in Crimson Park in midtown. That's where the heir apparent lives when he marries and starts his family."

Occasionally, I'd take a walk in Crimson Park. Or the gals and I would go there and have a picnic and beings watch. I'd been born and raised in Nocturn, and when I was younger, we'd sometimes have school trips to the park.

I'd seen Spikeback Castle probably hundreds of times in person.

It was a gothic fantasy in purple-tinged stone with a cerulean tile roof. It was compact, but tall (four stories), sporting an abundance of narrow, arched windows, dormers between turrets, and chimneys. Its famous features were the three turrets that adorned the front, one in the middle, the other two on the sides, and the eerily, always calm reflecting pool (not a fountain) in front of it.

The architect who built it had done it with an eye to intimidation and instilling fear.

It was beautiful, of course. But there were occasions, when the moon was full and falling behind it, it appeared dark, forbidding and otherworldly. And at all times, day and especially night, when the gothic spires and masonry were reflected in that pool, it seemed to trick the eye, making it mysterious and spooky.

It had been where the first Royals lived before they built Celestial Palace.

I loved Celestial Palace for its sprawling grace and elegance.

I *adored* Spikeback Castle because it was dark and ominous, even on a sunny day, and it spoke to the primal shifter in me.

But I didn't know if I wanted to *live* there.

"Are we going to do that?" I asked.

"We is plural, so I'll take you there, give you a tour, and then we'll discuss it."

At his words, everything, all at once, settled in me.

He was the one with the money, the status, the title, the prestige, the control.

But in that one sentence, he made it clear that *we* would make decisions about our life.

We.

While I was processing the heady fullness of that feeling, Aleksei continued talking.

"I failed miserably with my first business, Laura. I was young, had a university education, never worked a day in my life, outside my studies or royal duties. I thought I knew it all. I knew nothing. I had to find a partner to infuse capital into it, or I'd have to close it down, lay off one hundred and twenty-five employees. Fortunately, that partner was Sirk's father. He's a shark, but instead of forcing me out, he took me under his wing and taught me everything I really needed to know. He's still my partner in a number of ventures."

"Did you meet Sirk first, or his dad?"

"Sirk. At Red Lair. First year. We were both twelve."

I loved knowing that about him and his friend.

"My mother heard the business was failing, and she used that to try to force me back into the fold. It only made me more determined to figure it out," he shared.

"And you did."

He inclined his head.

I smiled. "Go you."

He smiled in return and explained, "What I'm saying is, I know it can be done, spending time in pursuits that nurture you, challenge you, along with doing your duty to the throne. Yes, if I were to give it all up, my time would be consumed with accepting more invitations, attending more events, taking royal trips, even spending more time in the Center, playing politics. But if that was my life, like it used to be, I would be deeply unhappy, as I was then. I'd put on a neutral face, but behind the mask, I'd hate every minute of it. If you find love it and wish to move out of your chosen field to concentrate on it, that will be your choice. But if you don't, then we'll find a balance for you, like I have."

It meant a lot he would back me on that play.

But he needed to know the fullness of it.

"Just before we start filming, and during filming, I'll need to be at the studio or on location. Some of the filming will be at the studios north of Nocturn, so maybe a half an hour craft ride away. I can come home every night. But we're also filming on location close to the Clan Caves. And that's a two-hour craft ride away."

"Not in a JetPanther that gets priority course routes. But just to say, I'm often away for business. Would you expect me to be home every evening?"

"No, but shooting can take two, three, sometimes even four months."

He pulled me up so we were eye to eye. "Darling, I can come to you.

You can come to me. You have access to transport that will cut the time it takes to make any trip in half. Save nefarious plots getting in the way, neither of us can fool ourselves that the rest of our lives are going to go as smoothly as we've begun. And when it doesn't, we'll work it out."

I was reminded for the first time in days about how angry he got after the assassination attempt, and how he'd communicated that.

I needed to share how that made me feel.

But I didn't want to. I didn't want to spoil this moment. I didn't want to cast a pall on what he thought of as our smooth beginning.

And I didn't want to make him feel bad.

It had been emotional. He'd given no indication before or since that was something he was prone to do.

He'd been murderously angry at his brother, and although he'd shared his feelings without a single attempt to sugarcoat it, he hadn't lost his mind shouting and cursing.

"Say it," he ordered.

I focused on him. "Sorry?"

"Whatever's on your mind that you seem hesitant to share, say it."

I gave him the side-eye, because I wasn't real certain how I felt about how quickly he was learning how to read me.

"Laura, we must be able to talk to each other."

"Okay then, you hurt my feelings, a lot, when you shouted at me after we got back from the gallery."

It reminded me of my parents, was the part I left out.

He nodded, not seeming offended in the slightest. "I can't say I'm always completely in control of my temper, but that was out of line."

It felt like every muscle in my body relaxed, and I hadn't realized how much tension I'd held about it since it happened.

Aleksei carried on, "My greatest hope is that we will never be in that situation again, and therefore, me losing my temper like that won't happen again. But I can't say I'll never get angry, or very angry. The difference is, you put yourself in the way of danger—"

He touched his fingers to my lips and kept them there when I opened my mouth to speak.

"No, darling, let me finish."

I closed my mouth, and he took his fingers away.

"In retrospect, I could see it was instinct, and I can just imagine how seeing the male who attacked you played with your head. You were panicked and shouting about a weapon before one was even produced. What you did was understandable. And maybe, when your creature fully awakens and bonds with mine, you'll understand where I was in those moments, because my response was instinctual too, and I was feeling it double. I saw my mate in danger, and my creature saw his. So my emotions were high. That doesn't forgive me losing my temper in that manner, but I hope it explains it."

I couldn't stop staring even as I asked, "How do you do it?"

"Do what?"

"Get more wonderful with every word that comes from your mouth."

Purple flame flickered in the backs of his sky-blue eyes.

"Germaine told me I had to act like each one formed a drop of nectar," I went on. "I haven't looked at the social tapes, but I figure I bested that and then some."

He rolled me to my back with him on top, at the same time his hands started roaming.

"I have seen the tapes," he murmured, dipping his head and scraping his teeth along my neck.

I shivered.

He moved his mouth to my ear. "Beings are rather enamored with that broach you were wearing."

"Mm," I said, making it my mission to memorize the swells and valleys of his back.

"Your ass in that dress though," he growled at the same time his fingers found a different target and curled around my breast.

"You looked fantastic in your suit too," I told him. "But then, you always do."

He ran his lips along my jaw and his thumb over my nipple.

I shoved my hands into his sleep pants and dug my nails into his behind.

That did it.

In the end, Aleksei had to comm Muriel to tell the beings he was meeting that he'd be half an hour late.

But I allowed myself time to laze and doze before I got myself together, commed Antheme, and headed to my studio.

CHAPTER 23

BLOBS

That evening, before I made my way to Madam Garwah's, I got a text comm from Aleksei sharing he had a late meeting he couldn't avoid, and as such, I should have dinner without him.

Although I was bummed he wasn't going to be home when I got there, I liked getting an everyday text from him about everyday stuff, like late meetings and dinner.

When I arrived back from class, I, with a tour guide of Comet, who seemed rather keen to show me the fullness of it (and he had a lot to say during the tour, but I was sensing his approval, many more places to find trouble) finally took a tour of the penthouse.

The back hall led to the freight elevator, along with a full complement of laundry units, and the two bots who'd unpacked me. They were shut down and plugged into their chargers.

And now I was seeing how the bed got made, the clothes were picked up from the floor, and Aleksei's mess when he was cooking was cleaned up, because he nor I did any of that. But apparently, they were programed to slip out and take care of business when we weren't around.

Pretty cool.

The upstairs, as noted, was his bedroom, but most of that level was taken up with his landing bay.

The rest was a cornucopia of awesomeness.

Yes, there were four fully kitted bedrooms with ensuites. And the wine room, which was large, stocked to the gills and had a sink, a small refrigerator and a full bar with all the complementary needs, like an array of sparkling clean glasses, and a drawer that opened that contained only ice.

There was also Aleksei's more formal office, which had a state-of-the-art holographic conference table (totally going to holo the girls in there one day).

There was a library with three walls of floor-to-ceiling books (real ones!) and a comfy seating area in the middle in which to hunker down and read.

There was a room that had a billiards and a poker table (and another full bar, wouldn't want to have to walk down the hall to grab yourself a whisky in the middle of a game).

And there was a media room with the biggest screen I'd ever seen, a massive square couch that was more like a couch-bed, a station that did have a Bev-Buddy, along with a Snack-Sensation, because if you were in the middle of bingeing a show or watching a vid, you wanted to program in the soda or popcorn you had a hankering for and not have to mess with making it yourself.

I'd camped out there with my Palm, doing some back-and-forth text comms with Monique, Gayle and Cat about the photo op, assuring them a task force was on the case about the gallery sitch (but not going into detail), and sharing the great news that my beast was stirring (I'd had two more flutters since that morning!). I also received some updates on their lives (Gayle was being closed-mouthed about Sirk, which meant I'd have to take it out of a group comm to get the skinny from Cat or Mon).

I finished it by telling them we needed a get together, because I wasn't going to go into detail over a text comm about Aleksei and me consummating our mating, and just how phenomenal that was. That had to be face to face.

We'd almost made a date before Monique reminded me, I was now one part of a couple, and we would need to confirm after I made sure it was cool with Aleksei.

This did not bother me at all.

Truth told, it was thrilling, thinking I finally had someone in my life to check plans and schedules and leave digi-notes for.

I left them holding for confirmation, and with all three of my cats in attendance, I was munching some sour cream and cheese flavored potato blobs, sipping a grape sparkle and watching *They Came in the Sunlight*, a vid about the Troll Invasion that was released a few decades ago (my troll skin was going to be *so much better*, if I did say so myself).

I felt his arrival (gods, I loved that), but stayed where I was, because I knew he could find me easily (and I was super comfy).

So this was as I was when Aleksei entered the room.

I lost interest in the vid in favor of watching my mate wander in in shirtsleeves, the collar open, but still wearing his suit vest and trousers.

Yum.

He stood at the side of the couch-bed, gazing down at me. "Is that your dinner?"

I looked at the blobs and caught sight of the cheese dust on my fingertips.

Comet, who had been quiet and content (for once) passed out on the back of the couch, got up and howled his displeasure at Aleksei's late arrival.

Nova made her approach, scrunch nose first, but thought better of it, because she was female, so she turned around and shook her booty at him.

She did not go wanting, Aleksei's long fingers scratched the base of her tail.

She lifted it further.

Yep.

Female.

Jupiter, who'd been lying at the foot of the couch-bed as far away from me as he could get, got into seated position, his tail sweeping the luxurious upholstery, his somber gaze on Aleksei.

"I was feeling lazy," I answered.

He moved around the arm of the couch-bed, then crawled in on all fours.

I watched, avidly, and managed not to have an orgasm, narrowly.

He lowered himself to his stomach, next to my legs, and reached into the tub of blobs.

"Vid pause," I called, before I asked, "How was your meeting?"

"First, did Germaine get in touch with you?"

"No," I answered cautiously because it was iffy I'd want to know why she would.

"You scored a ninety-seven percent approval rating in a poll she conducted after the pics from the photo op hit."

So three percent didn't approve of a woman they didn't know a danged thing about?

"I sense, since you mentioned this, it's important," I remarked. "So I hope to cause no offense when I say I'm not sure I care."

"Mom was the highest paid and most popular screen star at the time her engagement to Dad was announced. She was beloved. And she only scored an eighty-nine percent."

"Oh, so my score is good."

He swallowed the blobs he was chewing and just stared at me.

"Not good?" I asked, confused.

"*Bissi*, that is, for something like that, off the fucking charts."

Oh.

I beamed.

"My last approval rating was eighty-six percent," he shared.

I frowned.

"What's the problem with fourteen percent of the Fall?" I snapped.

He grinned and popped some blobs in his mouth.

"Do you do this kind of thing often?" I asked.

"All the fucking time."

Ugh.

"What's Timothee's rating?" I queried.

"Twenty-two."

That made sense, and actually, I thought it was on the high side.

Aleksei continued sharing. "Errol is at twenty-nine. Mom is seventy-nine. Dad is seventy-one. Aleece is eighty-three."

I smirked. "Seems the people of the Fall don't have a problem with me throwing myself in front of a beam for you."

It was Aleksei's turn to frown.

"Don't worry, baby," I murmured. "That will never happen again."

At least, I hoped not.

"My meeting was with the task force," he announced.

Now I was interested in our conversation.

"Oh my gods, are they making headway?"

He did more staring at me, then he pushed up so he was reclining beside me, crossed his ankles and stole my tub of blobs.

"How much of this do you want to know?" he asked carefully.

"All of it," I answered firmly.

He tossed some blobs in his mouth.

"Aleksei," I warned.

"They found Farlay. He's dead."

My stomach dropped.

"Shot in the face with a PR60, full beast stun," Aleksei continued.

"This is...not good," I replied.

"They already disposed of the female they used for gallery access, so it's their MO. When no longer of use, destroy. They put time into recruiting her. Inspection of her comms say she met the assailant three months ago, just after your attack, which did not have the end they wanted. They wasted no time putting a new plan into action. It was a full-frontal love bombardment, except obviously, he didn't love her. Flowers. Gifts. Attention. Talk of marriage. Pushing to move in together. He was well funded, those gifts he gave her were all high cost. Jewelry. A new vid screen for her flat. A long weekend at the Elysium Hotel at Black Beach. She has no history of any run-ins with law enforcement, save some docking tickets. Friends and family are stunned she was part of this, at the same time stunned he was too. They called it true love. As close to mates as you can get without being mates. The team is theorizing she had no idea what she was doing when she let them in, outside getting them into the hottest ticket in town to see Terrinton's work and hobnob with the rich, posh and trendy."

"Who faked her résumé?"

He shook his head. "No clue. It was faked so deep, they haven't gotten to the bottom of that yet. But it was uncovered he was the one who pushed her to go for it. Before, she worked as a dress minder at a boutique and lived in a flat with three roommates, and only two bedrooms."

I didn't know their rate, but my guess was, dress minders, who restocked the automated rods after customers tried on clothes, didn't make a whole lot.

I could see being dazzled by jewelry and the Elysium Hotel.

But I couldn't think on her very long, especially now that I knew she was an innocent victim in all this.

Her family and friends must be out of their minds.

I reached for more blobs. "Anything on Buildlore and Fitzgerald?"

"Not yet, but they're not thinking good things."

I was not the kind of person to wish ill on others, even if they had done me wrong.

But I *way* didn't wish either of those two to turn up with a blast in the face, even if they were horrid to me.

"Weapons are illegal, Aleksei," I told him something he definitely knew. "Unless you're law enforcement, or military, or you jump through a lot of hoops to get a permit for one. But those are normally collectors or hunters. How are they getting their hands on prison issue firearms?"

"They're tenaciously pursuing this line of inquiry and attempting to lock down who might be able to modify them in the hopes that, if they do, whoever that is can lead them to whoever is behind all of this."

I had a big question to ask, even if I didn't want the answer.

But it had to be asked.

"Could it actually have stopped your creature's heart?"

"We can't know unless someone tests it, which we won't be doing," he answered. "But the stream is at an intensity that they speculate it would easily drop wolves, bears, big cats, the hardest beasts to kill. And by drop I mean drop dead. Dragons are a different sort, but they're concerned."

"I am too," I admitted.

"I can't say I'm not, darling. But they have the weapon the male we captured was carrying. I incinerated one, but there's enough of it left, they can tell both weapons had the same modifications. The units are at the Royal Armory where they're studying them, and they're already at work on a defense weapon."

"A what?"

"A unit that can throw out an electronic shield that will absorb the stream. At the same time, it'll blast through and disable the PR60 so it can't fire, or if it already fired, it can't refire."

"And who would carry that?"

"RS agents. And me."

Oh boy.

Aleksei continued. "The good news, this takes so much power, it's essentially a one shot. That's why he only fired once. Because it has to recalibrate, and recharge, before another beam can fire. And it takes a full five minutes for this to happen."

"I guess that's good, unless whoever is modifying these things can one-up themself."

"If they can, this will narrow the field of possibles significantly. To be able to recalibrate and recharge a weapon of that small size for that amount of power in less time is something that hasn't been invented yet. There are maybe five scientists in all Twenty Realms who could pull off something like that, and they'd have difficulty doing it, because first, they'd have to invent the means to do it with."

Well, that was a relief.

"Anything else?" I asked.

He tossed some more blobs in his mouth, chewed, swallowed and answered, "No."

"Have *you* eaten dinner?" I asked suspiciously.

He lifted the tub and smiled.

"Want to watch a vid with me?" I asked. "I just started this one. We can go back to the beginning."

As answer, he handed me the tub, leaned in and kissed my forehead, then angled out of the couch-bed, saying, "I'm going to change. Program up some chocolate crackles, pop clusters and a cherry-lime sparkle, would you, darling?"

Prince Aleksei, the True Heir of Night's Fall, was going to hang and chill, eat crap and watch a vid with me.

Seriously.

Destiny knew what it was doing.

I rolled out of the couch-bed (a whole lot less gracefully than Aleksei did) and went to the Snack-Sensation. I got his chocolate crackles, pop clusters, and added cashew-caramel spots. I then went to the Bev-Buddy and programmed in another grape sparkle and his cherry-lime.

After that, I told the screen to cue the vid back to the beginning.

I had our feast spread out when he returned.

And second-best thing to do with Aleksei, king-to-be and my mate (after sex)?

Having him claim me in a cuddle while we lounged in front a vid, ate food that was not good for us, and did not one thing else.

Just us, the cats, and home.

Perfect.

CHAPTER 24

CRUSADER

I followed Rya down the stairs, my eyes on my mate leaning a hip to the kitchen counter, sipping coffee while he flipped through a digi-doc, again wearing shirtsleeves and his vest and trousers. His suit jacket was thrown around the back of a barstool.

My heart skipped because he was so handsome, but also because I knew he was waiting to start his day because I was getting IV therapy number three from Rya upstairs, and he didn't want to leave until he knew it was done and I was okay.

He looked our way and did a double take.

I knew why that was too.

Rya made it to the kitchen bar and nodded to him in a kind of succinct bow, before she turned to me, her face filled with compassion.

"I know you're excited about the increased activity of your beast," she said.

I for sure *was*.

"But in an effort to save you disappointment," she carried on, "I can't stress enough that, like the animals they are, shifter creatures do not like to be vulnerable. This has been studied extensively, and it is rare to unheard of that a beast will emerge before the drug is fully out of their host's system. If they did, it could cause them to force you to transform when they're in a weakened state, just because they won't have control over themselves, and they simply won't do that, because it would make you vulnerable. That is not their reason for being. In fact, it's the opposite. So you'll continue to sense increased activity, but you still have two or three days before the drug has fully exited your system."

"Okay," I replied.

She smiled. "And then it will be over, and you'll be whole again."

Whole.

I smiled a lot bigger at that.

Her expression grew serious. "When it comes closer, as I've already told you, you'll need to take care and hole up somewhere safe for you to transform. She'll have a lot of energy, and you might not be able to check her from taking over. She'll need to expend some of that before you can get her back under your control."

I nodded.

She smiled again.

"See you in a couple of days," she finished.

"See you, and thanks again for coming," I replied, following her to the lift.

She dipped her head to Aleksei again, got on the lift, and I turned to him when the door slid closed on her.

"Here," he ordered.

I fought an eyeroll and went to him.

He crooked a finger and touched it under my chin to lift my eyes to his.

"Did you hear what she said?" he asked gently.

It had been two days since I felt my first flutter.

And the time was short, but we'd fallen into a steady rhythm for our lives.

Wake. Work. Come home. Chill.

Last night, we'd hung out in the living room with the purple fire, ordered in noodles, drank wine, snuggled and read (real books!).

Oh, and there was a lot of lovemaking wedged in.

But I had not hidden the fact that I was increasingly excited at how much my beast was making herself known.

More flutters.

Tension in my chest like she was stretching.

Sensations of movement like she was rolling or changing position.

It'd been so long since I had all that, I was impatient to have her back in full.

"Yes, I heard her," I told Aleksei.

"We'll clear our schedules, hunker down here when the time is nigh," he said.

"You don't have to—"

"I'll be here when you get her back, Laura."

"Okay," I mumbled, fighting a grin because he was so...

Aleksei.

He removed his finger but swept his gaze down my feminine, stylish and pretty, but somewhat severe black suit. An ensemble I'd purchased to attend Cat's human grandma's passing ritual.

"Although that's fetching, albeit austere, you didn't have to go that far for the interviews," he remarked.

I wasn't dressed for the interviews I was conducting with Allain that afternoon to hire my aide.

I was dressed for something else.

Here we go.

"I'm going to Naylyn's ritual this morning."

His brows shot up.

Naylyn was the young female who'd been murdered at the gallery.

"Before you say anything," I began hurriedly, "I wasn't keeping it from you. I didn't know I intended to go until I was in my closet, programming my outfit for the day. But, *drahko*, I can't get her out of my mind."

His face softened and he stole an arm around me. "I've been experiencing the same."

Of course he had.

Because he was so...

Aleksei.

"Her family must be out of their minds with her loss," I said. "Not to mention the betrayal. And the way she's being portrayed on the news and the tapes. She wasn't a traitor. She wasn't a pawn. She was a young woman who thought she was falling in love."

"Indeed," he murmured. Then he said, "I'll go with you."

I was surprised at this decision.

"You will?" I asked.

"A statement needs to be made. Of course, it has, but no one has picked it up. The story was much more sensational when she was an accessory in an assassination plot. If you and I attend her passing ritual, that statement will be made."

"And it might provide some small balm to her family and friends," I added.

"Yes," he agreed. "But I'll warn you, love, this will be controversial. Beings have made up their minds about her. There'll be a great number of opinions about us doing this, and no one will have any compunction about putting them on a tape."

"Do you mind?" I asked.

He shook his head. "I don't, but you're very new to this. In the short time you've been exposed to it, you've enjoyed unprecedented popularity. You need to be aware that will turn, Laura. It isn't a maybe, it's a definite. There will be those who understand what we're doing and see it for what it is. There will be those who will not. Comments and speculation can be misguided and vicious. I want you to go in knowing that's not a possibility, it's what will happen."

"Not having experienced it, I can't say I'll be prepared. But I don't want to get into a zone where what people may or may not think dictates what I do. If I get in that zone, I'll never do anything for fear someone will get pissed about it. Or I'll surgically attach myself at the hip with Germaine so she can guide my every move."

"Let's not do that. The only female I wish in my bed is you. She's not welcome," he joked.

I laughed.

Then I had to quit laughing to get to the next part.

"Do you remember Nata?" I asked.

He still had his arm around me but had turned his head and was taking a sip of his coffee, and only his eyes came to me at my question.

He swallowed the sip, put his cup down and faced me fully.

"Yes," he said cautiously.

"Has...anything happened with her?"

"I informed Allain of my concerns."

"And?"

"And Allain investigated it. He found I was correct. Errol dallied with her. He also promised her he would announce they were formally courting. He did not deliver."

"And?" I pressed.

He sighed. "And Allain is looking to find her another post. Nothing is available for her skillset, so she's still working at the Catalogues for now, but she's been taken off anything that's sensitive or has great value."

"What does she do at the Catalogues?"

"Documentation and data entry."

"What does that mean?"

"That means she researches backlog papers and artefacts, verifies their authenticity and enters them into the database with thorough substantiation and descriptions before they're stored."

"And her skillset?"

"She has a university degree, double major, history and preservation."

"So she's pretty qualified."

"She wouldn't have been hired if she wasn't. It's my understanding her goal was to move out of authentication and into preservation. But she's young and was working her way up."

"Are there artefacts and papers held elsewhere in the realm?"

"Laura—"

"Are there?" I pushed.

"No," he admitted.

"So, if another post is found for her, it will be outside what she went to school and studied to do. What she found a job doing. All because she's pretty and Errol wanted to nail her."

"I hesitate to note this, but she has free will. It isn't appropriate for Errol to dally with staff. But she had a say in the matter, a choice, and she chose wrongly."

"I don't disagree. But it's my understanding truth serum is mandated for anyone that has anything to do with the Palace—"

"Laura."

He said no more.

But I heard him anyway.

Thus, I frowned. "So it isn't about her being dangerous around valuable items. It's about her being close, and Errol being done with her, and that potentially being awkward, that she's being moved."

"I'm afraid my father has also heard of this, and this is why the decision was made to transfer her," he said each word like it tasted bad.

They tasted bad to me, and I didn't even say them.

"How often has this happened?" My question was more of a demand for the information.

Aleksei didn't need a demand, I knew, and gave me the information freely and unhappily.

"Too often."

Ugh!

"Okay," I began, "if they were, say, working together in the same place, this happened and it was against company policy, as per the Equal Employment Decree, they *both* would be reprimanded the same way. And in essence, they both *do* work at the same place, but it's only Nata who will have to face consequences."

"What you say is true, but I'm uncertain why we're talking about her."

"We're talking about her because I want to approach her to ascertain if she wants to be my aide."

His brows shot up again.

He opened his mouth.
Closed it.
Took a breath.
And then he said, "Darling, this is unwise."

Okay, now we were getting into the big stuff.

"I know it's not her chosen field. But it would be me making a statement to her, and more importantly, your brother. She probably knows her days are numbered. She won't begin to expect that the True Heir's mate, and incidentally, a soon-to-be princess, and then after that, the queen, would go out of her way to offer a private show of support and a condemnation of the prince's actions. In the end, it'll be her choice. I saw the job description and the salary package. I doubt she's making that now. This will be more responsibility, an increased credit line, more prestige. It would be a promotion. My guess, a big one. She would be part of making history, not just conserving it. And if she refuses the opportunity to interview, that would be her choice, knowing it's highly likely she'll be transferred, and will then need to make the choice to accept the new post, or quit."

"I see there's something you're wasting no time getting used to."

I knew what he was saying.

I was exploring the newfound power of my position.

I knew the power I held wasn't much, but when it was important, I had to do what I could.

"Does that upset you?"

"I'll admit to being unnerved by it," he shared. "The stands you take will transfer to me."

"Not necessarily."

"In all things," he refuted. "We're a unit. Whether we were mates or not, we would be a unit. A united front. A united message. United in all things. If you do this, it's the same as me doing it. And if she should accept, and win the post, she'll be working even closer to Errol. The aides have their offices in the administrative wing of the Palace."

"That would be her choice too."

"I understand why you'd want to make this statement, Laura. However—"

"Honey," I said quietly, "I don't think you do. You never could. Yes, you were born with certain duties you can't escape, but even so, you had the power to find a way to build a life you enjoyed. This female's whole life is changing because she made a bad decision and trusted the wrong person. At the same time, the male who made that decision with her, and duped her into making hers by lying to her, gets to go on his merry way. I know

I'm putting you on the spot, especially since your father is involved, but is that the message you wish to send...*to anyone*?"

Aleksei made a frustrated noise.

I knew I was getting to him, but I didn't gloat.

"She might hold bitterness and be a danger," he warned.

"I would reply that I'd hope Allain or I would sense that, but as I mentioned, he's told me it's required anyone who works that closely to the Palace, and definitely a royal, has to take truth serum before they're offered the post, with the understanding this is administered randomly after they accept, so we'd find that out before she could get up to anything. And it isn't a given she'll get the job. That's not her field. The other applicants are very qualified. But if the opportunity is offered, I think she'll get our point."

"Yes, very unexpected," he muttered.

"Sorry?"

"When I first met you, you were a bundle of contradictions. Spirited, yet shy. Composed, yet awkward. Amusing, yet serious. Some of this was explained when I learned you'd lost your connection to your creature. But I'm being reminded of it now."

I was getting annoyed.

"Because you're surprised I give a shit about stuff?"

"No. Because the female who likes to cuddle in front of the screen with a tub of blobs, seemingly willing...no, actually determined to live in her own world and ignore the fact that everyone in four realms, or perhaps all twenty of them, is speculating about her, many of them sharpening their knives while they do so, is not the female who stands before me. This female is willing to hand them the whetstone as she sallies forth to do what she thinks is right."

"I'm not a crusader, Aleksei. But I still think you shouldn't hesitate to do what's right."

"I'm not a crusader either, Laura, but I am the True Heir. Right now, my mate is reminding me of that and showing me it's time to take it seriously. I have yet to start defining what will be my reign. And now is the time I should, and shall, start. With my mate at my side."

Gods!

He was just *the best*.

"The ritual is in forty-five minutes," I informed him. "We don't have time for me to show my appreciation for you being so danged awesome."

His lips curved. "I'll call that marker later."

"Deal."

He bent and touched his lips to mine.
Keeping them there, he said, "I'll go change."
His suit today was navy.
You wore black to a passing ritual.
"I'll pour myself another coffee."
He gave me a squeeze with his arm.
I watched him walk up the stairs to change.
Then I poured myself another coffee.

CHAPTER 25

NIGHT GOD

The door closed behind applicant number four.
I turned to Allain. "What did you think?"
"She won't be *my* aide," he replied.
This was number four of the refrains of these exact two sentences.

"Okay, yes, she'll be my aide," I said. "She and I will be a team. But I'm also a team with Aleksei, and you're on Aleksei's team, so we'll *all* be a team. Since Aleksei is Aleksei, and he'll want whoever I want, I need you to weigh in so I know you feel comfortable working with whoever is chosen."

Given permission, Allain didn't hesitate to share.

"I think she's stuck in her ways. She has a good deal of experience, but she and I will butt heads, because she's older than me, and even though I've been in this role with the prince for six years, and she has not ever been a royal aide, she's the type of female who thinks she knows everything, and always will."

I got the same impression.

"So, she's out," I muttered.

"And the first one was more interested in meeting the prince, or any of the princes, than she's interested in working for you. Her CV was exceptional, but the entire interview, she kept looking at the door, as if his royal highness would walk through it at any second, and she couldn't wait."

I'd noticed that.

"She's out too," I said.

"The second one would work, I suppose. There was just something..."

"Not right about her," I finished for him.

"Indeed. And the third—"

He didn't finish because the door flew open, Germaine barged in, and the door slammed closed.

By the by, in these hallowed halls, the doors were so old, they weren't automated. You had to open and close them yourself. They didn't sense you and had no audio commands. The entire compound had historical designation, and as such, these modernizations were illegal to make.

It was kind of mega.

Especially coupled with the fact the administration area was done up in genteel good taste with a massive dose of expensive.

If the admin area looked like this, I was excited to see the Palace (and Aleksei was coming to pick me up when we were done, and he said he'd take me on a tour before we left—I couldn't wait).

Allain straightened, and I did too, as Germaine bore down on the seating arrangement Allain had set up with rather comfortable, plush side chairs with tables positioned to rest drinks and digi-pads.

"Have you lost your mind?" she demanded of me.

"Excuse me," Allain huffed.

"Shut it," she snapped at him, his whole body jerked in affront, and she came back to me. "You went to Naylyn Biggerstaff's ritual? With *the prince*?"

"I—"

She threw up both her hands in exasperation. "It's flooding social media. It's a nightmare. A *disaster*. The next king and his mate attending the passing ritual of the female who plotted to kill said *future king*."

"She didn't plot to kill the future king," I bit out.

"*I* know that. *You* know that." She flung an arm out. "*They* don't know that."

"You'll remember who you're speaking to," Allain snapped.

"I'm speaking to the female who will be queen who made my job a whole fuckuva lot harder today," Germaine returned. "And what she did reflects on the entire Palace."

Allain stood and, surprising the dickens out of me, dropped his effete manner and clipped in full male, "Female, handle yourself."

Germaine opened her mouth.

But I spoke first.

"She's right. We should have given her a heads-up."

Both of them turned to me.

I looked to Germaine. "I'd like to say I'm new to this, but that isn't a good excuse. Aleksei and I discussed the fallout, and we should have brought you into our decision. This won't help, but I decided this morning, Aleksei agreed to come with me, and this happened forty-five minutes before the ritual began. We still should have told you, and you have my apologies we didn't. I'll do my best to make sure it doesn't happen again."

Germaine stared at me, stunned.

Allain sat down on a huff.

She whipped out a tablet. "I've written a statement. You need to approve it."

"The prince should—" Allain began.

She reared on him. "The prince is unavailable to me at this time. I've commed him repeatedly." She jerked a thumb at me. "She's ready to roll in her royal duties by making public appearances? Okay. But she stepped in it, so she has to help me wash off some of the mud," Germaine declared.

She was right about that too.

I took the tablet and read the statement.

Today, His Royal Highness, the True Heir, Prince Aleksei, and his mate, Mistress Laura Makepeace, attended the passing ritual of the victim in the recent assassination plot against the prince, Naylyn Biggerstaff.

They did this with heavy hearts that a beloved daughter, granddaughter, sister and friend lost her life to trust betrayed.

The prince and his mate ask the people of Night's Fall to bend their heads to the grief of Ms. Biggerstaff's family, mournful that such a young soul, full of hope and with a bright future, paid such a steep price for giving her heart to a male unworthy of it.

I thought of the family I'd met several hours earlier. The haggard face of a father. The lost expression of the mother. The swollen eyes of one grandmother, anger and shock in the fixed stare of the other. The defeated slump of the shoulders of a grandfather, and the etched grief of the other. And last, the abject, uncontrolled weeping of a younger sister.

It had felt unbearable, but standing at Aleksei's side, I bore up.

They'd been stunned at our arrival, and I didn't know if they knew it, but their curtsies to Aleksei were fit for the king.

He'd been marvelous, taking the mother's hand, lifting her up from her genuflection, and holding her hand between both of his while he murmured words of condolence.

I'd hugged her, and the sister, and touched cheeks with the father, thinking it sad and sweet he blushed.

They invited us to sit with them as the congregation slid into the curved pews circled around the ritual altar in order to watch the red flames consume Naylyn's swathed mortal remains in their glass enclosure.

And what did you say, even if you didn't want a front row seat to that?

We sat with them.

Aleksei had a meeting, and I had the interviews, so we didn't linger.

But with the family's response to us, the tearful but warm gazes of Naylan's other family and many friends that followed our every move, no matter what the chatter on the social tapes or news displays said, I knew we'd done the right thing.

"This statement is excellent," I said to Germaine.

"Allow me," Allain sniffed.

I handed the tablet to him.

"I have your approval to release it?" Germaine asked.

"If Allain is good with it, yes," I answered.

"Fine. Now we'll talk about Nata Livingston sitting out in the antechamber, awaiting to interview as your aide," she kept me.

Oh heck.

And yes, Allain went to the Catalogues to ask if she was interested in the position.

Obviously, she said she was.

But unsurprising news, it seemed Germaine had her finger on the pulse of everything at the Palace.

"I—"

"It cannot happen," Germaine decreed.

Allain's head came up.

My neck tensed.

"I believe we all know this is a sensitive issue for Prince Errol," she stated.

"She isn't interviewing to be Prince Errol's aide," I replied.

"He lives in this house," Germaine retorted.

"There are eight hundred and fifteen rooms in this *house*," Allain pointed out.

"He has his own aide," Germaine said to Allain. "And he meets with him in this wing. Where she will have an office."

"Then it's good they're both adults," I stated. "And should she be selected for the job, they can behave like adults. But as she'll be dealing with me, and Allain, the prince really needs to have nothing to do with her, except be courteous to her if he should pass her in the hall."

Germaine laid it all out.

"The king forbids it."

I gasped.

Allain did too.

She took her tablet from Allain.

"I'm sorry, but you're just going to have to tell her the position has been filled," Germaine concluded.

I didn't like candidate number three, so even if Allain did, right now, Nata was the only one who might have a shot before we had to go back to the drawing board.

"Comm his highness," Allain said.

I turned to him and saw his eyes on me.

"Me?" I asked.

"You," Allain replied. "Comm him and share this with him."

This was between a king and a prince.

A son and his father.

I felt strongly about what I was doing with Nata, but I wasn't sure I felt strongly enough, I was willing to cause (more) family discord for my mate.

"I don't think—"

"Trust me, Mistress Laura."

I studied his face, and even though I didn't think Aleksei would want to be disturbed with something like this, and what I read in Allain's expression didn't make me all fired up to do it, it still made me do it.

I reached in my bag, nabbed my Palm, got up and walked to the long windows behind the desk in Allain's office.

I pulled up his name and hit audio only.

I stared unseeing at the massive, formal courtyard garden situated in the middle of the Palace square and put the Palm to my ear.

Germaine might not be able to get through, but the tone sounded once before I heard, "Hello, love."

"Uh, hi. We have a little bit of a situation here," I told him.

The warmth had swept out of his tone, replaced with wary, when he asked, "What's that?"

"News got around about Nata. Germaine is here, and we'll talk about the response to Naylyn's ritual later."

"Bloody hell," he murmured.

"But...the king has forbidden me to interview Nata."

Silence from Aleksei.

No.

Such utter silence, I worried I'd never hear sound again.

Then he growled, "Interview her."

"Honey—"

"And if you like her, hire her."

"I don't—"

"I'm leaving shortly to meet you. I'll see you soon."

With that, he disconnected.

Oh boy.

I turned to Allain and Germaine. "He says to interview her."

Germaine started to say something, but Allain spoke first.

"Excellent. On your way out, will you tell Nata we're ready for her?"

Red hit her cheeks. "The king was staunch in his demand."

"Then he can take it up with the prince. The prince is *always* staunch in his decisions. They can battle it out. You have a royal statement to release. You do your job and allow us to carry on with our afternoon's business," Allain retorted.

After she shot Allain a venomous look, I worried my lip as she flounced out.

Then I went to sit down beside Allain.

"I don't feel good about this," I told him.

"Never you mind, Mistress Laura," he replied.

I was minding very much as the door opened and Nata came in.

She was very pretty.

But now, there was no attitude. She seemed nervous and guarded.

"Come and have a seat, Nata," I invited. She did that, and I asked, "Would you like some water or coffee or tea?"

"I'm good," she said.

"Excellent," I mumbled, and turned to Allain because he'd started each interview.

He raised his brows.

Okay then, I guessed it was me who was going to start this one.

I also knew why it was me.

Nothing for it, I got into it.

I turned to her. "Perhaps we should first dispense with the elephant in the room."

"You know," she whispered.

"It's of no consequence," I stated. "However, I have some say in what's happening in this room and the being I'll select to work with Aleksei, Allain and me. What I have no say in is what happens at the Catalogues."

She lowered her gaze. "Right."

Yes, she'd seen the writing on the wall.

"I've looked at your résumé, and your role evaluations, which are all stellar," I said.

Her chin lifted. "I like what I do."

"You can tell. You don't really have the, erm…well…experience we're searching for in regard to this position, but it's my understanding detail is essential to the work you do," I guided her to fighting for it, if she wanted it.

"As an intern, I was second assistant to the head curator at the Musée Histoire de Guerre for six term breaks during uni. That means this work spanned two years. Yes, I was second, and it was only for what amounted to six months. But the curator has a staff of nearly thirty, and she was working on an exhibit that had items from thirteen different realms the first year I was there, and another huge one on Pre-Unification weapons the second. It was busy. A lot was expected of me. I had important responsibilities. She wrote me a stellar reference, and I'm certain would do so again."

"I'm sure," I replied.

"She wanted to hire me after I graduated. I got the offer from the Catalogues, the enchanted moonstone of working in my field, so I took that instead."

Well, it was good to know, if she decided to move on, she might have somewhere to move on to.

But it sucked that it wouldn't be her first choice.

"And I'm young," she went on, clearly having given this some thought. She glanced at Allain then back to me. "But I don't feel my age is a detriment. Yes, there are things I'll have to learn, but I'm quick, and it's a personal goal for me to do my job well, pull my weight but also take initiative. So instead of my age and inexperience being a detriment, I believe I'll provide energy, fresh outlooks and an understanding of different generations of the citizenry of Night's Fall that will be beneficial to you. Not that you aren't of my generation," she said hurriedly (this was true, though she was younger, being twenty-seven). "It's just that"—another quick glance at Allain—"things can be a bit stuffy and outdated. I looked at the numbers, and nearly ninety percent of people aged thirty-five and younger feel the king is out of touch."

She scooched to the edge of her seat, now animated.

"What you did today, with his royal highness, was very brave. And if you don't mind me saying so, I personally think very beautiful. I'm not sure how the males will react to it, but many females have been conned by—" she cut herself off.

"I understand," I said quietly.

She squared her shoulders and got over it.

Good for her.

"We felt for her," she said. "It's all over the tapes. And there were some who were getting upset that it wasn't made clear that she was also a victim in that mess, and she paid the most of anyone," she continued.

"We do have a PR Director, leading a rather large team, who guides the royals in such issues," Allain put in.

Nata sat back, now seeming dejected. "I know. I didn't mean to infer I'd overstep my bounds."

"Actually," I said, "I'm new to this too. It's already been a ton of learning, and it'll be more. No matter who's selected for this role, I'll be relying heavily on his highness, and Allain, and so will she. I take your point. The prince and Allain are old hands at this, they know it inside and out, but fresh perspectives never hurt."

She brightened.

"It must be asked, considering your field of study and the work you now do, would it not be a disappointment to shift gears like this?" I inquired.

She stared a second before she glanced meaningfully around Allain's office and came back to me.

"I haven't had very much time to think about it. I've always had a passion for history, but it's never occurred to me I might have some small part in making it. Since Allain approached me, I keep asking myself that same question, Mistress Laura. But every time I think about it, all I can think is that it would be exciting." She gave me a tentative smile. "And the hike in salary would mean I'd be in a position to buy my own flat in a year, rather than the three my current saving schedule would allow."

Future-thinking. Thoughtful with her money. Considered. Forthright. Ambitious.

All right then.

"Okay, now, I'll turn it over to Allain, who can describe some of the duties involved and we can chat about them," I said.

We did this for half an hour, but I'd already made my decision before Allain even got started.

If we could get around the king, I wanted Nata to be my aide.

She had just over four hours to prepare for an important interview, and she made it clear she used them well. She spoke her mind. She wanted the job and let that be known. And she was right. Instead of the two of us bumbling along, she was sharp, motivated, would help me forge my path, but as she and Allain spoke, she gave clear indication she respected him, was eager to learn from him, and would defer to his experience when necessary.

When we were winding down, a sharp knock sounded at the door, and then it opened.

Aleksei strode in.

We all rose. We all curtsied (well, Allain bowed).

Aleksei ignored this, came right to me and kissed my cheek when I rose.

"Hello, darling," he greeted.

"Hey," I replied.

He turned to Nata. "Nata, lovely to see you."

At first, she gawped.

She got it together, bobbed and replied, "You as well, your highness."

"Allain," he said last.

"Your royal highness," Allain replied.

"I'm sorry to interrupt. I thought you'd be done," Aleksei said to me.

"We were just finishing up," I told him.

"I'll return some text comms while you do that," he murmured, kissed my cheek again, and then went to an armchair in Allain's huge office. He sat, crossed his legs and pulled out his Palm.

Seriously, just sitting in an armchair returning texts, he was gorgeous.

We finished up, and I walked Nata to the door personally.

"We'll make a decision soon," I promised her.

"Great and...Mistress Laura?"

"Yes?"

"Thank you," she said very quietly but with deep meaning.

"I'm glad I got the chance to know you better," I replied.

She nodded and walked out.

The minute the door closed on her, Aleksei requested, "Allain, may we have your office for a few minutes?"

"Already leaving," Allain replied, and he was. He stopped at me. "I can work with Nata, I believe very well."

He was impressed too.

I was thrilled we agreed.

I nodded.

He left.

I turned and gave out a little scream because Aleksei was right there.

"I've called a family meeting," he announced.

Terrific.

Ugh.

I was about to say something, but it was then I saw the banked amethyst fire burning behind the stars in his midnight eyes.

So what I said instead was a soothing, "Aleksei."

"Do you know the story of the first True Heir?" he asked.

Oh hells.

"Honey," I whispered, because I did. Everyone in Night's Fall did.

He launched in anyway.

"There was no king. We were still a clan. The Starknight clan. But the chieftain was a despot. The beings were suffering greatly under his rule. Due to the strength of his dragon, he was unbeatable. As such, he had absolute power. And he wielded it viciously. Entire tribes were wiped out. Beings starved while he feasted. He executed anyone who didn't agree with him."

"*Drahko.*"

"Everyone looked to his son to end their plight. He also had a powerful dragon, but not powerful enough to defeat his father. He despaired for his beings. So much, he left the Clan Caves, and as an act of sacrifice, on horseback rather than flying, he embarked on the treacherous journey to this very isle to beg the Night God to intervene. The Night God heard his pleas and infused in him the power of all the skies, this magic showing in his eyes. His dragon had vulnerable sheet wings hued blue. With this magic, he had webbed wings of purple. His dragon was handsome. With this magic, deadly spikes protruded from his head, down his spine and along his tail. His claws grew sharp as razors. He returned to the Caves and challenged his sire. He killed the king, took the throne, and the people knew abundance and harmony again."

"Aleksei."

"We discussed it and made our decision this morning, Laura. It was a considered decision. And in the end, the right one."

He'd been moved as well about the response of Naylyn's family.

"Yes, however—"

His tone was deteriorating, and a little of the Aleksei who lost it on me the night of the gallery sparked through.

Okay.

This wasn't good.

"I warned them," he reminded me.

"Maybe we should—"

"They do not trouble my mate."

I stopped trying to calm him down.

He took my hand in a firm grip.

"Come, love, it's time for my father to meet the True Heir."

I wasn't certain what that meant, considering his father had a hand in creating that True Heir.

But still...

Farg.

CHAPTER 26
THE TRUE HEIR

I wasn't even close to prepared for the impossibly high ceilinged, wide halled, crystal chandeliered, plush carpeted, gilded wonderland that was the Celestial Palace.

We were going at such a fast clip, and even if the journey was long to wherever we were headed, I didn't have much chance to do more than glance into the rooms that were studies of creams and golds, sea greens and sky blues, watered taffeta pink and champagne, ivory and porcelain blue... and the list goes on. And I certainly had no opportunity to peruse the plethora of paintings, portraits, sculptures, china, candelabrum and furnishings.

I also didn't have the headspace for it, considering Aleksei was a male on a mission and he was all but dragging me through the stunning opulence, all the while I raced beside him in three-and-a-half-inch heels.

Therefore, I was wildly relieved when he suddenly stopped.

I sucked in a breath.

As I did, it felt like my beast stretched, almost strained, toward him.

And good gods, I wasn't sure, but I sensed I felt the same coming from Aleksei.

My mind was taken off this when he asked curtly, "Do you wish to hire her?"

I blinked. "Nata?"

"Yes."

Oh dear.

How to answer this?

"She was the most impressive candidate," I said hesitantly.

He jerked up his chin angrily and started dragging me again.

"Honey," I called. "Please slow down. I'm in heels."

He slowed, but even so, his determination to get where we were going didn't ebb one bit.

We passed about ten more rooms, turned down a hall, went up some stairs, passed another five, and I was beginning to lament wearing my sleek, black, patent leather pumps, even if they were normally pretty comfortable. What they weren't was designed to hike two miles on plush carpet or otherwise.

Fortunately, Aleksei turned again, into a room that was a study of red and burgundy, gilt-edged furniture...and royals.

The king and Errol were sitting together on a silk damask couch the color of a red rose.

The king was scowling at Aleksei.

Errol was fighting a smile.

The queen was pacing the area behind the couch.

Timothee was slouched in an armchair to the side of the couch, one ankle resting atop the other knee.

He was smirking.

The princes thought their big brother was in trouble and neither seemed to realize this was not the case.

And my jangled nerves jangled more intensely, because there was also the glorious Princess Aleece, my first vision of her in person.

She was the picture of her mother, with her burnished-chestnut hair, generous mouth, upturned nose, soft brown eyes and peaches-and-cream skin (though, her features were more delicate, whereas Queen Calisa's were lush).

She was wearing one of the trendy new fly suits in olive green—boxy and utilitarian, the luxuriant silk that crafted it made it hang seductively and cling impishly, rendering it casually sexy, like the wearer didn't give a stuff that she looked fabulous, but she still looked fabulous.

Aleece was reclined on the arm of another chair, looking relaxed, but like she had places to go and things to do, so she had to be ready to pop up and do them at any time.

But the instant her oldest brother walked in, she straightened, and after a swift glance at me, her gaze locked on Aleksei.

She was reading her brother perfectly.

I already knew this, but this made it clear she was a far brighter bulb than the other two.

I couldn't think on Aleece much, because I was in the Palace and in the presence of the king and queen, and even though Aleksei didn't release my hand, I swayed an arm out and affected a curtsy.

I was barely down before Aleksei's hand was pulling me back up.

And Timothee was talking.

"She drags my brother to the passing ritual of a traitor, guess it's not a surprise she doesn't know she doesn't have to drop a formal when she's in the family's informal drawing room."

"Tim, take heed," Aleece said urgently.

Too late.

I'd lost Aleksei's hand.

And now he was a man on a different mission.

"Aleksei!" I cried, panic-stricken.

Timothee finally cottoned on to the threat, and he scrambled out of his chair just in time to be nose to nose with his older brother.

Though, to be nose to nose, Aleksei had to lean into him since he was three inches taller, and making matters worse, with the two of them that close together, I noted Aleksei had to have four stone more of pure muscle.

Timothee did not miss this, and he was no longer unclear about his brother's mood.

What he was, was visibly shaken.

"Outside. As males," Aleksei growled.

"Are...are you...are you being serious?" Timothee stammered.

The king stood and commanded, "Stand back this instant!"

Aleksei turned away from his brother, but it was far from a good thing his attention went to his father.

"Laura is hiring Nata," he announced. "However, if Nata wishes to stay at the Catalogues, I'll speak personally with the director and have her promoted to preservation."

I stifled a gasp.

Aleksei continued. "It will be her choice which avenue she wishes to take in the furtherance of her career."

"As you know, she deals with priceless treasures of the realm, and this is a delicate matter—" King Fillion began.

"What I know is that it was a delicate matter because you made it so, and after years of living in that particular level of the hells, I foolishly fell into that line of thinking, but now I know, this is no longer a delicate matter," Aleksei cut in.

The king focused fully on his son.

And the color ran out of his face.

"You wouldn't," he whispered.

"Yes, I would. And make no mistake, Father, *I am*," Aleksei retorted.

Okay, I was thinking I lost track of the conversation.

I had zero time to get a lock on it, because Aleksei turned to Timothee.

"I'll be taking over negotiations with the female you drugged. She'll be offered a year of your allowance, and as a result, you will lose that allowance. You will cost the throne not another mark for your bad behavior. You will also apologize to her, in person, for your lack of judgement, which resulted in misguided and malicious intent."

I felt my eyes get wide even as I noted the queen moving to the back of the couch. Curling her fingers around the gilt, she watched her eldest son avidly.

Aleksei was far from done with Timothee.

"You will also be suspended from your royal duties for six months, you will lose access to all the facilities of the Palace, save food, cleaning and laundry services. No transport will be available to you unless where you're going is approved by me. Visitors will also be approved by me. You will be banned from other royal properties, again, unless approved by me. You will lie low here and consider your course for the future. Once the six months is up, we'll discuss that future."

"You can't possibly—" Timothee tried.

Aleksei was having none of it.

"If you refuse, negotiations with this female will cease and your allowance will be revoked indefinitely, along with the property and facilities ban. Your royal duties will also be indefinitely suspended, including your attendance at the Council Chamber in the Center. Further, you will be disallowed access to royal legal representation, and if she chooses to press charges, you will stand before a panel of magistrates to do your best to try to convince them you aren't a piece of shit. You will also fail. This will happen in public. So the citizens of Night's Fall will know what you've done."

I swallowed.

Mine was about shock.

I watched Timothee swallow.

His was fear.

Aleksei turned on Errol.

"The same will happen to you if you ever play in the royal pool again," he warned. "And should Nata decide to move to the administration wing, and you see her, you will behave with the dignity of your title. Onward, you will respect the females who work for the throne. No. You will learn to respect females full stop. And if you do something outside the Palace walls that demands the negotiation of hush money again, the amount will be decided by me, and it will be deducted from your allowance. If you should continue to behave like an incorrigible, entitled brat, and this should go into arrears, your royal duties will be suspended."

He looked between the two of them and kept going.

"This stops now. If you don't learn from the consequences I've set forth, your royal privileges will be permanently revoked, and you'll be stripped of your titles. You will be removed from the Palace, and although residences will be provided for you, they won't be anywhere near what you're used to, and you will be required to find employment in order to sustain yourselves."

Everyone was silent.

The silence was heavy.

Timothee stupidly decided to break it.

"Who the fuck do you think you are?" he demanded hotly.

"You know who I am, Tim," Aleksei retorted unemotionally. "I'm claiming my right. I should have done it the moment I heard your latest villainy. Fortunately, the negotiations with this female are still happening, so I can intervene and try to do the impossible, everything I can to make it even a modicum of right by her."

"The Night God's choice, the chosen son," Timothee sneered, jerking his head toward his mother to indicate whose chosen son Aleksei was. "Do you not get what a headfuck it is to slink along in your shadow?"

"No, I don't," Aleksei returned. "Because I'm me, and you're you. I'd ask you to consider for a moment what it feels like to be in my shoes—"

"So tough, I'm sure," Timothee scorned. "I'd *so* hate to be you. The fiercest dragon. The best marks at school. Females throwing themselves at your feet." He jabbed a finger my way. "Destiny dumps a female with great tits and a perfect ass in your lap...*ulk!*"

Suddenly, the room was a flurry of motion as everybody moved because Aleksei had taken his brother by the throat and was lifting him to the tips of his toes by it.

"Son," Queen Calisa was at his side, and her word was a plea.

"*Drahko,*" I was at his other side, my hand on his arm, my voice soft, but my word was also a plea.

"You speak of the True Bride," Aleksei whispered sinisterly.

Oh gods.

I hadn't heard that term in ages because there hadn't been one in ages. But the True Bride was *me*.

"And your brother's mate," he bit off. "She will have respect, or you will regret your actions until your dying...*fucking...breath*. Am I perfectly clear?"

Timothee was choking, but also nodding.

Aleksei flung him into the chair.

I latched onto his arm, and he allowed me to pull him away two steps, but that was all he allowed.

"Am I clear about the rest of it?" he asked Timothee.

"Fuck you," Timothee spat, rubbing his neck.

"Is that a no?" Aleksei asked dangerously.

"No. I'm clear. Because I have no choice. Right?"

"Correct," Aleksei said. He turned to Errol. "Now you. Have I made myself clear?"

Errol turned to his father and whined, "Dad."

King Fillion was staring at his eldest son.

"Dad!" Errol called sharply.

Slowly, the king turned to Errol. "You wound me, every time you lay your weakness at my feet."

Uh...

Whoa!

That was unexpected.

Errol's pretty face went ashen.

"I despair, but you don't see it, what you do to me. You don't care. But you are my son, what am I to do?" the king asked.

"Dad," Errol said quietly.

"This family does not abide in this Palace because of the fortune of hereditary blood. It is because, from the first True Heir, we vowed to protect the people of Night's Fall, and the two of you,"—he looked to Timothee—"not only fail miserably in holding this promise sacred, you actively and repeatedly seek to break it. Is this my penance for showing you softness? Is this my penance for showing you love?"

Aleece made a sad noise, the emotion that was squeezing my heart.

Neither of the younger princes replied, nor did they meet their father's eyes.

"I've spent years, desolate, wondering where I've gone wrong," the king stated. "I was so proud of you in your youth. My fine four. So beautiful. But then you two took everything I gave and twisted it into something unsavory. Was it me, in the guilt I still carried at feeling my own siblings' envy of my status, that acted mistakenly because I wanted you to feel special? To feel heard? To feel seen?"

Neither male had an answer.

Then again, that was more than likely true on a variety of levels.

There simply was no answer. Their behavior was inexcusable.

"Fillion, my love," Queen Calisa murmured, her voice an ache.

The king's attention shifted to Aleksei.

"Is this official?" he asked confusingly.

"It doesn't appear it needs to be," Aleksei replied quietly.

"But in these chambers," the king pressed.

"We both know, in these chambers, it has to be," Aleksei said.

The king nodded. "Let there be no upset, son. Truth told, it's a relief."

And with that, saying nothing nor looking at anyone, with dignity I admired, the king walked out.

"Son," Queen Calisa called.

"Don't," Aleksei said tersely. "You know I don't want it."

"And you know it was an inevitability," she replied gently.

She moved to him, touched his arm, glanced at her two younger sons, her daughter, and followed her husband.

"Don't *even* open your mouth," Aleece warned.

Timothee's eyes had fired, and he was openly pouting. But he kept his mouth shut.

"Laura." She called my attention to her. "I've been looking forward to meeting you. But not like this."

"Same," I pushed out, so blown away by all that had happened and perplexed by a lot of it, I was unable to say more.

"So that's it?" Errol demanded of Aleksei. "One day, you just walk into a room, issue orders, act like a bully, and we're supposed to click our heels and salute?"

"Thank you for asking, I'm just fine after someone tried to kill my beast," Aleksei returned. "Thank you for asking, I'm extortionately happy I've found my mate. Thank you for asking, I'd love for you to get to know her and her friends better."

That said a lot.

And, right...

We were doing this now.

Since it needed to be done, I kept my mouth shut and my hold on my mate.

"Like you reach out," Timothee spat.

"I asked you to join my ring ice team. Then the team asked me to lose you because you're a dirty player and an inveterate cheat."

Color started to hit Timothee's face.

Aleksei carried on.

"I asked you both to stand up with me when I was engaged to Anna, and the night of our engagement party, you made a messy, inebriated pass at her," he said to Timothee, then he turned to Errol. "And you got drunk and were caught urinating on her mother's prized roses."

Errol suddenly was fascinated with the oval coffee table in front of him.

Aleece crossed her arms on her chest and glared between the two, and I had the distinct impression what Aleksei was sharing was news to her.

Aleksei, sadly, wasn't done.

"I asked you both if you were interested in working with one of my businesses. Tim, you threw that offer in my face. Rol, you took me up on it, and then I had to sack you for sexually harassing a colleague."

Errol now made a study of his shoes.

Ugh.

These males were a disaster.

And I was seeing Aleksei and I might need to spend less time having sex and more time talking (*might*).

"As ever, you're perfect, and we're fuckups," Timothee bit out.

"You said it, I didn't," Aleksei fired back. "But I'm far from perfect, Tim. You simply haven't bothered to try to get to know me. Also, I don't put everything I am into being a fuckup for whatever shitty reason you have for doing it. You are not me. You will never be me. You're you. That could take any form. Are you happy with the person you crafted yourself to be? Because if you are, we're dealing with something a great deal deeper here, because you're fucking insufferable, and anyone in their right mind would know the many ways you are."

Timothee shrugged. "You twist us into villains when we're just normal males. We're just not shining examples of glory, like you are."

"A normal male does not drug a woman to force her to have an abortion, Tim."

"You don't get this, but she was blackmailing me," Tim retorted hotly. "She got pregnant on purpose. She had me by the balls. What would you do?"

"I wouldn't have gotten her pregnant. It's a simple matter of taking the serum once a week," Aleksei returned.

"She can take the serum too," Timothee rejoined.

Aleksei sighed.

And I counted my lucky stars that my male regularly imbibed the birth control serum (and yes, we oh so had talked about *that*).

I did too, but you could never be too careful (until you didn't want to be, of course).

"I won't apologize to that bitch," Timothee decreed. "The rest, I don't give a fuck. Do what you have to do. You'll see what kind of female she is when you sit down with her. She was out to get exactly what you're giving her."

"And this is why you take the serum, Tim," Aleksei said with strained patience. "If she is indeed a female like that, you don't hand her the rope to hang you."

"I can't be fussed with remembering to take a freaking serum once a week," Timothee mumbled.

"For fuck's sake," Aleksei groused.

Aleece joined the conversation.

"You know, sometimes you make it really hard to love you two," she declared, aiming this at Timothee and Errol.

The first narrowed his eyes at her.

The other surprised me by having the good grace to look abashed.

Aleece kept at them.

"I'm mortified to my soul our future sister-in-law, new to our family, is standing there, watching you behave like this." She said this to Timothee, and then turned to Errol. "I'm chagrined she felt she had to step in and clean up your mess." She shook her head. "I've tried. I've really tried to understand where you two are coming from. I try, and then I hear about more shit you both get up to. I'm exhausted with the effort. I'm done. I can't beat it back anymore, make excuses for you. I also can't fight the feeling any longer that I'm just so fucking ashamed of both of you."

She moved to leave but stopped and looked back to me.

"I'm sorry for my family, Laura. We'll chat some other time."

I didn't get the chance to nod my acceptance, she was gone.

"Great. Thanks," Timothee said snidely. "Now you've turned Aleece against us."

"I'm curious," Aleksei said. "How does it feel to have the world land on you, and anything and anybody but yourself and your own actions are to blame for the shit that befalls you, which happens to absolutely nobody. Rather than your actions impacting you and those around you, which is what everyone else experiences?"

Timothee changed tacks.

"You blew it with that ritual, brother," he sneered.

"You're following the wrong tapes, *brother*. The impact of our attendance was overall positive," Aleksei replied.

It was?

Germaine didn't make it out to be that way.

"But even if it wasn't, we stood for compassion today and gave a family thrown into one of the hells no one wants to visit a thin thread to cling to, that we grieved with them and we didn't blame their loved one for something that wasn't her fault," Aleksei concluded.

"Always with the answers," Timothee retorted.

"Fuck, Tim, just let it go," Errol said on a sigh.

Timothee turned on his younger brother. "You'll toe the line, and now, instead of kissing Dad's ass, you'll kiss Aleksei's feet because you've got a dick the size of a toothpick and couldn't think yourself out of a paper bag."

For a flash, an expression hit Errol's face that set ice into my veins.

Then he shot back, "Fuck off."

"Gladly," Timothee returned and stormed out.

"I liked her," Errol announced, taking our attention to him. "I really did. She just wasn't marriage material."

He was talking about Nata.

I gritted my teeth, something that helped loads with me holding my tongue.

It didn't escape me that neither of those two males had directed one word to me yet.

It wasn't like we had dinner together every night.

But seriously?

"If they don't want you for you, Rol, and require promises you can't keep, then they aren't worth your time. Be the kind of male who makes that their loss," Aleksei advised.

Errol hung his head in a manner I suspected, in the past, got him out of some serious shit.

Aleksei didn't bother witnessing it.

He took my hand and off we went on another hike through the Palace, where I didn't see much more, just a rehash of what came before but in reverse.

I waited until we were in his JetPanther, and he was waiting for course approval, before I asked, "Our attendance at the ritual was overall positive?"

"When you mentioned Germaine, I asked Muriel to run some numbers." The onboard computer announced our course was cleared, Aleksei took the stick, and we had liftoff. "Females sixty years and under, overwhelmingly positive. Older, they're not happy. Males, the results are mixed. Sixty and over, they're pissed. Thirty and younger, about half and half. Males in between, we're at sixty-five percent positive."

Boy, Muriel could run some serious numbers in a short period of time (however you did that).

"Germaine made it sound dire," I remarked.

"She was riding the high of your approval rating and knows it's undoubtedly taken a hit. But regardless, she takes any negativity about our family personally. And a warning, darling, there is quite a bit of it, as we suspected."

"Ah."

"Therefore, anything negative sticks in her craw," Aleksei finished. "If it happened without her input, she loses it, like I'm guessing she did."

I didn't confirm, but I didn't need to.

With that out of the way, now the big stuff.

"I'm sorry, honey. My actions instigated what just happened," I said quietly.

"Don't think that for another moment, Laura," he replied tersely. "It feels like we've been racing to that scene since the first time Tim got the idea to douse me with ice water in the middle of the night, getting nothing but a mild dressing down. Whereas I got a chat with my father about how I need to buck up because that's the kind of thing that makes a boy into a male."

"I still need to learn that there might be larger ramifications for my decisions."

"No you don't. You already understand that. We should have told Germaine. That was my mistake. I mostly operate on my own, without her being involved. With you by my side, that has to change. But other than that, we can only be who we are, and if we're good beings, it will work. Does what we do reflect on an entire realm? Yes. But as good beings, the decisions we make will reflect positively. Like today. Not everyone agrees what we did was right, but we were there, we know what it meant to the people who mattered. And for the most part, the rest of them understood. But bottom line, in a day or two, no one will be talking about this. They'll find something else to be upset about."

This was true.

Moving on.

"I'm kinda confused about what just happened," I told him.

"I assumed the mantle of the True Heir."

No less confused.

"I thought you already were the True Heir," I noted.

"Back in the day, once the change occurred, the True Heir became de facto king."

Holy Hecate.

I knew this, of course. You learned it in history.

But that was what the ancients did.

"This proved ineffective," Aleksei told me something I'd also learned in history. "No thirteen-year-old boy should sit a throne, regardless that he was chosen by a god. Stupid shit happened. Laws were enacted. And the king, or queen, would continue to reign until the True Heir reached majority. Civilization advanced. Wars became less frequent. The need for a True Heir reduced, he seldom emerged, and we haven't had one for two hundred years."

"Yes." My word was breathless, because a good deal of heavy stuff was just occurring to me.

"I had no interest. And it'd been so long since the last Heir, people forgot," Aleksei explained.

"Are you saying...did you...just become king?"

"No. I assumed the role of patriarch of my family."

In these chambers.

Even if I was seated, and the path of the JetPanther was smooth, I felt shaky.

"Aleksei?"

"Yes, darling?"

"The True Bride..." I couldn't finish.

He glanced at me. "Laura, I already told you that you outrank my mother. The True Heir's mate, the minute he finds her, is known as the True Bride."

"Is that my title?"

"It is, and will always be, though on marriage, you'll earn another one, and on the sad day of my father's passing, you'll have another."

"I hadn't...remembered that," I said haltingly. "About the True Bride, that is."

"History hasn't focused on females. They didn't tend to start wars or order people guillotined, the juicy parts of history that are rabidly remembered."

True, indeed.

"Aleksei," I called again.

"I'm right here, *bissi*," he said quietly.

"Do we...there has always been..." I cleared my throat. "Throughout history, there's always been a need for a True Heir. War. Upheaval. Political strife. Tyrannical kings."

He said nothing.

I tore my gaze from the skyscreen to look at him. "Do you think you're True Heir because your father is a pushover, or he was, and your brothers are problematic?"

"We can hope so," he murmured.

He hoped so.

I hoped so.

But someone had gone to the trouble and expense of finding a witch to track me down. They'd tried to take my beast.

And then they'd tried to take his.

"Aleksei," I said again, shakily.

"Engage auto," he told the craft and turned to me.

Taking my hand, he held it firm, caught my gaze, and I saw in his what was now occurring to me had already occurred to him.

In fact, maybe he'd lived with it from the minute his eyes changed from his mother's melting brown to the color of the skies.

"We live our lives, Laura, and if there's something to know, we will know, we will face it and we will best it. But until then, we'll just live our lives and be happy. We have no other choice."

What he meant was, *he* had lived his entire life like this.

And now I was doing it with him.

"Yes, darling?" he prompted.

Again, I had no choice.

I was his. He was mine.

And we were in this.

I nodded slowly.

He held my gaze.

Unfortunately, until I could process it further, that was all I had for him.

He kissed my knuckles, let me go, resumed control of the craft and five minutes later landed us smoothly on the pad of our penthouse.

CHAPTER 27

STRUGGLING

"Shh."

"You shh."

"No, *you* shh."

We all giggled.

And yes, we were all tipsy.

My gals had come for a gals' night in. We'd stuffed our faces. Poorly played billiards. I lost a fortune in chocolate stars and corn nibbles at poker, because it would seem I seriously sucked at poker. Though, that might have had something to do with the fact, until that night, I'd never played it.

And we'd drank a lot.

Gayle, Cat and Monique had come to mine, because at the behest of Dr. Fearsome, backed by Aleksei, I was now under quarantine since my beast could emerge at any time.

That night, I'd finally gotten my updates from them (Cat and Bash were still dating (yay!), Gayle and Sirk were not (boo!) and Monique was still working so hard in order to be able to afford to remodel her flat, she wasn't doing anything (boo again! but also, good for her)).

I'd given my friends all the news, which was mostly about how I was falling in love with my awesome mate, with only a little bit about the rift and changes in the Royal Family and what I knew about whatever traitorous plot was unfolding.

I didn't share not because I didn't trust them.

I didn't do it because family business like that should stay in the family, and I had a strong feeling that threats to the realm shouldn't be discussed over bad poker playing and copious imbibing.

Aleksei had been with me when they arrived, and he'd checked in a couple of times during the evening, being his normal charming self, looking his usual gorgeous and making my gals oo and aah at how fantastic he was. But other than that, he'd left us to our gal time.

The night was just what I needed.

We were standing at the lift.

And the gals had been loudly discussing the fact I was imminently going to have tipsy sex with my mate (mm-hmm, I'd shared about how great Aleksei was at that too).

Now that our night was over, my friends were right. Aleksei would soon be giving me more of what I needed.

But the decibel level of our discussion caused me to emit the first "Shh."

"This makes me want to quest for my mate," Gayle said.

"You could quest Sirk, and jump on his big, bear shifter dick," Cat suggested.

"*Shh*," Gayle shushed her. "He's Aleksei's best bud, and Aleksei has shifter hearing."

"I've been glad I missed the mayhem at the gallery," Monique put in. "But the more I hear of this Sirk, the more I wish I'd risked being trampled in order to get a look at this male."

Suddenly, my beast shifted in my chest, and it made me turn my head toward the stairs.

"Everything okay, Laura?" Monique asked me.

I came back to them. "I'm sorry. I need to—"

My beast shifted again, and my skin started tingling.

"I need to get to my mate," I said earnestly.

Suddenly sober eyes lit on me, and I loved them even more because none of them had mates, but they still got it.

I received hugs, cheek kisses, and they loaded into the lift.

I waved at them until the door slid closed and then I hurried to the stairs.

I found Aleksei at the window in the bedroom, fully clothed even if it was late, and staring at the city lights of Nocturn.

Seeing him like that, instantly, I was sober myself.

When I entered, his gaze came to me.

I went right to him.

"Have a good night?" he asked, extending an arm.

I walked into that arm, and he curled it around me, pulling my front to his side.

"It was great," I replied and tipped my head. "Are you all right?"

His eyes moved over my face.

Then he looked back to the window.

No.

He wasn't all right.

"Honey," I whispered. "Talk to me."

"I just got a comm from the lead of the task force. Dr. Buildlore has been found. He's dead."

Oh farg.

"Blasted in the face?" I asked.

He shook his head before looking down at me. "He hung himself. The supposition is, he couldn't run anymore or feel hunted or both."

"Did he leave a note?"

"Yes. He apologized to his fiancée for being a weak male."

"That's it?"

He nodded.

"Please tell me his fiancée was the nurse he was showing favoritism to," I begged.

"It's my understanding she was not."

Stellar fellow all around, it seemed.

"Laura, he knew Anna," Aleksei informed me.

My body lurched at this news.

"Oh my gods," I breathed.

"They had a short affair a few years ago when they met on Anubis. They were both there for a holiday. It didn't last longer than that, but they kept in touch."

Anna certainly did get around to all the fabulous resorts of the Four Realms.

I'd always wanted to go to Anubis Island with its pink beaches, sprawling platinum-crown hotel and bungalows built on stilts in the azure waters of the Dolphin Sea.

The island was small, the resort the only thing on it, and there was nothing to do there but sit in the sun, eat, drink, go to one of their many spas, yoga or meditation sessions, hit one of their nightclubs, or browse through their exclusive boutiques. I'd even researched it (and as such, found there was no way I could afford it). Seven restaurants, three of them fine dining. Ten boutiques. Four spas. Two clubs. Oh, and a dinner theater.

This was where my mind turned, because it needed to have that brief respite rather than allowing what he was telling me to settle.

But then, what he was telling me settled.

Which was why I was feeling what I was feeling coming off of Aleksei.

He was reacting to the fact an old friend, a former lover, and his ex-fiancée put a hit out on me, and maybe him.

"That isn't concrete proof she's behind this," I tried.

"I'm telling myself that," he replied. "It's becoming hard to believe."

"Do you want to talk about it?" I asked.

He moved us to a seating area I'd yet to use. A charcoal velvet couch with an oval curve back elegantly edged in silvered wood, flanked by two blue velvet club chairs. These were situated around a silver and black marble table about ten feet from the foot of the bed, close to the wall that closed the room off from the downstairs.

"Activate fireplace," he called, and I stood in stunned silence as I watched the entire wall fold into itself, exposing a window with more of a view of Nocturn, but also the living area of the level below.

In the lower portion of the wall, purple and blue flames sprang up, and when they did, they danced high across the entire wall. Which meant, the wall was a fireplace.

Freaking *mega*.

I was sensing I should ask Aleksei to give me the full tour, rather than relying on the one I took with Comet, because I'd been missing things.

I decided against this because discovering them like I just did was a whole lot more fun.

"Service engage. Deliver whisky, three fingers," he went on as he seated us cozied together on the couch.

I curled my legs under me.

Aleksei looked down at me and lifted his brows.

"I'm on almondine sours," I told him.

"And an almondine sour," Aleksei said to the room.

"Um..." I hummed rather than asking the question about why he was talking to the room.

"I don't use the bots for personal service unless I can't be arsed to go get myself a fucking drink. And right now, I can't be arsed."

I nodded, noting his mood seemed to be worsening.

Aleksei brooded at the fire.

I let him.

A bot arrived with our drinks on a tray.

Once we took them, its mechanical voice asked, "Anything else for now, your royal highness?"

"No, but stand ready."

"Yes, sire," the bot replied, and walked out.

Aleksei drank.

I drank.

He launched in. "As I told you, Anna and I were friends. We became lovers. I should have taken pains to keep it a secret. I fear this wouldn't have worked, because Anna had no intention of doing so. My mother heard of it. She told Germaine. Germaine told Rytalf, the political advisor to the royal family. Rytalf brought my father into it. My father spoke to Dagsbrun. He spoke to their political advisor. And all of them decided, in the current climate, an alliance between realms would be a good thing."

"My first question is the easier one," I said. "And it is, why was that?"

"The magisterial system of Sky's Edge is a quagmire. A panel can make a decision, and if a barrister can poke a big enough hole in the reasoning behind their decree, it will go to another panel for a new decision. I honestly have no idea how they get anything done with this kind of setup, but demons love nothing more than to argue and pit themselves against things. So maybe it's that. In the years since King Riland's death, Tanyn has had six panels rule in favor of his question of succession. And Arnaud's barristers have found big enough issues behind the reasoning to call another panel."

I wasn't sure why we were talking about Sky's Edge, but I didn't ask.

I sipped my drink and listened.

"Now, Tanyn has jumped through enough hoops, his case is being prepared to go in front of the Premier Magistrate, and their decision will be final," Aleksei shared. "Arnaud will have no choice but to accept it, and it is in no doubt the decision will be his immediate abdication, and Tanyn will take the throne."

"This is good, isn't it?" I asked.

"It would be good, if our intelligence wasn't telling us there's an alarming rift in their military. There are those who back Arnaud. There are those who back Tanyn. But right now, Arnaud is king. So those who are found to back Tanyn have been disciplined, ousted, or even tried on trumped up charges and imprisoned."

Dear Lilith!

"This for sure is not in the media or on the tapes," I stated.

"This is because Arnaud is keeping it very quiet, and Tanyn has learned to caution his supporters to be covert. But that doesn't mean they aren't planning for the eventuality that Arnaud will refuse to abdicate, and that will mean he'll need to be forcibly removed. Which could mean he'd call on his supporters, and Tanyn will absolutely call his, and there'll be civil war."

This was not good news.

But I still didn't know why he was talking about it.

"And you're sharing this because...?"

"Because, if there was an alliance between Night's Fall and Dawn's Break, both the realms at Sky's Edge southern border would be of one mind, that being in support of Tanyn's claim to the throne. And if this was the case, even Arnaud might hesitate to do something stupid when he lost in the courts."

"Aren't Night's Fall and Dawn's Break already allied in this notion?"

"We are, darling, but royal marriage is a bond that does not break. With Anna and I married, there would be more discussion between realms about votes in the Center. We wouldn't be united, officially. But for the most part, there would be a united front. It is a subtle nuance of a shift, or in this case, consolidation of power. Subtle or not, it's there, and Arnaud wouldn't miss it."

"And this brings me to the more difficult question. You agreed to marriage with Anna because of these terms?"

He shook his head, but said, "It was put to me, and I considered it along with the knowledge we shared history, we shared an understanding of each other and the lives we live, and we were friends and enjoyed each other's company. She's amusing, carefree. Before things turned sour, she was almost always in a good mood. This is nice to be around. Someone who could find the good in everything or bounce back from something shitty happening and do it quickly. She's also beautiful. I was attracted to her before we became lovers." He gave me a squeeze. "And I've since learned that sex can be transcendent, but she was an excellent lover."

My beast trembled at that, and something else twisted, but he wasn't my first, I knew I wasn't his, I also knew we both understood on a primitive level we would be each other's last, so I had to get over it.

"I'm sorry. That was abrupt," he said low. "However, I'm putting this matter-of-factly, *bissi*, because I'm struggling here."

He felt my response.

And I knew he was struggling.

This woman had been his lifelong friend. I couldn't imagine Catla ever turning on me. Not ever.

I cuddled closer to him and urged, "Go on. And say it however you have to in order to get it out."

He nodded, sipped his drink and returned his attention to the fire.

"I was also of an age where it was time to marry, and she seemed a good match. But I can't deny that the political alliance didn't hold some sway. We've had an unprecedented period of peace. The only time this lasted longer was the Great Peace that began nearly eight hundred years ago. I've only experienced war in simulations at Red Lair. Even if those were only simulations, they were far from fun. The biggest lesson they taught me is that war is to be avoided at all costs. But the bottom line is, I'm True Heir, and it's my destiny to do what's right for Night's Fall."

"Of course."

"However, the more time I spent with her, the more it became clear that Anna is an elitist, like her mother. Since our break, I've come to suspect that Anna, or her mother, were behind my mother discovering our affair. They did this with the purpose of making it more than an affair, because Anna has few choices for a husband who matches her in status. Arnaud is out, he's a pervert, but even if he wasn't, he's a pretender. Tanyn has always disliked Anna. He's a broody, intense male who was deeply affected by his father's desertion of his mother, and the subsequent stripping of their status, which meant life changed for them greatly. Even so, he's highly intelligent, and I should have read his aversion to her as what it was. And Prince Cormac of Land's End is a throwback. He's more male than any male I've met. No chance Anna could lead him around by his dick."

"And she thought she could do that to you?" I asked in shock.

He turned to me. "When we spoke of her before, I mentioned the long con. Part of what I'm struggling with is she's given me reason to believe that even our decades of friendship were something she cultivated for the ultimate end of marrying me."

I gasped. "That's diabolical."

"So is sending assassins to murder the creature of a male's true mate."

Very true.

"Thus, you think she's behind it," I deduced.

"It was messy, ending things with her. However, once I explained the situation to Mom and Dad, they understood why I made it. Flurries of every form of diplomacy were dispatched, and things were smoothed over. Most of the mess was because Anna was livid. Without me on her leash, she'll have to turn to the Six Realms, Three Realms or Seven Realms to find what she considers an appropriate match, and she'd have to move there, for her husband would one day be king. It also might mean her husband would be a vampire, and she would not do well with her days turning to nights."

"Okay, Aleksei, but what could she possibly get out of harming you or me?"

"Revenge for being cast aside, something she is definitely not used to. Or a misguided notion that if you were not in the picture, I'd pull her back into mine. Remember, in the second attack, no one knew you and I had found each other yet."

"But that doesn't explain why the assassin turned his weapon on you."

His lips twitched with vague amusement. "I'm uncertain of the assassin's creed, but there could be dozens of reasons why he shifted targets. Bragging rights alone would be one."

I hated to admit it, but this was true.

"And now...what?" I asked. "What if you find proof it was her?"

He took another sip of his drink. "This is part of my struggle. I'm hurt I lost a lifelong friend. I'm angry at her along with myself that I didn't see through her and allowed it to go as far as it went. I'm stunned she may be behind this, because that puts her self-absorption and cossetted behavior in a bald and grim new light. And the last part is, this will be a diplomatic nightmare. We have one realm embroiled in an alarming internal struggle. Two more cannot be at each other's throats because the Princess Royal is a spoiled bitch."

He was so right.

And this was so messed up.

"I see why this is weighing heavily on you," I mumbled my understatement.

That brought me a fully amused smile. "Indeed. And this means, unless we discover all that is behind it beforehand, which we might not, this will make the Midnight Masque very interesting."

By the gods.

How had I forgotten?

The Midnight Masque, which happened at midnight on the first full moon of autumn, a night that was only a few weeks away, was a huge deal at the Palace. Everyone of consequence was invited, and they didn't miss it.

This included all the royals, not only of the Four Realms, but of the realms across the seas.

Which meant Anna would be there.

And this year, I would too.

"It's good Nata accepted the position as your aide," Aleksei remarked while studying my face. "Allain will have her up to speed soon, and I won't have to watch you freeze in shock at something someone will be attending to for you."

Latest news: when offered the choice, Nata surprised both Aleksei and me by choosing me.

Her reasons were that she had given the Catalogues six years of her life, her work had been exemplary, and her director had rolled right over and demoted her projects, if he didn't demote her role. Worse, he was prepared to let her go when a transfer position was offered to her, rather than fighting for her.

"It'll be nice to have a boss who right away demonstrates she believes in me and is willing to fight for me," she'd said.

Although I still worried that she'd miss it, I could see her reasoning.

Even if he done her wrong, the director had spluttered mild outrage that she left without notice.

He stopped doing that when Aleksei himself swung by the Catalogues to explain how things were going to be.

In other words, the True Heir had accepted his destiny not only "in chambers" but also at the Catalogues, which I assumed (and asked, and Aleksei confirmed) meant that "in chambers" consisted not only that he was the patriarch of the royal family, but that he was the big dragon of everything that had anything to do with the Palace.

"You'll need to get her on that," Aleksei warned. "It's my understanding it takes so long to create gowns, females decide on designers in the spring."

Dang it.

"I'll comm her tomorrow," I muttered.

He gave me another squeeze that was more akin to a reassuring shake.

"You needn't worry, love. If Anna is the instigator of this, Dagsbrun will be embarrassed, and therefore, he'll puff and prance. His ambassador will scurry and make demands and do her best to pick apart our evidence. But we won't go to them unless it's ironclad. So in the end, to avoid a massive PR disaster that might mean tensions between our realms, they'll have no choice but to privately apologize for Anna's actions."

I made a face, got another smile from Aleksei, and he carried on talking.

"That's not all. Night's Fall will leave the situation holding a very big marker from Dawn's Break. And Anna will be brought to heel, undoubtedly by marrying her off to a lesser aristocrat who will nevertheless be strong enough to keep her controlled. And this will be the height of punishment for Anna, I assure you. He could have masses of power and credit, and he still wouldn't be good enough for Princess Anna of Dawn's Break, according to her. But onward from this, I'll continue to have to put up with her in those rare times we're at the same events, which will not be easy, but I could do it. However, you'll have to do the same, and that will prove most difficult, but I have no choice but to best the endeavor."

"So this is a massive headache for you, but mostly, you're upset the female you knew and cared about might turn out to be one serious asshole, and you can't tell her to go fuck herself and be done with her."

That brought me a glamorous white grin. "Exactly."

I was not smiling when I said, "I'm sorry, honey."

He shook his head, took a sip of his drink, and replied, "Don't be. We're getting closer to the threat being neutralized, if, indeed, they intend to carry it through now that we've found each other. Your beast will emerge very soon. I've done that bloody interview, and both of our approval ratings are up, something neither of us care about, but it's making Mom and Germaine stay off our backs. We'll get through the engagement photo op and interview, we'll deal with your bloody parents, and then we can fucking relax for a while. At least until the Masque."

He might be able to.

I was way behind on work.

I didn't mention that.

I said, "Do you want to finish that?" I tipped my head to his drink. "Or do you want to go to bed?"

He leaned forward and set his glass on the table in front of the couch. He then took mine and did the same.

But he replied, "I don't want to go to bed."

I fought pouting.

Aleksei twisted into me, taking me to my back on the couch.

My belly dropped and my sex flooded.

"We're going to fuck right here," he murmured, his eyes lazy with banked purple fire.

"That's good for me," I wheezed.

That earned me another grin.

Then I got a kiss.

After that, I got well and truly fucked on the couch.

Mixed bag evening with the Anna news.

But for the most part, our couch action put the cherry on top of an awesome night.

CHAPTER 28

ONE

The next evening, we were on the couch, and I was multitasking, because I was screwed.

I had my tablet hovering in front of me (Aleksei showed me it also had hovering capabilities, which was so cool it was *unreal*) and I'd entered the measurements of the heroine of the movie I was working on into the Seam-Stitch at the studio. Now I was selecting the textiles to go with each part of the pattern and entering all her costumes into the queue, so the Seam-Stitch could build them.

What screwed me was, I'd left it too long. The Seam-Stitch had a big backlog that had been programmed in by other productions. With each costume I was entering, the estimated time of completion was just the day before the fitting appointment I had with the actress playing heroine, which was four days from now.

I needed to get all of them entered before someone else threw something at the system and slowed my roll.

I also needed to get the other characters' designs entered, because the fitting appointments were stacking up and I didn't need the stress, or what it would say to Bodi that his suddenly very famous costume designer was falling down on the job just weeks before we were to begin filming.

I had a feeling he cared more that his actors had something to wear than he did about me finding my mate.

Aleksei was on his back on the couch beside me, his head on my thigh, reading a book (yep, a real one!), his long legs up, calves resting on the back of the couch, ankles crossed, showing again his capacity to be cute.

Nova was lounged on him, stomach to stomach, purring loudly because she was with her chosen one, and he was stroking her, head and booty (again with the cute).

And my multitasking included my work with the Seam-Stitch, my fingers playing with a curl of Aleksei's hair (see? hover capacity with tablets ruled!), and I was on a comm with my friend, the designer, Lancet.

"I've been *waiting* for you to *comm* about this since the minute I saw you on the dragon's *back*!" he complained. "Now, I don't even have a *month*."

I'd had a conversation with no less than four people that day (Nata, Allain, Queen Calisa and Germaine) about whether I should design my gown for the Masque or honor another designer with outfitting me for my first public and official event as Aleksei's mate and the future queen.

Allain and Queen Calisa said designer, because this would highlight the talent of a citizen of Night's Fall, something I would need to consider doing on the regular.

Nata and Germaine said me, because they felt it would show the realm my talent, and make them feel they knew a little more about me.

I decided Lancet, because he was immensely talented, but his label was relatively new, and he needed the exposure.

And because he was a friend.

"I have some ideas," I told him, touching my stylus on the enter button on my tablet to send off another costume, then pulling up the next one.

"No you don't," Lancet returned. "I know you. I knew you'd be loyal to me. Do you think I've been twiddling my thumbs the last week?"

I sensed something from Aleksei and looked down at him.

His eyes were on his book, but his lips were tipped up.

He liked I had good friends.

It was safe to say, I did too.

"I'm sending you my thoughts. I've designed three looks," Lancet said, then warned, "The first one is my favorite, so you better pick that."

The little screen he was on in the corner of my tablet shifted to the pic of a gown, so I said, "Enlarge," and it filled my display.

I gasped.

"I knew you'd love it!" I heard Lancet's voice crow over the vision of the gown.

I didn't love it.

I'd begun *living for it*.

A massive skirt of impossibly rich amethyst ombréed up to the strapless bodice of crystal-encrusted lilac. The precisely corrugated folds of the skirt, as well as the front of the bodice, were adorned by spikes of intricate, sparkling silver filigree. There was a narrow crystal belt at the nipped-in waist. But the showstopper was the dozens upon dozens of little butterfly appliqués that danced along the hem and up the skirt in every hue from the deepest amethyst to softest lilac.

It was ridiculously feminine. Utterly fantastical.

It was the fantasy dream dress of every little girl who grew up not expecting much, but in the end she found her prince and became a princess.

Best part, the theme for this year's Masque was "Soaring," and Lancet's take on that with the butterflies was *genius*.

"Look at the mask," Lancet said, and my display changed to a mask that appeared like he intended it to be made of actual silver.

One side was an elaborate butterfly wing adorned with amethyst jewels. The other side was just the eye mask, but it was covered in shimmery purple scrollwork, save for a swirl of latticework that burst out of a corner.

"This gown needs to be handmade, Laura," Lancet warned. "No Seam-Stitch could do it justice. So it's going to take weeks."

With that elaborate of a gown, I didn't doubt it.

A Seam-Stitch could usually pump out any number of items of apparel in just hours, depending on the difficulty of the pattern and the capacity of the unit.

The studio had an industrial level Seam-Stitch.

I had a mid-level business unit at my studio (and I was probably going to need to use it as backup to get some of my costumes done).

Lancet, I knew, had an artisan level, which was slower, but not that slow.

All that said, nothing beat handmade. Not ever.

"And then there are fittings," Lancet went on. "I need to start immediately. And the metalwork on the mask also needs to be handmade. I've made inquiries, and the craftsbeing I want says it'll take at least two weeks, but probably longer."

"Get started," I gushed. "We're done. I love you. It's perfect. I don't know where you got the butterfly idea, but it's life. I'm actually *living* for those butterflies right now. I'd marry you if you weren't mated, and I wasn't too. I can't believe you pulled my fat out of the fryer on this one. I'll never forget it."

The gown disappeared and Lancet's face came back on my display.

"You'll never forget it when it comes to your wedding gown?" he hinted.

Aleksei grunted.

Hmm.

"Aleksei kind of wants me to design that."

I watched Lancet frown.

"In a couple of days, I have to stand in a garden or somewhere for our engagement announcement and do an interview after. You have anything for that?" I offered.

"Dearest Laura," Lancet sighed. "Did you miss the fact that my staff and I will be busy making your Midnight Masque gown? You really cannot throw these things at me at the last minute."

Aleksei grunted again.

I fought laughing.

"I have a new aide, Lance. So you'll get far more notice in the future," I assured him.

"I'll re-jig the queue on my Seam-Stitch. What color are you thinking?" he asked.

"You can use the one at my studio," I told him.

That unit was going to be busy, but my engagement photo/interview ensemble was definitely a priority.

It seemed like everything was a priority.

"And it should definitely be purple," I continued. Then got to the tough part. "It has to be—"

"If you think I can't do classic and understated, but *divine*, watch me," he declared.

And then without saying goodbye, the screen went blank.

He tended to be fanciful and embellished, or willowy and mysterious (yes, he could be both, that was why he was so talented), so if he didn't tone those down, things were going to get real.

But I couldn't think on that now. I'd worry about it later.

I had other things to worry about presently.

I switched gears to focus to the costume and returned to work, thinking I hated to admit it, but I couldn't wait for Nata to get a handle on my life.

Things were ramping up with work. I had an appointment for tea with Queen Calisa the next afternoon (if my quarantine was lifted, which it didn't seem it would be, my beast was taking her sweet time). And Aleksei had decided to double that up, since I'd be at the Palace, with he and King Fillion meeting with my parents (and that was the only thing that would make me not want my wee beast back, using it as an opportunity to postpone that nightmare).

I had yet to decide if I would attend that meeting, but it was scheduled after the tea.

There was also the Masque on my mind, of course. And Aleksei wanted to take me to Spikeback Castle (and I couldn't wait to go). Not to mention, the next photo op was looming, during which I'd be wearing my engagement ring, something I didn't have yet, and something that I worried about because, well…I was me.

That being picky when it came to stuff like that.

The entire collection of royal jewels was available to pull up on a digipane. I'd located the purple topaz set Queen Calisa referred to, and the ring was a cushion-cut topaz, surrounded by unusually large round diamonds intermingled with perfectly same-sized pearls. The coronet was narrow, but lovely, and the matching necklace and earrings the same.

It was from the Revivalist Era of the 1700s, when the style was to be compact, but the gems selected were sizable in an effort to pack a punch that screamed how much money you had.

It was pretty, but I didn't love it.

No, I'd stumbled on a pleasantly not too big, and definitely not too small octagon aquamarine stacked side to side with four long (though the outer ones were shorter) diamond baguettes. The matching coronet was more like a priceless aquamarine and diamond headband, and it came with no other pieces, just those two.

The design was from the Insouciant Riche era, one of my favorites, where the look was cleaner, geometric, but opulent and, for the time, very (even shockingly) modern.

The realms then had been moving away from horses and carriages and into automobiles and technology, and art moved with it.

To me, it said things didn't have to be formal, overly worked and ornamented to denote luxury and class.

So, to me, it made a statement, and not just about my taste.

Of course, I'd happily wear whatever Aleksei gave me.

But I wished I'd never seen that ring (just in case he didn't pick that one).

I focused on my costume and entering textiles.

"Is your comm done?" Aleksei asked.

"He disconnected me, yes," I answered.

"Do you want me to get started on dinner?" he asked.

I kept my attention on what I was doing on my tablet, but answered, "I have two more costumes to enter into the program. Then I'll get to it. It's my turn."

"Darling, work. I can cook."

At that, I looked down at him.

And dang.

Prince Aleksei, my heart's desire, was lounged on a couch with his head on my leg.

I am so totally and completely and limitlessly and enormously falling in love with you.

This thought warmed me, toes to tendrils, as I gazed down at his male beauty, consumed by all I was feeling.

"I thought I'd make creamy garlic pasta," I said softly.

A glow came from his dusky gaze.

He heard the words I spoke.

And the ones left unspoken.

Before I could react to that, my body jerked violently, and I rasped out a coarse breath.

Nova took a dash as Aleksei shot up to sitting.

My body caught fire.

"Alek—" I started.

He grabbed my hand, pulled me out of the couch and dragged me to the steps to the sunken room.

"Clothing, love," he warned.

He let me go, and still moving, I whipped off my top.

He yanked off his shirt.

We were racing to the steps to the landing pad.

"Doors open!" he barked.

I pulled down my lounge pants, just as all that was happening became too much, thus I nearly fell over.

Aleksei swung me up in his arms and sprinted up the stairs.

I felt the night air coming in through the doorway above, but it was happening, and I couldn't stop it.

Panic coursed through me.

There wasn't going to be enough room.

"Aleksei," I whispered urgently.

Two steps from the top, he hurled me bodily through the door.

My world burst in pearlescent pink stars.

And I landed on her clawed feet.

Her long neck turned just in time to see the ferocious black dragon explode from the stairwell, immediately taking flight.

He made a half circle and banked, coming back in.

Seeing him right there, with the excess of energy bounding through her, she hunched, then took to the skies.

He glided to her side.

He soared.

She rolled, spun and dipped.

When she dipped, he zoomed under her, his wingspan wide, his body powerful, guiding her to the airspace above the courses of crafts zipping around the city.

Mindlessly, finally free, she gloried in the movement, the wind whispering through the silken strands of her long, pearlescent pink fur, caressing the sheer coral and gold feathers that burst from the back of her head in the place of horns or spikes, the night breeze rustling through the opalescent feathers of her wings.

She played with the wind.

She played with him.

Swooping and gliding and climbing and bombing.

He kept her safe, away from tall buildings, out of the path of crafts.

She made flight a dance.

He made it a sentry.

She teased him, gliding below him, her wingspan half of his, she reached, twining their long necks, her silken fur tangling with his fearsome spikes.

At the touch, his dragon roared.

She detached on a delighted whinny and ascended toward the quarter moon.

He followed her.

Flight was a frolic. A scamper. A romp.

And he kept her safe through it, until he sensed her energy waning.

And then he guided her home.

They landed, and with a pretty sneeze, she became me again.

He shook his body and became Aleksei.

We looked at each other.

And then I was over his shoulder.

Down the steps, with the doors whooshing closed behind us.

Up the steps, with the door to our bedroom remaining open.

My hair flew as he tossed me on my back on the bed.

Then he fell to his knees on the floor, pulled my behind to the edge, opened my legs, buried his face between them, and his mouth was gorging on me.

I came on contact.

He still fed, and fed...and *fed*.

And I came...and came...*and came*.

Then, with a hungry gasp, I was off the bed, on my feet.

He turned me roughly, shoved my torso forward and my hands hit the mattress.

He entered from behind.

And I cried out as I came again.

His fucking was staggeringly brutal, totally complete.

It cemented in me then. Our bond. Our mating.

I would never take another cock. I would never have another lover. I'd never want another male.

We were four, and two, and only one.

Forever intertwined.

Forever the others.

He fucked me onto the bed, took me to my belly and fucked me into it.

He planted his hands in the cheeks of my behind, arched into his final thrust, burying his cock to the hilt, and roared his release.

I felt the erotic strain of his body through his immense orgasm, and at the power of it, I shuddered beneath him.

He fell to me, his weight in his forearms at my sides, his chest covering my back, my legs splayed, his hips between them, his cock still hard inside me.

"Fucking hell," he grunted.

I smiled into the duvet.

"She's a menace in the skies," he groused.

My smile got bigger. "Not usually. I had zero control over her."

He slipped out gently, pushed up, turned me, then lowered himself to me again.

"She nearly flew straight into the Titian building," he bitched.

I sucked my lips in and gave him big eyes.

He was genuinely disgruntled, because he'd clearly been alarmed.

But I was both elated and exhausted. I didn't know how long we flew, but I did know it was for a while.

And let us not forget, I'd just orgasmed about fifteen times, so I was further seriously mellow.

"She's also fucking gorgeous," he went on. "A million times more beautiful than the pic. Bloody fucking hell, all I could think, and he could think, was getting you back here so I could fuck you, and off she goes, dive-bombing a TrailLiner."

"Sorry," I whispered, trying not to laugh.

"Do you know how hard it is to stop a creature from crashing into a building when all you can think about is your cock?" he asked irritably.

"If it makes you feel better, you did an admirable job. We're both here, safe and sound."

"Fucking bloody hell," he grouched.

I sucked my lips in again.

It took him a bit, but he got it together, his face softened, and he ran his knuckles along my hairline.

"Gods, *bissi*, she's beyond stunning."

That meant...it meant...

The whole wide world to me.

I smiled at him.

"And she's back," he whispered.

My eyes filled with tears.

"She's back," I whispered in return.

Then I lost it.

He held me as I cried.

She nestled contentedly in my chest.

He flapped off his lingering displeasure and settled in Aleksei's.

Finally.

We were four.

We were two.

We were one.

✦ ✦ ✦

The lightest touch on my chest woke me in the middle of the night.

"Shh, love, don't move," Aleksei murmured so low into my ear, I barely heard him.

I was on my back.

His long body was curled into my side.

What was happening filtered through my sleepy brain.

And I remained perfectly still while Jupiter got the courage to step fully onto my chest, whereupon he curled into a little cat ball.

My beast pulsed her warm welcome.

Jupiter started purring.

Aleksei started petting.

More tears filled my eyes (these I managed to control), as I whispered, "Yes, baby. She's home."

✦ ✦ ✦

"Darling, wake up."

I pried my eyes open and squinted against the bright sun.

"Gluh," I muttered, and I was surprised I could, because the rest of my body refused to move.

"Roll over, Laura. I have coffee," Aleksei said.

"I can't."

I heard his chuckle.

"Seriously," I mumbled into the pillow. "I was there, but still, how hard did you fuck me?"

His chuckle turned into a laugh.

I heard two coffee cups hitting the nightstand, then I was moved, pillows were adjusted, fluffed, and I was positioned to partially upright but draped into Aleksei's side as he rejoined me in bed, propped up on pillows.

With no other choice, I let him take my weight.

"Do you want your coffee?" he asked.

"In a minute," I mumbled.

"You didn't get your work done last night," he reminded me.

"Ugh," I moaned.

"I'll go make you an energy lift smoothie in a minute," he murmured.

That might help.

Might.

I felt him sip coffee.

Then he set the cup aside and the edge of a tablet came into view.

"*Beauty and the Beast,*" he said like he was reading something.

I put superhuman effort into tipping my head back to look at him, and yes.

He was reading.

"*Yesterday evening, as if they were intent to give us a preview of their upcoming engagement announcement but were determined to outdo themselves with their spectacular flight, His Royal Highness, the True Heir, Prince Aleksei took to the skies with his mate, Laura Makepeace.*"

I pushed up further, breathing, "Oh my gods."

I focused on the pic that accompanied the article.

A perfect telephoto shot, in color, of my beast gliding, neck intwined with his creature, against a backdrop of a gleaming crescent moon and the pinprick of stars in the night sky.

"*No two beasts could seem more incongruous, thus more perfectly matched, than the mightiest of all dragons, and the most uniquely stunning. Crafts ground to a halt. Beings stopped on the streets or ran to windows, Palms raised, as a fairytale played out in the skies. It is a surety that the words 'Long Live Prince Aleksei and his Future Queen were not only on this writer's lips.*"

"Stop reading," I begged.

"They got the 'Beauty' part right, I'm a little stung by being the 'Beast.'"

I looked at his face and was relieved to see he was teasing.

"People saw us," I said.

He was smiling when he replied, "Of course they did, darling. You nearly ran into twenty buildings and about a hundred crafts."

I buried my face in his neck.

My beast tittered.

His surged and settled.

Okay, those two reacting to each other took no time getting used to, not to mention understand completely.

It was easy.

And perfection.

Aleksei dropped the tablet to his lap and curled his fingers around the side of my neck.

"*Uniquely stunning*," he said into the top of my hair. "It's not only me and my creature who think so. It's all over the news, all over the tapes. I'd say you're back in the nineties for your rating, darling. Germaine is probably doing back flips in the admin wing."

"They like her."

"Did you miss the 'fairytale played out in the skies' part?" he asked playfully.

"They like her," I repeated.

His fingers tensed at my neck.

And his voice was vastly different when he vowed, "I will tear them apart."

I lifted my head.

And yeah.

His expression was vastly different too.

"Aleksei—"

"Not physically, but that doesn't mean I don't want to."

"I'll get used to it," I promised.

"Medical science bested the removal of scars over a hundred years ago," he stated. "The kind you have never disappears. Not unless you have your memories scrubbed."

"I don't...I can't." I shook my head. "It made me *me*."

"I don't say that because I advise it, Laura. It should only be used for the most traumatic of traumas, because you're right, any scrubbing alters a being, and I'll take you any way you come, but the you I have in bed right now is perfect, and I want to keep her like she is."

"Oh my gods!" I exploded, pushing away from him. "Lancet's perfect princess gown. Getting her back last night. The Jupiter thing. Stop it. I can't take any more. Don't make me cry again!"

His brows rose. "Perfect princess gown?"

I slapped his chest.

He wrapped both arms around me and pulled me to it.

"First, you captivated a realm with your bravery," he said. "Then you set it alive with your compassion. And you've done it again with your beast's beauty."

"You're not helping me not to cry," I warned.

"How's this? Your vid won't have any costumes if you don't get your ass in gear."

"That's better," I mumbled.

"Drink your coffee. I'll get your tablet. Work in bed while I make breakfast. I'll bring it up."

I was seriously down with this plan, and because I was, I reached beyond him to my coffee cup. "You could also stop being so awesome, it's giving me a complex."

He pressed his lips to my temple before he said, "You weren't called the 'Beast.'"

He got out of bed.

I took a much-needed sip of coffee and asked his departing back. "Is that really bothering you, *drahko*?" When he turned to me, I added, "Because I think he's handsome. Scary as farg. But handsome."

"He's hideous and terrifying. Because he needs to be. Cretins like Arnaud wouldn't quake in their boots if he wasn't." One side of his lips went up. "I'm teasing, darling. I am gladly the Beast to your Beauty. We are a fairytale after all."

Dropping that world-rocking nugget, he strolled out.

I am so totally and completely and limitlessly and enormously and endlessly falling in love with you, I thought.

My beast sighed.

Comet jumped up on the bed and shared Aleksei didn't give him enough breakfast.

I set my coffee aside, reached, snatched him to my chest, shoved my face into his soft fur and decided it was good I lived a life with no dreams.

Because when they came true anyway, it sure was something.

CHAPTER 29
VALUES

"Oh my gods! It's stunning! The butterfly detail is *lie*-yeef!" Princess Aleece exclaimed. "Look, Mom. Isn't it perfect?"

She passed my Palm to Queen Calisa.

I took a sip of tea.

Queen Calisa had invited her daughter to our get together, which I thought was cool since I wanted to get to know her better, and she was so down to earth, it helped with my nerves at hanging with a queen.

We were in another room on the second level of the Palace. This one was decorated in salmon, butter yellow, and bone. It was feminine and refined.

We sat on sofas opposite each other and perpendicular to a fireplace edged in gold-veined, ivory marble. The layout of a traditional tea, complete with finger sandwiches, biscuits and little cakes, was on the table between us.

I'd since learned that I didn't have to formally curtsy in times like these (Aleksei told me what Timothee's mention of "dropping a formal" meant, and further explained Madam Garwah probably didn't mention it because, "She's not family, love. I doubt she knows the inner workings of the things we do that are unseen by the public.").

I still needed to curtsy. But just a bob.

This I'd done when I'd arrived, and weirdly, it seemed natural.

Queen Calisa squinted at my Palm in a way I wondered if she needed her eyes lased.

"It is quite stunning," she murmured, then offered my Palm to me.

I reached across the table and took it.

"Who is the designer again?" the queen asked.

"Lancet," I answered. "He's just emerging on the scene. Me wearing a design of his, I think, will be helpful to him."

"Rest assured, it will," she replied, vaguely wafting off the essence of pleased that I went with her advice before she shook it off and daintily sipped tea.

I was beginning to like Aleksei's mom unreservedly. She wasn't a warm female, but she was danged cool.

But I fought checking the time on my Palm.

My parents would be headed here soon.

And I had a decision to make.

I knew Aleksei's ploy with this. Tie me up with his mother and sister, something I would think I couldn't get away from, and that way I'd let him non-physically "tear them apart" without being there.

But before he went to a breakfast meeting that morning, I'd put my foot down. I made him promise he would connect with me before meeting with them.

He promised by kissing me deeply first, then giving me the words after.

It was a good way to make a promise.

But since then, no matter how often it clogged in my brain (and it clogged my brain often), I hadn't made the decision.

"You've needed to defer instruction with Madam Garwah, considering your quarantine," the queen broke into my reverie. "But now that the unpleasant business that muted your beast is concluded, you'll be resuming, yes?" And this last was an order veiled in a question.

"I only have a couple of sessions left, and I'm back on it this evening," I assured her.

"Excellent," she murmured.

"Your beast and Aleksei's are so perfect," Aleece mooned, sitting back in the corner of their couch, crossing her legs, her expression dreamy. "I'm totally waiting until I find my mate."

Queen Calisa gave her daughter a sharp look.

Mm.

Seemed the queen had other plans for the princess.

"Destiny obviously knows what it's doing," Aleece decreed. "Sure, it makes me throw up a little in my mouth to say this, but there's no denying my big brother is not hard on the eyes. He's all dark and big and male, and you're all blonde and rosy and female, and your beasts are just the same."

She frowned. "Not to mention, Anna used to complain all the time that it annoyed her he preferred to stay in, cook, read, chill. She was a nightlife kind of female."

For a bright moment, I forgot about my parents' imminent visit and considered this.

I considered it more as Aleece continued speaking.

"He's always been like that. He liked the quiet spaces. Preferring to be in his suite, reading or studying. Out taking the dogs for a walk. Holed in the corner of the library. He was all about perfecting the art of the chill. Tim and Rol teased him about it all the time, but he didn't care. That was just who he was. The fact you two have that in common is double, ultra mega. Everyone thinks Aleksei is this whirlwind. He's not. He's a long storm." She grinned. "Sometimes a thunderstorm, but that doesn't happen very often."

There was a lot there: the annoying fact his brothers teased him about enjoying the things he enjoyed, a deepening understanding of why he bonded with my cats so easily (he was clearly an animal person).

But I was taken aback she knew this about us, even if I knew that Aleksei was close to his sister. Apparently, they talked. Somewhat deeply.

I was also silently reeling, because I'd been living this with Aleksei for days, and it hadn't occurred to me he was a homebody.

Just like me.

I was feeling all warm and squishy inside when Queen Calisa said, "Quite. Now, Laura, it's come to my attention you intend to continue working. I can understand you wish to honor your obligation on your current project but—"

"Mom, give it up," Aleece warned. "I know you want to pretend, since he stepped back from royal duties and put effort into making his own money, that every time Germaine unleashes a poll about why Aleksei's popularity continues to soar, respondents don't say it was because he stepped back from royal duties and put effort in making his own money. But they do."

Queen Calisa's mouth formed a mew, but she said nothing.

Aleece turned to me. "Days gone by, our ancestors filled their chests with gold, silver, copper, you name it, taxed from the people. Then again, we used it to build roads and schools and whatever. We were also the first to fly and put ourselves in danger when some idiot, usually from Sky's Edge, did something stupid. And it was all on our heads to make laws and carry out punishments and stuff, which had to be a royal pain." She smiled again. "Pun intended."

I smiled back at her.

She carried on, "But some bright bulb in our past invested in real estate and stuff like that, which made buckets. Now all of us and the entire Palace run on residuals and interest. We don't cost the citizens of the Fall a single shilling."

I had no idea that was the case.

Actually, it never occurred to me to wonder where their money came from.

But seriously, those investments must have been stellar for the residuals and interest to fund this setup.

"Still," she continued, "part of why Timothee and Errol languish in the polls, notwithstanding their penchants for acting like twits..."

The queen made a genteel sound of disapproval.

Aleece ignored it and carried on.

"Is that they're considered wastrels. It's half what they get up to when they're out living it up, getting drunk and femaleizing, and half the fact that they're constantly out getting drunk and femaleizing." She turned to her mother. "People work, Mom. Most people work hard. And they respect other people who do."

"They respect me, and I don't *work*," Queen Calisa retorted.

Aleece scoffed. "You work harder than any of us, it's just that the estate pays you an allowance instead of some boss giving you a salary. I mean, how many appearances do you have scheduled this week?"

The queen didn't answer her daughter.

She said to me, "It's a fulfilling way to spend your time, Laura. And there is much good you can do without putting much effort into doing it. Like how you'll benefit that designer by wearing his gown. It might even change his life."

"Keep your job if you love doing it, Laura," Aleece encouraged. "We've got it covered on our end."

"I'm actually a little worried about this," I admitted. "I'm not super outgoing. I have friends and I like going out, it's just that, like your brother"—I smiled at Aleece—"I prefer quiet time at home, and there are times I can be shy."

Queen Calisa seemed to be considering this, but Aleece immediately replied, "Then do you. I promise, your ratings will stay high if you do."

I was feeling a tad bit alarmed at all the ratings talk.

"Is this, uh...*ratings thing* a, well...big deal for you all?" I asked.

Aleece shot a pointed look at her mother.

Queen Calisa answered, "As my daughter explained, our dragons do not fly, and we no longer bear the entire brunt of the governance of this land. But we do have votes in the Center, and we must understand how our citizens wish us to cast them, something you can learn by being out among them. Though, you can learn more by conducting polls. Also, we continue to reign at the pleasure of the people. If that pleasure should wane..."

She let that trail.

Aleece picked it up. "Then we'd just be a super-rich family that lives in a palace and owns all sorts of stuff. But Mom and Dad, me, Tim and Rol wouldn't have anything to do."

No less alarmed.

I mean, my mate was the first True Heir in two centuries.

Was something up I didn't know about?

"Is there something I've been missing? Is there some threat to the monarchy?" I asked.

Aleece shook her head, but said, "There are anti-monarchists, for sure. Folks who don't think we've got the right to represent Night's Fall in the Center and think we embody a dead, antiquated system that needs to be cast aside. But there have always been those kinds of beings. That said, they're right. There is no real purpose for us. Except, like Mom said, we do good. We open hospitals and shine light on issues and make beings feel special, just because they shook our hands. It doesn't seem to have much meaning, but it does."

"We represent this realm, and its values," Queen Calisa put in. "Think how Sky's Edge is perceived. The vast majority who live in the Edge are probably very lovely people. But their current king is a deviant and a tyrant. So the beings who live there are colored by his brush."

I set my teacup in its saucer and put it on the table, saying, "I hadn't thought of it like that."

"And straight up, after we've had the throne for *forever*," Aleece began, "it would suck if we were the ones who let it come to nothing."

I smiled at her. "I hadn't thought of that either."

My head tipped to the side and my smile became private when my beast and I felt them coming near.

Both women looked beyond me, but I knew who was entering the room before I twisted to peer over my shoulder.

Aleksei and his dad were walking in, King Fillion's gaze on his wife, mine was on my mate, his was on me.

I started to stand, but the king said, "Please, please, stay comfortable," before he bent to kiss his wife's cheek.

When he arrived, my male touched his mouth to my lips.

My beast wiggled.

His flexed.

Gods, they were so cute together.

Aleksei reached out, taking a little iced cake, greeting his sister and mother before he lounged in the couch beside me and popped the cake in his mouth.

I took him in.

This was a new Aleksei. The prince of the realm who was perfectly comfortable eating a tiny cake, slouched on a sofa that was also probably a priceless antique, this sofa in a massive palace.

It was hot.

He turned his head, caught me staring at him, and his eyes changed.

And now he was hotter.

"Enjoy tea?" he murmured.

"Yes," I replied, still sitting primly, because the king and queen might be his mom and dad, and they would be my mother- and father-in-law, but they were still my king and queen.

His gaze raked the length of me, the look in his eyes deepened, and it took a lot not to visibly shiver, or alternately throw myself at him.

"If you two would stop having eye sex across the table from us—" Aleece began.

My head whipped her way, and I felt my cheeks warm.

"Aleece!" Queen Calisa snapped.

Aleece ignored her, grinning at us and finishing, "It'd help a lot with my sudden urge to vomit all over the tea service."

"Our children, Fillion," the queen complained.

King Fillion, however, was studying his watch unit.

He looked to Aleksei and nodded.

Aleksei straightened.

Oh boy.

"Your parents are at the guard terminal on the mainland," he said quietly.

Dang, heck, dang, and *farg*.

"What's this?" Queen Calisa inquired.

"Aleksei and I have granted the Makepeaces an audience," King Fillion explained.

"You've done *what*?"

The ice in her words frosting the entire room took my mind off the decision I no longer had any time to procrastinate in making and brought my attention to her.

"Dearest," the king murmured.

"Why wasn't I informed of this?" she demanded.

"It's not a formal visit," the king explained. "We'll speak to them in the receiving room—"

"You will do nothing of the sort," the queen snapped. She clicked open a handbag tucked at her side, pulled out a Palm, glared at the display and instructed it, "Comm Dita."

"Caly," the king clipped.

I felt Aleksei's mouth at my ear. "When we discussed giving them an audience, I explained things to Dad. My guess with Mom's reaction, he explained them to her as well."

I wasn't sure I understood what was going on, outside the fact they knew of my history with my parents, something I didn't know how to feel about it, but I didn't have time to figure it out.

"Your majesty." A voice came from the queen's Palm.

"There are beings at the guard terminal. They're expected. When they arrive, take them directly to the throne room."

"Caly!" the king bit.

She didn't miss a beat and kept issuing orders. "Two chairs at audience distance. Do not offer them refreshments."

"Yes, your majesty," the voice replied.

"Tick me when they're settled," the queen said.

"Will do, your majesty."

The queen tucked her Palm back in her purse as the king blustered, "This is precisely why I didn't tell you. I knew you'd horn in just like this."

She took a sip of tea and, completely unperturbed, replied, "You know me so well."

"They're Laura's parents," the king stated. "We're meeting them like civilized beings in the receiving room."

"The receiving room is for honored diplomats," she retorted. "Elected officials. Nobles of good standing. It is *not* for the likes of *those two beings*."

I was suddenly feeling a lot, but I didn't have time for that either.

"What's this about?" Aleece asked.

"You will come with us," the queen told her instead of answering. "United front."

On the words *united front*, Aleece gave Aleksei big eyes.

"It'll be Aleksei and I," the king stated.

"It will be all of us, Fillion. *All of us*. And you know why," she retorted.

Aleksei took my hand before he said, "Laura has yet to decide if she'll join us."

"Pish," the queen returned. "She will stand with her family."

Stand with her family.

Oh yeah.

I was feeling a lot.

Aleksei's voice was inflexible when he started, "Mother—"

"She'll stand with her family, son," she repeated.

"I'll go," I said softly.

And I would go because, one day, I was going to be Queen Calisa. One day, I was going to stand for the values of this realm.

No, I already did.

I couldn't hide from this. I couldn't let others face it for me.

I had to stand for myself.

If this family intended to stand for me, I would stand with this family.

Aleksei's hand squeezed mine.

"You don't have to, darling, no matter what my mother says," Aleksei assured.

I looked to him. "I'll go, honey."

His study of my face was a veritable examination, and I knew he wasn't certain of his conclusions when he asked, "Are you sure?"

No, I was not.

Though, I also was.

I nodded.

"If you're uncomfortable in the slightest," the king said, "you shouldn't go. Or if you feel uncomfortable while it's happening, you should feel free to leave." He looked to Aleksei. "Comm Allain. Tell him to wait outside the door. If Laura needs to leave, he can escort her to your suite."

Aleksei pulled out his Palm.

"I'll be fine," I asserted.

The king sat on the arm of the sofa by his wife, his focus on me. "My dear, there will be many times in the service of the throne you'll be uncomfortable. When some old windbag has your ear and doesn't want to give it up and you can't get away. When some pompous ambassador pontificates ad nauseum, and you don't agree with a single thing he says, but you have to keep your mouth shut. When some aristocrat gets on a tear of self-aggrandizing, and all you want is to tell him to be quiet, but you cannot. However, this is not one of those times." He peered down at his wife. "And no, Caly. I don't care what protocol dictates. These beings aren't meaningful. If she wants to leave, she'll go."

"I didn't say a word, Fillion," the queen replied. "Goodness, of course, if she wants to leave, she'll go."

Aleksei and Aleece were exchanging meaningful glances, but my parents were right then being processed to enter the castle (whatever that entailed, I'd ask Aleksei later).

I needed to focus on the fact I was going to see them for the first time in over a decade, that they probably weren't expecting me, and the reason they were here was because I'd landed myself the mate to end all mates, so they were probably going to ask for something.

I also had to focus on the hope that Aleksei wouldn't go back on his assertion he wasn't going to literally tear them apart.

"We should address what has so far been left undiscussed," the queen declared.

I pulled myself out of my thoughts and focused on her.

"Timothee and Errol," she went on.

Oh dear.

The king seemed to tense. Aleece was gazing with great interest into her teacup. Aleksei sighed.

"First, our apologies to you, Laura, for how terribly they've behaved in your presence. Twice," she said.

"Family is family, these things happen," I replied.

"They do, but the apology is deserved, nevertheless," she returned.

I nodded.

She looked to Aleksei. "Your father and I have spoken to them. They understand you have our full support. As I can never predict their behavior, I can't say how they'll react. I do know both of them have kept to the Palace, because Timothee is sequestered here, but even Errol has done the same. It seems Timothee is sulking, but I have hopes that Errol is considering the error of his ways, and I have further hope for good things."

"Perhaps they're not too old to learn," the king murmured.

"They'll have to be, because they have no choice," Aleksei stated.

Aleece was watching me with unhidden curiosity mixed with concern.

I smiled at her, though I wasn't sure how effective my smile was.

I became sure when her concern visibly deepened.

The queen lifted her hand and looked at her watch.

She then lifted her head and said, "Your parents have arrived."

Ugh.

Here we go.

Dang.

CHAPTER 30

HOME

There was nothing informal about the way we promenaded to the throne room (for your information, that room was down and just beyond the majestic sweep of the stairs, situated at the back of the grand foyer at the main entrance of the Palace, and unfortunately, in these circumstances, not too far of a hike).

The king led with the queen on his arm.

Aleksei, with my hand in his elbow, came next.

Aleece trailed behind.

I saw Allain loitering outside the tall double doors to the throne room.

However, before we entered, when it felt like my lungs had forgotten how to breathe and each step was an effort at endurance—this meaning Aleksei tensed more and more at my side, my beast was jittery, and his was pitching aggressively—the king stopped.

He turned.

He left the queen where she was and came to us.

He put his hand on my shoulder and looked in my eyes.

"They were never your family, Laura. From your birth, you were destined to be with us. Before we enter that room, understand this, dear."

Great.

Now I was also fighting tears.

Safe to say, the king didn't give good first impressions, but he was totally growing on me.

I couldn't do anything but nod.

Aleksei drew me closer.

King Fillion looked to his son and then returned to his wife.

The king's words helped my lungs to breathe, and my legs to be stronger beneath me.

This was a good thing when we walked into the enormous, intimidating but nearly empty throne room.

It was painted daffodil yellow.

Straight ahead, there was a line of massive rectangular windows dressed with extravagant goldenrod curtains replete with silk fringes. They exposed a view of the colorful but austere beauty of the formal gardens of the courtyard.

To the left, against the wall, there was a dais dressed in plush, amethyst carpet, which shone stark against the bright yellow all around.

Atop this, were two thrones with royal-purple velvet upholstery. The larger one was framed in gilt fashioned to look like scales with spikes jutting out dramatically, the smaller one, the same gilt, but this was fashioned as feathers. Adorning the back and sides of the dais, there were sumptuous velvet curtains of amethyst and gold, pulled back with thick silk cords ending in tassels.

And there were two gold chairs situated ten feet in front of the dais, in which my parents were sitting.

My heart squeezed as I watched them come to their feet.

My father bowed. My mother curtsied.

And neither of them did it correctly.

Something about that penetrated my anxiety, calmed me and made me feel...

Well, dang.

It made me feel like I belonged.

The king and queen strode to their thrones (King Fillion, spikes, Queen Calisa, feathers), sat, and Aleksei, Aleece and I arranged ourselves standing around them. Aleece on the queen's side. Aleksei on the king's, with me at his. He had his hand curled firm on the dent in my waist.

"You may sit," the king said.

My parents did this, both of their gazes darting around, taking in the show before them and adjusting to it when they thought they'd only be dealing with the king and Aleksei.

It was then, I understood why Queen Calisa set it up like this.

This was not only a statement of family; it was a statement of status. It was a show of power.

It was intimidation.

It was putting my parents in their place.

Struggling to keep my expression neutral, I took them in.

It was clear they spent money on maintenance. They, like the king and queen, looked much younger than their years.

I had my mother's coloring, my hair honeyed like hers and unlike my father's dark blond. I had my father's body, proportionate with long legs (my mother was petite).

And seeing them after this long, I was struck with what I felt.

No.

With how little of any emotion there was.

Neither of them met my gaze.

No one said anything for so long, it started to feel weird, and then the king spoke.

"You do not wish to hail your daughter?" he asked.

My father's gaze darted to me, and he said, "We wish to...we had hoped..."

He stopped talking, raised his hand as if to adjust his collar, dropped it and said no more.

It struck me he appeared nervous, which was not something I'd seen him be in all the time I knew him.

My mother shot him a look of pure disgust (and that was very familiar), before she said to me, "You're named after her."

My spine went rigid as I understood exactly what she was saying.

Aleksei's fingers dug into my waist, and he clipped, "Unless given leave, you will not address Laura directly."

Mom's lips parted in astonishment.

"Explain this statement," the king demanded.

"I had a mate, your majesty," Dad said. "She passed."

"This is not unknown to me," the king replied.

"He named our daughter after his dead female," Mom spat.

And that was exactly what I understood she was saying.

Oh my *gods*.

Why on earth would he do that?

King Fillion turned to me and asked gently, "Did you know this, dear?"

I shook my head.

"The point of you sharing this?" Aleksei all but barked.

"The point—" Dad began.

"Every time I saw her, or talked to her, or spoke her name," Mom cut in to say, "I was reminded that I was not *her*. I was not the one he wanted.

And every time *he*"—she snapped her head to the side to indicate my father—"did it, he was reminded she was dead."

"And this explains why you broke her wrist, her ribs, and assaulted her beast?" Aleksei asked.

I heard Aleece's sharp gasp.

I watched my father grimace.

"He thinks, now that she has a mate, she'll get it," Mom said.

"She'll understand emotionally and physically abusing a child because she's found her mate?" Aleksei didn't hide his angry incredulity.

"Consider if you lost him," Dad urged me.

My beast curled into herself, probably because Dad was around, but also at the thought of losing Aleksei.

Aleksei's beast, feeling this, pulsated adamantly.

"What did I say about addressing my mate?" Aleksei bit.

"She's my daughter," Dad returned.

"No, sir, she is mine," the king retorted.

I jolted.

Dad visibly did too.

Mom's eyes narrowed.

"Tread carefully from here, understanding this," the king warned.

"Yes, your majesty," Dad acquiesced (Dad! Acquiescing!). "Please, let me assure you, it is agony, losing your mate. Ask your son."

"I would be inconsolable if I lost my queen," the king replied. "And, of course, angry at the gods for taking her from me. But I would not take the anger of my loss out on a single being, especially one of my children."

"With respect, sire, you cannot say that without having experienced the loss, and without having—"

"Your mate," Mom finished for him. "It's all about *his mate*."

"Be quiet, Cetra," Dad whispered harshly.

Here we go.

"I didn't even want to be here, Tern," Mom hissed.

Yep.

Here we go.

"If you two intend to start bickering," the queen warned, "you can do so on your way home. Now explain. What is your purpose here?"

"I've had time to think on it, thirteen years of it, and I simply want Laura to understand," Dad said.

"Our daughter is the True Bride," Mom said at the same time.

Queen Calisa chose to focus on Mom.

"This has not escaped us," she drawled.

"We are her parents," Mom asserted.

"This is debatable, but I have no interest in debating it," the queen returned. "Though I would like you to explain why you said it."

"We received the no contact order," Dad informed them.

"Yes, it is procedure for you to be notified when a no contact is filed against you. And yet, here you are," the king said.

"We didn't know Laura would be here," Dad replied.

"We won't be calling the constabulary, rest assured," the king told him. "However, whether you knew or not, you contacted her mate's family. This is not illegal, but it is dishonorable."

"This is also not bringing the matter forward," Queen Calisa put in.

"We are the parents of the True Bride," Mom reiterated.

"I have no understanding of why you persist in asserting that," the queen retorted.

Mom squared her shoulders. "We have a place in—"

"Don't fucking finish that." Now Aleksei was absolutely barking at them.

I saw Mom's face pale at his tone, and I turned to look at my mate.

Those veins had popped out, and his eyes glowed purple.

"Honey," I whispered.

"We wish to inform you we're filing an intent for reconciliation," Dad announced, but although it was an announcement, you could hear he was nervous.

And again, I jolted.

"Laura?" the king called me.

I looked to him.

He raised his brows.

I shook my head.

He turned to my parents. "Denied."

I could tell it took a lot out of Dad to assert, "With respect, yet again, your majesty, you do not have the authority to deny our request. When an intent for reconciliation is filed, we're guaranteed at least one meeting with our daughter, attended by an adjudicator, before the question of a no contact order is considered valid...or rejected."

He was correct, but they could not be sitting there, doing this, thinking I would reconcile with them when they only came forward because they thought they could get something out of it.

"Allain!" the queen called.

Allain immediately came through the doors.

"Get the Minister of Law and Justice on a comm," she demanded.

"Your majesty," he said and pulled out his Palm.

"If you try to go around this, pull strings, we'll talk to—" Mom began to threaten.

But I cut her off.

"What do you want?" I asked.

With no hesitation, pure and unadulterated Mom, she bitterly fired back, "Oh, can we talk directly to you now?"

"What do you want?" I repeated.

"You're our daughter," she snapped.

"Wait, did we enjoy roast pork by candlelight all the while exchanging presents last Dead Winter and I've forgotten?" I queried.

"You left us, we did not leave you," Mom returned.

"You didn't ask me back," I reminded her. "In fact, I heard nothing from you at all for thirteen years."

"So it's our place to plead and kneel before you after we spent seventeen years providing for you and you simply up and leave without that first glance back?" Mom asked.

I could feel Aleksei, but more, his beast, responding to this, so I had to shut it down.

"Fine. I'll attend a reconciliation meeting," I conceded.

Aleksei's fingers bit into my waist.

I kept talking.

"You can assert to the adjudicator what great parents you were. And then I can share my medical records. I can ask Mr. and Mrs. Truelock to testify regarding how often I was at their house because I couldn't bear being around you and your constant arguments with each other that you never hid from me, and the ugly things you said to me. I can comm the Vinestrongs, and they can tell tales of how you never came to the school plays I designed the costumes for, and sometimes didn't even bother to pick me up after rehearsals and performances, so they had to take me home. I can ask Cat to share the loving story of how Dad lost it and shouted at me for half an hour right in front of her when I accidentally dropped my school tablet, and he had to buy me another one. I'm sure Gayle will be happy to tell the delightful tale of you ripping my Summer Solstice gown to shreds, not because of anything I'd done, but because you were angry at Dad for the seven millionth time. I'd designed that gown. I'd stitched it with my own fingers. You refused to give me the money to buy the materials to replace it, so in the end, I had to borrow something from Cat to wear on my date. Shall I go on?"

"Excuse my interruption, Mistress Laura," Allain called.

Everyone looked to him.

He had his Palm turned our way and there was a male's face on it.

"Please note," the male's voice came from the Palm, "the Ministry of Law and Justice considers this a reconciliation meeting, and any request to reject the no contact order has been denied."

"Thank you, minister," the queen called.

"Your majesty," the male said, and Allain turned the Palm back to himself.

"This is a travesty," Mom declared.

"Again, Mom, *what do you want?*" I asked.

"We have a rightful place in your life," she stated.

"What you mean is, you have a rightful place as parents of a princess of the realm," I amended.

"That is what you'll be, and that is who we are," Mom declared.

"All right, I'll ask a different question," I returned. "How on earth can you think you deserve that respect with the disregard you used in raising me?"

My mother's face twisted. "I didn't want to do this, coming here. Tern has been riddled with guilt since you left…"

My gaze darted to my father to see his riveted to the step of the dais.

Mom kept talking.

"Losing her, it twisted something in him. It was like he thought you'd be her, born again. And then when you weren't, he blamed me."

"He also blamed Laura," the queen pointed out.

"Whatever," my mom returned. "That's what I lived with all my life. A husband who wanted someone else."

"So you came here because you thought you deserved to get something out of the fact that you…*you*…decided to marry a man who had lost his mate, and whatever you were expecting to get out of that didn't come to fruition, so you acted like a bitter cow to everyone around you, including your own daughter? Is that what I'm hearing?" I asked.

"I thought I could make him love me," Mom snapped.

"Newsflash, Mom, acting like an absolute bitch all the time isn't really loveable,' I shot back.

I heard Aleece stifle a laugh.

The king stood.

"Laura, have you said your piece?" he asked.

I opened my mouth, but Mom got there before me.

"We—"

That was as far as she got.

"Aleksei." The king said my mate's name like an order.

Aleksei accepted that order, and he delivered.

Boy, did he.

"You will return to your lives," Aleksei declared. "You will resume them as you've been living them, with no contact with your daughter. You will not contact the Palace for any reason. You will also not speak to any media, even if they're stubborn in their requests for you to do so. You will cease to exist for her, and you will consider her the same for you."

Mom played her ace.

"And we will confirm the interview we have scheduled after this, which we have been assured will be aired precisely after your engagement interview with our daughter."

Dad scowled at Mom like he could burn her to cinders with his gaze.

Aleksei inclined his head as if conceding.

But then he said, "Therefore, I'm sorry to say, if you do that, I will be forced to release the pics I have of you fornicating with Shivell Chevalforce, which I can assure you are quite indelicate."

Dad's inhale of outraged shock could be heard throughout the massive room, and that was good, because it covered my surprised one.

I didn't know him very well, but I did know Shivell Chevalforce was a jerk. He was in my parents' circle, married to a friend of my mother's, but none of them really liked him, he was that much of a jerk.

Mom's face became devoid of color.

"And you, Mr. Makepeace," Aleksei continued, "will shortly be receiving the news that the Revenue Department is right now in the process of administering a warrant for the seizure of all comp units from your home and office."

Dad sat very still.

Aleksei kept going.

"As well as those of a Mr. Neeru Sandslot, who I believe is your partner in a few ventures that have not been appropriately reported on your tax forms."

Dad's face was now devoid of color.

But...*dang*.

Aleksei didn't mess around when he tore someone apart.

"Underpayment of taxes once garners a much different penalty than when it happens twice," Aleksei informed him. "And it's my understanding that the amount left unpaid is much more substantial this time. You could be looking at a prison term of no less than a year, as well as full repayment of the taxes, along with penalties."

"It's revolting that you would use your superior resources to invade our privacy like this," Mom snapped.

"You find that revolting, and showing here to assert your position in this family, which, in case you aren't getting this, you do not have one, after you snapped your daughter's wrist *by accident*, not even caring enough for your child to take heed as you handle her, isn't revolting?" Aleksei asked.

Before Mom could answer, I said, "I'll be releasing my medical history to the media."

Mom closed her mouth.

"I'll do this tomorrow, and this will be a topic of discussion during Aleksei and my interview."

I felt him close in on my back, murmuring, "Darling."

I kept my attention locked on my mother.

"I thought it would be embarrassing, everyone in every realm knowing how you raised me, what you did to me, how you treated me, but I'm coming to understand the fullness of my destiny," I shared. "And there are without a doubt far too many beings who will understand my experience intimately, and who will feel no small assurance we share that in common, no matter how unfortunate it is we do. But more, I survived and thrived, which might, if they're struggling, encourage them that they can too."

"I don't believe that's necessary," Dad said swiftly.

"You would be wrong," I replied. "My decision is made. I'll also be discussing this with the Truelocks and the Vinestrongs. I've been a member of Cat's family since I was eight, Gayle's, since I was nine. They've seen things, they know things, and they can corroborate any assertions I make along with Dr. Fearsome explaining about my remodeled bones. I doubt my friends will mind sitting in front of a cam and sharing their memories. The visit from the RVPB is on record. Your tax penalty is on record. And if Aleksei releases what he has, you'll both have to move to the Three Realms to escape the ire of those of the Fall."

It was all coming to me now, everything, the entirety of it.

And I shared that.

"I have a ninety-four percent approval rating. Go ahead, try to fuck with me. We'll see how that goes. But my advice, once you deal with whatever the HMRD turns up, find somewhere far away, go there and forget you have a daughter. Once I walk out of this room, I can promise, I'll do everything I can to forget about you."

With that, I ignored the enraged expression on my mother's face, the sick one on my father's, and I took Aleksei's hand.

I walked him to the king, where I got up on my toes to kiss his cheek (and he blushed too, like father like son cuteness). I smiled at the queen, Aleece, then Aleksei and I stepped off the dais and exited the room.

I caught Allain's grin of sheer glee and not-minor approval.

Once we left the room, however, it wasn't me guiding Aleksei.

It was Aleksei guiding me.

Up two flights of stairs and to the left, around a corner and into a room that was more like a vestibule.

He turned me into his arms.

I put my hands on his shoulders and looked up at him.

"That was bloody brilliant," he growled, his eyes shining again with amethyst light, but this wasn't anger, it was pride.

I smiled, but my legs were shaking.

He cupped my jaw in his hands. "Are you okay?"

"I'm not sure."

"You don't have to follow through with your threats, darling," he assured.

"I think I need to. I think those of the Fall need to know what they're getting with me."

"If you're absolutely sure, I need to get Allain and Nata on discussions with the being who'll be interviewing us so we can agree a new set of questions."

I nodded.

Aleksei didn't immediately get out his Palm.

He said, "*Bissi*, this is your story to tell, and you can choose not to tell it. I can handle your parents."

"I don't think you understand, Aleksei. I *need* to be the one who handles them. Anyway, stuff like this finds its way out of the darkness. If we get in front of it, we can put it to good use."

He bent as he pulled me up and touched his lips to mine.

"I'm seriously fucking proud of you," he whispered.

My smile was firmer after he said that.

He touched his mouth to mine again.

He let me go, pulled out his Palm and walked us into what had to be his suite of rooms.

It started with a sitting room that was a masculine display of dark, heavily carved wood, a color story of aubergine and myrtle green, the fixtures and furnishings the same as everything else I'd encountered in the Palace, except more welcoming and lived in.

As he spoke to Allain, I noted again how entirely comfortable he was here.

This was his space. His place in the world. His home.

And now, for the first time, I realized it also was mine. It always had been.

Since the day I was born.

I went to the window and peered out to the view of the outer gardens (no less formal, or spectacular, than the courtyard) and the sparkling Dolphin Sea beyond.

I was home here.

I was home at the penthouse.

I was just home.

Because I was Aleksei's.

And Aleksei was mine.

CHAPTER 31
CLOUDS

The next afternoon, I found myself a thirty-year-old female in the middle of a hand slapping fight.

"Laura," Lancet snapped, planting his hands on his hips. "You promised. And may I remind you, you don't have time for this."

He was right. I did promise, and I didn't ever have time for a bitch slapping fight. Especially right now.

I was running late. Not super late, but for what was planned this afternoon, any late was too late.

But in my defense, Lancet was making a big drama about this, and my anxiety was on overload.

"Then let me do it," I tried.

"Do you not trust my vision?" he demanded, pulling out the big guns.

Gah!

I reclined on the killer-cool curve of the chaise in my closet and pouted.

Understanding his victory, I saw his smirk, and for my sanity, I ignored his smirk. I then heard the beeping as Lancet entered the settings before he put the cosme-mask on my face.

More beeping and a, "Sit up," order from Lancet. I sat up and the mane-mate hood was slipped over my hair.

I felt the patting, buffing and brushing on my face, and the tugging and twisting on my scalp.

"I cannot believe you live here," Lancet said. "This place is so mega, it defines a whole new level of mega."

I couldn't speak, because you couldn't move your face when the cosme-mask was at work. The results were always horrifying.

But he wasn't wrong, so I gave him a thumbs up.

"And I can't believe Prince Aleksei is your mate," Lancet continued. "He's so mega, it isn't a redefinition of it. There hasn't been a word invented yet to define how mega he is."

He was so right about that, I gave him two thumbs up.

"I also can't believe you are imminently going to announce your engagement," he went on. "And last, I can't believe you don't have your ring yet!"

That last part got a major thumbs down (though, only in my head).

I couldn't believe it either.

In fact, I was beginning to get worried about it.

Had Aleksei forgotten?

His day was even busier than mine, so he wanted me to meet him at his office before the photo op and interview. We were going from there to the Palace to sit down with Germaine to hash out how I would answer the questions we'd agreed for the interview. After that, the photo op (ugh) and vidding the interview (ulk). I would have my last class with Madam Garwah, and then we were going to swing by for a quick look-see of Spikeback Castle (well, I would be looking and seeing, Aleksei had been there before).

I was a nervous wreck.

I was also far too busy.

Fortunately, my classes with Madam Garwah were ending, I only had that one more (although her classes had become a hassle because of my busy life, truth told, I'd miss her). So that would be something to tick off my to-do list.

But Nata was quickly getting up to speed. This meant I was going to need to accept some invitations, consider what charities I would become a patron of, get on with my royal duties, and Germaine had warned I needed to make a statement with my first choices because they would define my reign.

No pressure there.

I managed to get all my designs in the studio's Seam-Stitch. They would be ready by the skin of my teeth. But once the fittings were done, the shooting schedule was set to start within a matter of days, and I'd be expected on set for the entirety of the three-month shooting schedule.

Intermingled with all of this, I had the Midnight Masque. There would be an engagement party shortly after. And I had a wedding to plan.

I wasn't sure I was going to be able to find the balance Aleksei said we'd find.

In fact, just thinking of my scroll through of the invites in the file Nata created, I was thinking it might be impossible.

I wasn't twenty people. Even if I did this as my full-time gig, like Queen Calisa, I'd have to decline the vast majority of them. The beings who sent them had hope I'd care about what they cared about. It was going to suck to have to tell them, essentially, I didn't have time for them.

The mask beeped it was done, and Lancet said, "No peeking. You promised."

And again...

Gah!

"All right, no peeking," I agreed, wishing I hadn't because this look was too important, and giving in to Lancet's drama was ratcheting up my anxiety.

But he was my friend. This was important to him as well, possibly more important, and he was excited about what he'd designed for me.

I didn't have the heart to put a damper on that.

He swept the mask away.

Thirty seconds later, the mane-mate beeped, and then that was gone.

He took my hand and pulled me out of the chaise while I made the prodigious effort of avoiding spying myself in any of the mirrors in my closet, of which there were a lot.

"Okay, close your eyes, I got you," Lancet said.

I closed my eyes, and he untied and divested me of my robe.

"Step in," he ordered.

As he guided me, I stepped in. I felt a garment shimmy up my hips. There was some tugging, and my arms were engaged. I felt fastening, adjusting, a featherlike touch at my left collarbone, cinching at my waist, and then Lancet placed my hand on his shoulder so I could balance as he slid what I could tell were slingback pumps on my feet.

He took my hand and guided me where the three-angle mirror stood.

"Okay, *look*!" he cried.

I opened my eyes.

And yes.

I should never have worried.

Lancet was my friend too, and I should have trusted him. He'd break his back not to disappoint me.

Fortunately, he didn't have to do that.

I was wearing a plum-colored dress in a delicious crêpe. It was ultra-feminine, had a short flutter sleeve, a thin, patent belt at the waist the color of lapis, the same as the sleek, sexy slingbacks on my feet. There was a large flower brooch made of soft-pink organza and wispy blue feathers pinned over my left collarbone so the feathers tickled my neck.

My makeup was natural, but sophisticated, fresh, with only a hint of dewy, and very feminine. My hair was pulled back in a soft, but complicated chignon at the nape of my neck.

I'd already put my diamond studs in.

It was perfect.

I was perfect.

There was flair. Panache. Style. Color. Personality. Delicacy. But it was refined.

"I think the brooch should be your signature, at least for a while," Lancet decreed, reaching in to fluff the feathers while he studied his work in the mirror. "I'm seeing them all over the streets already, since you wore your last one."

I turned to him. "Lancet, honey, it's sheer perfection."

He looked to me. "You think?"

I didn't confirm.

Well, I did, by hugging him.

His arms went around me super tight.

"Laura, this is a huge opportunity you're giving me," he said in my ear, and I could hear from the huskiness in his voice how much it meant to him.

Even so, I pulled out of his arms and gave one a playful slap. "Shut up. You deserve it." I turned back to the mirror and lifted my hands to my sides. "See?"

His eyes got bright with tears.

"Don't you cry, or I'll cry," I warned.

"I set your makeup to waterproof," he returned.

"I don't need bloodshot eyes."

"Any home Medi-Aid would take care of bloodshot eyes in two seconds."

He was right about that.

"Excuse please," we heard from the door.

We both looked that way.

Antheme was standing in it.

"We should have left five minutes ago," she said.

Crap.

I had a super busy schedule, and I knew Aleksei had packed it like that so I wouldn't have time to think about all that was going on.

I'd never tell him this, but his plan totally backfired, but it was sweet because the thought always counted, right?

Lancet went to the built-in vanity and brought me a clutch that matched my belt and shoes.

"All packed and ready to rumble," he said.

He was the best.

I kissed his cheek.

Antheme led the way as we left my closet and headed to the lift.

I hugged Lancet before he got into it to go down.

The door was barely sliding closed before Antheme was marching to the stairs to the landing pad.

I followed her.

We were in the craft (a cushy, roomy, luxurious, black, armored UtiliSport, the kind all the celebrities used), and waiting for course approval, when I asked, "How is your day going?"

"It was going well, until my charge made us seven minutes late."

Well, there you go.

As ever, Antheme was feeling like being Antheme that day.

This didn't upset me. I liked that it wasn't "Mistress Laura this" and "Mistress Laura that" with her. She did her job. She took it seriously. She wasn't a fan of me making it harder for her. She was down to share that. The end.

We were lifting off when I heard the chimes of my Palm in my bag.

I pulled it out and the screen said VIDEO COMM FROM THE OFFICE OF DYT LINSTAR.

Dyt Linstar was the executive producer of the vid I was working on.

I'd met him, briefly. It wasn't often (as in ever, except in hiring, and after, in passing) the costume designer brushed shoulders with the head honcho.

I wasn't sure this would be good news (maybe he was some kind of micromanager and heard I got my costumes programmed in at the last minute and he was going to give me a dressing down?).

I didn't want to, but I took the comm.

Mr. Linstar's tanned face filled my display.

"Laura," he said expansively, smiling widely.

"Uh, hello, Mr. Linstar," I replied, surprised by his jovial opening.

"Dyt. Call me Dyt," he invited.

"Of course."

"I have some good news and some bad," he announced.

Oh boy.

"And what's that, Dyt?"

"We've run into some trouble with Mardel's schedule. We thought we could get him out of a commitment, but they were having none of it. Bodi is dedicated to Mardel for the part, so now, I'm afraid, everything's going to have to be pushed back six weeks, giving him time to see to this other project. We'll have a new shooting schedule, shooting around him for two weeks before he can join us. But he's our hero, that's all we can do before we have him on set. Unfortunately, we've no choice but to postpone production."

I was sure this was bad news for him, but it was crazy good news for me, and it came with the best timing in the history of the world.

"I'm so sorry," I said, not sounding very sorry at all.

The thing was, Dyt didn't seem sorry either.

"It's a nuisance, but this kind of thing happens all the time."

He wasn't wrong about that. This had happened on other productions I'd worked on.

Scheduling talent was a nightmare.

The weird part about this was, normally, some assistant would comm, or they'd just send me a mail to explain things.

"It's my understanding you have the fittings scheduled. We'll carry on with them unless you need to postpone them too. You have time," Dyt continued. "And can I say, we are just so delighted with your recent mating. Thus, we're thrilled that this nuisance can be a boon for you as we're sure you need some time to get used to your new situation."

I was such an idiot.

I'd been so in the thick of all that was happening in my life, I hadn't realized practically everyone else was in the thick of it too.

I was carving out time to spend on watching social tapes, and it hadn't escaped my notice that the work I'd done before was being alternately exalted and reviled, and this meant more people were watching those vids and shows so they could have an opinion.

Not to mention, there was quite a bit of speculation about my work on the current vid, which was nothing but good PR for Dyt and Bodi.

"That's very kind of you," I said.

"We've found a little wiggle room in the budget, so we'd also like to offer you the use of a personal assistant on the production. Someone qualified to see to your duties if you should be called away."

What he meant was, they were worried my new situation might make me quit, and in order to keep me and what I offered their vid by being the new me, even though they were going to bleed money on this postponement, they were finding some to give me a personal assistant I didn't need (I'd have two assistants when it came to dressing the actors) so I wouldn't quit.

However, I was not going to let the weird feeling he was so blatantly kissing my behind stand in the way of a good thing.

"This would be lovely," I told him. "I must admit, things are very busy for me."

"Of course, of course," he intoned. "And you'll be directly involved in hiring."

"I appreciate that."

"And we appreciate you."

"Thank you for personally sharing this information," I said. "But I'm afraid I need to let you go. I have a busy afternoon."

He chuckled, and if he twiddled his fingers like a mad, greedy business mogul, I wouldn't be surprised, as he saw the future of the credit line he was tapping for this production expand when beings flocked to the vid I designed the costumes for, partially because of what I was busy doing that day.

"Indeed, you do. Thank you for taking my comm, Laura."

"My pleasure, Dyt."

He smiled blindingly.

I disconnected.

"Kiss ass," Antheme muttered.

I burst out laughing.

Oh yes.

I totally loved when Antheme was Antheme.

"I suppose I have to get used to that kind of thing," I remarked.

"As far as I can tell, Aleksei is the total shit. That male has it all together. But I think his greatest talent is not hurling when people line up to try to shove their noses up his ass."

I watched as she descended to land in front of the gleaming, black, severe, one-hundred-and-fifty story, pointed spear of the famous Spire Building.

It was new, only about a year old, and had changed the skyline of Nocturn in what I thought was an awesome way.

Was Aleksei's office in the Spire?

This question led me to the uncomfortable realization that we'd been together for weeks, and I didn't know where Aleksei's office was. Or, really, what he did in it.

Because I hadn't asked.

Oh gods.

Was I making us all about me?

"A sobering thought," I murmured in reply to Antheme, but it was also a note to self, as she set down on a spot on the street that had indisputably been cleared just for us. "My life has changed a lot in a short period of time," I pointed out the obvious (considering that spot was indication of just that).

The craft powered down, and I noticed members of my detail positioned outside the building. I usually had four, including Antheme, Fannon, Diablo and Geleena.

Fannon was coming toward my door, when Antheme spoke.

"You're doing great."

I turned to her. "You think?"

"Aleksei's a male I could get a serious hard-on for," she stated bluntly.

I couldn't stop my surprised chirp of laughter.

"But I'd never do it," she continued. "Even before he found you, because getting involved with my charge screws with my ability to do my job. Also, he isn't into females like me, so I'd never have the shot. But mostly, his life is a nightmare. You either gotta get off on the attention, like the princess did, or you're in for a world of hassle. You didn't have a choice. You had to accept the hassle. Honestly, I didn't think you had it in you. But you do. And you make him happy on top of that. So a double score."

It meant a lot more to me than I would have expected, having Antheme's approval.

I didn't say that because she wouldn't care.

Instead, I said, "You really don't beat around the bush, do you?"

"Nope." She said that hilariously popping the P.

I laughed again as she jutted her chin toward my side window and my door opened.

I caused quite a stir, not only on the pavement, but in the busy lobby of the Spire, and it wasn't the first time I noted how uncomfortable it was to simply walk through a space and be the object of everyone's attention.

I totally got what Antheme was saying.

And I couldn't imagine how Anna would like this kind of thing all the time.

Of course, we didn't bother with any of the public areas.

Instead, I was directed around a corner to a private lift.

"The hand thing again," Antheme said once we were in it.

I put my hand on the palm plate, felt the prick, smiled to myself that

Aleksei had programmed me in to get to his office, and the lift zoomed upward.

The doors opened to Muriel, who smiled, came out from behind her console desk and took charge of me. After giving me a warm cheek brush, she guided me to a set of stairs, and up them, to the next floor.

From the view, I assumed it was the one-hundred-and-fiftieth one, just below the pinnacle of the spear.

The entire floor being Aleksei's office.

Plush, charcoal-gray carpet.

Another console desk, this one lacquered black and massive.

Interesting art on plinths situated in the perfect spots.

A holo conference table that was twice as big as the one in his office at home.

Three-hundred-sixty degrees of the view of the city.

Aleksei rose from his desk, smiling at me.

I didn't go to him.

Feeling a little shy and a lot like a bad mate, I went to a window, tucked my clutch under my arm and crossed both of them, staring at Nocturn, the off-coast islands, the Sceptred Isle and the white caps waxing and waning on the blue of the Dolphin Sea.

This wasn't Prince Aleksei's office.

This was Aleksei Knightstar's office.

He earned this.

I turned to him to see he was resting a thigh against his desk, and his arms were crossed too, but his eyes weren't to the view. They were on me.

That tall, broad, handsome man casually leaning on his expensive desk belonged here.

Because he worked to put himself here.

"So, you don't have *an* office in the Spire Building, you have *the* office," I remarked.

"That's what happens when you own the building."

Of course he owned it.

"So, I'm not meeting you at your office because your day is busy and it helps you out. I've met you here because you're a big showoff," I quipped.

His grin was cocky (and panty melting). "I'm always busy, darling. But I'm also showing off."

I turned back to the view.

He had a lot to show off.

"I know about the dock project on Thoth, but what do you do that gets you an office like this?" I asked.

He didn't hesitate to reply. "I have three arms of interest. Commercial real estate, development and lettings. Other construction projects. And tech with a focus on communications. For instance, one of my labs developed that tablet I gave you."

Of course it did.

I looked back at him and asked quietly, "I can't believe I didn't know this. Has it been always all about me?"

His expression grew soft. "Darling, for me, everything is always all about you."

So sweet.

"You know what I mean," I replied.

"I'd say you have a fair bit more to get used to in a life with me than I do having you in my life."

This was true.

Even so.

"But on the whole, no. It hasn't always been about you," he finished.

That was being kind.

I mean, I didn't even know he owned the Spire and had his office there.

"You're pretty fascinating, Aleksei." I indicated the room with a sweep of my arm. "I've been missing out."

"Most people think what I do is tremendously boring. They're only interested in the amount of money I make doing it."

"Well…" I said no more but I did make a show of taking in his incredible office, something his money bought him.

He chuckled.

I walked to him, tossed my clutch on his desk and rested my hands to his chest, my weight into them, as he curled his long fingers around my hips.

"I'm duly impressed," I said.

"I hope so," he replied.

"I get a kick, learning about you," I shared.

His sky-blue eyes warmed. "I hope so with that too."

"Beware, I'm intent to do more of it," I told him.

"Consider me warned."

"I'm crazy nervous," I admitted, abruptly changing the conversation (yes, back to me, gah!).

"You look beautiful. Your outfit is perfect. You'll be fantastic."

I took in a big breath and asked what I had to ask, but didn't want to ask, and further, didn't want to care about the answer.

"Any news?"

Now his expression grew understanding and he gave me a squeeze. "No, love. Your father's units are in a queue. I don't want to give your mother any ammunition to fire at us, so we're doing this by the book, and I can't pull any favors to jump that queue to give you quicker answers. We won't know for a couple of weeks if he's committed a crime."

I nodded.

He placed a hand on my jaw and stroked my cheekbone with his thumb.

"There's still time to change your mind about the content of the interview," he said.

I shook my head. "No, I'm determined. I think this might be the perfect bent to what Germaine calls my 'brand within a brand.'"

"You don't have to make your life about being abused, Laura," Aleksei stated firmly.

"If I do, then I might be able to make something good come of it. Right?"

"Right," he whispered on another stroke of his thumb.

"I was late arriving. We should go. Are you ready?" I asked. Then I teased, "And on the way to the Palace, I want to hear about whose brilliant idea it was to make that tablet hover."

"I've been wracking my brain about how to do this."

I was confused at his words.

"Sorry?"

"It's selfish of me to do it here, in my office, in the building I built, and I own."

I felt my forehead crinkle. "Aleksei—"

"But for some reason, I need to do it here. For it to happen in a place removed from all of that. For it to happen in a part of my life that's just mine. The life I would have given you when I found you, even if that other part wasn't who I am. Do it in the life I made, that would always be ours, not the one that was given to me."

I remained quiet, because I wasn't exactly following, except I knew whatever this was, he had to do it like he was doing it, say the things he was saying, and it was big deal.

He took a half step away and tucked a hand into his pocket. "I also can't take credit for the choice."

He took my left hand, brought it to his lips, then held it between us as he slipped the Insouciant Riche aquamarine and diamond ring on my finger.

My heart stuttered to a stop.

"I asked Gayle and Cat to help," he shared as I stared at it. "They said this was the one. But I hope I get points that I would have chosen it anyway. Because it matches your eyes."

"Thank the gods for waterproof makeup," I mumbled stupidly, not knowing what to say, unable to find the words with all I was feeling, at the same time sniffling and staring at my beautiful engagement ring.

He'd asked Cat and Gayle (so danged *Aleksei*).

But he would have picked it for me anyway.

Gods, my Aleksei.

He brought my hand to his lips again and kissed the ring. Then he pressed my palm to his chest.

"This isn't very romantic, *bissi*, but I hope you understand it has meaning for me," he said gently.

I looked into his eyes through my watery ones. "Are you crazy? You brought me to the top of the world to give me my engagement ring. How is that not romantic?"

He smiled and didn't hide the relief in his eyes.

Gods, *my Aleksei*.

"And take note, my prince, if something has meaning for you, it has meaning for me."

That made the look in his eyes intensify.

And his silky voice was gruff when he said, "Whatever it brings, I look forward to the life I'll share with you."

Seriously?

"Ugh!" I grunted. "Males so do not get that romance is not flowers and grand gestures but meaning and feelings. And you are killing me with all the meaning and feelings you're giving me, your highness. My face might be waterproof, but even the Ultra Paint 5000 can't withstand the effects of me bawling for the next thirty minutes."

"Is that your way of telling me to shut up?"

"Yes."

"Can your makeup withstand me kissing you?"

If he didn't kiss me in short order, I would just *die*.

So I said, "Heck yes."

He smiled before he pulled me in his arms, angled his head and kissed me.

When he finally broke the kiss, and considering he took a good deal of time doing it and making sure the job got done thoroughly, we were definitely running late.

"Time to share our joy and my message with the world," I said, sounding exactly like I felt, as if that was the last thing on earth I looked forward to doing.

"Indeed," he replied, moving as if to do that.

I stood still and he stopped.

"But first, I have to tell you, I'd say I can't wait to share my life with you too, but since you moved me in, catnapped my cats, stole Nova's love forever and exposed your good taste at liking chocolate crackles, I already am. And just so you know, even with some crappy times we had no control over, so far, it's been everything."

After I finished saying that, Aleksei was kissing me again.

This meant we were seriously late meeting Germaine.

She was in a tizzy.

But me?

I was walking on clouds.

CHAPTER 32

SPIKEBACK

I slipped Aleksei out of my mouth, then got off my knees on the floor beside the bed, climbed to straddle his lap and held his gaze as I took him inside.

He wrapped his arms around me and pressed his face between my breasts.

I wrapped my arms around his head, holding him there, as I rode him, taking my time, feeling the clench and release, the sumptuous friction of us, the delicious fullness of him invading and retreating.

He unwrapped his arms to glide his big hands up either side of my spine, pressing in, and I arched for him.

He took full advantage of my offering, sucking my nipples, rolling them with his tongue, nibbling them sensually.

I moved faster.

He pulled me off and tossed me to my back in the bed. Looming over me, he hooked my ankles on his shoulders and drove back in.

His eyes burned flames of purple fire, holding mine captive until I couldn't watch the beauty of him fucking me anymore because I was coming.

Not long later, he joined me.

He gently pulled my legs from his shoulders, slid out and rolled us, so I was flat on top of him, straddling his hips.

With his hands moving over my body, he murmured, "I'm assuming from the fact we've been fucking here for the last eleven hours, you want to move to Spikeback."

I started giggling.

One could say, the minute I was introduced to the medieval pointed arched windows, carved stone, stained glass, ostentatious columns, flagstone floors, and brooding-broken-misunderstood-hero-lives-here décor, I was a goner.

It was ridiculously well-preserved, and just ridiculous. It was like I'd walked eight hundred years into the past.

It was so not my thing.

But there was something about it.

Something gloomy and mysterious and magnificent.

Something that said, "Stay away, the beings who live here do not want you here."

It felt safe to me.

It seemed like the place, if his dragon was a human (which he was), would drag my dragon if she was a human (which she was), to keep her sheltered, protected, happy.

In fact, it was my beast who signaled her adoration of the castle before I'd stepped foot over the threshold.

Sure, it was situated in the middle of a public park.

But the airspace above it was a no-fly zone, there was a tall, spiked, iron fence around the perimeter, the gardens and grounds were enormous, so there was a sense of privacy, no matter how public its situation, and it was protected 24/7 by the RS, even when no one was in it.

It felt like an island of protection surrounded by a stormy sea, a lot like the Celestial Palace, but without all the staff bustling about, and, well...an actual sea.

I loved it.

We arrived here for a tour yesterday evening after our media thing was done (we didn't get to a Palace tour, the queen and Germaine wanted to have a post-interview "debrief"). Also, after Madam Garwah came to the Palace for my final instruction. And last, after we had dinner with the king, queen, Aleece, and Errol joined us (on his best behavior, and the male actually spoke to me this time, but since it was "Can you pass the butter?" and my subsequent attempts to engage him in conversation came to naught, I decided it didn't count).

Timothee took dinner in his room (no surprise, and I suspected, no loss).

During our tour, once we hit the master bedroom, with its huge bed draped in swags of glimmering pewter velvet, flanked by massive crenelated black columns, the headboard a work of art of silver inlay, immense shields and rosettes, all of this beckoning me to do naughty things to my mate, the tour stopped and the sex-a-thon started.

Aleksei was not telling the full truth about fucking for eleven hours, though.

I'd passed out somewhere in there but had awoken that morning to pop to the loo and returned to deliver a blowjob upon my mate and start the sex festivities again.

I lifted my head to look down at him. "Color me stunned. I guess I have a hint of a goth gal in me."

"No," he murmured. "I'm not surprised, *bissi*. Outside of the Clan Caves, this is the only royal property where I ever felt truly at home."

Interesting.

"I'm not surprised about that either. It's all the black and purple in the design scheme," I teased.

He smiled. "My creature is definitely comfortable here too. Yours as well."

I nodded to confirm what he sensed from my beast, something I sensed from his as well.

"So we're decided?" he asked.

I frowned.

He slid a hand between us to cup my breast, idly thumbing my nipple.

Idle for him, not so much for me.

I squirmed.

"You'll miss the penthouse," he guessed.

"It's kind of our place," I said.

"You can have a studio here," he noted. "There's plenty of room to set one up."

I shook my head. "I don't want to give up my studio, if that's all right. Everything is just as I need it there."

"You can have what you want, Laura. And we can keep the penthouse. It's in the north of the city, your loft and studio are in the south. This is in midtown. We can use whatever is convenient."

I grinned and joked, "Only a royal prince would find a ten-minute craft trip inconvenient."

"Depending on traffic and what course you're given, it could be half an hour," he returned.

"A half an hour? How would we live?" I asked, still joking.

He smiled even as he tipped his head on the pillow. "This might be a lot for the cats."

I tipped mine too, considering this.

"Too much?" he asked. "They could get lost."

I grinned at him again, loving how he worried about my pets. "Nova would find you in a blinding snowstorm with you being a thousand miles away."

He grinned in return. "She does seem to like me. And we can implant trackers. They're harmless and painless. Though, it'll make it much more difficult for Jupiter to hide from us."

I grinned yet again.

I loved it how well he knew my fur babies.

His gaze suddenly went hooded, and the silk of his voice turned velvet when he ordered, "Get my cock in you."

My breath stuttered, but I wasted no time reaching between us to do as told, grabbing hold of him, positioning and bearing down.

Oo, so nice.

"Fuck, your cunt is magic," he growled, the purple radiating out of his iris that had already turned dark as night.

"Aleksei," I whispered.

"Don't move, just lay there, talking to me, doing it full of me."

I shivered.

His thumb at my nipple was joined by a finger and he started rolling.

At that, I trembled.

"I'm delighted your schedule has cleared," he said, like I was not squirming on his big, hard body while sitting on his big, hard dick.

"Me too," I pushed out. "The better to have eleven hours to fuck you with."

His grin was wicked this time as he pinched my nipple.

That shot between my legs and my body jerked.

"Stay still, darling," he murmured.

Oh gods.

He was testing me.

"Honey," I breathed.

His hand left my breast, and I was happy for the respite, but that wasn't what he intended.

Both his hands traced down my back to my behind, where he seized my flesh, digging in, the pads of his fingers pressing maddeningly into my cleft.

"We'll move here," he decided.

"All right," I panted.

He squeezed my behind.

I clutched his cock with my pussy.

He grunted, then growled.

"With this change in your schedule, do you think you can take an engagement trip?" he asked.

I wasn't sure.

"Yes," I forced out.

"A week? Two?"

"However long you like."

He lazily thrust his hips up.

Oh *gods*.

I whimpered.

His lips twitched.

Gah!

With one hand, he stroked my cleft.

That brought me up to a quiver, and it was a really good quiver.

"After the Masque. I'll ask Muriel to plan it. Anywhere you'd like to go?"

"Anubis Island. The Elysian."

"Not a space station?"

Beelzebub, his fingers were driving me crazy.

"Beach," I moaned, wanting to give him what he wanted, but I was nearly at my end.

My Aleksei, he sensed it.

"Kiss me, darling," he ordered thickly.

I kissed him with everything I had.

He broke it with a swat on my bottom and commanded, "Pleasure yourself, Laura."

No hesitation, I sat straight up and rode his thick cock like a woman possessed, orgasmed on a cry and an arch of my back that made me plant my hands in his thighs.

I was yanked off, rotated, positioned so I was straddling his face, and his big cock was right in front of mine.

From between my legs, he demanded, "Suck me off while I eat you."

I took him in my mouth, tasting me and him, with Aleksei doing the same between my legs, and in a rare simultaneous climax, he jetted down my throat and groaned up my pussy at the exact same time I came on his mouth.

He was lapping, and I had my cheek to his hip and was stroking when he repositioned me again, this time, throwing the covers over us while we were face to face, tangled together.

I nuzzled his throat and made purring noises.

"I think we'll be happy here," he said into my hair.

"I think we'd be happy anywhere," I said into his skin.

Suddenly, I had no breath because his arms locked around me so tight, I couldn't force any in so it could come back out. He also buried his face in the side of my neck.

"Aleksei," I wheezed.

His hold loosened (but not that much), and he took his face out of my neck to catch my gaze.

"I want to spend the whole day with you here, just us, we'll order in food," he stated. "Can you do that?"

I loved that he wanted that. But I would find a way to do anything for him.

Definitely that.

"Yes, baby," I whispered.

An expression moved over his beautiful face I did not like.

He didn't make me wait to explain it. "I have to share you with everybody. I hate it, Laura."

Oh gods.

I lifted a hand and stroked his jaw. "I'm just yours."

"I wish that was the case," he muttered.

"It is," I asserted.

He shook that off and said, "I was proud of what you did yesterday. You were remarkably honest, but self-possessed."

Ah.

Understanding was dawning.

"You didn't like me sharing that part of my life," I took a wild stab at guessing what his recent reaction was about.

"Your pain that I can't assuage, giving it to the entire world?" he asked.

My gods, this beautiful male.

"You have things I can't fix either," I reminded him.

"Does it burn in you, threaten to consume every thought, control every action?"

Holy Hecate.

"It bothers me, a whole lot," I told him, beginning to feel a gnawing sense of worry. "But it doesn't do that. Is that how you feel?"

"At the audience, it took everything I had not to shake them until their necks snapped. Even so, I had to find more, so my creature wouldn't release, clench them in his jaw, fly over the sea and drop them in the middle of it."

Whoa.

He was talking about my parents.

"It's primal," he grunted.

I froze.

"It troubles me," he admitted.

I stared at him.

So I saw him wince and felt his hands move soothingly on me as he said, "I shouldn't have shared that. It's not something I should burden you with."

"You love me," I stated impassively, and it was impassive because, if I let just a hint of what I was feeling loose, I would explode with it.

His hands stopped moving, but he didn't say anything.

"You love me, and your creature loves her," I said.

"Laura, we're mates," he pointed out. "But I don't wish to alarm you. It's too soon."

It wasn't too soon.

It just was.

"I love you, and she loves him," I declared. "Effortlessly. Limitlessly. I don't love the True Heir. I love Aleksei. I love the male who lets my cat lay on his stomach while he strokes her and brings me coffee and breakfast in bed so I can work. I love the cute Aleksei who hovered through a flyby to bring me Captain Jacques's and I love the fierce Aleksei who wants to shake my parents until their necks snap."

"That last isn't my finest urge, love," he said quietly.

I shook my head vehemently. "I don't care. It's a part of you. They all are what makes you. You've given me a family. Sure, they're a king and queen, a princess and a couple of emotionally stunted princes, but it isn't about that either. It's about them, who they really are. You've given me a sense of belonging. You've given me a home." I pressed into his chest. "*You* gave me all of that, Aleksei."

"You had all of that, Laura, with the Truelocks, the Vinestrongs."

"I love them to my soul, but it's not the same. You have a family, and you all have issues, that's true, but you still have a family and there's love and care there. You can't know how it feels to live your life not having that. It's about belonging to someone. It's about how I know I belong to *you*. Who we are, the strength of what we feel, it isn't about the True Heir and his True Bride, it isn't about being mates. It's because I'm Laura. And you're Aleksei."

He rolled so he was on top of me.

"You love me," he said, like he was just processing my words.

"I knew I was falling. I just realized I landed. And when I did, I did it hard." I rested my hand on the side of his face. "You've given me the sky and stars, baby, in so many ways. And I treasure it."

A sound rumbled from his chest that was so predacious, I wasn't sure if it came from Aleksei or his creature, before he took my mouth and kissed me, then we made love again.

Right, well, it was too energetic and desperate and communicative to be considered making love, but you get the gist.

When we were done, and I was recovering (okay, sweating and panting), he rolled from me to reach his suit jacket on the floor and pull out his Palm.

He made an audio-only comm, commanding, "I need you to contact Muriel and clear my schedule for today. And Laura and I need almond croissants and fruit bowls from Lesendre's."

At the mention of Lesendre's, the best patisserie in the city, I suddenly found the strength to roll toward him. "Oo, and four religieuse and a dozen madeleines for later. And pain au chocolat for tomorrow morning. Oh, and some of those swirly, vanilla frosted things, just because."

"Did you get that?" Aleksei asked. He paused and then, "And two large café au laits. We'll want Benninden's for lunch."

Yes!

The sandwiches at Benninden's were *to kill for*.

Aleksei looked at me.

"The turkey and salami melt. And their toffee cookie," I ordered.

"Add beef and Emmental to that, and a cashew chocolate cookie," he said into his Palm. "I'll comm later about dinner." Pause then, "Great. My appreciation."

He tossed his Palm casually to the irreplaceable silver-gilded black nightstand and turned back to me.

"Okay, Lesendre's and Benninden's, maybe I love you just a little bit because you're super farging rich and titled so you can order your aide to bring us the city's finest food we'll be eating in a castle while we have a sex-fest," I admitted.

Aleksei snatched me to him as he burst out laughing.

The sound rang out in the cavernous room.

Honestly?

As much as I loved it here, I hadn't been sure about Spikeback.

The penthouse was totally our place.

But hearing his laughter echo in that room, I realized I was wrong.

Every place was our place.
But this was where I learned he loved me, and I told him I loved him.
So this would be our new place.
And whatever life brought us, we'd find the same thing there.
Always, with my Aleksei.

CHAPTER 33
HERO

"Well?"

Antheme looked to Gayle, then to Cat, then to Monique. Once she did that, she put her finger to her chest and inquired, "You're asking me?"

"Yes, I'm asking you," I replied.

"I haven't worn a dress in my life," she told me something that did not surprise me.

"It's not a dress, petal, it's a *gown*," Lancet huffed.

We were at my final fitting.

The Masque was only a few days away. And although I was a little anxious to put all of Madam Garwah's training to use on such a big stage, and a little more anxious, because tons of people around me, almost all of them strangers, definitely all of them curious about me, wasn't my thing.

But I had to admit, I was also a little excited.

This magnificent gown would make any female excited.

Except Antheme.

On that thought, along with riding the crest of the Aleksei wave that had become my life, I smiled.

Not much but normal stuff (or, my new normal) had happened since Aleksei and my love fest at Spikeback Castle over two weeks earlier.

And that was good.

The fittings I had scheduled for the vid were done, the adjustments made, and I was ready to roll when we were ready to shoot (except getting

Mardel outfitted, he wasn't available to me, but his costumes were constructed).

I'd scheduled my first royal appearances, these to happen after the Masque.

Thankfully, Aleksei was going with me to these appearances.

The first was at a school's theater department in the city, the second to the Royal Vulnerable Person's Bureau to meet their overworked staff and bring attention on the vital work they did.

We hadn't moved to Spikeback yet.

It was even more historical than the Palace, so any modernization that could be done (like electricity and plumbing) had been done.

But it required a full staff, and Allain and Nata were going to take offices there. This meant they were busy hiring, and settling in themselves, then, again after the Masque, Aleksei and I were moving.

The plans for the engagement party were in full swing, a much smaller affair (seven hundred and fifty people attended the Masque, Queen Calisa was thinking two-fifty for the party, but I'd been warned the wedding would be a thousand, so obviously, I wasn't thinking about that now, I'd fret about it later), and we'd even made inroads into planning the wedding.

If that wasn't enough (and it was, but the idea was so good, we just couldn't sit on it), Nata and I were also working on a project we wanted to present to the king and queen.

This included offering the history of royal wedding garments to the Musée de Vêtements for a limited-time exhibition and working with the other museums around the realm to display items of historical significance from the Catalogues.

This was Nata's idea, and I loved it.

So much was going on, but she was on top of it all at the same time taking the initiative.

I'd *so* made the right decision with her.

Totally.

I wasn't sure how the king and queen would take to that idea, but I did know Aleksei thought it was an excellent one, because he told me.

The only downside was that my father had indeed been hiding money from the HMRD. He'd been charged and was awaiting trial. And I was perplexed by the consolation I felt that his trial was scheduled months from now, so he was free and living at home, and Aleksei told me he'd retained very good representation.

It had been a big news story for a few days, and I was further confused at the complicated emotions I felt whenever I saw him on the newsfeeds, scurrying to avoid the cams.

My mother didn't appear, but then again, Aleksei's sources shared either she'd left him, or he'd kicked her out.

As far as I was concerned, this happened twenty-nine years too late (I couldn't say thirty, because, obviously, that would mean I wouldn't exist).

One could say I understood the depths of his grief at the loss of his mate. And I couldn't deny that his remorse and hope for some kind of reconciliation had seemed genuine, and not about me being the next queen.

But one could not say I condoned how my father treated me all my life. I'd had to wait thirty years for him to show even an iota of care for me, and in the time he had me, what he'd shown was habitual inattention, punctuated by bouts of fury with instances of physical abuse.

See?

Complicated emotions.

His arrest, albeit very public, had not had any effect on me, except to put a fine point on what I'd shared during our engagement interview.

My approval rating remained steady at ninety-four (I'd been very right about being so open about my childhood, and not only my rating proved it, the outpouring of mail I was getting at the Palace did). Aleksei's had climbed to ninety-one. And even the king, queen, Aleece, and both princes had seen upticks in their ratings.

Add to all of this, the very not insignificant fact I was in love with the finest male on the planet.

Not to mention, I was getting great sex on the regular.

And I was right then wearing the most beautiful gown ever created.

In other words, life was good.

"You've known Aleksei a long time," I said to Antheme to explain requesting her opinion about the gown.

"You could wear a potato sack and he'd like you in it," Antheme replied.

That was sweet (and true, and again, I was in love with the finest male on the planet).

But she wasn't getting it.

"It's about me wearing this dress and being on his arm," I explained.

She rolled her eyes. "Stop stressing. You look gorgeous. And that dress is...fit for purpose."

Cat snorted.

Gayle choked.

Monique outright laughed.

Lancet gasped in affront and snapped, "*Fit for purpose?*"

"Anyway, there's no going back now, right?" Antheme ignored Lancet and asked me.

She was very right.

"I do not know why you subjected me to this creature's opinion," Lancet complained.

"Because I'm going to have just shy of eighteen million pics taken of me in this gown. I love it. It's stunning. But those pics are going to travel twenty realms, live forever, and I'm freaking out," I explained.

His mood changed immediately, though I didn't know if it was about wanting to console me, or the reminder that eighteen million pics would be taken of his gown.

"Oh, dearest," he cooed. "You'll wow them all."

I turned on my gals, my heavy skirts swirling with me, almost taking me off balance (note to self, don't move too fast at the Masque or I was going down).

"You three are set with gowns?" I asked.

"I was set two months ago," Cat drawled.

"Only because, after you very belatedly invited us, the aide to the True Bride made comms and got the two top designers in the Fall, not including you, of course," Gayle said her last to Lancet, "to rush gowns for us. Mine is nowhere near as lush as yours, but it's *mega*."

"Mine is a shooting stars theme," Monique shared. "I thought that was an awesome idea, but butterflies beat it by a mile. Even in Nocturn."

"Laura, you need to be at the Palace for your weekly tea with the queen in less than half an hour," Antheme warned.

Oh.

Right.

That had also been added to my schedule.

I couldn't say Queen Calisa was warming up to me, as such. I had a feeling she was already as warm as she'd ever get. But I could say I loved our chats, mostly because Aleece always joined us, it felt nice getting to know them better, and it felt fabulous being inducted in their crew.

Although the queen wasn't a demonstrative person, her closeness with Aleece was clear, and the indication they wanted me to be a part of it meant the world to me.

I was going to ask if I could take the gals to one of our teas, and I loved knowing I had to ask, but the queen was going to say yes.

I stepped down from the dress platform. "I'll change."

Lancet bustled after me.

I got changed, hugs, cheek kisses, gratitude that they took their lunch hours to show at Lancet's studio for the fitting were exchanged, and we all rolled out.

"Are you working the Masque?" I asked Antheme as we left Lancet's building, me waving at the gals who were walking down the pavement (sadly, not every craft had a ready-made landing spot at the doors of every building, but they'd all taken the Subterra to get there).

Antheme was scanning as we moved toward our craft. "I'm where you are if you're in public."

"Right," I said just as she tensed.

Then I cried out as she shoved me sprawling to the pavement, shouting, "*Weapon!*"

I heard the zing of a laser stream, the thud of what sounded like a body landing right beside mine, another one not too far behind me, and then I was being dragged.

I kicked and struggled before I heard a terse, "Fannon, mistress."

I switched to working with him instead of against him.

Beings were screaming. There seemed to be too much movement. I was pushed into the back seat of the craft, the door slammed down, a sharp rap sounded on the top, and we were lifting off.

I righted myself in the seat, looked out the window and saw Fannon crouched over a prone body.

Antheme's prone body.

My heart rate spiked and my gaze darted to the pilot. It was Diablo.

"Buckle in," he ordered.

Absently, I did as told.

"Antheme," I whispered, looking back, trying to find Gayle, Cat, Monique.

I saw nothing but a pavement cleared of panicked people who'd run away, Antheme's body, Fannon working on her, and another body, a male, just down the pavement.

"Emergency route cleared," the on-dash computer said. "Proceed to Celestial Palace at crisis velocity."

The sudden burst of speed plastered me to my seat as we shot through the sky.

I pulled my bag off my arm, fumbled in it and yanked out my Palm.

I didn't know who to comm first.

I was saved the decision when Gayle's came into mine.

I took it, seeing her pale face and wild eyes on my display.

"Are you okay?" I asked.

"Geleena got us down, then back in the building," she answered. "Are you?"

"Physically, yes. Can you see Antheme from where you are?"

Her expression shifted and my stomach clenched at what I read in it. "Laura—"

"*Can you see Antheme?*" I shrieked.

"Honey, she's not moving. But the ambu-lift is already here."

Another comm came through.

Aleksei.

"Aleksei's comming. I have to go. Do what my team tells you to do, nothing else. Promise me."

"Promise," she said.

"Love you," I replied.

"Love you too."

I took Aleksei's call.

"Are you safe?" he barked.

"We're heading to the Palace. Honey, Antheme—"

"I'll meet you there."

Then he was gone.

"Landing cleared," the on-dash computer said.

My heart skipping every other beat, I stared at the Palace looming before us.

And then we landed.

❖ ❖ ❖

Due to my beast expanding so much, she felt like she would burst out of my chest, I knew he was arriving not only because she and I felt him, but because the room darkened as his flight blocked out the sun.

I jumped off the sofa.

"He'll be met with clothes, dear, and—" Queen Calisa started.

But I was already racing out.

Down the hall, the stairs.

To the front door.

Out of it.

Allain was there.

As was Aleksei, naked, but tugging on a pair of jeans.

I let him get them up before I hit him like a rocket.

He picked me up and carried me into the Palace.

He dropped me on my feet in the entry and started buttoning his jeans.

"What's happening?" I asked.

He took a shirt from Allain and shrugged it on, not meeting my gaze.

Oh gods.

No.

"Aleksei!" I shouted.

He turned and moved so fast, I didn't see him do it, but suddenly my face was in his hands and his face was all I could see.

"We lost Antheme," he whispered.

The tears sprung to my eyes.

"Lost, as in...*dead*?" I asked.

"*Bissi*." He was still whispering.

Lost, as in...*dead*.

The tears spilled over.

He pulled me into his arms.

"They were aiming at me?" I asked his chest.

A hesitation and then, "Yes, darling."

"She died for me."

He held me tighter.

"She died for me," I repeated.

"She will be remembered for eternity, an honored hero of Night's Fall," he decreed.

I yanked away. "I don't want her to be an honored hero!" I yelled. "I want her to live a full life and retire to a beach."

He hauled me back into his arms.

The spurt of anger extinguished as fast as it came, the sound of Antheme's body hitting the ground so close to me reverberating through my head.

I melted into him and sobbed.

"Son?"

I felt Aleksei shake his head.

I peered out from his chest to see they were all there, Fillion, Calisa, Aleece, and even Timothee and Errol.

I was in no state, but Timothee appeared sad and shocked, and Errol, shaken.

I couldn't deal with them now.

I couldn't deal with anything now.

I turned my face back into Aleksei.

"You're moving to the Palace," the king decreed.

"Yes, we are," Aleksei agreed.

I just kept crying.

✦ ✦ ✦

The curtains on the windows had been closed, and I was lying in the dark in his bed that was dressed in aubergine velvet, feeling cold through to the bone, but so listless, I didn't bother dragging the bedclothes over me.

This is how I was when he came to me.

My body was limp as Aleksei adjusted it into the bend of his while he rested against the headboard, his long legs in front of him.

"What do they know?" I mumbled into his shirt.

"Let me get some food in you first."

I couldn't eat a thing.

"Please tell me," I begged.

My torso rose as Aleksei drew in a huge breath.

Then he let it out.

"The team was scattered. Antheme down…"

I closed my eyes tight against the sound of her hitting the pavement assailing me for the millionth time.

"…Diablo and Fannon were on you, Geleena was on your females," he continued. "Once she got them secured, she gave chase, but it was too late. The killer got away."

Got away?

I tipped my head up to look at him. "I saw a male lying on the pavement."

"An innocent bystander, caught in the stream that got Antheme."

Oh no!

"Did he…?" I couldn't finish that.

"He passed too, love."

And it gets worse.

I swallowed my grief for that unknown male.

It didn't go down easy. Not at all.

"How could he get away? There are cameras all over the city, Aleksei," I pointed out.

"Yes, and they caught him jumping into a craft that launched without course approval. It also had its tracker disabled, so traffic control couldn't follow it, it had no identi-tags, and it disappeared before they could lock a trace on it."

I lifted my head to look at him. "Do you think Anna has gone this far around the bend?"

"No. I think something else is happening, and I thought that before Prince Tanyn commed and asked Father and I for a meeting."

By Lilith.

"Arnaud?" I asked.

"I don't know. Tanyn's flying down tonight. We're meeting first thing in the morning. Whatever it is, he has something to share, and the timing cannot be coincidental."

I nodded, because he was correct. Nothing was *that* coincidental.

"It was a fucked-up thing to say," he admitted. "That Antheme was a hero to the realm. I just didn't know what else to say."

It hit me that he'd known her longer than I had, but it was me who was bringing the drama.

I pulled myself together, doing this the easy way, by cuddling closer to him. "Are you okay?"

"I'm fine," he said tersely.

He was so not.

"Your creature flew," I noted carefully.

"When I got the news there'd been another attempt on you, it was a miracle I kept him contained before I heard your voice over comm."

"Who's telling her family?"

"They live down in Skull Bay. Set went down to talk to them."

Not an easy task.

Poor Set.

I nodded again because I didn't know what to say.

"I've talked with Mammon and Tomahs. They're moving their females to the Palace. Monique is being moved too."

Tomahs was Gayle's dad. Her mom, by the way, was named Elayne.

My body went solid at this news. "What? Why?"

"Whoever is behind this is targeting you."

That was in no doubt.

"Yes."

"And you'll be at the Palace until we get to the bottom of this, and the Palace is impenetrable."

I didn't like where this was going.

"So, if whoever this is means to hurt me, or hurt you by hurting me, and I'm not available, they might cast a wider net by hurting someone close to me," I deduced.

He pulled in a sharp breath through his noise, but he didn't confirm, because I didn't need him to confirm.

Yep.

I didn't like this at all.

"Do you think this is Arnaud's super farged-up way of saying, 'You're messing with me having the female I want, so I'm going to take out your female'?"

"Darling— he started, then stopped.

"What?"

"Fuck," he said under his breath, turning his gaze from mine.

I pressed into his chest with my hand.

"What?" I demanded sharply.

"Fuck," he repeated. But before I could ask again, he shared, "Fannon saw the shooter."

"And?"

"He says he could swear he wasn't aiming at you."

"So, this was some random shooting on the street? That hasn't happened since weapons were banned over a hundred years ago," I said.

"No, he says he thinks the shooter was aiming at Antheme. Geleena didn't have an open angle, but from what she saw, she shared it looked the same as Fannon claims."

I blinked. "Why would someone be aiming at Antheme?"

"What I believe, the task force believes, and the agents at the RIC believe is that Arnaud is gearing up to do something. What, we haven't been able to figure out. But even as insane as he seems to be, no one wants the dragons to fly."

This was without a doubt. Even now, with modern weaponry, our dragon squadrons were feared in twenty realms. That said, our military was nothing to sneeze at. Even with no war for nearly a century, we were a warrior realm, and always had been.

We didn't have the magic of the witches and the fae. In our human forms, we didn't have the brute strength and speed of the demons.

But the creatures we shifted into were exponentially more powerful than their animal counterparts.

And our dragons were nearly unstoppable.

"And so?" I prompted.

"And so, while Four Realms are tied up in all that's going on with me and my mate, he might have an opportunity to do it while no one is paying attention."

"I can't imagine everyone in Sky's Edge cares that much about what's happening between you and me, Aleksei."

I said this, but the social tapes were worldwide, and we did seem to be on a lot of beings' minds if the tapes were anything to go by.

"Yes, but the male who was engaged to the Princess Royal of Dawn's Break, a female who is beloved by her people, is now engaged to another female, just three months from their breakup."

"I still don't understand."

"And as such, the only other realm who is feeding off of us, perhaps in a different way, but just as ravenously as Night's Fall, is Dawn's Break."

"Again, I'm not getting it."

"There are two possible scenarios," he shared. "But we feel the first is part of the last."

"The first?"

"Dr. Buildlore was recruited because of his past with Anna. We've found he was a male who was easily bought. The hysterectomy he performed outside his patient's knowledge was purchased by her ex-husband after a highly contentious divorce."

My eyes grew huge. "Oh my gods."

Aleksei nodded. "If he was indeed recruited in the current plot for this reason, this would lead us to believe Anna was behind these things, and it did lead us to that. This would mean tensions would be strained between Night's Fall and Dawn's Break, even strained to a breaking point, pitting us against Dawn's Break."

"The point of this being?"

"Distracting us from what's going on in Sky's Edge, at the same time lining us up to be an ally."

An ally?

An ally in what?

"And?" I pressed.

"That brings us to the second scenario."

"That being?"

Another deep breath from Aleksei before he asked, "What causes a military, and a country, to band together under one leader?"

Oh hells.

I finally got it.

And in so doing, I felt the blood run out of my face and repeated, "Oh my gods."

"Yes, darling. The writing is on the wall. Arnaud's reign is nearly at its end.

He's exhausted all legal remedy. He's out. It's a poorly kept secret Tanyn is gearing up for a coup if Arnaud doesn't step down, and he has a tremendous amount of support. This means, unless Arnaud can find another way to stay in, and at this juncture, that way has to be dramatic, rallying his beings behind him, he'll be deposed. Therefore, I think Arnaud intends to solidify his rule by finding or creating some reason to invade Dawn's Break. I further think Dawn's Break has no idea this is going to happen. But once it does, the Fall and Land's End will start with sanctions. However, if Arnaud doesn't pull back, which he won't, we'll have no choice but to get involved in the fighting."

"Do you think he's that insane?" I asked, my voice pitched high, because I for sure thought he was.

"What I know is, his mother was, and still is, ambitious. Queen Tatra did everything she could to oust the female that was in her way in order to claim her position. She succeeded in this endeavor. Part of this was so she could be queen. Part of it was so she could be mother to a future king and continue to hold some power because she was. She then spent Arnaud's whole life teaching him the same. Power is a drug. Some believe status should be protected at all costs. Add his need to assuage his aberrant tendencies, which includes having the power to satisfy these urges with no repudiation, and yes. I think he's that insane."

Cold had invaded my insides after Aleksei laid me in bed when I'd cried myself out, and he'd left me to learn more about what was going on.

That cold, right now, got so, so much colder.

"Historically, Sky's Edge and Night's Fall have been enemies, and Dawn's Break has been their ally," I reminded him. "An invasion of Dawn's Break by the Edge would seem entirely out of the blue."

"They're the better target. Witches and conjurers, for the most part, are peaceful people. Although there has been some bad blood throughout history, especially with Land's End, it was their alliance with demons, or at times shifters that helped them win wars. If not for us, there would be no Dawn's Break."

"But we don't war all the time anymore, so anyone would see through his scheme."

"Perhaps. Though I introduced the bill in the Center that would keep Arnaud from his supposed love, Prince Bainon of the Break has been far more vocal about his revulsion of Arnaud's tendencies."

I couldn't say I'd missed this. There was no love lost between those two. Arnaud often took potshots at Bainon as well, though, to my way of thinking, with a lot less success. Bainon was nearly as gorgeous as Aleksei (nearly), and although a bit of a playboy, he was respected among the realms.

I just didn't think their enmity might lead to war.

"We cannot, and are not, discounting the idea that he might also, or instead, be considering invading Night's Fall," Aleksei concluded.

Dear gods!

"So this whole thing is—"

"Yes, Laura. This whole thing may well be an elaborate distraction."

"Which means—"

"There might be a possibility you were not the intended target today. We're supposed to think that, but they killed who they intended to kill. As such, their mission succeeded. Night's Fall is glued to their displays, and beyond, in all four realms, it's probably mostly the same. Theories are flooding the tapes. And in a few days, all eyes will be on the Palace, because the Masque is being thrown. And Arnaud as well as Tanyn and Dagsbrun, and incidentally, Anna, are all coming."

Surely, after what happened that day, the Masque would be cancelled.

I didn't get into that, because my temper was rising, temporarily beating out my fear. "So Antheme was just a pawn."

"No," he growled. "I didn't lie earlier. Antheme was a hero. She took that blast thinking it was meant for you. But whoever is behind this thinks she was, Laura, and if I discover what the top minds in our law enforcement and intelligence communities are considering to be true, our dragons will fly, and it will be me leading the bank."

He was serious.

Deadly serious.

The purple in his eyes and the vein pulsing in his forehead told me so.

This meant I was still angry, but that wasn't winning out anymore.

Because I was also scared.

No.

I wasn't scared.

I was terrified.

✦ ✦ ✦

It was Germaine's idea (naturally), and it was a good one (also, although I hated to admit it, naturally).

And therefore, an hour after Aleksei's and my chat in bed, I had to do triple duty with my Medi-Aid (for bloodshot eyes and swelling), my spavisor (for blotchiness and also swelling), and my Ultra Paint, programming my mane-mate to arrange my hair in a simple ponytail at my nape.

I did all this before I donned a somber sky-blue dress that Germaine had found somewhere (it was not in my closet, that's for sure, though not unattractive, it wasn't me at all...and obviously, I didn't put on a flower broach).

And then I sat with the king, the queen and my mate on a couch, with his siblings standing behind us in a room on the family's more informal floor (that would be the second), three cams aimed our way.

King Fillion spoke, and I noted for the first time he was very good at it.

The speech was prepared, and when I walked into the room, I saw him pacing and scrolling through it on a tablet, talking to Germaine and his aide, a female named Allina, as he did.

But when he spoke the words to the cams, it sounded off the cuff. Sincere. Determined. Angry. Wretched. Each emotion assigned to whatever the words referred to (concern for the state of mind of the realm after what had happened; that we would find the perpetrators; that this had happened at all; about the loss of Antheme and that poor male who was in the wrong place at the wrong time, respectively).

I had little doubt he was all of those things, genuinely, it was just impressive he could pull them off at the same time saying measured, prepared words.

Aleksei spoke briefly about how Antheme had been on his detail for years, she was an exemplary agent, and as such, he selected her personally for my detail. He also shared what a loss she was personally to the royal family, to him and to me. And he expressed sympathy for the male who had fallen after getting caught in the stream.

And I had a very brief statement to say, sharing I was all right, albeit devastated at Antheme's loss, saddened that one of our citizens who was simply going about his day got caught in the beam, but there were no words to express how grateful I was to the Royal Service for acting quickly to be certain I was whisked to safety.

All of that was prepared, but genuine too, and I hoped I delivered it as well as the king.

I was told our transmission would break into anything being displayed, streaming in real time, therefore, once the green light went off on the cams, my relief was great.

But me sitting with them earned me the first hug I'd received from Queen Calisa, and a pat on the cheek while she murmured, "I'm very proud of you, Laura."

And with that, as I suspected every royal family in Night's Fall did throughout history, no matter what was going on...

We got on with it.
In this case, we went to dinner.

✦ ✦ ✦

Even though the table was full of normally interesting, lively people—those being the king, queen, all three princes, the princess, me, the Truelocks, the Vinestrongs and Monique—the mood at dinner was somber.

I specifically noted how Queen Calisa's attention frequently turned to Aleksei.

It wasn't hard to understand why, since mine did as well, considering his mood seemed to deteriorate palpably as the night wore on.

Before the desert course, a male walked into the room, directly to the king, bent and whispered in his ear.

The king stood immediately and left with him.

Aleksei didn't hesitate to follow.

I made moves to do the same, but Mr. Truelock, who was my dinner partner, took my hand.

"In a time like this, my lovely, one must tread cautiously around a male shifter," he advised.

Considering the last "time like this," Aleksei had acted like a big jerk (though, understandably, still...), I saw the wisdom of this and kept my seat.

It wasn't long before Aleksei came back.

He stood in the door, his eyes beckoning me.

"Go," Mr. Truelock murmured.

I got up and went to my mate.

Wordlessly, he took my hand and guided me through the Palace.

We came out on a balcony on the south side.

I heard it before I saw it when he opened the door.

I only took two steps out before I halted.

The mingled sound of wolves howling and big cats and bears roaring was a low din that carried across the water to the Sceptred Isle.

And the air was rife with dragons.

"What's happening?" I whispered.

The king turned to me, and my breath caught when I saw the fierce expression on his face and his eyes glowing gold.

"Their True Bride was threatened. The shifters of Night's Fall prepare for war."

Farging *farg*.

CHAPTER 34

SUITE

It was still dark the next morning when I felt Aleksei pull from my arms and leave our bed. When I heard the door to the bathroom close, I turned to my back and stared into the murky room.

We'd both had a restless night.

Not a surprise.

It was also the first night since we lived together where we did not make love.

That wasn't a surprise either.

Then again, Aleksei had been called away, so I'd gone to bed alone and had been so dead asleep, I hadn't felt him join me until I woke due to him shifting.

Commence our restless nights.

And as I lay there, I thought much the same thoughts as had assaulted my brain over and over through the dark hours.

Primarily, remembering one of the last things Antheme said on this earth was that she was going to protect me.

Yes, she'd been referring to the Masque, but the message was the same.

Our conversation wasn't me sharing how much I liked her, gruff and distant and blunt as she was, or the fact that her being gruff, distant and blunt were big reasons why I liked her.

It wasn't about how much I appreciated her looking out for me.

We'd shared throwaway words. Nothing important. Two females walking to a craft and talking.

And then her lifeless body thudded to the pavement on a city street, and she was no more.

I wanted those last moments back for so many reasons.

To grab hold of her and pull her down with me so she would still be here.

To shift time so Antheme, or Fannon, or someone saw the shooter and stopped them before they released the blast.

Or simply to have our final conversation be about something meaningful.

To shut down these thoughts, I turned to my side, claiming Aleksei's pillow and holding it close, breathing in his scent.

I felt that nearly imperceptible shift of the bed when a feline lands on it, and sensing my mood, Comet shared none of his usual complaints when he approached. He just allowed me to add him to the pillow I held in my arms.

The cats had been brought from the penthouse (obviously), as had a ton of my clothes, and other things I'd need.

Palace staff moved me in.

Seeing as I didn't want my fur babies to get lost in this palatial maze or get stressed at another big change, the cats were sequestered in Aleksei's suite, which was more like a flat, and not a small one.

There was the vestibule, and the sitting room. There was also a study, which was large, and a library, which was small.

The library had three walls full of books (yes, real ones, but they were so old, I was afraid to touch them for fear they'd fall apart), a comfortable armchair, foot stool, lamp and table, and that was it.

It was a cozy nook I could see Aleksei using and wondered if he had. If this was one of those quiet places where he retreated in order to escape his brothers and the duties he'd been born into.

I hadn't asked him about this last night before he'd gone off to do whatever it was he'd been called to do. His mood didn't invite conversation.

But, because I wanted to know all about him, I made note to ask him about it later.

In the suite there were also two bedrooms, both sumptuously appointed, but Aleksei's was bigger. Each had attached bathrooms and rooms that used to be dressing chambers that had been converted to closets.

The bathrooms were old-fashioned, though they'd been modernized since the Palace was built, but before it was historically designated, so now, there could be no more changes. As such, they didn't have bath pods, instead, bathtubs and showers.

The bedrooms were situated at opposite sides of the suite, and Aleksei explained there were two, because in olden times, husband and wife didn't sleep together.

That said, my stuff was moved into his room, and it was my mate who directed it there.

The last rooms were found off the old dressing chambers. They used to be the bedrooms of the prince's valet and his princess's maid.

Aleksei's valet's room had been fitted with a state-of-the-art Body-Tone unit.

The room where my maid would have stayed had been set up for Queen Calisa to be her personal retreat when she was a princess.

That room was my favorite in the suite.

It was a stark contrast to the heavy masculinity that dominated the rest of the space (save the princess's room, but even that was a feminine version of the rest, featuring furnishings and fittings in deep wines and bright roses).

The princess's retreat was decorated in soft, cool tones of delicate green and misty blue, with a lush daybed, a big display and a cleverly crafted cabinet that held a small fridge and cupboard for drinks and snacks (due to Bev-Buddy and Snack-Sensations needing access to supply tubes, they couldn't be outfitted in the Palace).

I wondered if Queen Calisa had a room like that to get away from it all in her current situation in the Palace, and I hoped she did.

Knowing I'd never get back to sleep, I kissed Comet on his downy head (he mewed mildly angrily at the indignity of that) and he scampered when I slid out from under the covers.

I went to the bathroom and gave Aleksei a sleepy smile as his stormy gray eyes (apparently, the weather boded rain that day) followed me in the mirror on my trek to the little room that held the loo.

He'd showered and had a towel wrapped around his waist, and my vintage-loving mate was shaving rather than using a Beard-Raze.

This made me smile again.

I did my business, came out and used the basin beside his to wash my hands, doing so watching him wipe off shave foam.

"How are you doing, honey?" I asked.

"Shit," he answered.

Hmm.

At least that was honest.

"I was wondering if you thought it would be appropriate for me to contact Antheme's parents." I inquired. "To tell them—"

He cut me off. "Ask my mother about that. I've no fucking clue what you should do about it."

With that, he prowled out of the bathroom and into the closet.

Seemed Prince Aleksei got cranky when he didn't get decent sleep.

Understandable.

Especially after yesterday.

I fit my Denti-Clean in my mouth and hovered over the basin so the water that often dribbled out didn't wet my nightgown. A quick donning of the Ultra Paint on cleanse setting, and then I headed to the closet.

Aleksei was wearing suit trousers, shoes and buttoning a light-blue shirt.

I wanted to ask about what he'd learned when he'd been called away last night, but other pressing things were at hand, so I asked about that instead.

"Okay, I was also wondering if maybe I could go to this meeting with you this morning," I queried.

"No," he replied.

I waited for him to say more.

He did not.

This made my head titch. "Just...no?"

"These are affairs of state, Laura."

"I'm aware," I replied. *But yesterday, a female I liked and respected dropped dead beside me after taking a stream for me or taking it to manipulate my mate and his realm. So I'd kinda like to be in the know about what's happening*, I did not say.

"The Masque will go on," he announced. "Security will be heightened, of course. You being here at the Palace and available, with nothing else to do, can help Mom with that."

I couldn't get into his mentioning the Masque would go on, something I wasn't sure was a good idea, but it also wasn't my choice, nor did I suspect I had any say in the matter.

No, I had to dive into the other thing.

"Help your mother with the Masque?" I asked like he said, *Help Mom dig up the entire garden and replace the flowers with rutabagas.*

He stopped shrugging on his suit jacket and asked in return, "Am I speaking the old language and you aren't following?"

My beast curled into herself, his swelled, and I tried not to get angry.

Aleece had told me last night that Antheme had been on Aleksei's detail for three years.

I'd known her weeks. And as mentioned, it was Aleksei himself who appointed her head of my team.

Thus, he liked and respected her too, so I had to give him some room to grieve.

And Mr. Truelock had warned me to be cautious with Aleksei now.

I'd already learned that lesson, but I didn't quite know how to balance being supportive to him in his loss and cautious with him considering his mood.

In this vein, I thought it was safe to request, "You'll brief me on what's said?"

I was wrong about it being safe.

"Have I been keeping anything from you?" he asked sharply.

"Honey," I said softly, "I'm trying to be there for you."

He adjusted his cuffs under his jacket with short movements. "It's interesting how you trying to be there for me is all about what you want."

It felt like I'd been slapped.

And it felt like it happened again when he didn't notice.

Instead, he informed me, apropos of nothing, "The Palace works on an old bellpull or phone system. You can pull one of the cords in any of the rooms, and a member of staff will come up and attend to your needs. Or if you want something, say, to order breakfast brought up, pick up the receiver on the apparatus by my bed, hit the one button, and a member of staff will answer. Tell them what you want. If you don't fancy that, there's always a buffet in the breakfast room. That's not the one we eat dinner in. That's the informal dining room. If you don't know the way, call a member of staff to escort you."

It had been over a century since we'd moved to Palms and wrist units, etc. As such, I'd never used a phone in my life.

But I knew what telephones were.

I didn't share that.

"Okay," I whispered.

"Again, since you'll be here with little to do, you should arrange to have a detailed tour so you don't need to trouble a member of staff to show you where to eat breakfast. This will eventually be your home. You should know how to get around in it."

He and I hadn't yet found the time for that tour.

However, I'd been looking forward to Aleksei giving it to me, and although his suggestion was a good one (of course, I did need to learn my way around the Palace), the way he suggested it wasn't so good.

He gave me a close look and ordered, "Don't act wounded, Laura. I have a lot on my mind, we both lost someone important to us yesterday, and for once, this is not all about you."

I felt my lips part at this insult.

Delivering it, and all the rest, he didn't want me to act wounded?

Was he mad?

Patience, Laura, patience.

"It isn't your place to sit in on meetings like this," he went on. "Like it isn't your place to attend sessions in the Center and cast votes for the realm."

"I know that," I replied as evenly as I could.

"So why are you looking at me like I rehomed your cats?"

"Because I don't know the male I'm talking to," I retorted before I got control of my mouth. I took in a deep breath, reminding myself to be calm, rational and supportive, and continued, "Honey, I understand you're grieving—"

"I'm not grieving, I'm angry," he bit out. "It's clear I'm not the True Heir because my brothers are fuckwits. Something is happening, and for some fucked-up reason, you and I are at the center of it. But even if I might be part of it, you always seem to be in the thick of it."

I could see this was a lot for him.

I decided to address that.

"Can we talk a little about what happened last night?"

"What happened last night?" he asked.

"With the dragons, cats, wolves, bears," I explained, deciding to start with that first.

"Dad told you."

"I sense there's more to it."

He shook his head. "I also don't have time to do what your mother should have done and give you an understanding of the mind of a male shifter."

As I thought, there was definitely more to it.

"Okay, I'll ask your mother about that too," I mumbled.

"Are we done with this?" he asked tersely.

Patience, Laura, patience!

"We haven't been together for years, Aleksei." I tried a shaky smile. "Even if it feels like it, in a good way. So I don't quite know how to navigate this, but I'm doing my best to support you."

"Your best would be not waylaying me from important matters in order for you to take my time to point out how hard you're working to support me."

Perhaps it was his suggesting the unthinkable, rehoming my cats, even as a for instance.

Perhaps it was him weaponizing what I'd said weeks ago about how I worried I'd made us all about me.

Perhaps it was that this wasn't a heat-of-the-moment reaction to traumatic events, which plausibly would cause tempers to flare, but instead a cold distance while delivering seemingly calculated cuts meant to draw blood.

Mostly, it was all of that.

So I didn't lie. I didn't know this male.

And I didn't like him.

Whatever it was, I was less cautious with my words than I should have been when I retorted, "I do understand you have important matters on your mind, and though I'll never understand what a heavy burden you have to bear, I know it's there. That said, it might be nice if you understood I *haven't* been taught how to deal with a male shifter in times like these, and as such, perhaps you might put some small effort into not behaving like a dick."

At that, his head ticked, and his gaze darkened to a starry night.

Dang.

Then he spoke.

"And maybe we can have this discussion when I haven't been up all night, knowing the citizens of the Fall are riled, they want blood, but before that, they want answers we *do not have*. Not to mention, finding it impossible to sleep knowing that my mate has been in the sights of a stream *twice*. I've seen the vid from the cam on that street, Laura. I know how close you were to Antheme, thus I know you could have been hit by the stream that burned a hole through her gods-damned heart. I've also been in a cold, clinical room and seen for myself a lifeless Antheme with a hole burned through *her gods-damned heart*."

Oh gods.

He'd seen her?

"And the last thing I want on this earth is to lose my mate and turn into a weak, bitter piece of shit like your fucking father," he concluded.

With that, Aleksei was done talking, I knew, because after he finished speaking, he walked out on me.

CHAPTER 35
CAELYN

The member of staff (a chambermaid named Linzy) quickly retreated from the pandemonium that was going down in the breakfast room after she escorted me into it.

I didn't blame her, because this pandemonium included Timothee shooting from his chair, angrily tossing down his napkin, then leaning toward his mother, his face red with anger, his eyes glowing blue, and his mouth shouting, "You've lost your fucking *mind*!"

"Timothee, for goodness sakes, calm down," Queen Calisa replied.

"Tim, let's go take a walk," Aleece suggested.

Timothee turned on his sister. "Fuck that. You know she's insane to even consider this."

"I know you needed to fly last night," Aleece said carefully. "And you didn't. Maybe you should do that now."

"I can't." Timothee's accusing gaze swung to me standing in the door, like it had been me who'd confined him here. "I've been forbidden."

"I'll talk to Aleksei. He'll understand," Aleece said.

"Fuck Aleksei too," Timothee ground out, then he stalked toward the door, which I was still standing in.

I jumped out of his way, and he stormed right by me.

"If you'll excuse me," Queen Calisa said, rising far more genteelly and making her way to the door. "Good morning, dear," she greeted as she swept past, like her son hadn't just thrown a huge strop.

Right.

Seemed like emotions weren't just running high in the prince's suite.

I wandered toward the buffet, forced myself to make some selections (I wasn't at all hungry), then sat down beside Mr. Vinestrong.

Through this and what had come before, the non-royal members of the breakfast party, that being Mr. and Mrs. Vinestrong, Mr. Truelock, Monique and Gayle, had been studiously eating their breakfasts.

Aleece was the only royal left at the table. Aleksei and the king were in the meeting. And Errol wasn't there.

"What's happening?" I asked Aleece.

She flicked out her fork that had a chunk of pineapple speared on its prongs.

"Mom has an appearance today. She's not canceling."

Oh dear.

"It would be a tactical misstep if she did," Aleece continued.

"According to Germaine?" I asked.

"According to Mom," Aleece answered.

"She's right," Mr. Vinestrong put in. "It is now about demonstrations of strength. It would not send a good message if the royals cowered in their palace."

And now I was seeing why they were going ahead with the Masque.

Two assassination attempts on the True Heir and his mate, but all's good. Nothing to see here.

I saw the reasoning.

I still did not like Queen Calisa heading out that day.

But I was surprised at Timothee's reaction.

"Timothee doesn't agree?" I inquired.

"Tim's beast has been roused," Aleece shared. The earnest little sister who wanted to believe her brothers were good beings made an appearance as she said, "He was really upset about what happened to you yesterday. The loss of Antheme. But his mother putting herself out there is a sitch that isn't going to be easy for him to retain control. Dad and Aleksei will feel the same, but they'll get it, so they'll be able to control it."

"And Errol?" I asked.

"I think Errol is avoiding all of us because he's trying to keep it together," Aleece answered, but she did it in a way where it sounded like she wasn't so sure.

However, I took note that Aleece had lived her whole life with shifters, so, with the queen off to an appearance that day, maybe I could sit down with Aleece and have a deep chat.

On this thought, she pushed her chair back, stood and said, "I should probably check on that. Errol, I mean. See you all later."

And with no further ado, she was off.

Okay, I guessed she was out for me to ask her to provide some insights. At least for now.

I heaved a sigh.

"You doing all right?" Gayle asked.

I looked at her to see this was aimed at me.

With our company, I couldn't tell her no, I wasn't. My mate was being a dick again and everything was farged up.

I'd have to wait until later.

"I just didn't get very much sleep," I said for now.

Gayle gave me an understanding look. "I don't think any of us did."

"I don't suppose so," I mumbled.

Monique looked at her watch unit and said, "My transport is here. Gotta go."

Wait.

What?

I tensed. "You're leaving?"

"They've set up offices for the rest of us because we can work from here," Gayle answered for her.

"But Cat and I can't," Monique added.

I'd thought Catla was probably having a lie-in or availing herself of the ability to pull a cord and have someone bring her breakfast.

That was very Cat.

Now I took in the table with no small amount of concern.

At the expression on my face, Monique continued, "They're giving me protection, Laura. I'll be okay."

We had protection yesterday, and we were not okay.

"Are you sure?" I asked.

"I have clients who depend on me, hon," she answered. "And bills to pay."

She did.

Not to mention, as Aleksei reminded me earlier, it wasn't all about me and what I wanted.

"Of course," I mumbled.

"Aleksei wouldn't let anything hurt me," she assured. "And I'll come right back to the Palace after my last client."

I nodded, even if I didn't like it.

But I got it.

It wasn't long ago that I would have done the same. It was just that now, I was no longer in her position. Through my mate, I was filthy rich. I had four homes in one city alone. I could walk away from my vid and my career, never look back and never want for anything.

But it wasn't my credit line to tap into, it was Aleksei's, and the Palace's, so I couldn't tell her I'd cover her losses so she could stay safe in the Palace.

And it was because of me that she might not be safe.

"Is Cat in the city?" I asked.

"The gallery has been repaired. She's working with Terrinton on the next showing," Mr. Truelock said.

I examined his face, searching for signs of worry his daughter was out in the world, a possible target.

But either he was very good at hiding it (which was a possibility), or he trusted the RS (also feasibly genuine).

With Monique going first, one by one, they all took off to find their new palace offices and get to work, and I lingered alone at the breakfast table, sipping coffee, trying not to think, and thinking too much.

In an effort to curtail that, I left the table and wandered the Palace by myself.

I definitely needed a guided tour. There were a number of rooms, but none of them had plaques outside that said "this is the room the family uses to do so and so."

I did notice that everything on the second floor seemed more lived in, even if it was imposing and refined, bearing testimony to what I'd already figured out, it was the family living area, whereas what I found on the first floor was more formal. Meaning the first floor was where they did their royal business.

And I already knew the third floor was where they had their private spaces and where some guest rooms were located (I didn't peruse that floor).

I was out in the courtyard, trying to enjoy the nip in the air that was brought on by the gray skies and the coming autumn and giving myself the opportunity to see the lush but exacting layout of the garden close up, when I heard the mighty flap of dragon's wings.

I looked up to see a dragon, smaller than Aleksei's, but with a goodly number of horns and spikes, the ridges of his wings, his brow and his breast an iced blue that looked fierce against the rest of his black.

He flapped down to land behind some shrubbery not close, but not far from me.

I saw a member of staff scurry behind the shrubs with an arm full of clothes, the proud dragon's head I could see over the top of the neatly clipped shrubbery disappeared, and within minutes, Timothee was stalking out from behind the bushes.

Toward me.

I said nothing as he approached, because I was a little surprised how awesome his dragon was.

Okay, so maybe he wasn't a massive, powerful, fearsome beast, like Aleksei's.

But he was still beautiful.

And fearsome.

I then said nothing as he came to me, his face a mask of fury, and immediately grabbed my arm.

I didn't have to pull it away. He yanked his hand from me while shaking it.

"He's keeping you marked, which is good, but you need to get your ass inside," Timothee decreed.

"Why?" I asked.

"They're after you, in case you hadn't noticed," he returned.

I looked stupidly to the sky. "Isn't this airspace protected?"

"Yes," he clipped. "Do you want to see if they can penetrate that?"

Considering an all-out affront on the Celestial Palace would be an open act of war, I thought he was being a mite overprotective.

And then I had to give a thought to the fact that he, *Timothee*, was being overprotective...of me.

When I didn't move, he threatened, "I can text comm my brother and tell him you're in the gardens, meandering about under the open skies."

I didn't want to give Aleksei anything more to be angry at me about, so I headed toward the door I'd come out of.

Timothee followed me.

Once we were inside, I decided to make an effort.

I turned to thank him.

He was already stalking away.

"Timothee," I called.

He stopped in a manner that he wanted to make it clear it was taking all of his effort and patience to do so, and he aimed his attention to me.

"Thanks for"—I drifted a hand toward the door we'd come in—"looking out for me."

"Whatever," he muttered and made to leave again.

"Timothee," I called, moving toward him this time.

He stopped and bit out, "What?"

"If you have some time today, maybe we could—"

"I have all the time in the world, Laura. As you know."

Okay then.

He wasn't going to make this easy.

Not a surprise.

And so be it.

"Then perhaps we could, I don't know, chat or something," I suggested.

"About?" he asked.

"You're my mate's brother. I'd like to get to know you."

He leaned back and crossed his arms on his chest. "Would you?"

"Well...yeah." I gestured to the door again, this time indicating the garden beyond. "That's the first time you've spoken to me."

He looked at the door but didn't say anything.

"Okay, here's the deal," I began to lay it out.

He returned his attention to me.

I kept going.

"All my beings are working. I don't know where Aleece is, and I don't want to comm her if she's busy. Your mom..." At the ice-blue flare in his eyes, I decided not to get into why she was unavailable. "And Aleksei was a big jerk to me this morning. Also, unless you aren't paying attention, you know I didn't exactly have a loving mother who sat me down and explained the many nuances of living with a male shifter, so all I know about it is my dad alternately not giving a dang about me or doing other not-so-fun things when it came to me."

Was that a slight flinch I saw on his face?

Hoping it was, I powered on. "So you're all I've got."

"All you've got for what?"

"To explain about male shifters."

He blinked. "You want *me* to explain to *you* about male shifters?"

"You are one, who better?"

A long hesitation (very long), and he asked dubiously, "What do you want to know?"

"You could start by explaining why the dragons flew last night, and the wolves howled, the bears roared, etcetera."

"Someone shot a stream intended for the True Heir's mate and killed her bodyguard," he said like I was a dim bulb.

"Yes, I get that, but I'm not their mate."

"Do you not know history?" he asked, again with the dim-bulb tone.

"Of course I know history," I answered, thinking maybe I wasn't the brightest, considering it was clear using this to try to make inroads with him was not a sterling idea.

His head tipped to the side as he muttered, "Do females not get this?"

"Get what?"

It took him about twenty beats, throughout all of them, I didn't know if he'd march away or stay.

Finally, he said, "Follow me."

I wanted to crow in victory that maybe I'd made a break in the walls around Prince Timothee.

I didn't do that.

I followed him.

He took me into a cavernous room on the first floor that had its walls covered entirely in a magnificent mural.

This included the ceiling.

I'd heard about this mural. It was famous.

But I hadn't gotten to this wing of the Palace before I got sidetracked by the gardens, so I hadn't seen it yet.

He went to a corner and pointed at the wall.

"This is Battle of the Chasm, which happened about a hundred and fifty years before the Troll Invasion. And this"—he did a circle, his finger still pointing, indicating the entire room—"is the history of the Starknight Clan."

Slowly I turned, taking it all in, knowing I was going to be in that room for hours, inspecting every inch of Aleksei's family history in mural form.

"You know shifters adapted from humans before recorded history?" Timothee asked as I studied the dragons flying with eagles, hawks, ravens, owls, all of these clearly battling demons who were on the ground trying to stave off wolves, bears, snakes and a variety of big cats.

"Yes," I replied.

"The Battle of the Chasm is the first resounding defeat of the demons who populated what's now Sky's Edge," he shared.

I looked to him. "I know that too."

"Do you know the reason we won is because Caelyn Knightstar devised a strategy that's known now as the first militarized bank of dragons?"

I nodded.

Even so, he continued his history lesson.

"He synchronized this with land-based creatures. Before, the different shifter creatures battled among themselves. We were not united as one species but broken up into clans of the beast we carried. Further, war tactics were not that advanced. It was race into the clash, kill or be killed, and the leader with the most standing at the end won. In other words, it was chaos. Casualties were always huge. Caelyn not only amassed all the species together, he ordered reconnaissance and did not attack unless he knew everything he could about his enemy. He devised the first aerial sorties. He organized battalions, created flanks, trained commanders, planned battles to the last warrior, with secondary and tertiary strategies that could be called if he saw one failing. In essence, he created modern warfare."

"He was also the first to treat all species of beasts equally, in battle and out of it," I added.

Timothee nodded and pointed again to the wall. "He wasn't made chieftain until after that victory. And the reason that war was fought was because his mate had been captured by a band of demons."

"I know that too."

Then, Timothee pointed to the very top corner of the wall, where, on the ceiling, flying creatures hovered, and on the wall, land-based ones milled, but it clearly depicted a gathering.

And they were all looking up to a nebulous being in the night sky.

"The night before the Battle of the Chasm, Caelyn called all his warriors together, and together, they all beseeched the Night God for bravery, victory and glory, and not insignificantly, the return of Caelyn's mate. It isn't known if the Night God answered their prayers, because they won, obviously, but she was killed by the demons in retribution for the routing of their troops. But all the male shifters suffered her loss like they'd lost their own mate."

What he was saying started penetrating.

Because I knew all of this.

I just didn't *understand* it.

Until now.

"And all the male shifters vowed, from then on, to fight and die for the protection of the chieftain's mate," Timothee said. "And that vow was definitely heard, and as such, bonded into the males by the Night God. Since, if the leader of Night's Fall's mate is threatened, we all rally to her defense. It isn't a choice. It's ingrained in us. And in doing so, we experience a significantly heightened sense of protection to the females of our own clans or families."

"Okay, I get that," I said. "So why didn't it happen the first time there was an attempt? The one at the gallery?"

"Because we didn't know you were Aleksei's mate yet. But that beam was aimed at him. No one would want the True Heir, or simply the next king, harmed. But, right or wrong, he is not as vulnerable as a female. He's considered a warrior, and you are not. He's better able to defend himself. Though, the bottom line is, the Night God instilled in us all the uncontrollable drive to protect our queen, or the one who would be her, and at the same time, it ramps up our already seriously developed inclination to protect the females in our clans."

"So is this why Aleksei is acting like a jerk?"

I was lulled by our precarious camaraderie, I saw, after asking that question, and I regretted it the instant he smirked.

"Aleksei's acting like a jerk?" he asked.

"Forget it," I mumbled, turned from him and studied the wall.

The Troll Invasion was the next thing depicted.

I feigned fascination (well, not feigned, exactly, the mural was *insane*, it was so cool), and in so doing, hopefully, I dismissed him.

"I don't have a mate, Laura," he said.

"I'm aware," I told the wall.

I heard his heavy sigh.

"In other words, I've no idea why he's acting like a jerk," he went on. "And I'm surprised he is. In a time like this, I'd think he'd be acting the opposite."

I would think so too.

That said...

I looked at him. "You shouted at your mother in front of people she barely knows at the breakfast table."

His chin ticked to the side in visible shock at this, like he didn't realize he'd been a jerk too.

"So is this a thing with you males when you sense your females are vulnerable? Letting your hormones dictate your behavior?" I asked.

"I'm worried about her," he returned.

"Okay, but she's an adult female who doesn't make a move unless she considers the consequences to this family and the entire realm. Maybe you can share your feelings without yelling, throwing your napkin on the table and marching from the room."

He was no less shocked when he shared, "I didn't really...have any control over that."

Interesting.

"So, she told you she was..." His eyes flared blue, and again I skipped that part, but I did it this time noting that it was clear this was an uncontrollable response to the mere suggestion a female in his family was in danger. "And it just happens?"

Timothee shrugged, but I could tell he was unsettled by this.

"It's pretty mega, not the shouting part, the you caring about your mom so much part," I told him.

He stared at me with even more shock.

"Also, you shouldn't hide your dragon from the people. He's gorgeous."

Timothee's mouth dropped open.

"Scary as farg, but gorgeous," I amended.

"You think he's scary?" he asked.

"Have you seen your dragon?"

"We don't tend to look in mirrors," he returned.

"A pic?"

Another shrug and I could swear it was uncomfortable when he said, "Sure."

"I don't know what this is about, but from an objective observer, he's fierce and terrifying."

He brushed my words aside. "Dragons tend to be that."

"Mine isn't."

His smile that time was another smirk, but I was sensing, not a bad one. "No, she isn't."

"It isn't about size. It isn't about status. It isn't about anything but what you make of what you've got," I educated him. "The thing is, what you've got is a lot, and I don't know, I haven't been around for very long, but I suspect the reason beings are annoyed with you is because you're smart enough to figure that out and do something with it."

His face closed down. "You're right, you don't know."

"I know. I said that. But be this guy." I jabbed a finger at the wall. "The male who helped me out. Not the other one, who would have walked away in the hallway and made me try to sort it out myself. I'd trust my life to your dragon. It'd be nice to know I could trust a piece of my heart to you."

There seemed to be a variety of emotions battling it out in his expression, before he settled on one.

Incidentally, it was the wrong one.

"Do you think you can come into our family and fix us?" he asked, a hint of the snide Timothee in his tone.

"No. But that doesn't mean I won't try. It's using what I've got. I might fail, but it would suck more if I didn't bother to try."

As his stare turned into a scowl, and I sensed the other Timothee coming to the fore, I again studied the depiction of the Knightstars in the Troll Invasion.

Timothee didn't engage me in further conversation.

He also didn't say goodbye when he walked out.

But at least I had a sense of why Aleksei got so hot and bothered after our flight from the gallery.

I still didn't know why he was so cold and cutting in the closet.

I just knew one thing.

I was in this by choice and destiny.

So eventually, I'd have no choice but to find out.

CHAPTER 36
WRONG

I was ensconced in the daybed in the Princess's Retreat Chamber (I named it that myself), reading (not really, I couldn't concentrate) and cuddling Nova (I was doing better at that) while Jupiter lay on the back of the daybed, his tail swinging lazily, and Comet was giving his pudge the opportunity to spread by laying on his back on the floor.

I was waiting for everyone to be done with work so I'd have people to hang out with, but more to the point, I could grab my gals and get their take on what was up with Aleksei.

I was also recovering from the two comms I'd just made.

I'd asked Nata to get me the sequences for Antheme's family, as well as the wife of the man who'd died yesterday.

I hadn't had the opportunity to ask the queen if this was the right thing to do, and I didn't ask Germaine because I didn't want her to say no.

I could imagine both families being angry with me, because if not for me, their loved ones would be alive.

But no matter how hard it was going to be (and I knew it was hard before I found out exactly how hard it was), I also couldn't ignore the fact, because of me, their loved ones were no longer alive.

During the comms, I got the opposite of anger, which weirdly made it worse.

Both were openly moved I took the time to connect, express sympathy and chat with them.

And Antheme's mom and dad were both reduced to laughing tears that heartened, at the same time broke me, when I shared how much I liked their daughter and the reasons why.

In the end, it was the right thing to do, but it was horrid all the same.

It was on this thought Aleksei walked in.

After my convo with Timothee, I'd decided to give him his bad mood of the morning, considering all that was going on, and pretend it didn't happen.

So I smiled at him.

He did not smile back.

He took us all in, looked to me, and asked, "Enjoying your day?" in a tone that said, *The rest of us are taking this threat seriously, and you're in here, chilling out.*

I ignored his tone, put my book down and replied, "I've been waiting for your meeting to be over."

I did not share it was nearly three in the afternoon, his meeting was at seven in the morning, and maybe it lasted that long, but I was guessing it didn't.

And if it didn't, in between times, he didn't come to me.

"Did you get anything accomplished today?" he asked.

I was in a holding pattern with work, something he knew.

His mother was away from the Palace for an appearance, something I suspected he knew.

So I wasn't sure what I was supposed to accomplish.

But I offered, "Timothee and I had a conversation about Caelyn Knightstar and the Battle of the Chasm."

"You asked *Tim* to explain the instincts of a male shifter?" he all but sneered.

No.

It wasn't "all but."

He straight-up sneered.

It was hard, but I ignored that too.

"I couldn't say he was leaping for joy at the opportunity to tell me, but he was helpful," I said.

"A miracle shines out of the murk," he muttered.

Do not ask me why, but a protective instinct surged in me regarding his brother.

"He helped me out, Aleksei. I had a question, and he took time to answer it."

Something you did not do, I left unsaid.

He ignored that and inquired, "Did you get a tour of the Palace?"

"I wandered myself."

"That isn't a tour."

"No," I agreed. "But staff have things to do. Aleece disappeared after breakfast, she was checking on Errol. I didn't see her after, and I didn't comm because I didn't want to bother her in case she was busy. Your father was otherwise engaged. Your mom was gone. So I did the best I could do."

An odd brittleness seemed to infuse his features when I mentioned Errol, but he didn't explain that or say anything.

He simply inclined his head.

"I also spoke to Antheme's mom and dad, as well as the wife of the male who was lost yesterday," I told him.

His brow creased. "Did Germaine approve that?"

"No."

He put his hands on his hips, like a father preparing to educate a small, dull child. "Laura, I believe you've already learned, in sensitive matters like that, you need to discuss them with Germaine."

Do not rise to the bait, Laura.

"They were moved I took the time to comm," I shared.

"We're lucky for that," he murmured and then declared, "I have a meeting in ten minutes. I'll be in my study and shouldn't be disturbed."

"Is this meeting about what's happening?"

"No. I still own controlling share of twenty-seven businesses, regardless of what happened yesterday. And in so doing, I'm required to discuss issues and render decisions on how they operate."

And now I was not a small, dull child, but I was getting another you're-a-dim-bulb tone from a prince of the realm.

Patience and understanding. He considers his mate in danger and vulnerable. Don't add fuel to the fire.

"Will you share about your meeting this morning after your imminent meeting?" I asked.

"I said I would."

More odd, I sensed he was lying.

Since I couldn't understand why I had that sensation, I didn't call him on it.

I nodded and said, "Okay. Can you tell me why you were called away last night?"

"No."

I waited.

Nothing.

So I guessed that was again all I was going to get.

"Are there any more questions you have in order to detain me before you get back to reading, and I return to doing important shit?" he asked.

Patience and understanding instantly took a swan dive out the window.

"I'd appreciate it if you'd stop throwing in my face that I confided in you I was worried I was self-absorbed when we got together. I'm not Anna, Aleksei."

"You are, indeed, not," he agreed. "And I'm not doing that."

"It feels like it."

"So there are issues you wish to use to detain me," he noted, his voice beleaguered.

Beleaguered!

I was beleaguering him!

I picked up my book, saying, "Go. I'm not a fan of you in this mood."

"I'm not in a mood, Laura. I simply have things to do."

"Fine. Awesome. Feel free to do them," I muttered to my book.

"It didn't take you long to learn to be a princess. Now that, love, is *very* Anna."

My attention snapped back to him.

Nova slunk away.

Jupiter jumped off the daybed and disappeared under it.

Comet rolled to his belly and stared up at Aleksei.

My beast retreated.

His bulged.

"Did you just say that to me?" I asked.

"It seems to escape you that I'm not a fan of your mood either."

"And tell me, Aleksei, what is my mood?"

"I almost lost you yesterday."

"That might be an explanation of *your* mood, not a good one, but an explanation. It isn't your take on mine."

"You seem not to understand there are pressing matters at hand. Very pressing."

"How exactly have I shared with you I don't understand that?"

"I don't know," he drawled. "Maybe something like, I told you I have a meeting in what is now less than ten minutes, I have to prepare for that meeting, something that will take longer than the time I have, but I've no choice but to do what I can, and I'm not doing that. I'm having this conversation with you."

"As I said earlier, your highness, you are free to go. I'm not detaining you. You're not leaving but instead hanging around in order to throw barbs."

"And now she plays the victim," he murmured under his breath, turning to leave.

That was it.

I was done.

I slapped my book down on the daybed.

Comet dashed under it.

"Oh my gods!" I cried. "I am not playing the victim."

He turned to me, all too eager, despite his assertions that he wasn't, to be detained.

I shook my head and did it hard.

"No. Nope. I'm done with this discussion. You have pressing matters. We'll reconvene when you have time."

I picked up my book again, opened it, and it wasn't the page I was on, but I pretended it was.

"I'll warn you now, there is much that was discussed this morning that I can't tell you," Aleksei said.

This did not make me happy.

I absolutely didn't share that at this juncture.

"Consider me warned," I replied to my book.

He didn't leave.

I continued pretending to read.

He still didn't leave.

I quit pretending to read and looked at him. "Anything else, your royal highness?"

His eyes sparked purple, and he growled, "When you call me that when you're pissed, it takes everything I have to stop myself from turning you over my knee."

"I'm not a child," I snapped.

"Darling," he purred. "It wouldn't be that kind of spanking."

Drat it all, my sex dampened.

He sensed it or smelled it and the spark in his eyes became fire.

"Though, you'd learn your lesson," he finished.

He wasn't to be believed.

I stared at him.

He stared at me.

I continued to stare at him.

He kept staring at me.

I carried on staring at him, and I did it resolved it wouldn't be me who spoke the first word.

He broke our staring contest. "I'll see you at dinner."

No, you won't. I'm dialing one, ordering food, eating in here and giving you loads and loads and LOADS of time to get over whatever this is.

"Later," I replied, turning back to my book.

He left.

I suddenly felt like crying.

I didn't.

I needed to pin down the queen.

Or I needed to talk to Mr. Truelock. He seemed like he might know where Aleksei's head was at.

Either way, I needed someone, anyone, to tell me what was going on with my mate.

I needed this so I wouldn't kill him.

I put my book down, found my Palm and text commed Mr. Truelock, asking if we could have a chat when he was done with work, but before dinner.

I knew him better, that's why I picked him.

I also didn't have the queen's number. Anytime we made plans, we did it through aides.

I barely set my Palm aside before the tone sounded.

It was Mr. Truelock.

He was just the best.

I took his video comm. "I didn't mean to disturb you."

"Are you all right?" he asked, appearing concerned.

I looked to the door.

It was open.

I got up and walked to close it, saying, "I have something personal to discuss." I shut the door and said quietly, "About Aleksei."

"Is he all right?"

The answer to that was a big fat no.

"Can we talk after you get done with work?"

"We can talk now, Laura."

Totally the best.

"It might take a while," I warned him.

"You're concerned because his instincts have engaged," he deduced.

"Well, I think so, except that they're weird."

"I can imagine it's very intense."

"More like...cold, distant, argumentative." *Mean.*

"I'm sorry?" he queried, now appearing confused.

"It's like with every conversation we have, he's picking a fight. Like, he's going for all the vulnerable spots, prodding them, even pushing at them to force me to react."

"*Your* vulnerable spots?"

"Mine."

Mr. Truelock said nothing, but now he appeared contemplative.

"It's only been today, and yesterday was a lot," I explained. "I get the sense he's more upset than he's willing to let on that we lost Antheme, so that might be part of it."

"I'm not a shifter, as you know," Mr. Truelock said. "But I do know, when their protective instincts have engaged, the males are very unpredictable. But shifters are creatures of action. For dragons, to that action, you can add fire. Either way, it's known this runs hot. For a dragon, I would suspect very hot. Not cold and argumentative."

Hmm.

"Freya is not my mate, demons don't have them," Mr. Truelock continued.

"I know."

"So I fear I may not have any answers as to why Aleksei has retreated to this behavior after what's happened."

"So you think it's a mate thing, not a shifter thing?"

"I could ask some of my shifter acquaintances," he offered. "And some of my mated ones."

"Do you think they might figure out that you're asking about Aleksei and me?"

"I think they know I've been moved to the Palace for my protection because you're my family, so yes. Although I'd do my best to shroud it, if they have a brain in their head, and they all do, they would likely make that leap, considering it isn't a far distance to land."

So that was out.

"And I can't ask the king or queen, because they aren't mates either," I mumbled.

"This is true. But you could look it up on a digi-pane."

Oh my gods.

I was such an idiot.

Of course I could.

Why hadn't I thought of that?

In fact, why hadn't I done it weeks ago?

Aleksei had even mentioned how poor my research was, since I got everything I knew about mates from romance novels.

"I can't believe I didn't think of that."

"It's as if you have other things taking your time and other matters on your mind," he teased.

He was totally the best.

"Thank you, Mr. Truelock."

"I wonder, perhaps when you become princess, if you might consider acquiescing to one of my many offers to call me Mammon."

I scrunched my nose.

He smiled at me.

"It feels weird," I told him.

"I suppose after all this time, it's become somewhat of a nickname, as it were."

"Yeah. Look at it like that," I encouraged.

He smiled at me, then sobered. "Have patience with him. Sadly, the male gender is not good across species at dealing with emotion."

"I'll try," I promised, even though I thought I *was* trying.

I was just failing.

And it was Aleksei's fault (so said me).

We disconnected and I went to find my tablet.

I returned to the daybed, holed up in a corner and got to work.

I searched *Male Fated Mate Reaction to Female Mate Vulnerability*.

And I got a lot about volatility, unpredictability, and in some, the tendency to bait other males into a challenge. In others, though it was rare, physical abuse of their mate and/or young.

I stared hard at that one, rereading it repeatedly, until I let it go, because Aleksei wasn't doing that, and I knew he never would. But my father definitely had.

Though I did note all the articles said that a fated mate would continue in these behaviors, with changes in the intensity depending on his ability to control it, until he sensed the vulnerability had passed. Or, until he found a release of tension, and physical activity (including copulation, which was an intriguing concept), sparring or shifting were all suggestions on how to release said tension.

It was in this search I found myself sliding down a rabbit hole, skimming or reading full articles about the psychology of mates.

This was a fascinating, but not always fun place to be.

One of the fascinating parts was that the prevailing theory of the origin of fated mates was that the Night God, Sky God, Dawn God and Land God all got together to create them for the purpose of the continuation of the species.

They didn't explain why this was the theory, considering nature for all creatures was to procreate in the first place, but it was clear it wasn't to keep species pure, because from the dawn of time, inter-species mating was a thing.

The next fascinating part was that there were different reactions to finding your mate, depending on your species, or if your mate was of another species, or if there was mixed blood.

Shifter beasts made it easy, because they recognized their mates instantly.

It wasn't so easy for fae or the magical, even manifesting itself as unexplainable enmity, at first, until something happened when the mating became clear.

The not-always-fun part was an article I read (definitely in full) about how there were mates who should not be.

The article was titled *When the Gods Get It Wrong*.

It explained, in modern times, this was sometimes a conscious decision, say, should I have turned away from Aleksei because I wanted no part in his complicated life.

However, there were some who simply didn't get along, couldn't find harmony, their lives didn't naturally intertwine, or they found they simply didn't like each other.

And the authors of that article encouraged those mates to part and find contentment elsewhere, at the same time cautioning they'd do so feeling the loss for the rest of their lives.

Though, they assured the pain would become manageable, like a chronic illness of the past that had no cure: for instance, migraines.

In other words, the pain was debilitating, but you had no choice but to learn to cope with it and carry on, and this you would do.

This brought to mind that Aleksei and I had few things in common.

Sure, we both liked quiet and being at home, reading, cooking, yadda, yadda.

We also liked having sex.

But was that a basis for a relationship?

He was wealthy. Titled. He had an intact family, which had some dysfunction, but there was love, care, support.

I had none of that.

He had a drive to make something more of himself, doing this making scads of money.

I liked nice things, and I didn't mind working for them, but I'd never been ambitious that way.

He was business minded.

I was creative minded.

He was determined to find balance in doing what he wanted with his life and performing the duty he was born into.

I was struggling mightily with that, and I honestly didn't know if I could take on another job and do it to my exacting standards, at the same time fret about all the appearances I was going to have to make, but I had to make them anyway because that was expected of me, and I couldn't demur.

Truth be told, if we were not mates, we would never have found each other.

Like the article suggested, had the gods got it wrong?

Was that why Aleksei was behaving like this, because with all that was going on, he was realizing it?

It couldn't be denied, even if it wasn't my fault, I was trouble, a weakness that was not his own, one he didn't really need.

All of this messing up my head, I searched *Male Shifter Dragon Fated Mate Reaction to Female Mate Vulnerability*.

And the results rendered much the same but included spontaneous or uncontrolled shifting to their creature.

Nothing about picking fights, remoteness, coolness, or overall dickish behavior.

I tapped my fingernail on the edge of the tablet until I got a brainstorm.

True Heir Reaction to True Bride Vulnerability.

There were a number of panes about the history of the True Heir and his Bride, but the only ones about any reaction harked back to general information about shifter mates.

But on the third pane of search results, there was an article about Prince Aerin and his True Bride, Princess Iphelia.

There was a famous play about Aerin and Iphelia. We'd put on a production of it when I was in school (and my costumes for it rocked).

The reason they were famous was that Aerin's and Iphelia's love affair was known as being explosive. She was a warrior herself, which didn't help things in their relationship, because he was big on wanting to make her stay at Spikeback Castle and go off to battle on his own, and she wasn't so hot on that. They clashed, she won and was eventually wounded at the Battle of Peak Neige, which made Aerin lose his mind.

They shocked realms by separating. But during this, they were both miserable.

The legend went, they eventually couldn't deal with being apart and set out from their respective castles at the same time, met in the middle, and their activities there created the next True Heir.

I called up the article to read it just as a bubble drifted down from the top of the screen.

It announced a vid comm from Cat.

I took it. "Hey."

"Where are you?" she asked.

"I'm in the Princess Retreat," I told her. "Where are you?"

"I just got back from the gallery."

Thank gods.

"The Princess Retreat?" she queried.

"We're having drinks in here ASAP. Seeing as I'll be princess, I decree it, but we also have all sorts of stuff to talk about."

"I'm in," she replied. Then asked, "Did you know Prince Tanyn is here?"

"Yes," I answered.

"Have you met him?" she asked.

"No," I answered.

"Well, I just did. In the hall. And he's a massive asshole."

I felt my eyes get wide. "Really?"

"He thinks the Truelocks are demon traitors."

I sat up and asked angrily, "He said that?"

"Not in so many words. But when I introduced myself, his lip curled."

I sat back.

This was not a new thing. In the past (the *way* past), demons of the Edge made it known their feelings about the First Families of Night's Fall.

And yes, it was that they thought they were demon traitors.

But that was *way* past.

That said, how that was made known was so ugly, I knew Cat, as well as Mr. Truelock and all the First Families, had some sensitivity around it.

"It was five hundred years ago. He needs to get over it," she groused.

"Aleksei says he's broody," I told her.

"I'll say," she replied. "Why are we doing drinks there?"

"Because I need a drink, and I also need to suss out stuff with my gals."

She knew me, so she knew what I was saying, and she proved this by mumbling, "Uh-oh, trouble in paradise."

Absolutely.

"Just come when you're ready," I bid. "I'm going to text Gayle and Monique. This is about Aleksei, and Aleece knows him better than I do, but even though she'll give good insights, I don't know if it's wise to invite her."

"One hundred percent no," Cat advised. "I get she digs you, but if you talk shit about her big bro, that'll go out the window."

"It won't be talking shit. He's genuinely acting weird."

Her brows knit. "What's going on?"

"Just come here after you're done chilling a bit from getting back from the gallery. Do you know where our suite is?"

"No clue."

"North wing, third floor. Just text when you've made it to the floor, and I'll stand in the hall."

"Cool. I just need to get changed and I'll be on my way."

"Thanks, Cat."

"See you soon, babe."

We disconnected. I sent my text comms. I got replies that Gayle was done with work (seemed I did fall down a rabbit hole, it was well after five) and on her way to my suite, and Monique was in a craft heading back to the Palace, and she'd join us when she got there.

I decided to take advice from Cat and not invite Aleece.

After all this, I sat and wondered if Aleksei was still in his latest meeting, which had started two hours before, or if he was being a dick again and not coming to me after it was over.

Since I had no intention to seek him out to discover the answer to that question, I picked up the receiver from the apparatus that sat on a table by the daybed, and I ordered drinks to be sent up.

CHAPTER 37
RELATIONSHIPS

"Bollocks," Gayle spat, throwing my tablet on the miniscule free area on the daybed where we were all curled and crunched together with martini glasses (in which, there were martinis).

FYI: I'd cued up the *When the Gods Get It Wrong* article and shared it with them all.

As such, she concluded, "The gods didn't get you and Aleksei wrong."

Although I was heartened by the vociferousness of her response, I said, "You have to admit, we don't have a lot in common."

"Tell me one couple, mates or just lovers, who have everything in common," Gayle returned.

Hmm.

Food for thought.

"You both like animals. You both like hanging out at home. You both don't like big crowds or attention," Cat intoned. "You both like real books and get off on vintage things and doing stuff they invented tech to save us from doing. I mean, cooking?" She pulled a face. "Hells no."

Aleksei and I did like all that stuff.

And it didn't seem like very much, but maybe it was.

"You both also have a lot to get used to," Monique put in. "And you would, whether he was the future king, and you were surviving assassination attempts, or not. Relationships aren't always free and breezy."

"Actually," Cat chimed in again, "I was wondering when you two would get out of the first blush phase. It was lasting so long, it was beginning to get weird."

"Totally," Gayle agreed.

Moniqe nodded.

"You all thought we were weird?" I asked.

"Not in a bad way," Cat said. "It was awesome, how loved up you were, how well you got along. But couples fight."

"There are misunderstandings," Gayle added.

"Shit happens," Monique summed it up.

"I'm not sure this is just fighting," I said. "He's being so un-Aleksei, I don't know who this male is."

"Have you asked him what's going on in his head?" Monique inquired.

"Not straight out, but I've noted his mood and—" I stopped speaking when they all groaned in unison. "What?" I asked.

"Telling someone who's in a mood that you've noticed they're in said mood isn't a good way to help alleviate that mood," Gayle advised, like she had a side hustle as a relationship expert.

Although she didn't have this side hustle, she wasn't wrong.

"It's more about digging into it to see what's *causing* his mood," Monique added.

"I've mentioned Antheme, he says he's not grieving, he's angry," I remarked.

"He has a dick," Cat said. "People with dicks don't get sad, they get mad."

Gayliliel and Monique nodded.

This wasn't wrong either, and Mr. Truelock said much the same thing, without referring to dicks, of course.

"He's also mentioned me almost dying, which obviously would put him in a crappy mood, but he's taking that out on me," I pointed out.

"Suck it up," Gayle said as Monique reached for my tablet.

"I'm trying," I replied.

"Well, if giving him grace isn't working, then give him space," Cat counseled.

I was all the way down with this option.

Sure, it was avoidance, but that could be good sometimes.

Right?

"I'm considering avoiding dinner," I told them. "I don't want anyone else to notice we're not getting along. And I agree, he needs space. Maybe he'll sort himself out."

"You don't have to avoid him at dinner. I passed Timothee in the admin wing, and he said that Princes Bainon and Cormac had showed," Gayle informed us all. "He didn't seem happy that the king and Aleksei were going to be holed up with them in a meeting that would probably go through dinner. But that was probably because he wasn't invited to the meeting."

Timothee wasn't happy about much of anything these days.

Though, I thought it was interesting he shared this information with Gayle, rather than being a jerk and ignoring her or something.

Maybe Aleksei sequestering him to the Palace was making him think on things.

These were my first thoughts because I wasn't going to allow myself to think my next ones.

Those being why Princes Bainon and Cormac were here now, since the Masque was still two days away, and Aleksei probably knew they were coming when we last spoke, but he didn't tell me.

But if they were already in a meeting, at least that explained why he didn't come to me after the last one.

"Yikes," Cat said as she looked at her watch. "We need to get on that. Pre-dinner drinks are at six thirty, and it'll take us an hour to walk there, but we only have ten minutes."

I smiled at her, not feeling totally better about Aleksei and me, but it felt good to hammer it out with my gals.

And I did feel better, even if just a little bit.

Aleksei and I were new. We did have things in common. We were facing scary, unknown issues that we had no control over.

It didn't excuse Aleksei getting cold and quarrelsome, but it explained it.

My gals were right.

I just needed to suck it up.

"Why were you reading about Aerin and Iphelia?" Monique asked, waving my tablet at me.

"That article came up in a search about how the True Heir would react to the vulnerability of his Bride," I shared.

"Well, an epic fuck-fest is always fun," Monique said on a grin, waggling her eyebrows. "But you two don't need to plant the next beast in the burner just yet."

I one hundred thousand percent wanted to give Aleksei babies.

I mean, little black-haired baby females and males?

Definitely.

But she was right.

Not just yet.

"And anyway," Gayle put in, "Iphelia was a kickass warrior. No shade, babe, but you are not that. Your talents lie elsewhere. So her 'vulnerability' and yours are two different things."

I felt no shade, seeing as she spoke truth.

"Okay, before we head out, I want updates on Bash," I said this to Cat and shifted my attention to Gayle. "And Sirk."

"Bash is still on," Cat shared with a smug smile that turned wonky. "And I'm nervous. He's escorting me to the Masque. So he'll meet Dad."

We all gave her understanding looks, because Mr. Truelock might be pressing Cat to get her life sorted (meaning, in demon dad terms, find a husband), but he was even more picky about the prospects than she was.

And it seemed Cat actually liked Bash.

It had been just over a month since she met him, and they were still together.

It wasn't a record for Cat, but it was promising. Especially since he shared her love of art, fine dining, he was generous, he had an impressive credit line, and pedigree (the last two more important to Mr. Truelock than Cat), and reportedly, he was very good in bed.

"Sirk?" I asked Gayle.

"Okay," she replied, throwing up her hands. "I'll admit. I'm into him. I'll also admit, he was comming, but he's stopped, because I've planted us firmly in the friend zone."

Another collective groan rang out.

"What gives with that?" Monique asked.

"He's Aleksei's best friend," she explained.

"It's very sweet you'd worry about that," I told her. "But we're all adults."

"There was something..." she looked away.

"What?" Monique pushed.

She returned her attention to us. "When he got all pissed on my behalf when they took me in for questioning, it felt..." Her focus homed in on me. "I think it felt a little like what you feel for Aleksei."

Oh my gods!

"Do you think he's your mate?" I asked breathlessly.

"I know he's not," she replied, and my face fell, because she sounded sure of that. "And that's just it. Feeling that little feeling I had when he was trying to protect me, watching you and Aleksei fall in love, I want that. I want my mate." She squared her shoulders and announced, "So, I've decided, after this plot gets thwarted, I'm going on my quest."

Whoa!

Awesome!

But wait.

"I did a lot of reading this afternoon, and it said sometimes fae don't recognize their mates right from the jump," I told her.

She nodded. "I know. You have to be open for it. And with Sirk, I'm *so* open for it. I've searched deep because I really like him. But he's not the one."

She lifted a hand our way to stop us speaking, because we all were about to say something, and continued.

"I want to go there. I'm attracted to him. I think he'd be great company." She gave us a small smile that was a bit melancholy. "And he'd feed me well. But then, what if he finds his mate? What if I do? What if it doesn't end well? We can't have one of Laura's best buds being weird around one of Aleksei's best buds. We're all in this for a lifetime. And it shouldn't be weird."

It was beautiful she understood we were all in this for a lifetime. But it still made me sad, as much as it made me proud she was mature enough (Timothee and Errol could take lessons) to consider herself, Sirk, their futures, and how something like this might affect them and the beings they cared about.

It still sucked.

"I'm super excited you're going on your quest," I said.

"Me too," Monique agreed. "Once I finish pumping my credit line enough to get the renos done on my flat, and if you haven't found him yet, I'll join you for a month. Though, then I'd have to pump my credit line up enough to be away from clients for a month."

"That would be awesome," Gayle replied, her green eyes lighting.

"I'm down with meeting you for some long weekends and mate trawling," Cat put in.

It occurred to me then that the idea the problem with Aleksei and I was space, actually was part of the problem.

But only part of it.

He needed space *and* time.

He and I both worked. We weren't together 24/7, but we were together a lot, and that togetherness had been intense from the start. He enjoyed work, but now he had all of this other stuff weighing on him too.

So perhaps he not only needed space to see to all the things he needed to see to, without having to worry about looking out for or paying attention to me, we also both needed time.

Time to deal with the loss of Antheme. Time to get to know one another better. Time to settle into our lives together.

The thing about that was, all of that made sense, but it didn't feel right.

And it hurt my heart, and my beast didn't like it either (at all), to think of giving it to him.

But everyone needed a break.

And they needed those on the regular.

Anyway, I wanted to support Gayle on her quest too.

"I'm in for long weekends as well," I said. "And maybe we can ask Alchemy if she could narrow down the search area."

Alchemy was the witch that had her mystic sanctum in my building.

Gayle scrunched her nose. "Do you think she's actually a witch?"

"No, but it doesn't matter. We'd have fun wherever we went," I replied. "She could just offer vacation suggestions, and I'd be down."

"Too true," Cat agreed.

Monique raised her glass. "Suck 'em back. I need dinner to soak up some of this vodka."

I should have requested snacks, because she was very correct.

We all lifted our glasses and did as told.

Then we all hoisted ourselves out of the comfortable but tight fit on the daybed.

Cat linked arms with me as we walked to the door.

"It's going to be okay," she said.

I took in a deep breath, let it out and nodded.

"Also, you totally need to tell the staff to stock your fridge and snack cupboard up here," she went on.

I turned to her in order to refute this assertion.

"Don't say it," she said before I could say anything. "It's their job. They like to have those jobs, since they get paid to do them. And you have a job as well, actually, two of them. The point of having staff is so they'll do things to give you time to do the things *you* have to do." She jostled my arm. "There are lessons Madam Garwah can't teach you but you need to learn, because you aren't Laura Makepeace anymore. You're her, of course. You always will be. But you're also the True Bride."

I absolutely was.

And I needed to remember that in all the things that were swirling around us.

Destiny put me here. Destiny gave me Aleksei.

And I needed to embrace my destiny.

"These include offloading and delegation," Cat continued. "I know it doesn't seem like it's any skin off your nose to wait until someone can deliver the ingredients of martinis to you. But first, it takes them a lot less time to stock the snack cabinet than it does to constantly be running up here with stuff you order."

I hadn't thought of that.

"Also," she kept at it, "time is our most important commodity, and you need to learn how to stretch yours as much as you can, because you'll have tons of stuff pulling at it, and when you need to work things out with your gals, you don't need to be placing a call and waiting for vodka and olives."

There it was again.

Time.

She pulled me closer to her as we kept walking.

And she finished, "Trust me."

I always trusted her.

But this was excellent advice.

It would feel weird at first, but I'd get used to it.

I hadn't really thought I'd get used to living in a penthouse and being looked after by bots.

But once I was in, I barely noticed it.

And now I was living in a palace.

I nodded to Cat.

We then followed Gayle and Monique to the parlor where the family had drinks before dinner. Fortunately, a room I knew.

Then again, after last night, we all knew it.

Because—and I had to remember this above everything—something amazing had happened.

A gift I'd always wanted, I had received.

Through destiny and circumstance, we were now one big family.

CHAPTER 38
DISMISSED

A leksei and the king did not join us for pre-dinner drinks.
They also didn't join us for dinner.
Though, the king came into the parlor we'd all retired to for after-dinner drinks, mostly, it seemed, to show his face to his guests, give his wife's cheek a kiss and leave.

He appeared distracted and troubled, which meant the queen's gaze was sharp on him, but he did at least show his face.

Aleksei didn't do that.

By the by, Timothee had come to dinner, and he seemed aloof, but there were no outbursts, and he didn't act like a horse's behind once.

Errol was still MIA.

I'd been feeling better about things, but with Aleksei a total no-show, I was back to more than a tad insecure.

Thus, when the queen announced she was going to bed, I decided to leave with her.

We said our goodnights, and my insecurity lightened when she curled her fingers around my elbow as we walked out of the room.

It wasn't the gal-clutch Cat and I'd been in on the way to pre-dinner drinks, but I sensed it was Queen Calisa's version of it.

"Dita had a conversation with Nata today," she shared as we walked to the staircase.

"Yes?" I asked.

"Nata mentioned to her your idea of loaning the wedding garments to the Musée de Vêtements."

Oh boy.

"I was going to talk to you about it at tea yesterday," I told her. "And it wasn't my idea, unless your use of 'your' was collective. The idea was Nata's. But I thought it was a good one."

She nodded to indicate she heard me, but she didn't address that.

"Alas, we didn't get to have that riveting conversation over tea," she replied as we started up the steps. "But I think it's a marvelous idea. So does Germaine. I've spoken to Fillion about it, and he agrees with me and Germaine. The timing couldn't be better."

Timing?

"Sorry. What timing?" I asked.

She stopped us when we were halfway up the steps and looked at me.

"If you'd be willing, we'd like to send someone with you to the Catalogues. Tomorrow. They can vid you among the displays, and you can talk about the different eras of the garments, who wore them, pick two, maybe three to focus on. Then explain that there will be an upcoming exhibition of them, and the royal family will be discussing more such exhibitions of the priceless relics of our realm, introducing them to our beings in the coming years."

I saw this play. And she was correct, it was great timing.

Another indication of, *All's well here, no worries, onward, and look! Something fun is coming your way.*

"Dita has already spoken with the Director of the MdV. They're ecstatic about the opportunity," she informed me.

As they would be.

"We'll do a ball. A fundraiser for the musée," she decreed. "Along with a contest. Citizens can buy tickets, maybe five marks apiece. A chance to win two entries to the ball. Perhaps for ten beings, five winners. Then we can seat them with dignitaries, noblebeings, celebrities. Raise more money but make it inclusive. Share the message this is not just for those who can afford it. Everyone can feel involved."

This idea terrified me, because I'd be the face of it.

But it was an excellent idea.

"I can do that."

It was then, she removed her hand from my elbow and took my own, giving it a squeeze.

And that was out-and-out affection that, in my current state, made me want to burst out crying.

I did not.

What she said next, though, didn't help.

"I know these types of things will be hard on you, Laura. I've always been an extrovert. Gregarious. I get my energy from being around people, thus, I don't understand, but I do understand it's there."

"I'll be okay," I assured.

"That is not in question. You've done swimmingly so far. I simply wanted you to know I understand."

Okay.

Yeah.

I totally dug Queen Calisa.

"Thank you, my queen," I whispered.

She gave my hand another squeeze before letting it go. "And as for that, I believe we're beyond it. You may call me maman from now on. In private, of course."

Yep.

Still on the verge of tears.

This time, my nose stung with holding them back, but I managed a smile and mumbled, "Of course."

She took my elbow again and led me up the rest of the stairs, turning toward the north hall, where, apparently, her and the king's suite was also situated.

"I need an official tour of the Palace," I told her as we went. "Who should Nata arrange that with?"

"I'll have Dita talk to Nata."

"Great."

Aleksei's suite was getting closer, and it was the perfect time to stop and ask her about his behavior.

But now that the time was nigh, I realized, like with Aleece, I didn't know how to say, *Your son is being a jerk. Can you explain?*

I tried, "I think Aleksei is struggling."

She nodded. "I suspected." She then sighed. "It is often not easy with a dragon shifter."

"It's been pretty smooth sailing so far."

She laughed softly, and listening to it, I wasn't sure I'd ever heard her laugh.

It was very pretty.

She also stopped us again, a good two doors down from Aleksei's suite.

"I cannot tell you how much it's delighted me to see my son so settled with you. So content." She took her hand from my elbow and wrapped it around my upper arm. "But these are troubled times, dear. We will all need a good amount of patience to deal with each other through them." Her fingers tightened, almost painfully, before she said, "He loves you."

"I love him too," I whispered.

She released the pressure on my arm by releasing me.

"I know. This delights me as well. Just remember, at your beginning, not even thinking, the love had not yet blossomed, but even so, you put yourself in front of a stream for him. However, my son was not there when you were in danger. As I said, after a life where I sought as much attention as I could find led me to a life where I had more attention than anyone could need, and I thrive in that life, I don't understand your aversion to it, but I know it's there. You might not understand how his struggles manifest, but you must give him room to best the struggles."

I nodded, but asked, "Is there some way I can help him?"

She took my elbow again and started us walking. "My son, he was always one to retreat and lick his wounds. They healed, and he moved on. I can't know, but my suggestion would be, make sure he knows he can count on you, but let him sort his own head out."

Another vote for space, it would seem.

"Thanks…um, Maman."

She smiled at the hall instead of me and stopped us at Aleksei's door. It was a small smile, but I adored it.

That was when she looked at me. "Sleep well, *ma fille*."

Jeez.

She was killing me.

She patted me on the arm and continued down the hall.

I turned to the room, opened the door, walked through the vestibule and stopped dead when I saw two of the staff carrying my clothes across the sitting room toward the princess's bedroom.

Uh…

My heart thudded painfully, my senses clicked in that Aleksei was in his study, and my voice sounded strangled when I said, "Good evening."

"Good evening, mistress," she replied.

Her face flushing, her eyes averting, she scurried away and disappeared into the bedroom.

Now my pulse was hammering as I walked on unsteady legs to the study.

The door was open.

And Aleksei was indeed in there.

He was sitting behind the desk, had stylus to a display and didn't look up at me even as my beast reached to his, his surged in return, and I knew he knew I was there.

My throat closed and I knocked on the doorjamb.

His head came up.

"Hey," I pushed out my greeting.

"Please come in. Close the door," he said perfunctorily.

Space, patience, space, patience, let him sort his own head out.

I walked in, closed the door behind me, then moved to stand between the two chairs in front of his baronial desk.

"Did you get dinner?" I asked.

"We had food brought in," he answered.

"Good," I murmured. Then louder, I noted, "I heard Bainon and Cormac are here."

"They are."

"Um..." My attention drifted to the wall beyond, which was the princess's bedroom. I looked back at him. "There are staff moving my clothes."

"I'll be busy with a number of things," he stated. "Very busy. This will mean I'll get to bed late, wake early. And my sleep will be fitful when I have time for it. I'd like to save you from having to deal with that."

This was a weak excuse.

I didn't call him on it, and that wasn't entirely about giving him room to sort his head out. It was also about me being in so much pain at this decision, I couldn't address how weak his excuse for it was.

Instead, I inquired, "Has something happened?"

"Take a seat," he invited, like I was an employee standing before my boss.

I didn't want to sit. I wanted to stand. The easier to run if I needed to.

But considering this was far, far worse than his fractiousness had been, and I didn't want to irritate him to see how much more fractious he could be, I took a seat.

He rested back in his own, studied me a moment, his expression bland, and that was yet another cut, because I didn't think he'd ever looked at me without open interest, warmth, amusement, desire, or, more recently, love, since we met.

"Nurse Fitzgerald turned herself into the authorities at Sheer Drop this morning," he announced.

My torso jerked in surprise at this news.

Sheer Drop was a city in the Center.

"She's been transported to Nocturn," he carried on. "She's not saying anything, but instead, demanding a trade of information for leniency."

"Oh," I said stupidly because I didn't know what else to say.

"I'm against this. Ideologically, I have an issue with this practice across the board. You do something heinous, you shouldn't get a deal to experience fewer consequences because you rat out your accomplices. I understand it can be expedient, as it saves time and resources that are always stretched too thin, but committing a crime is committing a crime. You should pay the penalty for it."

"Okay," I said, simply because he stopped talking.

"In this instance, since her crimes were perpetrated against you, I'm experiencing even deeper emotions around it, and have no desire in the slightest to be lenient."

Well, at least it was good he could say, even in the monotone he was using, that his feelings for me made this difficult for him.

"However," he continued, "we're piecing the puzzle together, and the more pieces we have, the clearer the picture, so I might not have any choice. I've ordered them to use threats first, in the hope she'll understand I will use all my power to see she gets the maximum penalty, which, for high treason, since she's the first to commit it in centuries, would be the resumption of the guillotine."

Lord in hellfire!

I was so shocked at this, even my beast lurched at the news.

"Obviously, we won't be doing that, but she doesn't know it," he concluded.

I pushed out the breath I was holding. "You're, uh...piecing it together?"

"What I say next, you can tell no one," he warned.

"Who would I tell?"

"Your females."

"I don't tell them this kind of thing, Aleksei," I said softly.

"Continue in that vein," he ordered inflexibly.

I pressed my lips together.

When he said nothing, I nodded to confirm I would tell no one.

"After we lost Antheme, we had a rogue agent of the RS, infuriated, as he would be that one of their own was brought low, who defied law and administered truth serum to the assassin caught at the gallery," he informed me.

"By the gods," I whispered.

"This agent is being dealt with. But it can't be denied, the information gleaned is crucial."

"What is that information?"

"I'm afraid I can't tell you that."

Space, patience, space, patience.

"Simply rest assured, the picture is becoming clearer, Laura," he carried on. "You'll be safe in the meantime. And the best minds in four realms are working together to handle it."

The best minds *in four realms*?

By Lilith, it had been confirmed.

It was Arnaud.

Arnaud was up to something.

Something big.

And terrible.

"I don't mind you coming to bed late or sleeping fitfully," I said quietly.

"I won't sleep at all if I must worry I'm disturbing yours."

I was down with space, but I wasn't sure about *this*.

"Aleksei—"

He cut me off.

Unwaveringly.

"The decision has been made, Laura." He said this like what was left unsaid was, *And now you're dismissed.*

"If you need to talk—" I began.

"I'm fine."

"Even so, so much is going on, if you—"

"I said, I'm fine, Laura," he clipped.

Okay, back off and *patience*.

I wanted to find it, but there was so much fretting and yearning and aching going back and forth between our creatures, along with me feeling all those same things (crushingly), it was muddling my head.

I honestly wasn't sure I could sleep without him. I couldn't imagine being just rooms away, and not being with him when the stars were out.

Oh yes.

In all that I'd gotten used to without even noticing it, sleeping with Aleksei by my side was the one that was the easiest.

Because us tangled together through the night was the most natural thing in the world.

"I'm setting up a Palace tour for tomorrow," I forced out. "And your mom has agreed to the loan of the royal garments to the MdV. I'll be taping an announcement that's going to happen tomorrow as well. Along with sharing there'll be a fundraising ball."

"Excellent."

"Would you like to..."—I flipped out a hand—"share a drink before we both go to bed?"

"I need a clear head. I have some business comms to return before I retire."

So, that was a no.

"Right."

He said nothing.

I said nothing.

This continued as my heart grew to feel like it weighed a ton in my chest.

I stood. "I'll just...go read for a bit."

He nodded.

All right.

This was the hardest thing I'd had to do in my life.

I hadn't even been "giving him space" for a whole half an hour, and this was torture.

"Can I kiss you goodnight?" I requested timidly.

A flicker of something warm and lovely glimmered in his eyes before he murmured, "You may always kiss me, love."

Okay, at least that was good.

Right?

I moved around his desk.

He didn't get up, just tipped his head back.

I bent in and touched my mouth to his before pulling back.

"Try to sleep well," I bid.

"You too."

"Love you, *drahko*," I said softly.

He didn't say the words, he jerked up his chin.

And that was bad.

Totally torture.

I gave him a smile that trembled, that flicker came back to his eyes as he watched it, but he turned to his desk and picked up his stylus.

And...

Yeah.

I was dismissed.

With no choice, I walked out of the room.

A stroke of luck, when I got to my bedroom, I noted the staff were done moving me.

So when I got there, I could close the door, bury my face in the rose silk of the pillow sham, and cry shamelessly.

CHAPTER 39

DEEPEST PIT

My eyes puffy from crying, scratchy from lack of sleep, lying in a bed of sumptuous bedclothes, my eyes to the tall window, I watched the sky move from night to a murky dawn.

The weather, it would seem, was continuing to align with my mood.

I gave three fluffballs (yes, even Jupiter remained close) some pets before they were forced to scatter when I pushed the covers back and got out of bed.

The cats stayed with me last night. And although I loved them for their show of loyalty, it was another stab in the heart that they'd had to choose, and they, too, didn't get to spend time with daddy.

Especially Nova, who always had a doleful look on her face, but now she seemed miserable.

I wandered to the window, not the bathroom, sat on the cushion in the window seat and looked out at the sea.

I caught a school of the sea's namesake dolphins leaping and playing while swimming south, toward the Three Realms, seeking warmer water for the winter. The barely-there sun still glinted off their glossy skin.

Normally, this would enchant me.

I'd felt Aleksei's presence leave the suite an hour before, and he didn't even bother to stick his head in, so nothing was delighting me.

I'd maybe snoozed for about an hour. The rest of my night was sleepless, so his goal of not disturbing it was for naught.

I needed a serious stint with my spa-visor.

I also needed to buck up, suck it up, and get on with it.

Tour first. Shoot vid next. Have a meeting with Nata to get stuck in on the MdV ball, which I had decided I was going to spearhead. We needed more to do like we needed holes in our heads, but farg it.

I, too, was sequestered at the Palace, and I'd go nuts without something to do.

That was something to do. And I'd never organized a ball, but I figured I'd be good at it.

Time to get on with it.

I turned from the window, headed to the bathroom, my Denti-Clean and my spa-visor.

✦ ✦ ✦

"And we'll be delighted to host five lucky winners, with their plus ones, at this event, along with providing feeds on social tapes, so you can tour the exhibition and be a part of the ball, even if you can't travel to Nocturn."

I took a short breath, lifting both hands to hold them, one over the other, at my chest, my smile still pinned to my face, and I continued.

"I've lived my whole life fascinated by clothes, not only style, but function, construction, the textiles that make them, and history. This particular fascination of mine is something I cannot wait to share with all of you. I also cannot wait to open the door to the Royal Catalogues and share the treasures we store here with the citizens of Night's Fall with the hope you'll be just as fascinated as me."

I dropped my hands, holding them together in front of me, and I tilted my head very slightly.

"Thank you for watching. See you at the Musée."

I kept smiling, not too much, not too little, at the cam.

"Annnnnd...*we're out*," the cam operator called.

Germaine hurried forward.

"That was a good one. We'll go with that one. Perfect," she gushed.

Standing in the sublevel of the Catalogues, in front of Queen Mathilde's gown, I hoped it was perfect, since that was the eighth take, my feet were hurting, and I wanted nothing but to get out of there, get in the hover-cart, be whisked to the Palace and get into my retreat where I hoped they'd stocked the fridge and snack cabinet as I'd requested.

It was only early afternoon.

I still had every intention of kicking off my shoes, mixing myself a drink and getting the next item on my day's agenda done and behind me.

For that one, I'd need a drink.

I'd had my tour of the Palace. It had lasted three hours. It was fascinating. And there was so much of it, I was sure I'd need a refresher in a week.

After that, a quick lunch with Aleece, who seemed even more distracted than her father had the night before. And there was a melancholy to her that was not a small amount of alarming.

I didn't press her on it. We were all feeling it in one way or another, especially with the Masque fast approaching, when we'd all have to be on, no matter what was happening. But I also didn't know her very well, so I didn't know if I should.

Seemed to be the case all around with the Knightstar clan.

And the quickness of our lunch was due to Aleece's distraction, because, no other way to put it, after she ate a few bites with disinterest, she barely looked at me while mumbling words of farewell and wandered out.

Commence an hour-long meeting with Nata to go over invitations and correspondence I'd received and our pitch to the MdV about me being chair of the fundraising ball committee.

At that time, I gave her a task so I could finalize the last item on my day's agenda before we headed to the Catalogues. And now that item was up next.

I'd heard nothing all day from my mate, though I'd text commed him that morning to share I was starting my tour.

Aleksei did not reply.

I didn't try again.

Space.

Now, one last thing to do, something I absolutely, one hundred percent didn't want to do, but the idea came to me, and I couldn't get it out of my head. It might be a huge mistake, but I was doing it.

Because I also might get some answers.

And then, maybe I'd get drunk. I didn't know, I hadn't planned that far. But I suspected getting drunk was going to be etched onto my agenda after I got my next line item over and done with.

"We'll release this on social tapes after the Masque," Germaine decreed. "It'll be the perfect follow-up. Everyone is always in thrall about what beings wear to the ball. We'll give the Masque a couple of days to run its course, so this announcement doesn't compete with it, and then we'll release. I'll let Nata know when it's scheduled."

"Add another day or two."

"It really would work better on the heels of the Masque," Germaine disagreed.

"And it would also seem like I don't give a dang about the fact my bodyguard was streamed down in broad daylight, and I'm skipping joyfully onward in planning a ball just days after she died protecting me," I retorted.

I noted immediately Germaine saw my point.

"You're right. A week?" she asked.

I nodded, but said, "Let's keep in touch, play it by feel."

"You got it," she replied.

At this point, Germaine began bossing the cam crew around, so I made my way to the lift, outside which Nata was dallying.

When she saw me, she ordered the door to open.

"Hey," I greeted as I stepped past her into the lift.

"Hey. I was watching. You did well," she said, joining me in it.

"Thanks," I mumbled as the lift started to ascend. "Did you get the sequence?"

She nodded. "I sent it in a text comm." She then regarded me closely before she asked hesitantly, "Are you sure about this?"

No.

"I'm sure," I lied.

"It's not my place..." She didn't finish that.

But I knew what she thought wasn't her place.

My heart pitched when I turned to her and stated words akin to ones someone wise said to me not too long ago.

"No offense, Nata, truly, please believe that before I say what I'm going to say next. But we're not going to be friends. It's not our job to be friends. The jobs we have are important, and we can't let anything get in the way of them. Even so, we can be friendly, and we definitely need to be honest with each other." The lift door opened, but neither of us stepped out. "But we're in this together. So you need to feel like you can be forthright with me."

"This isn't about my job," she replied. "This is personal."

Oh yes.

I knew what that personal was.

"Okay, say it anyway," I invited.

"I don't know why you needed that sequence, but I'm afraid there's no good reason for you to have it, and I'm worried that you asked for it."

I couldn't tell her why I needed it, so the only thing I could do was nod and say, "You're heard." Then I lowered my voice and added, "And thank you for caring. I'm sorry you're worried, but I promise I'll be okay."

And I hoped I could keep that promise.

"All right," she mumbled, realizing, accurately, that I was done talking about this.

Not done, exactly.

More like, if we kept talking about it, she might talk me out of it.

And as much as I didn't want to do it, I couldn't shake the sense I had to.

We walked out of the lift, out of the building, and we both got into the back seat of a covered hover-cart.

It was open on all sides. The nip in the air was now straight-up autumn chill, the skies were still gray, and it had rained or drizzled on and off all day (but it wasn't now), and I wished I'd worn a coat, but too late.

Regardless, it didn't take long for the driver to zip us into the tunnel under the hill that led from the Catalogues to the Palace.

While we glided, Nata briefed me about the various designers sending clothing and accessories to consider for appearances.

I knew she did this to get my spirits up, because I wasn't hiding how down they were, and normally, it would.

But I hadn't gone this long without connecting with Aleksei since we met.

So pretty much nothing would brighten my spirits.

"We'll go through them the day after the Masque," I told her as we alighted from the cart in the cavernous area under the Palace.

It was replete with walls that were fortified by shiny black steel, other parked hover-carts, a few glide-cycles, a moto-bike, and alarmingly, six armored combat-crafts.

Not to mention, one whole wall was lined all the way across, three rows up to the ceiling, with at least a hundred powered-down defense bots resting (but doing it like they were at attention) in charge pods.

They were not humanoid, though they did have two arms, two legs, a torso and a head. They were made of a shiny opalescent black and purple metal with a sight screen that went all the way round their oval-shaped heads.

And they were killer cool, but totally terrifying.

Though, knowing they were there gave me an increased sense of safety.

I ignored them (not really, they were hard to ignore, but I tried) as we headed toward the lift up to the admin wing.

"I've already had some clothing delivered," Nata said as we moved. "We could go through those now."

Definitely trying to distract me from the next item on my agenda.

I gave her a smile I knew was wan, but I couldn't make it anything else, as we stepped into the lift. "The Masque is tomorrow. We'll do it the next day. Okay?"

She nodded despondently.

She was a very good female. I made the right choice with Nata.

This made me feel minimally better (*minimally*).

We bid adieu in the admin wing, and I executed the long trek to Aleksei's suite on my fabulous Eduardo Navasco, ankle-strap heels that had the big, fabulous bow at the side. They were lethally stylish, girlish and sexy, but murder on your feet.

Once I hit the suite, knowing from the emptiness I felt, Aleksei wasn't there, this added to the emptiness I'd carried with me all day because I'd heard nothing from him.

I went direct to my tablet, grabbed it and headed to the Princess Retreat.

I checked the fridge and snacks first.

Grape sparkle, cherry-lime sparkle (ouch, but I had to order it for him for those times, hopefully soon, when he'd hang out with me here), sparkling water, white wine, and mixers in the fridge. The cupboard had bottles of booze and a variety of nuts, blobs, crackles, bars, snaps, stars and clusters. Slid into sideways slots also in the cupboard were bottles of red wine.

In the small freezer department, there were four small tubs of stem ginger ice cream.

It was all perfectly organized. So perfectly, it was good enough to pic.

And it was full to the edge.

The top of the cabinet now had a tasteful array of glasses, a drink shaker, bar tools, linen napkins in colors that coordinated with the room and a cool-tub filled with chipped ice.

It seemed when the True Bride made a request, the staff of the Celestial Palace didn't mess around.

I decided against a pink fizz or an almondine sour, a martini or wine.

I wanted one (or all), but like Aleksei last night, for what I was about to do next, I needed a clear head.

Instead, I poured a grape sparkle over chipped ice in a heavy, tall, cut-crystal glass that probably was worth a quarter of the fee I made for my entire last contract. Then I put a fancy bent straw constructed of glass with a crystal star affixed to the bend in it.

I set this on the table by the daybed, sat, let out a sigh of relief, but kept on my shoes, because I wanted to be totally together when he saw me.

I sucked in more oxygen.
I released it.
I sucked in even more.
I released it.
I was procrastinating.

"Just do it," I bit out my impatience with my own danged self.

I nabbed my tablet, pulled up the text comm from Nata, powered beyond the nerves I felt when I programmed in the sequence, then requested the holo comm.

I stared as the bubble opened and closed on the display, and it didn't take long before the word Accepted filled it.

I clenched my teeth, let them go because I had the need to suck in more oxygen, and finally, I set the tablet beside me on the daybed before I tapped the display.

My father's holographic form sat across the room from me.

"Laura?" he said carefully, anxiously, and maybe a hint hopefully.

"I need something from you," I announced.

"Are you okay?" he asked.

"This isn't a social comm," I shared.

"Sweetheart, you were shot at two days ago."

My entire frame froze at the endearment.

He'd never called me anything like it.

"Are you okay?" he demanded.

"As you can see, I'm fine," I said stiffly.

"I've been mad with worry. Even your mother commed, asking if I'd heard from you."

"The family did a vid that very night, Dad," I reminded him.

"You can fake things with makeup and vid-shopping and"—he skimmed a hand out in front of him—"holos."

"Well, this isn't vid-shopped. This is me, live and in person."

"All right," he replied. "What do you need?"

"I need to know about her."

Even his holo paled. "What?"

"Obviously, I learned my lesson the very long and hard way about the depths of your loss."

He flinched.

I refused to process that, or how painful it obviously was for him, and kept going. "But I need to understand...her loss."

He got even paler. "Is the prince okay?"

"Aleksei's fine," I snapped. "I'm fine. We're all fine. Except Antheme. She's very dead."

"Oh, Laura," he whispered. "Were you close?"

"She died for me, so I'd say that's pretty close."

More whispering with, "Honey."

I could not take this.

"Okay, let me be clear," I bit out. "I'm breaking the no contact for a reason. I'm not telling you that reason. And after this is done, we'll go back to that. But I need this, and you're the only one who can give it to me, so I'm asking for it, and then we can go back to regularly scheduled programming."

"Everyone is right in what they're saying. This is something big," he guessed (correctly).

"No," I lied through gritted teeth, giving the party line that Germaine had released after the incident. "As I said, everything is fine. Yes, there's a disenfranchised faction that's doing stupid stuff. But the RMI is all over it. I can't say more, I just know they have it under control now."

"Then why are you asking about me losing..." A long hesitation. "Her?" he queried.

It sucked that it hurt he could barely even say the word "her" while referring to *her*.

I couldn't feel it.

I had to stay on target.

"If you want to ask questions, I'm out, Dad. We're done and we can return to—"

I was reaching to the display to end the stream, but he said quickly, "No. No. I'll tell you."

I sat starchily on the side of the daybed, folded my hands in my lap and stared at his holo.

"I sense you already understand it's agony," he started.

"Yeah, Dad. I got that part," I drawled sarcastically.

"Can I...will you allow me to show you something?"

Of course, he wouldn't just *tell me*.

"Fast, Dad. I have things to do."

He nodded quickly, reached for his Palm, murmured some things into it, and then...

By all the gods...

A 3D pic popped up from his Palm, not full size, obviously, but...

Hecate save me...

The extraordinary dragon with silky fur the color of creamy buttermilk, brilliant amber eyes, sheer taffy-pink feathers streaming back from the sides of her head, her long, sinuous neck curled in an elegant S, her intelligent face, which resembled a doe more than a dragon, was stunning.

The coloring was wrong. My beast's face had more of an equine shape.

But there was no denying the similarities.

"Is that her?" I breathed.

The image blinked out.

"It was a mugging gone wrong," he said tersely. "We were so connected, she was fifteen blocks away, and I could feel her fear. I transformed. I flew. She was still alive when I got to her. She died in my arms."

I closed my eyes and dropped my head.

"It doesn't excuse what I did to you," he said swiftly. "She would...she would hate me. Absolutely *loath me* for what I did to you."

I lifted my head.

"But your beast so looked like her, when she appeared, something fractured in me," he whispered.

I couldn't bear this.

"This isn't what I want to talk about."

Again, speaking swiftly, he offered, "What do you want to talk about?"

"Could you not control it? How you were with Mom. How you were with me?"

"Your mother and you are two different stories, Laura."

"I need to understand how a male acts when his mate is in danger," I ground out.

His expression infused with understanding, and for the first time in both of our lives, it became fatherly as he let out a long, "Ahhhh."

"Dad," I snapped.

"Laura, it's excruciating," he stated. "Females, they bear other burdens. Males, this...if I'm reading it right, what you're asking about, then I can tell you. Right now, Prince Aleksei is in the deepest pit of all the hells."

My heart lurched.

My beast rolled.

My eyes raced to the door.

And Aleksei stalked through it.

I took one look at his face and...

Uh-oh.

CHAPTER 40

BROKEN GLASS

I had no chance to move or utter a word before he was in, he'd seized the tablet, and Dad's holo blinked out because Aleksei hurled the tablet across the room.

It shattered against the wall, falling to the floor in bits.

I shot to my feet, shouting, "Aleksei!"

"Have you lost your mind?" he asked.

"Aleks—"

His torso spiked toward me, and he raged, "*Have you lost your fucking mind?*"

Keep calm and calm him.

Keep calm and calm him.

"I don't know any fated mates. I needed to talk to him about having a mate," I explained.

"You don't know any fated mates?" he asked acidly.

"If you're suggesting I should have talked to you, right now, you aren't really talking to me."

Drat.

That sounded accusatory.

"I mean, I'm giving you space," I corrected.

"Fuck space, Laura," he bit out. "*That male broke your gods-damned ribs.*"

"I know," I said soothingly.

"When you were *nine*."

"I know, honey."

"You do not comm that motherfucker," he ordered.

"Listen—"

"Ever."

"Please, if you'd—"

"Fucking *ever*, Laura. Do you *gods-damned hear me*?"

Calm went out the window because…

Enough!

"I can't *not* hear you since you're shouting!" I shouted.

"Were you not fucking there when we pulled royal strings to circumvent a reconciliation meeting?" he demanded.

"Please calm down," I snapped.

"You are no contact with that male."

"I know."

"You know? He was just a holo in *your gods-damned lounge*!" he thundered.

"I know, Aleksei!" I yelled. And then I kept doing it. "Calm *the farg* down!"

He didn't calm down.

"If you need to know something, you talk to *me*." He pounded his chest on the "*me*" in a manner, if it was anyone else but Aleksei, it would leave a bruise.

"You're dealing with things," I pointed out.

"Fuck yes, I'm dealing with things," he agreed furiously.

"And I'm letting you deal with them."

"By comming your motherfucking piece-of-shit father?"

"I think he's…I think…I might be understanding him a little."

Wrong thing to say.

Big time.

If his eyes burst dragon fire and incinerated me with the look he was giving me, I would not be surprised.

Instead, he roared, "*You do not understand that weak waste of life!*"

"If you'd—"

"That's not going to be us, Laura."

"I agree. But I have to—"

"It's not fucking going to be us."

"Gods!" I cried. "How do I get through to you?! I've talked to Mr. Truelock. My females. Your mother. I even did two hours of research and talked to *your brother*. And I still don't know what to do with you!"

"There's nothing you need to do with me."

"We're not sleeping in the same bed, your highness," I pointed out snottily.

"Do not fucking call me that," he clipped.

"Why not?" I clipped back. "You're throwing a royal testosterone tantrum just like a gods-damned *prince*."

"Errol was the one who discovered you were my mate."

I stood perfectly still, except I blinked.

"What?" I whispered.

"He's right now under lock and key, benzoed, in the dungeons at Spikeback."

"Holy Lilith," I breathed.

"*That* is what we learned from the assassin when he was given the truth serum."

I didn't know what to do with this.

It was impossible to process this.

But my lips still formed the words, "Oh, Aleksei."

"Errol has been interrogated. And yes, he was given truth serum, at my command, against his will. Fortunately, my father agreed, but it wouldn't have mattered if he hadn't. Dad's crushed. Destroyed. I don't know how he's walking around."

My heart broke for the king.

And for my mate.

"Can I come to you?" I asked.

"No," he said curtly.

I didn't like it, but I stayed where I was.

"It was retaliation," Aleksei carried on with his tale of treachery. "Apparently, Tim fucked with him too, but no one knew. Of course, Rol didn't say dick, so how we'd know, I've no fucking clue. But it's fucked up his head."

My eyes closed slowly.

I reopened them when he kept talking.

"It was the same shit as with me, what Tim did, but it stopped years ago. Rol got it twisted up, or he twisted it up on purpose, I don't give a fuck. Bottom line, he's twisted. Aleece and I, according to him, were Mom's favorites. Tim was Dad's. He was cast adrift, his words."

It had to suck to feel that way.

But for the gods' sakes.

Aleksei carried on, "He knew I wasn't happy with Anna. He knew I'd end it. He didn't want me happy with anybody. Years ago, someone came to him from Arnaud's camp, but he didn't know they were from Arnaud's camp. Unfortunately, the RIC didn't know it either. A sleeper, they say. The male has been in Night's Fall for nearly a decade with the mission to get close to Rol. He accomplished this. He helped this shit to fester. And they came up with the idea to fuck with me by fucking with you. Killing your beast."

"Dear Hecate," I whispered.

It was like I didn't speak.

"Rightly, when they paid the witch to find you, and learned you were in Nocturn, your best friend was Catla Truelock, and Mammon and Freya considered you a daughter, they knew there was a good possibility our paths would cross. They wanted to mute our bond by killing your beast. And when that didn't work, they arranged for the benzobytines to be pumped into your water supply until they could take another shot at her. For that first attack, the PR60 hadn't been modified yet. But, according to Rol, he had no idea how deep the plot went. He thought he was getting his own back from me for being a favorite. So he was blindsided when they turned the weapon on me at the gallery, that it had been upgraded, how it had been upgraded, and he was fucking floored when Antheme was killed."

I remembered Errol's face that terrible day in the entry of the Palace.

Shaken.

And now I saw, terrified.

But he was a shifter.

He had to know how devastating it would be to lose your beast, even lose contact with it.

He had to know.

And he did that to me.

"So there it is, my True Bride," Aleksei said snidely. "I can't even protect you from my own fucking brother."

"This isn't on you," I said carefully, but fervently.

"Your father was right about one thing. You in danger is agony. You don't get it. It's not the same for females. I know you feel it, but for males, it's pure fucking torment."

"You told me," I remembered. "After the first time. How deep this feeling went."

"I didn't scratch the surface then, because I thought that was anguish. But seeing Antheme's body, her face morphed to look like yours, and it fucking broke me."

Gods, now he was breaking *me*.

"Please, can I come to you?" I begged.

"No," he returned.

"Aleksei—"

"Dad's telling Mom now. I told Aleece this morning. She's rocked to her core. We had to dype Tim. When he learned, he tore apart the blue salon, tried to get out a window to transform and fly to Rol, and fuck knows what he'd have done if he made it to him."

Okay.

All right.

Time to listen.

Time for him to let it out.

Time for me to take it.

I nodded.

"His memory is being scrubbed."

Oh *gods*.

"He has to go to the Masque. This spy from the Edge will be there. Rol can't disappear. We need to set him up to use him. They're scrubbing his time at Spikeback, the truth serum, but keeping parts intact and implanting things he'll need so this spy won't know we know, and we can get what we need to have."

Memory implantation was also illegal, unless signed off by a physician, and backed up by government approval, and this was usually in the most extreme cases of trauma.

But I had no issue with this, or Aleksei ordering the truth serum to be used.

Because, to put a fine point on it...

Fuck Errol.

Aleksei kept going.

"Rol will wake up at the Palace, being told he's caught a flu and was delirious for two days. He'll be injected with something else to make him weak in order to sell that story."

Shifters didn't tend to be brought too low by flus. We got them, but our immune systems were mega.

But a little pipsqueak like Errol?

Yeah.

I could see that.

"He'll continue to be benzoed," Aleksei said. "Possibly for the rest of his life. We haven't decided what to do with him after this is over. But it's likely to be swept under the rug. No digi-docs. Not even redacted. This event will not exist in Starknight Dynasty history. But Dad knows I can't let it stand. So we're going to have to figure that out. And in the meantime, we're all going to have to find it in ourselves to act like he isn't a treacherous fucking jackoff."

Gods, this was so *farged up*.

"I didn't want to tell you any of this because it's so fucked up, what my own damned brother did to you, I didn't want to admit it. But I also didn't want to tell you in order that you wouldn't give anything away," he explained.

"I'll do my very best not to give anything away," I promised. "Anyway, Errol and I aren't close. We haven't even exchanged any words, except 'pass the butter' and 'here you go.' So it won't be hard. At least for me. But for you...honey, I'd really like to come to you."

"I was there, when he was given the injection, Laura. I saw how deep this went. His hate for me. His years of manipulation of Dad. Then he'd cry, begging my forgiveness, saying you were lovely. He didn't know you. He didn't think about you. He didn't think about what it would do to you. He didn't know what your parents had done to you. He didn't think about you at all. He just thought about his twisted, fucked-up shit. When Dad asked why he didn't talk to him, to Mom, Rol said 'I'm your son, you should have just known.' What the fuck is that horseshit?"

"I don't know, baby," I said gently.

"The night Antheme died, that was when they called Dad and I in to tell us the assassin had indicated Errol."

Everything was making sense now.

"When Tim tore the room apart, I wanted to join him. It's been a gods-damned *ache* since I learned. Standing in that cell with my brother, listening to his bullshit and not tearing his fucking head off feels like it cost me everything."

Okay.

Farg this noise.

I went to him, pressed close, wound my arms around him and tipped my head back to keep hold of his gaze.

He was holding himself so still, his body felt like it was made of steel.

My poor Aleksei.

"You need to step back," he warned.

"I'm sorry, honey. I tried. I can't."

"Darling, if you don't, I might fuck you in two, I need so gods-damned badly to be balls deep in you."

Yes, everything was making sense to me now.

"Then get balls deep in me, Aleksei," I invited.

He needed no further encouragement.

His fingers fisted in my hair, yanking my head back, a move that saturated my sex, and then his mouth slammed down on mine, and that left me soaking.

In short order, I learned what a male with a vulnerable female needed to do to release tension.

It was rough. It was fevered. There wasn't an item of clothing on my body that didn't end up torn, tattered and flung across the room.

He didn't take off a stitch of his, simply tore down his zip to release his cock before he buried it in me.

My beast unfurled her welcome. His rushed to accept.

Aleksei marked me with his teeth.

I marked him with mine and my nails.

It was savage, and in some faraway part of my mind, I knew it would frighten me if he wasn't mine.

But he was.

So I understood.

I knew.

I knew what he needed.

I didn't give it to him.

I let him take it.

And Aleksei took it.

So we both got what we needed.

For my part, it was a world-rocking orgasm that forced his name up my throat on a sob.

For his, the dragon roared.

Oh yes, he roared, and I soared.

Make no mistake, this wasn't use, this wasn't intense sex.

This was making love.

The dragon's way.

And it was beautiful.

He stayed inside when it was over and I took his weight, but I also took the spikes of my heels (the only thing I was wearing) out of the backs of his thighs, because those things were lethal.

I wrapped my calves around them instead.

His voice was guttural when he asked into my neck, "*Bissi*, did I—?"

I squeezed him tight. "Don't even ask. Your ache and mine are different, and mine was just assuaged. I needed to do that, Aleksei. *Needed* it. So we aren't talking about it because it's just the way. Okay?"

He lifted his head, took some of his weight into his forearms and looked down at me.

It was then I saw it and settled.
Yes, I needed to do that for him.
Two days ago.
Which irritated me.
So I ordered, "Next time, though, just fuck me. All right? And we'll skip the you-being-a-dick part."
His lips hitched.
"I'm in no mood for you to be amused," I warned.
"Darling, you just came so hard, I thought you'd rip my cock off, your pussy clutched it so tight. How can you be in a bad mood?"
Was he serious?
"I slept alone last night," I snapped.
He trailed his fingers down my hairline and murmured, "I know, love. I'm sorry. I was scared shitless about the possibility of hurting you. I'd never needed to fuck anyone that badly before."
And another nuance of why he was being so argumentative surfaced. He was dealing with some serious shit, but he was also trying to push me away from him in order to protect me.
"Well then," I huffed. "Now you know. So this won't happen again. Because it wasn't just me. The cats also had to pick sides, and that's not cool. Nova might never recover."
His lips hitched again.
My eyes narrowed.
He got serious and asked, "Where are they?"
This was a good question.
"I don't know," I said, all of a sudden panicked, because I hadn't seen them since I hit the suite. I hoped they hadn't escaped the room while the staff was cleaning or filling my snack cupboard.
He kissed my nose (really, he *had* to stop being sweet when I wasn't feeling it), pulled out (ugh, I hated losing him), rolled away and tossed a throw over me before he did up his slacks and sauntered from the room.
I turned to my side and reached for my grape sparkle because I was parched.
He came back carrying Nova in his arms, Comet trotting and complaining at his heels.
He'd taken off his jacket and was in waistcoat and shirtsleeves.
Aside from naked, that was my favorite Aleksei.
And we were back.
"They were in our bed," he told me.
"I didn't see them when I came in."

"*Our* bed, Laura," he said, sitting down beside me.

Ah.

So my babies kept me company last night, but for naptime, they sought comfort in daddy's scent.

Comet hopped up and yelled at me.

"What's wrong, baby?" I asked, reaching out to stroke.

Comet ducked his head, stepped away and shot me the evil eye.

"I woke him up," Aleksei told me.

Oh boy.

Comet took his naps seriously.

"Silly Daddy," I said to Comet.

He jumped to the arm of the daybed, over to the snack cupboard, and as payback for his nap being interrupted, batted at the glass straws in their holder, making them clink.

"Stop him from doing that, he'll break one," I demanded of Aleksei.

"He's fine," Aleksei refuted.

Now look who was spoiling the children.

"Those straws probably cost twenty marks each." *Or more.*

"He's fine, darling."

I heard more clinking.

Whatever.

Time for other things.

I reached out and ran my finger along the side seam of Aleksei's trousers at his thigh.

He looked down at me.

"*Bissi*," he groaned when he saw my face.

"I'm not a flower," I whispered. "A bruise doesn't scar me. A fierce wind doesn't tear my petals off. The end of a season won't make me wither to nothing. I'm a star, Aleksei. I'll shine bright until the day, a long time from now, when I blink out, which will be the second before or after you do. You know it hasn't always been good for me, but I didn't survive. I just lived. That's what I do. I get on with things. I don't understand the power behind your drive to protect me, but I know it's there. And I promise to be cognizant of it. However, I need you to understand that I'm in this *with* you. I count on you, and I need you to count on me too. Don't shut me out again. Please."

He kept hold of Nova (of course) even as he caught my hand and bent to it, pressing his lips hard against my engagement ring.

He kept hold of my hand (and Nova) when he promised, "I won't do it again."

I squeezed his fingers. "Okay."

"Do you need me to run you a bath?" he asked.

I totally did.

That was some intense, awesome, crazy sex, and momma needed some soothing oil and a hot soak before she had to drag herself to dinner with a family torn asunder with all of us pretending they hadn't been torn asunder.

"Will you get into it with me?" I asked.

"Yes."

"Then yes."

He smiled at me. "I love you, Laura."

Gods.

Gods.

I let out a breath it felt like I'd been holding for two days.

"I love you too, honey."

He bent and kissed my temple.

Then he got up and strolled to the hall (with Nova) and past the bathroom.

"You missed the bathroom!" I called.

"We're bathing in our bathroom," he returned.

Yes, we were back.

Aleksei wasn't out of sight for a second before I heard a crash from the snack cabinet.

And there went the straws.

I heaved myself out of the daybed to find my robe, because I needed to quarantine the cats until someone could come up with a vac.

I couldn't have them slicing their paws on broken glass and crystal.

But first, I had to take off my shoes.

Then, quarantine the cats.

Then, I had to take a bath.

CHAPTER 41
DRONES

I was in our closet, strapping on my pink high-heeled sandals (maybe one day my feet would get used to the torture), the ones I'd worn the night I met Aleksei.

I was doing this because, while we were in the bath, we both got a comm that we would be having a semi-state dinner that night, considering Princes Tanyn, Cormac and Bainon were joining us.

So it was going to be fancy.

That was why I was wearing my silvery-pink dress in a material that looked like molten metal.

The other reason I was wearing it was because I had love bites all over my neck and shoulders, and it had long sleeves and a turtleneck.

I could attach a Medi-Aid to them, and they would fade, but no way I was doing that.

A part of me wanted to show Aleksei's marks to the world.

But not at that night's dinner.

The dress came to just below my knees. My hair was down. And I'd scanned in a photo and set the Ultra Paint to evening, semi-formal, sultry.

I did this because Aleksei and I were back, we'd had some more fun in the tub (just not the dragon sex kind), and even if everything was still a mess, I was feeling all kinds of sultry.

The dress also needed it since it was skintight.

While we were in the bath, staff came up to move me back to Aleksei's room.

I refused to allow people knowing my private business to affect me.

Spikeback Castle would have a full contingent of breathing (not bot) staff, so this was my life.

Aleksei had explained this was for two purposes.

The first, it was important for the royals to employ actual beings.

The second, although the time was long gone when bots had glitches and bugs, and as such, could cause unexpected damage or do things in error, these two properties were too significant to take that chance.

The bottom line, as mentioned, this was my life now, it would be when we moved, it would be forever, so I had to get used to beings in my business.

Twenty realms of them.

I wandered to the sitting room where Aleksei (and Nova) was lounged on the sofa.

But only Aleksei was sipping whisky.

He took one look at me, his eyes darkened, I congratulated myself for the sultry idea, and he set his glass aside and rose to his feet.

He came to me, his gaze devouring me from top to toe to top again (one could say mine were doing the same with him, and I'd already seen him in his suit before he left the closet), and he rested his hands on my hips.

"That's quite a dress," he murmured.

"Hmm," I hummed, pleased with the pinprick stars in his eyes.

"I remember those shoes," he purred.

Of course he did.

He took his gaze off my dress and aimed it at mine.

"Royal testosterone tantrum?" he teased.

I wanted to shout my joy that he was teasing. That we were here, not where we were. That he liked my dress, and he had his hands on me, and Nova had her daddy back.

I didn't.

Because after he left the closet, a few things had occurred to me, and we needed to have them out before we went to pre-dinner drinks.

I arched into him and cupped his jaw in one hand. "Before we go, I'd like to talk about a few things."

He sighed. "We need to talk about a number of things. I'll fill you in with what I can after dinner."

He was referring to political intrigue.

I wanted to talk about something else.

"Real quick, can I get into mine?"

"Of course, darling," he murmured.

Gods, I loved this male.

"I think I made...not a mistake, but I said something which might have made you concerned about something else, and it was right at the time, but now, not so much."

One side of his lips tipped up. "Laura, I'm not understanding."

"I told you how upset I was the last time you got angry at me."

No humor in his face now, and the pads of his fingers dug into my hips.

"Part of what we need to talk about is your father," he stated. "But you're right. I should have gone somewhere to cool down before I confronted you."

"No. That's not what I'm saying. What I'm trying to say is, when you're angry, you need to be angry. You need to express it. You need to share it with me so we can work it out."

His attention had drifted to my ear.

So I cupped his jaw in both hands and called, "Aleksei."

He looked again at me. "It upsets you."

Yes.

What occurred to me in the closet was yet another nuance of what he'd done the last two days.

"As I think I've made clear, I can hold my own," I told him.

"I don't want you to fear me."

"I've never feared you, not once, not even when your dragon came out and tossed me on its neck. When we argued before, it wasn't fear I felt. Never. Upon contemplation, I realized it was shock, because I hadn't seen that side of you. But also, anger, because, well...just because you pissed me off."

I wasn't going to tell him I was also triggered due to how my parents treated me.

I wasn't doing this because I was keeping it from him.

No.

I was seeing now that was a false alarm, and more, I was safe with Aleksei in an argument, and we needed to be free to have them.

I couldn't fight back with my parents. I could with Aleksei, with no ramifications.

It was a style of communication for a couple, a passionate one, that, if done right, could lead to working things out.

Both times for us, we did it right. We'd worked things out.

"Darling—" he started.

I moved my hands to his chest and pushed in. "Part of the last two days was that you needed to do what we did in the daybed. Part of it, I'm sensing, is that you couldn't let loose like you needed to for fear you'd upset me. And yet, nearly every conversation we had, you were goading me, so I'd get mad and we'd start fighting, and that way you would either manage to push me away in order to protect me from your attentions, or alternately, you could feel free to let loose like you needed to."

His lips thinned.

Mm-hmm.

I sensed right.

"I didn't do it consciously, but yes," he said. "That was what I was doing."

"I want you to be you, honey," I told him. "What's happened with Errol is too much to bear on your own. You needed to offload." I smiled. "Pick a fight with me. I can take it. And then we can make up."

"That isn't fair. It wasn't you I was angry at."

"I'm not a flower, remember?" I asked. "I'm a star. There is not one thing in the universe that makes a star burn less bright. Right?"

At my words, he groaned, pulled me up his chest and shoved his face in my neck.

Okay.

I was taking that as he got me.

"You're *my* flower," he murmured into my neck.

So farging *loved him*.

He lifted his head. "You're also my star."

I got up on tiptoe to touch my mouth to his.

When I settled back on my heels, I said, "We best go."

He didn't want to, I could tell, but he nodded.

He tucked my hand in his elbow, so it was me who slid it up to his biceps and leaned into him as we walked to the door, Aleksei being careful to close the cats in behind us.

As we made our way to the stairwell, I noted, "I know we'll get into it later, but I take it from the little you said in regard to Arnaud and Errol, and the fact all the princes are here, Arnaud is behind all of this, and something not-so-fun is brewing."

"Tanyn has some spies in Arnaud's inner sanctum. When things started to go down with you and me, he directed them to ferret out if Arnaud might be behind it. Unfortunately, they learned of the plot to take out a member of your detail only minutes before it happened."

That was unfortunate indeed.

However, since time travel hadn't been invented yet, I couldn't do anything about it, so I had to set it aside.

We continued walking even as he said, "We'll have this conversation now, since there really isn't much more I can tell you, because most of it is tactics, diplomatic discussion and details, and although I'm interested in that, for most, it would be boring. Though, if you're interested in the details, I'll share them."

I had a feeling I'd be part of that "most" because I could get down with the detail in every stitch of an elaborate gown from the Dark Epoch, but I wasn't sure I could get fired up about details of tactics and diplomatic discussions.

"Tanyn is poised, Laura, should he need to take action," Aleksei informed me. "Bainon and Cormac are on board. They all have few doubts, if something sparks in Sky's Edge, all their reps will vote to support Tanyn, and this has been confirmed because many of the ones those males can trust have been polled, confidentially."

"Good," I murmured.

"It's just that we can't be sure what else Arnaud might get up to in the meantime," he warned. "And he'll be in this Palace tomorrow night. So we must be wary."

"Great," I pushed out sarcastically.

"They've lost their tie to us and our family, love. He won't know it, until we share the memories that were scrubbed after it's over, but Errol is our agent now. Whatever comes in Sky's Edge may be ugly, but it shouldn't last long."

I was a lover of history, and not just the clothing part of it, so I knew many had said that before, and something ugly lasted far longer than anyone could expect.

I didn't share that.

If Aleksei was going for optimism, I was going to stick with him.

By the time we made it to where we were to have pre-dinner drinks (it wasn't the parlor this time), I wanted to throw my shoes out the nearest window, but the vibe of the place took my mind off my feet.

The king and queen were there.

He looked tired. She looked drawn. They were both talking to the Vinestrongs, with Aleece, who probably took some time with a spa-visor because she appeared her normal self, but her eyes were haunted.

This was expected.

What was unexpected was that Cat was alone on a couch, arms crossed over her chest, poison in her eyes aimed at Prince Tanyn, who was talking to Mr. Truelock, as well as Prince Bainon and Prince Cormac.

Gayle and Monique were in another group, speaking to Mrs. Truelock, and although Monique appeared normal, high color was in Gayle's cheeks, and her eyes seemed unnaturally bright.

If this wasn't enough, having Tanyn, Cormac and Bainon in the same room with Aleksei was too much for your average female to bear.

I'd seen pics of them too, of course.

But like Aleksei, the real thing packed one serious wallop.

Tanyn was tall, with that lithe, muscular demon frame, and elegant features. His thick hair was a lustrous dark brown. His expression seemed like it was never anything but different degrees of very serious, which was somehow hot. And he had electric-blue eyes that weren't even aimed at me, and I felt the sizzle.

The Dayrise Dynasty was famous for its members having sunny, golden hair.

However, Bainon's tousled mane was a dark gold that was almost brown, like the color of caramel. He, too, was tall (in order of tallness, Cormac, (shocker! he was even taller than Aleksei), Aleksei next, then Bainon, and Tanyn last—still, they were all taller than average).

Bainon had the fit, athletic body of a male who spent a lot of time in the surf. His skin was tan. His features skimmed pretty, but the maleness of him was so off the charts, they didn't go there. And his eyes were a warm, dark brown.

Cormac was a revelation.

The male was *huge*.

He had hair the opposite of Bainon's (it didn't make sense unless you saw it). It was brown and golden, and this was due to natural highlights that flirted with the dark. He had a beast of a body that gave him the look of a shifter. His features were ruggedly hewn. And his eyes were a startling bottle green.

I wasn't recovered from the glory that lay before me, along with wondering what was wrong with Cat, considering it didn't look at all like Tanyn had a problem with Mr. Truelock, or what might be up with Gayle, as Aleksei took me to the king and queen.

I performed my bobbed curtsy as Aleksei did his short bow.

Then, to hells with it, I leaned in and kissed each of their cheeks.

I knew they knew I knew with the tears that shimmered for a moment in the king's eyes, and the sniffle the queen barely gave (but I heard it).

So I quickly turned to Aleece to kiss her cheek, same with the Vinestrongs, and Aleksei ordered drinks for us from a hovering member of staff before he made his apologies to our current company and took me to meet the princes.

Seriously, they got better the closer we got, so my legs were trembling by the time we stopped among them.

I got four short bows (including Mr. Truelock), gave a bob and Aleksei launched in.

"Bain, Mac, Tan, allow me the pleasure of introducing my fiancée, Laura Makepeace."

"Pleasure," Tanyn murmured.

"Nice to meet you," Bainon said, seeming alert, aware, but not like there was any bad blood due to me replacing his sister.

Cormac just dipped his chin.

I nodded to each and then went in for a cheek touch with Mr. Truelock.

"Dearest," he said softly as I did.

I pulled back, smiling at him, and Aleksei wrapped his arm around my waist.

"Are you well?" Tanyn asked.

I shot him a *What can you do?* look. "I'm hanging in there. Thank you for asking. And you?"

"I will be," he stated soberly.

Hmm.

Poised and serious indeed.

The staff member came carrying a tray with our drinks. Aleksei took them and handed my almondine sour to me.

I lifted it to my company. "As lovely as it is to meet all of you, if you don't mind, I'll excuse myself. I'd like to greet my friends."

"Of course," Bainon said.

I gave them a small smile, shot a larger one to Aleksei, accepted the lip touch he dropped, and when he let me go, shooting another smile to Monique, Gayle and Mrs. Truelock, I moved directly to Cat.

I sat beside her.

"Are you okay?" I asked under my breath.

"Look at him."

I turned my attention to the males across the room, the ones she was glaring at. They appeared to be in relaxed conversation, except Tanyn, who I sensed was always on the alert. So much so, it was a wonder his eyes weren't red.

I turned back to Cat. "What about them?"

"Lording over Dad and me, like he's better than us."

I felt my brows knit and surreptitiously glanced again at the males.

"Who?" I asked.

"Prince Tanyn," she hissed, then took a sip of her drink, but she went right back to crossing her arms when she was done.

I took a sip of my own before I noted, "He seems fine to me."

"You don't know demon nature."

"I went to school with demons. I've worked with demons. And I was adopted into a family of demons when I was eight," I pointed out.

"Huh," she puffed out.

"Is there something you're not telling me?"

Her eyes slid to me, then away, and they did this too fast.

"Catla," I warned.

She puffed another breath out, this time without sound.

Then she uncrossed her arms, turned to me and asked, "You remember that time we went skiing in Glacial Bay?"

Did I remember?

I'd never forget.

We were fifteen. It was between-terms at school. Glacial Bay was (and still is) *the* premier ski resort in all of the Four Realms. It was situated at the northernmost point of Sky's Edge.

They'd asked me to join them, and I'd wanted desperately to go.

My mother had flatly refused, and it had devastated the teenaged me.

Now, though, I remembered my father had agreed.

I also remembered my father had agreed to everything I'd asked, including giving me the marks to buy the insanely expensive material I'd wanted for that Summer Solstice gown I'd made, the one Mom had eventually destroyed.

But even back then, I had the thought that Mom had shredded it *because* Dad had given me those marks to buy that material.

I couldn't process this now.

Something was up with Cat. I had to focus on that.

"I remember," I told her.

"Well, Arnaud was holidaying there too."

Oh boy.

"He heard we were around," she went on. "And he asked us to join him for dinner at his chateau. We went." She leaned in closer and dropped her voice. "And you would not believe how *foul* he treated us, Laura. Dad was livid. Mom was so upset because Dad was. I was embarrassed. Arnaud was a dick, but *I* felt embarrassed."

"Why didn't you tell me?"

She was back to hissing. "Because I was embarrassed."

You didn't cross the pride of a demon, I knew.

"Well, honey, Tanyn is not Arnaud."

She sat back, decreeing, "They're all like that. You know those family reunions we go to up there every five years?"

Oh boy!

"No," I said, not that I didn't know they went up there for the reunions. I was saying no to the knowledge that even her blood family treated them badly.

She jerked her head down in an affirmative. "Oh yes."

"Why do you go?"

"Because Dad has scads and *scads* more money than they do, and they treated him like dirt even when he was a kid, so he likes us to go up and rub their faces in it."

I couldn't help but laugh.

Because that was *so* Mr. Truelock.

And yeah.

You didn't cross the pride of a demon.

"The only good demons live in the Fall, the Break or the End. Period. Dot," she declared, crossing her arms on her chest again and returning to pouting.

"Well, I sense Tanyn is of a different sort. I think you need to give him..."

I felt something, looked to the side, and caught Tanyn staring our way.

Nope.

I caught Tanyn staring at Cat's bare legs, and I couldn't tell at this distance, but there seemed a hint of a ruby glow in his blue eyes.

My attention skittered to Mr. Truelock, who was sipping his vodka tonic, his position meaning he could see us, and Tanyn, even if he was listening to something Cormac was saying.

In other words, he was at an angle he could see it all, and a small smirk was on his face.

He didn't miss this.

Okay, Bash seemed like a cool male, but I was absolutely loving this.

I looked back to Cat. "Honey—"

She peered over my shoulder, straightened and mumbled, "Oh shit."

I turned that way and saw Timothee was stalking in.

He looked tired. His eyes were swollen.

And he was determined to get *to me*.

I stood swiftly. Cat came up with me. And Aleksei was there before Timothee, his attention glued to me, stopped three feet away.

"Tim," Aleksei murmured.

But I pulled in a sharp breath as Timothee executed a formal bow, arm wrapped around his stomach, the kind that was fit for a queen (Madam Garwah had demonstrated the male bows in class too).

And he did this to me.

I swallowed down a suddenly tight throat.

And I had to do it again when Timothee rose, and the instant he was straight, Aleksei's hand shot out.

He caught his brother by the back of the neck and yanked him into his body. He rounded him with his other arm, and I fought whimpering as Timothee wrapped his arms around Aleksei as well.

They pounded backs, Aleksei said something into his ear, Timothee nodded, he said something, then they let go and stepped away.

"One moment, ladies," Aleksei said, and he and Timothee walked right back out of the room.

The instant I lost sight of them, Gayle and Monique were there.

"I take it that was big?" Gayle guessed.

"That was big," I confirmed.

"I thought so. Queen Calisa is the master of keeping her cards close to her chest, but I thought she was going to bust out crying when Timothee bowed to you," Gayle explained.

I turned to look at the queen.

She was still in conversation with her group, but it now seemed avid, and there was color in her cheeks.

In fact, all three Knightstars appeared to be feeling better about things.

Mark one in the good column for Prince Timothee, and I hoped there would be more.

"You walked in with Aleksei like it's all good," Monique remarked. "Are you in the wrong profession and should be in front of a cam, not behind the scenes, or has something changed?"

There was too much to get into there, particularly about my dad (obviously, I wasn't going to tell them about Errol), so I said, "We had a huge dustup and then had sex twice, and now it's all good," I shared.

I got three big smiles.

"Are you okay?" I asked, narrowing my eyes on Gayle.

"Later," she replied right before Aleece joined our group.

We chatted, and about ten minutes later, Aleksei and Timothee came back into the room.

Catching the look my mate aimed at me, I excused myself from my company and made my way to him.

He slid his arm around me, tipped his head down and held me where I was at his front, our bodies not close, but not far, though I knew our position put me as a kind of shield, even if the others could see him because he was so tall.

"All good?" I asked.

"Tim might have been zoned out on drugs the last four hours, but I believe even before that, he's had a chance to think on things. He just admitted that he'll be attending the ball with Anna on his arm."

I wanted to roll my eyes at another indication of how petty his brothers were (and petty was kind when it came to the rot Errol had gotten up to).

But I didn't

I just nodded.

"He's into her, of course. But mostly, it was to be a jackass. He reports she's still pissed at me, but he doesn't care that she's using him, because she's going that extra mile, and they've been fucking."

"For goodness sakes," I snapped.

"He's going to end things with her after the Masque. But considering the current climate, he didn't want to do it before."

"Good call," I bit off.

"I sense some guilt, because Tim thinks what he did to Errol set him on this course."

And another mark in the good column, an indication that Timothee could consider his actions and their ramifications.

Even so.

"I refuse to condone his behavior, but sadly, the truth is, until they learn better, boys *will* be boys. The thing is, he did the same to you, and you didn't turn into Errol. So that's on Errol, not on Timothee."

"Precisely what I said to him."

"Did he listen?"

"Maybe," he murmured, and his eyes wandered, to his brother no doubt, but I didn't check because he kept talking. "I thought they were close. I think Tim thought they were too. He's taking this hard."

"Of course he is, honey. I'm stunned all of you are doing so well. I'd be a mess."

Aleksei returned his attention to me, and there was surprise in it. "You would?"

"Undoubtedly."

"Well, love, I hate to point this out since you seem so sure, but it *did* happen to you. You bore the brunt of it. And there you stand, entirely too fuckable in that dress and those shoes, chatting with your females and being nothing but the wonders that are you."

I felt my eyes get round.

Then I smacked his arm and sniped, "Have you not learned not to say marvelous things and get me all emotional when I can't do something carnal to pay you back for the compliment?"

He adjusted me to his side, his gaze again moving to the room, as he murmured, "You can pay me back for the compliment later." He gave my waist a squeeze. "Thoroughly."

He'd barely finished his last word when a throat clearing could be heard.

It was the king.

"If you would all accompany me outside," he said.

We were in the room with the balcony Aleksei, the king and I had gone out on the night we lost Antheme. The room was bigger, slightly more formal, and now I realized we were there because of whatever this was.

We set our drinks aside and followed the king out.

The air was super chill so Aleksei held me close.

I watched the king move to the balustrade, look down and nod.

And then I watched thousands, maybe hundreds of thousands of tiny drone lights lift into the air and head out to sea.

Once there, they danced, they whirled, reflecting off the cloud cover, glistening on the sea. And they did this a long time.

It was gorgeous.

At first, I thought this demonstration was a show for our distinguished guests, and a bonus for the population of Nocturn. A surprise treat from the Palace the night before the Masque.

Then I realized this preliminary light show was to get attention before the real purpose came clear.

And I was in the position of fighting emotion again, this time, I did it curling into Aleksei's warm, solid side and pressing close even as his arm tightened at my waist.

Because the drones eventually formed words, melting apart to form more.

And this was what they said:

AGENT ANTHEME FALLGROW
YoD 2084, 11, 2 – YoD 2118, 9, 18
ROYAL SERVICE
DIED IN SERVICE TO THE REALM

Mr. Richard Tayor
YoD 2073, 5, 4 – YoD 2118, 9, 18
Leaves Behind a Wife and Two Daughters

Now in the hands of the Night God.

Eternally at peace among the Stars.

They will be missed.

I was peeking at the sky lit up for what seemed like miles over the Dolphin Sea, my cheek pressed to the lapel of Aleksei's suit, when the lights blinked out and the sky went dark.

It took a minute, but like they were all one, the sounds of shouts and cheers, vocal tributes to the fallen, drifted to us from the mainland and the offshore islands.

Antheme would hate this.

But I loved it.

King Fillion turned from the balustrade and announced, "Now, we live. We love. We celebrate those lost. We count our blessings we're still here. And at this very moment, we enjoy good company and eat."

CHAPTER 42
FORGIVENESS

"I think Tanyn has a thing for Cat," I announced.

Aleksei and I were in bed.

It was after dinner and after we'd made love (yes, again, but I did have payback to give after his lovely words earlier).

I was in a satin nightie and nothing else, lying on my back at a slant, my head on Aleksei's pillow.

Aleksei was naked (yum), on his stomach, down the bed with his head on my belly, his arm tight around my hips.

Jupiter was communicating his happiness Mom and Dad had worked it out by sticking close, even if it was Jupiter's version of close. He was curled into a circle next to me on my pillow. Nova was tucked against the base of Aleksei's spine. And Comet, still not over his nap being disturbed with the added affront of him being banished from the Princess Retreat, was at the end of the bed, leg up in the air, cleaning his unmentionables.

Aleksei lifted his head and looked at me.

Gods.

Would I ever get used to how beautiful he was?

I sifted my fingers through his hair.

"You caught that?" he asked.

I nodded. "You did too?"

Aleksei nodded. "But Cat didn't. She acts like he slithered up from the last level of hells."

"She has some ugly history with the demons of the Edge."

"Hmm," he hummed.

Wow. That felt good.

"If she cottons on and is interested, she should go with that. Tan loves nothing more than a challenge." Aleksei advised. "The more she avoided him or glared at him like he was a fly who landed on her dessert, the more I sensed his interest grew."

I noticed that too.

I also smiled and filed this away for future use.

"So noted," I said.

His arm around my hip tightened on my smile.

Then all three cats' heads turned our way as he surged up so we were chest to chest and face to face.

I liked the other position a whole lot.

But this one worked too.

I slid my fingers through his hair again, ending the journey this time by playing with a curl at the end.

"I have more to tell you about Errol," he announced.

Oh farg.

I frowned.

How could there be more?

"I'm sorry, love," he murmured, gaze to my frown.

I was sorry too.

For *him*.

I curved my arms around him. "Right. Let's get it over with. Give it to me."

He rested his forearm on my shoulder so he could stroke my jaw with his thumb.

And then he said, "He didn't just fuck with you and me. He's the one who paid that female to get pregnant by Tim. He even arranged for them to meet. He set the whole thing up."

My mouth dropped open.

"Indeed," he muttered. Then shared, "He knew Tim doesn't take the birth control serum. He paid her and then told her she'd get more on the other end either from Tim, to pay her to get rid of it, or Dad, when she refused. Although he didn't know that Tim would douse her drink, Tim had confided in him he was going to do it, so Rol was the one who told her it was done. Even so, she meant all along to rid herself of the child."

Lord in hellfire.

"Does Timothee know this?" I queried.

"We were going to tell him. But he lost it simply hearing what Rol did to me and you. Dad and I discussed it after he was sedated and decided against it. At least until we figure out what to do with Rol after this is all done."

I sensed this was a good decision.

But I was doubly angry, because the negotiations with this female were complete. Weeks ago, she'd signed what she needed to sign to be kept quiet, and she'd been given Timothee's entire yearly allowance, which was three and a half million marks of credit.

"Are you going to do anything with her?" I asked.

He shrugged. "There's nothing we can do. If we confront her with it, or renege on the agreement, she can share Rol's involvement widely."

Now I was angrier.

"So you're forced in the position of having to protect Errol."

Aleksei said nothing, but his eyes did. A flash of purple shot through the night sky of them.

"As infuriating as this is," I began, "the more I hear of the width and breadth of his treachery, the more I think Errol needs some serious help. I mean, what he did with us...nothing more needs to be said. But what's the purpose of doing that?"

"We asked the same thing. He didn't consider I'd do what I did and assume my place at the head of the family. One thing Errol is adept at is observation. He knew that wasn't something I wanted. Instead, he thought Mom, and even Dad, would consider this as Tim going too far, and they would do what I did. Either way, he got what he wanted."

"Are you going to lift Timothee's punishment?"

"I'm considering it. Though he'll have to avail himself of Palace resources until his allowance is reinstated a year from when the payment was made to her. He may have been set up, but he played his part in it, and it was far from good."

"True," I mumbled.

"Darling, I want to go over one more thing before we sleep."

I focused on him, not a huge fan of his new tone.

"Your father—" he began.

I sifted my fingers into the hair on both sides of his head to stop him from speaking and said, "Let's discuss this later. It's been a lot today, but we're back, the cats are good, I love what your dad did for Antheme, and we have a big day tomorrow."

"This has to be said, Laura. Now."

Ugh.

"What?" I asked.

"It isn't lost on me that a child, no matter the age, would want to understand the behaviors of their parents. Especially if they had a detrimental effect on your childhood."

"Okay," I said when he stopped speaking.

"And you might come to some understanding of his. Because I also know that a parent is a parent, there is a yearning for them to be that, again, no matter your age. And it's my experience, you never stop wanting them to be a good one."

Yes, that was his experience.

And fortunately for him, his did.

Mine?

We'd have to see.

Though, I was sensing Mom was a lost cause.

"You're saying this because...?" I prompted.

"Because, again, you might come to a point where, what you learn, how he explains, how he behaves with you, you forgive him. But you must know, I will not. Not ever."

Oh boy.

"It's your life," he continued. "And your choice who to welcome into your life. But he will never be welcomed into mine. And when we have children, we'll need to have another discussion."

Oh boy!

"Aleksei—"

"I want to be open to this exploration with you," he said, his voice rougher. "I've searched myself these past hours since I saw his holo, and for you, my love, I can and will search more. But you must know, I fear there will be no change in how I feel about this. If you find it in your heart to attempt some kind of relationship with him, I might get to the point where I'm capable of being cordial, but I doubt even that."

"She died in his arms, Aleksei," I whispered, and he flinched.

Yes.

He very much understood how painful that would be.

So when he asserted, "It doesn't matter," I was taken aback.

"I'm learning how deep our bond is," I replied. "And I'm seeing how devastating that had to be for him. He says he was fifteen blocks away from her, and he still felt her fear. Their bond must have been—"

"It's no excuse."

"Aleksei—"

"Darling," he bit off, "I stood in a cell and listened to my brother share how he conspired to murder your beast. I wanted to tear his head off. It took every ounce of control I had not to do so. And I didn't."

"And he didn't succeed in his plans," I pointed out.

"No, he didn't. But consider this. Many years ago, it was a viable defense of rape when a male asserted he was under the influence of alcohol or drugs when he committed the act. Until it was made clear that there are vastly more males who could become inebriated and their instinct was not to violate a female, in fact, they'd never consider it and would find such an assertion of themselves repugnant, that this defense was successfully disputed."

This was true.

Aleksei wasn't done.

"We touched on this discussion tonight with the guilt Tim is feeling. He was a punk, playing pranks on his brothers, and his parents didn't put a stop to it. I hated it, but I didn't let it dig deep so I harbored it for years in order to use it as an excuse to commit unspeakable acts. In other words, what befalls us is not an excuse to commit unspeakable acts. If you do that, it's in your character, whether you're drunk, or you've experienced some trauma. A monster commits rape. A monster abuses his child. A monster conspires to commit murder. The murder Rol was conspiring to commit was of your beast, it's still murder."

He swept his thumb over my cheek and continued.

"They both have a monster within, love. As such, I'll also share that it will be very difficult for me should you find it in your heart to forgive him, because I know this about him, which is why we'll be discussing things further when we have children."

What he said was food for thought.

But on my first chewing, I didn't totally agree with him.

"I think you're right about sexual assault, honey," I said. "And I can't say you're wrong about Errol. But I also can't say that anyone can discount loss or trauma and how it affects your psyche and how that will further affect your behavior."

"He put his hands in anger on a child," he gritted. "There isn't a being alive who doesn't understand that's unconscionable."

"I know," I said, running my hands soothingly up and down his back. "But Timothee has behaved in manners reprehensible, and I sense forgiveness in you, because you sense he's feeling regret and taking responsibility." I gave it a beat before I finished, "My father is feeling regret and taking responsibility."

A muscle jumped up his cheek.

He saw my point.

"I love how much you love me," I whispered, and felt his big body relax in my arms. "And I know it's intense, and sometimes can be troublesome for you, but for me, it feels amazing how deep your need is to protect me."

"Laura," he murmured.

"And I'll tell you, I don't know if I can forgive my father either. But if I do, and that need interferes with you being able to be there with me, so be it. It's a consequence of his lack of control, or whatever took him to the place to take his grief out on me." I lifted up and kissed his jaw before I fell back to the pillows. "It will be what we need it to be. And I promise, I won't ask you to do anything it goes against your instincts to do."

"This is all I need," he whispered.

"Then we're good," I said.

"Yes, we are," he said much more firmly.

Then he kissed me before he called to the lights to go out, pulled the covers over us and tangled us up in bed.

Proof.

I couldn't sleep without him, because last night, I didn't.

But in the dark in his arms, within seconds, even after our most recent deep conversation, after we murmured goodnight to each other, I was out like the lights.

CHAPTER 43
FIREWORKS

One could say, over the last month, I'd learned a good deal about what my life would be as Night's Fall's next queen.

And most of that was awesome.

But some of it wasn't all that great.

And the worst of it, I found that next evening, was having to stand in a receiving line.

Okay, meeting the royalty of the realms from all the other continents who'd flown in for this fête, after seeing them in pics and on tapes for decades, I'll admit, I was starstruck.

And since I was a homebody and didn't get out that much at night, I'd never had the opportunity to hobnob with many vampires, but everybody knew, they were the glam of the *glam*.

Done up for the Masque, they took your breath away.

All the rest?

Good gods, it was horrible.

Standing there, in heels, wearing a heavy gown, a perfect smile pinned to your face, having people bob and bow and blather and slaver. The speculative looks. The constant attention.

Totally the worst.

Fortunately, there were staff to keep the line moving along so we could get through as many guests as the hour we were to stand in that receiving line would allow before we joined the rest in the Masque. Therefore, it wasn't like I was forced into seven hundred conversations.

It still sucked.

What didn't suck was that we wore our masks through it, considering there was a big ta-do later when everyone would be taking them off, which meant I had a modicum of protection against the attention.

What sucked a whole lot less was Aleksei's mask.

He wore a black, silver and purple dragon mask that had a long, proud nose that covered his own as well as part of his mouth, horns shot up from the top and curled spikes came out of the sides.

I didn't care how kinky it made me, I wanted him to fuck me while wearing that mask.

Seriously.

This was such a good thought, it got me through the first fifteen minutes of the receiving line.

The rest was mostly torture, but outside the glitzy vampires and toney royalty, there were a few bright spots.

The first was the parade of all the masks and gowns others wore, some of them slinky, some of them inspired, some of them miracles of construction, all of them fanciful.

This was due not only to an extreme level of one-up-beingship, but also the many photographers who would broadcast each to every corner of the planet. They'd been given access to the proceedings, their flashes constant outside the Palace and along the receiving line, as the trail of crafts cruised down to let the noblebeings, aristocrats, diplomats, dignitaries, businessbeings and celebrities onto the silver-dusted black carpet that looked like a welcome of stars.

The second was Madam Garwah coming through the line. I'd missed spending time with her, of course. But also, she was wearing this swan getup with a mask that had a swan neck and head that rose three feet above her own. It was outlandish, and not altogether attractive, but it was attention-getting and so very her.

The deep curtsy she gave me choked me up. And the affectionate clasping of my hand in both of hers nearly had me losing it.

The last was meeting the royal family of Land's End.

King Niall, Queen Laoise and Princess Rowan were warmly greeted by Aleksei, Queen Calisa and King Fillion, and they warmly greeted me. My dinner partner the night before had been Bainon, who I found was an interesting and often amusing male. Even so, throughout dinner, I'd noted Prince Cormac seemed quiet, watchful and reserved, almost broody, like Tanyn.

His family was the exact opposite, which was a relief.

But that was the end of the list of the highlights of the receiving line.

The day had been busy. I'd made the decision to trail the queen and Aleece around, because this would one day be my responsibility, so I might as well dig into learning how to pull it off without delay.

This meant I hadn't had any time for my gals that day, and since they were staying at the Palace, they hadn't gone through the receiving line.

I was dying to see what they were wearing.

Though, Errol was back, looking peaked and discombobulated, even with this obscured by his raven mask.

I was surprised at how easy it was to pretend I didn't know all he'd done to me. But he'd laid the groundwork by not being friendly or approachable, so I just kept playing at that.

As time wore on, I noted a certain someone hadn't gone through the receiving line.

This being Arnaud.

But sadly, only a few minutes after Aleksei bent to me and whispered in my ear, "Only ten more minutes of this, love," *she* hit the line.

I felt her the minute she did.

She wore a gold and ivory feathered mask tied to her golden-haired head with ivory satin ribbons (her ensemble was dove themed, and it might be petty, but her coming from the Dayrise house, I thought that wasn't very inspired). This mask matched her gold and ivory gown that was a miracle of feathers which also highlighted her every curve, and significantly highlighted her cleavage (and okay, so her gown was inspired).

Even through her mask, I knew her eyes were blazing hatred at me.

Princess Anna.

Behind her were King Dagsbrun and Queen Delanta.

Aleksei noted her too, I knew this when his lips came back to my ear.

"Remember, you outrank her. She curtsies to you. You do not do the same."

I was sure that would go over well.

"And your status means you do not offer a formal curtsy to Dag and Delanta," he concluded.

I nodded.

Timothee, standing at my other side, glanced across me to his brother.

Aleksei nodded to him.

When the royal family of Dawn's Break arrived at him, he bowed to the king and queen, then left the line and took Anna's hand.

Anna's perfectly formed lips curled in a butter-didn't-melt smile, her chin dipped, but her eyes floated from Timothee to Aleksei to gauge his reaction.

Behind my mask, I rolled my own.

I saw Errol, who was on the other side of Timothee, jerk in response to this.

So he didn't know some of Timothee's tomfooleries either.

This made me happy.

But then she was standing before me.

She stared at me.

I glanced at her, looked to her parents and dropped a bob to them.

Both inclined their heads, Dagsbrun curiously, Delanta dismissively.

Anna didn't curtsy to me, but instead, kept staring at me like she was expecting it from me.

It was Timothee, not Aleksei, who intervened.

He muttered loudly, "Anna, Laura is the True Bride."

Anna's face took on another mask, one of outrage, before she bobbed the quickest curtsy known to beingkind.

Aleksei's silk flowed through us. "Laura, meet Princess Anna, King Dagsbrun and Queen Delanta of Dawn's Break."

"My pleasure," I said for the five hundredth time (literally).

"Mistress Laura," King Dagsbrun replied.

He was the only one who did. Delanta was also staring daggers at me.

Suddenly, Bainon was there.

"Mother. Father," he greeted. "Anna," he said, not hiding the disapproval in his tone as he took in how his sister was grasping Timothee's arm.

By the by, Bainon's mask was a take on the wings of a body glider.

And it was mega.

"Son," Dagsbrun replied.

"Dagsbrun, Delanta, Anna, so lovely you came," Queen Calisa called from Aleksei's other side in a manner that stated they were holding up the line and they needed to get a move on.

I didn't know how she managed to state that without actually stating it, but she did.

I took note of how she did that too.

Dagsbrun, Bainon and Timothee moved their party along.

Errol shifted closer to me to fill the gap left by Timothee.

I tensed.

Aleksei put his hand to the small of my back and pressed in briefly, but reassuringly.

I relaxed.

Five minutes later, the rest of the guests were directed away from the receiving line and into the Palace, and we were given the notice to disperse.

Thank Hecate.

Aleksei tucked my hand in his elbow and led me down the hall.

"Arnaud didn't show," I said under my breath.

"He registered in the king's suite at the Imperial this morning at eleven seventeen," Aleksei muttered back. "He'll be here."

He guided us into one of the Palace's three ballrooms.

All three were in use that night.

The largest had a live band and open space for dancing. The second largest had extravagant buffets down the middle and on tables set up around the sides, along with four bars. The last was set up with tables and chairs for people to sit and eat, another two bars, and sofas and armchairs arranged in seating areas, giving beings the opportunity to sit and chat.

Each ballroom fed into the other, with small antechambers here and there. All the antechambers were regularly set in seating areas.

And yes, my heels were already killing me, my gown was gorgeous, but I made note of its weight for future consideration, so I was delighted to know there would be plenty of places to sit down.

Of course, along with a plethora of the most amazing flower bouquets and installations, Queen Calisa had settled on dragons to denote the soaring theme in the décor.

As such, there were massive, elaborate dragons made of silk and streamers hanging sinuously from the ceilings. Down the middle of the center buffet table, a dragon's head rose, then the arch of its back could be seen arising from the middle, with its tail flashing at the end. Dragon heads and necks taller than two men were affixed to the sides of the doorways between ballrooms, their jeweled eyes facing each other, one side the dragon was dark and male, the other was light and female.

And in the room with the band and dancing, a colossal set piece that resembled Aleksei's dragon sprung up from behind the band, wings spread, like he was about to take flight.

Although the theme was expected, as you could tell, Queen Calisa's follow-through was outstanding.

Even with the amount of food available to peck at (and there was a lot), there were servers wandering (they wore dragon masks too, just not as elaborate, or hot as Aleksei's) with trays of hors d'oeuvres, glasses of champagne or the signature cocktail of the evening, the soaring dragon (gin, egg white, lemon juice and violet liqueur in a martini glass rimmed with glittering purple sugar dust).

And fortunately, one of these servers approached us *tout de suite*, so Aleksei grabbed two soaring dragons for us.

He handed one to me and I took a sip.

I wasn't one for the taste of flower, but the lemon cut it, the sugar sweetened it, thus, in the end, it was delicious.

I lifted my glass to Aleksei. "Your mom knows her stuff. This is perfection."

He smiled at me.

Then he smiled beyond me.

I turned and gasped.

Monique's gown of midnight blue shot through with silver shooting stars tracing stardust was *mega*.

And Gayle's body-hugging gown of brass-and-nickel-colored parachute silk stitched in panels, the edges frayed giving a feathery effect, that trailed a train that floated behind her several feet was *insane*.

But it was Cat's gown that was the showstopper. It had steel disks on padded shoulders, and encasing her arms and on her body, sheets of steel-colored silk skimming her every curve to end in a fishtail hem, all of this representing an old-fashioned airplane.

And it was a *miracle*.

As such, I couldn't help but squeal, hand my drink to my mate and throw my arms toward them.

Gayliliel got to me first and we did the double cheek touch.

"You're perfect," I told her.

"No, *you're* perfect," she replied.

Monique came next, with the refrain of perfects, then Catla, and we said it again.

"Oh my gods, Aleksei, that mask is *hawt*," Gayle exclaimed as Aleksei returned my drink.

"My thanks," he replied, his full lips under the mask twitching.

"Where's Bash?" I asked, craning my neck to see if he got lost in the crush on their way to us.

I didn't think it was good that my question had Monique and Gayle exchanging a glance behind their masks (Gayle's, parachute silk, frayed at the edges, wrapped around her eyes like a superhero mask, Monique's a study of silver glitter, one eye a star with a trail of stardust shooting out the top side).

"Trying to impress Dad. And failing," Cat told me.

As he would, since undoubtedly, Mr. Truelock had set his sights on a very-soon-to-be king for his daughter.

I looked up at Aleksei. "Maybe we should save him?"

Before Aleksei could reply, all of my gals got tense, closed in, then surged back.

And Anna was there.

Well, one could say she didn't dally.

Though, I wondered where Timothee was because he wasn't with her.

"Aleksei," she buzzed cattily, completely ignoring me and my gals. "In the receiving line, I didn't get a chance to ask if we could have a brief word in private."

Um...

Hells no.

I was about to stake my claim, but I would find quickly I didn't need to, because Aleksei spoke.

"If this word is you sharing you're fucking my brother, Tim already told me. And if you have concerns this hurts my feelings, rest assured, it does not," Aleksei replied frankly.

Three collective gasps came from my females at this Timothee/Anna news.

Anna's head jolted like she'd been slapped.

"Outside of that, Anna," Aleksei continued, "there isn't anything we need to discuss in private."

"There were things left unsaid," she asserted.

"You mean unscreeched," Aleksei corrected blandly. "Although I knew going in you would not take my message well, I'm afraid listening to a female shriek at me for an hour, after not listening to a word I said, doing so further proving my point that we were not suited, is an experience a male can stomach once in his life. But only once."

Her gaze behind the mask darted to the four members of her audience before she said, "Could we discuss this in *private*?"

"As I said, we have nothing private to discuss," Aleksei denied. "You're sleeping with my brother. And I've found my mate. With our history, privacy isn't appropriate."

"Tim and I are dating. Not *courting*," she pointed out.

"And I've found my mate," Aleksei repeated.

"Yes, you have," she sniped. "And what I would like to know is, if you hadn't ended things with me, and you found *her*, would you have left me for her?"

"Quest your own mate, Anna, and you'll answer your question," Aleksei returned.

"I think, with our history, this going back to when I was practically a baby, I deserve an answer to that," she snapped.

"Our history?" Aleksei asked dangerously.

Uh-oh.

I got closer to him.

My females sidled away.

"We could have salvaged something, Aleksei," she told him. "But not after you rubbed her in my face. Could you not have waited at least a few more months before announcing to the world you replaced me?"

"I'm afraid an assassin took that opportunity away from me," Aleksei retorted. "But allow me to remind you, you're sleeping with my brother, Anna. And along with him, you carried on with Windstalker, and you did this publicly. Both of these happened before I met Laura. Although I'm unsurprised you find you can behave any way you please and expect others to dance to your direction, this is actually not the way the world works."

She looked side to side, got closer, so I got even closer, and she hissed, "Beings can hear us and they're listening. *Please*, can we speak privately?"

"Again, *you* aren't listening. I will, however, repeat myself. We have nothing to say to one another," Aleksei returned.

She assumed a pretty, pouty expression underneath her mask.

"Lexy, *please*," she begged.

Lexy?

Blech.

Unfortunately for her, "Lexy" had lost patience.

"For fuck's sake, Anna, you killed what we had by doing everything in your power to stop me from being me and mold me into what you wanted me to be. Then you made certain it could never be resurrected by using my brother in an attempt to hurt me. I have no interest in this conversation, and even less in anything you could say to me, privately or not. What we had is done. What we shared before that, you stained. For the love of all the gods, let this be done. Live your life and allow me to have mine."

She stood woodenly, staring up at him before she said through stiff lips, "I guess I know where we stand."

"I hope so," Aleksei muttered impatiently.

She didn't move.

But we did.

After Aleksei bid a dismissive, "Enjoy the Masque," he took my elbow and led me away.

I noted a great number of guests pretending they hadn't been watching what had just gone down, but my gals had retreated to the next ballroom (the one with the food).

Aleksei and I ignored people poorly pretending to ignore us and met them there.

Bash was with them, so Cat did the introductions between the two males.

We chitchatted.

Everyone avoided speaking about that altercation with Anna.

But we didn't need to. It happened. It was clear Aleksei didn't enjoy it. It was also clear he wasn't dwelling on it.

I still stayed close to him, and I was pleased he felt my support, even more so when he lifted my hand apropos of nothing in order to kiss my knuckles, communicating he appreciated it and he was fine (okay, so our beasts humming contentedly to each other told me that, but either way, I got the message).

"Would you like me to make you a plate, darling?" he asked me.

"I can get it," I told him.

He grinned. "I know you four are dying to tear Anna apart, so allow me to give you the opportunity to do that."

I nearly started laughing as he ended this by tipping his head toward an antechamber.

"Hungry?" Bash asked Cat.

"Would you?" she replied.

He dropped a kiss on her lips, and it was sweet, so I was a little bummed because I'd been rooting for Tanyn to get in there. After witnessing that, I wasn't sure.

The males moved off and Monique latched onto me, Cat doing the same to Gayle, and they all but dragged Gayle and me into the antechamber.

Boy, it seemed they really wanted to tear Anna apart.

There was no one in the chamber, which was nice and gave me the opportunity to go to a sofa and sink into it.

Ahhhhhhhhhh...

Yes.

"Tell her," Cat demanded before I was even settled.

My attention perked, and I noticed they'd all sat as well, putting us in a circle.

"Now's not the time," Gayle returned.

"Oh my gods, you have to tell her," Monique said.

"She just got Princess Anna'ed," Gayle snapped.

"Okay, I'll tell her," Cat stated, turning to me.

"No!" Gayle cried. "It's mine to tell."

Oh my gods!

Now, with all of this, I was dying to know whatever it was.

"Someone tell me," I demanded.

Gayle looked over my head and didn't say a word, so I sent a questioning glance to Cat and Monique.

Monique beamed.

Cat pitched to the side and elbowed Gayle.

I ignored Monique's beam and focused on Gayle's face behind her mask.

I couldn't tell for sure what it was, because of the mask, but I could tell something was up.

"Are you okay?" I asked.

Her eyes came to me, and she blurted, "Prince Cormac is my mate."

My body jolted and I blinked.

I did the blinking part again.

Then a rush of excitement raced through me, I leaned forward and breathed, "*What?*"

"You know, I've opened myself to it," she said. "So I felt it."

"I know...and he...it's *him*?" I asked.

This was...

This was...

Super, double, extra *mega*.

But wait.

"Why aren't you with him?" I asked.

"Because, apparently, he isn't open to it," Cat answered for her.

"He doesn't know I exist," Gayle said miserably. "Okay, he does, since he's been introduced to me. And he's been cordial, but distant. To him, I'm just a female that's important only because I'm your friend."

"Not even a spark?" I queried.

She shook her head. "Not that I can tell."

It was lucky I read up on mates because I'd learned just this.

Though, somewhere inside Cormac, he had to know, but perhaps due to all that was going on, he wasn't tapping into it.

That said, Gayle felt it and...

Dang.

That had to sting.

"I'm so sorry, honey," I whispered, reaching out to take her hand.

She squeezed it and said, "Now, I don't know what to do. I can't be me, a huge nobody, and walk up to a prince that will one day be a king and say, 'Hey, we're supposed to spend the rest of our lives together. You wanna start doing that now?'"

No, she couldn't do that.

My attention drifted to the entrance to the alcove. "Maybe I can talk to Aleksei."

"No!" Gayle cried.

I looked back to her.

"I don't...I want it to happen like..." She shook her head. "He should figure it out himself."

"But if Aleksei—"

"Aleksei knew right away," she reminded me. "He called you to him, what? Maybe five minutes into us being at the club? And then you got Captain Jacques's and after, all of this..."

She explained "this" by flitting her hand toward the ball, the Palace, and also my dress.

She ended with, "I want that, Laura. All of it."

I couldn't say I blamed her.

"All of it" was danged awesome.

Still.

"Cormac isn't Aleksei," I noted.

"Well, he better pull his head out of his magnificent, tight, muscular ass, or he's going to have some groveling to do," Cat decreed.

This was true, and in the romance novels, the groveling was the best part.

But Gayle looked no less miserable, which, of course, was why the male had to grovel. It just never occurred to me how miserable the female had to be to deserve it.

I didn't want that for Gayle.

Alas, we could speak of it no longer, nor could I get into Tanyn with Cat, because Bash and Aleksei joined us carrying two piled-high plates between them, so we could all munch.

This we did, and it was good to have this fortification before Aleksei turned to me and said, "I'm sorry, love, but our respite is over. I'm afraid we have to mingle."

Ugh.

I nodded, bid adieu to my friends, and Aleksei helped me out of the sofa, onto my aching feet and guided me into the ballroom.

I wanted to tell Aleksei about Cormac and Gayle, but I found right away he was correct.

The respite was over.

Beings were no longer ignoring us. We barely got two steps out of the antechamber before we were descended upon.

Commence nearly three hours where I learned the different, excruciating levels of foot pain and hoped my face didn't space out as my mind tried to figure out how mad Lancet and Nata would be if I didn't send this gown to the Catalogues, and instead burned it in the courtyard. It weighed a ton when I put it on, it began to feel like ten and growing as the night wore on.

Though, from the two-hundred and eleven (literally) compliments I had on it, and the number of pics taken of me in it by the varied royal and media photographers Germaine had working the event, it was a hit.

Making matters worse, I had to dance.

Doing it two times with Aleksei was sublime.

While he whirled me around the dance floor, my feet didn't hurt a bit, and the gown felt like a cloud swirling around me.

He was an excellent dancer (of course) but having that alone time with him in a sea of people was a revelation. It was like a recharge to my flagging energy and the constant race to the limits of my endurance with the crowds, the conversations, the attention.

I made note of this too: be sure to take time with my mate, even if only a few minutes, just the two of us.

And then I could face anything.

The three times I had to dance with other people (a count named Hoyt who did business with Aleksei and also played in their ring ice league, a male I found I liked very much (he was also a vampire); an actor who laid it on so thick about how great my designs were, it was all kinds of sycophantic gross; and last, Sirk, who was another respite, because I was glad to see him, he was also an excellent dancer, and I was happy he didn't seem too broken up about Gayle, since he was his normal gregarious, affectionate self and he'd brought a slyly elegant demon to the Masque as his date).

The receiving line had formed at eight, when the doors to the Palace were open.

And I'd been warned that the Masque could go until two or three in the morning.

But we were homing in on midnight, when we could remove our masks, after which there would be a magnificent, old-fashioned fireworks display that was so big, all of Nocturn would see it.

And I'd also been told by the highest authority (Queen Calisa) that I would be expected to remain at the Masque for an hour after, but then I could feel free to retire whenever I wished, which I would do after that hour was over.

I knew Aleksei would be all the way down with leaving with me, and I knew it because we'd already made this plan.

So when six uniformed footmen stood across each other at the entrance to each ballroom and blasted a tune on horns to get everyone's attention, then called out in unison that guests who wished to unmask outside before watching the fireworks should make their way there, I knew we were closing in on the end, and I could not wait.

The night would be chill, but there were heat coils under platforms that had been laid outside so people could stand without sinking into the grass (or destroying it) and be warm.

But the royal family weren't headed that way.

We went to another balcony. This one ran along the front of the Palace, and I'd only been on it during my tour.

Aleksei led me there.

When we stepped out, I found it too, fortunately, had heat coils snaking around the perimeter, which was good, since Queen Calisa told me the fireworks show would last for twenty minutes.

As they were royals as well, Dagsbrun, Delanta, Bainon and Anna also joined us there. As did Tanyn and Cormac, King Naill, Queen Laoise and Princess Rowan.

Arnaud did not, and I didn't know if he'd even made it to the ball.

If he hadn't, I found it odd, since he RSVPed in the affirmative, and Aleksei knew he was in town.

And odd with that male was concerning.

Queen Tatra had RSVPed no, which didn't seem odd, since Queen Calisa hated her, and Aleksei told me she hadn't been to the Masque since Riland brought her to her first. There was history there, I could tell, but Aleksei didn't get into that.

We watched as the guests filtered out to the platforms erected through the gardens at the front of the Palace, until King Fillion moved to the balustrade, placed a small mic-unit to his throat, and commanded, "It is time to show our faces to the Night God! Unmask!"

Gratefully, I lifted my hands to the bow of the purple satin ribbon at the back of my head above my elaborate chignon that sat at the nape, but Aleksei murmured, "Allow me."

With a smile, I allowed him.

My mask loosened, my face rejoiced, he took it and handed it to me before he took his off.

"Don't you dare throw that," I warned as, per tradition, the rest of the congregation in the gardens—as was their wont as the richest of the rich, and the elitest of the elite—threw their ridiculously expensive, painstakingly crafted masks into the air with abandoned glee.

Aleksei's head tipped to the side and a sexy smirk hit his face as he deduced why I wanted him to keep his mask safe.

And then the boom of the first fireworks exploded above our heads, lighting my mate's glorious face in a burst of color.

He snaked a hand around my waist, pulled me to his side, and we looked up.

Drones were amazing. Truly.

But nothing beat a big ole vintage fireworks display.

We ooed and aahed at not only the spectacular show in the air, but the one that was for guests only that happened closer to the ground.

It was unreal.

I loved it.

I loved standing at Aleksei's side watching it.

I forgot about my shoes, my dress, and just how taxing the evening was. About Cormac and Gayle, Tanyn, Cat and Bash. Errol. Arnaud.

I was rooted in that brilliant moment, marveling about how a life of living had turned into an extravaganza of fireworks and ballgowns and balconies crammed with royalty, standing close to the male I adored.

No, I wasn't a huge fan of crowds, attention or small talk.

But this evening taught me something.

At Aleksei's side, I could face anything, and eventually, it would be worth it, because he'd given me something beautiful.

These were my happy thoughts when I felt Aleksei tense beside me.

I turned to him, seeing the fireworks lighting his face, his frame, and all around us.

And I noticed how alert he was.

Really alert.

Hyper alert.

And his eyes were cast down to the garden.

He released me and moved closer to the balustrade when I heard the first scream pierce the sound of the detonations in the sky.

On the heels of that scream, like a wave, the confusion washed over us, then the tsunami of fear as I watched Aleksei tear off his tuxedo jacket while flipping off his shoes.

He turned to me, his eyes glowing purple, and thundered, *"Inside!"* before the studs of his shirt went flying as he pulled it off.

He didn't bother with his trousers before he put his hands to the balustrade, leaped over it, and the slap of his dragon wings extending hit me like a physical thing.

His dragon soared over the rushing, frenzied beings rushing frantically toward the Palace.

The king's dragon followed Aleksei's.

Timothee's dragon followed the king's.

And I stood still and staring in the direction of where they were heading.

Because I could not believe the sight that met my eyes.

Trolls.

CHAPTER 44
STREAM

I stood fixed to the spot, even as someone tugged on my arm desperately, and I heard Queen Calisa demand, "Laura! In the Palace! *Now!*"

But I couldn't move.

I could only stare as Tanyn, Cormac and Bainon all leapt over the balustrade like we weren't a story up, and in the Palace garden, shifters shifted, sparks of witch, conjuror and fae magic flew, blazes of dragon fire rained down, and flashes of demons and vampires raced, all of this lanced by screams of terror and shrieks of pain.

Catastrophic pandemonium was playing out in front of me.

But no matter what they threw at them, nothing touched the trolls.

They were even immune to dragon fire.

Gods.

How could it be?

Trolls.

"*Laura!*" Aleece screeched right in my ear.

But I was watching a golden-brown bear I knew had to be Sirk tear across the garden. He barreled into a troll who had hold of a female. The troll went off balance, dropped her, and Sirk reared up and slashed with his mighty claws at its chest.

His claws did not perforate the troll skin.

However, the troll backhanded Sirk so hard, he flew ten feet in the air and twenty feet across the garden, landing on grass and skidding uncontrollably into a bed a of flowers.

That was when I heard a familiar dragon's roar and watched in terror as Aleksei divebombed the troll who struck Sirk.

He got too close to the ground and two trolls jumped on their mighty legs into the air, clasping him around his neck, just as another one caught his tail and swung it. Off balance, Aleksei lost control and went crashing to the ground.

NO!

My beast thudded violently in my chest.

"Unzip me," I demanded.

"What? Laura get inside!" Aleece replied on a shout.

I looked to her, and the instant I did, she reared back.

"*Unzip me!*" I screamed.

She unzipped me, my heavy gown fell away, I jumped out of it, raced to the balustrade, went as if to dive headfirst over it, and she burst from me.

She glided low, listing and banking to avoid the grasp of troll hands.

When she got close, Aleksei's creature was already on his hind feet, sending trolls flying with tail, wings, and he clamped one in his maw, biting down, and three bits of bloodied, ravaged dead troll fell to the turf when he opened his jaw.

She dove into the troll who'd had his tail, and she heard Aleksei's creature's roar, but it didn't stop her.

She caught the troll in her jaw in mid-flight, ascended, and even as the creature struggled in her mouth, beat at her snout with his fists, she soared over the sea, faster, farther, faster, higher, faster, and then she dropped him.

A ferocious, unearthly wail escaping the troll's mouth as, limbs flailing, he fell to the depths from a height that would likely shatter his bones on impact with the water, but even if it didn't, he was in a place no creature could swim back.

She turned and he was there, sending a line of infuriated amethyst dragon fire over her head.

And then she did something she'd never done.

She opened her mouth, and a stream of white-hot flame streaked out, aimed well below his magnificent body.

His wings flapped back, exposing his claws and breast. He bellowed, but she ignored his surprised fury and beat a tattoo back to the Palace.

He soared into place beside her.

By the time they returned, the defense bots had been unleashed, and the flashes of laser beams coming straight from the ends of their limbs were downing trolls all over the west gardens.

He bumped her and tried to guide her, but she ignored him, so he had no choice but to allow them to fall into sync, releasing distraction streams of dragon fire in aid of still-battling shifters, demons, fae, vampires and witches.

And he dispatched another two trolls by divebombing (to her fury) in order to capture them, severing them in his teeth and fangs: one who'd cornered a fighting female fae, and another who looked to be besting a male demon.

They circled and blasted, Timothee's blue and black beast and the king's fierce golden dragon with its amber eyes took their wings until it came clear the defense bots had it in hand, and Aleksei's creature guided us to the courtyard.

The other two dragons sought their own shrubbery, he and she landed behind a line of conical arborvitae.

He shook off his creature.

She let out a cute sneeze and I stood naked with Aleksei in the garden.

He had blood around his mouth and down his chest.

Along with murder in his eyes.

But two could be pissed right the heck off.

"You need to stop divebombing!" I shouted.

"She streams?" he asked with clearly barely controlled calm.

Some dragons had fire, some did not. It wasn't about gender or class, it was about genetics.

Until that night, mine did not.

I shrugged. "She hasn't before. It's new."

I tensed when he suddenly whirled, and Aleece rounded the shrubbery with her arms full of clothes.

Gaze averted, she handed him what looked like a sweater and jeans, then she came to me, her eyes avoiding mine, but she was smiling, so I didn't think she was protecting my nudity, but instead, hiding her insane amusement (what was amusing, I ask you!), and she gave me the same.

"I'll just..." She hooked a thumb to the shrubbery and skedaddled.

"Never again." Aleksei's voice was vibrating with fury as he spoke and yanked up his jeans.

"Honey."

"*Never do that again!*" he thundered.

Okay.

I was learning he had to shout it out, so did I, and then we could carry on like adults.

But now, he had to pull it together.

I was also dressing as I said with as much calm as I could muster in the face of his pulsating wrath, and frankly, all I'd just seen and *done*, "We'll battle it out, but we can't right now. We need to see if our loved ones are okay and find out what the farg is going on."

My mate agreed with me, I knew, because he yanked down his sweater, snatched up my hand, and dragged me through the courtyard to the Palace.

Once inside, there was still pandemonium. I could see the green and orange flashes of constabulary craft outside the opened front doors, defense bots standing at attention just inside, ambu-lift medics were hard at work, beings were milling about in shocked stupors, and some had fainted and were on the floor. To my despair, the latter were intermingled with those who were battered and bloodied. And worse, some who were obviously dead.

I saw Dr. Fearsome, Rya not too far from him (they were guests), both of them administering to some wounded.

And then I lost sight of them when Aleksei pushed me into Timothee's arms and ordered, "Take her to the king's study, and I swear to fuck, Tim, she steps one foot out of it, I'll hold you responsible."

Timothee nodded, but he also looked like he was fighting a smile, when, *again*, I had no idea what could possibly be funny, and he started pulling me to the stairs.

I didn't want to go. I was no medic, but I could wield a Medi-Aid, for goodness' sake.

But my mate was in a state, so I said not a word and accompanied Timothee to the king's study.

✦ ✦ ✦

The first to join us were Monique and Mrs. Truelock.

Right.

Two down.

Good.

Seven to go.

"The others?" I asked after I rushed to them to give them hugs.

"In the crush to get back to the Palace, I lost track of Gayle and Cat," Monique told me apprehensively. "I...I don't know about Mr. and Mrs.

Vinestrong. But Mr. Truelock was talking to a constable when we were located and escorted up here."

Right, three down, six to go.

"The queen?" Mrs. Truelock asked, glancing at Timothee.

"I don't know. I believe she went inside at the beginning of the attack. But Aleksei, Aleece, and the king are okay," I said.

"We saw Aleksei, Aleece and Fillion," Mrs. Truelock said. "But we haven't seen Calisa," she finished as the door opened.

"I'm here. I'm fine," the queen announced.

I hurried to her and threw my arms around her.

She gave me a brief squeeze, pulled away but kept hold of one arm, patted my cheek with the other hand, her eyes moving over my face, a strange light in them.

And she murmured, "My little Iphelia."

Whoa.

"I should have read it," she said mysteriously, just as the door opened again.

Cat and Gayle came in.

I hastened to them too.

After we embraced, I looked to Gayle. "Your mom?"

"She refused to come up. Somehow, she got her hands on a couple Medi-Aids and she's slapping those babies on anyone who has the faintest bruise."

Gods, I adored Mrs. Vinestrong.

"Did either of you see Sirk?" I asked.

Cat nodded. "I saw him. He was helping to load wounded onto ambu-lifts."

Okay.

All nine were good.

I could relax, at least a little.

"Now that we're all together, can someone tell me I had a drug slipped into my drink and I'm hallucinating the fact that there are a slew of dead trolls with blast holes strewn all over the west garden of the Celestial Palace?" Cat drawled.

"I wish I could," I told her.

"I can't believe you flew," Gayle said.

I shrugged. "They'd downed Aleksei."

"Wow. Really?" she asked, obviously having missed that part.

"He was down for less than five seconds," Queen Calisa announced. She narrowed her gaze on me. "If it wasn't so magnificent what you did,

Laura, I would be lecturing you on how tremendously foolish it was, you doing it without a hint of training."

"What it was, was fucking *epic*," Timothee muttered.

The queen whirled on him and snapped, "Timothee."

"Mom, you said it yourself," he retorted.

Although I felt the breakthrough Tim and I had in the mural room strengthening, and I thought that was awesome, there were other, more important things afoot.

"What'd you do?" Cat asked me.

"One of the trolls that downed Lex is fish food, for starters," Tim told her.

Cat, Gayle and Monique all gaped at me.

We'd get into that later.

"Um, can we talk about the trolls"—and not me—"for a bit?" I requested.

"I would like to talk about that too," Queen Calisa sniffed. "But since they haven't been sighted in nearly eight hundred years, until tonight, I don't have that first clue what to say."

"Credits to croissants, those demons up at the Edge have been breeding them for *forever*," Cat remarked.

This would be my guess.

But wouldn't Tanyn have known about that?

Though, perhaps not, considering he was banished from Berg Castle when he was only a year old and confined on an island until he was old enough to go to school. And he'd famously never been let back into the Castle, or his father's orbit, even if he'd been given a prince's education, and he and his mother lived in a citadel on the island that wasn't a castle, as such, but it was nothing to sneeze at.

"Timothee, your mother needs a brandy, if you would be so kind," Queen Calisa ordered.

"And I need a whisky," Tim muttered. "Anyone else?"

"Shot of tequila," Cat said.

"Times two," Moniqe put in.

"Snifter of almondine," I requested.

"I'll help," Mrs. Truelock said.

"No need. I have it," Tim told her.

Yeah.

He just said that he'd make a bunch of females some drinks.

I stared at him because...

Who was this male?

"I need something to do, sweetheart," Mrs. Truelock told him.

Tim jerked up his chin.

"Can you make me a martini?" Gayle asked. "Stiff. Olive."

"I change mine to that," Cat said.

"Me too," Monique added.

Tim and Mrs. Truelock headed to a bureau that had the makings of a full bar on top of it and got to work.

They made our drinks, and we settled in, only for Mrs. Vinestrong to arrive ten minutes later on a massive eyeroll to her daughter and the words, "Your father commanded I remove myself from the melee." She turned her attention to encompass Queen Calisa and Mrs. Truelock and griped, "Males."

"Indeed," Queen Calisa agreed.

"So things are still crazy?" Gayle asked.

Mrs. Vinestrong nodded as she collapsed into an armchair. "Not like at the beginning, of course. They're restoring order. I think every constable in Nocturn is interviewing guests. And two banks of army dragons have arrived. There are beasts sitting sentry all around the island, and more flying overhead."

Suddenly, Gayle asked, "Where's Errol?"

I tried not to meet Tim and Queen Calisa's eyes as they did the same to me, because he couldn't shift, though he didn't know he couldn't shift, and now he probably wondered why, which was not good.

They far more successfully avoided my gaze without looking like they were, and Queen Calisa answered breezily, "Helping, I'm sure."

Under the guard of some defense bots so he wouldn't put two and two together and make an escape, I was sure.

"Okay, is it only me who noticed that King Arnaud didn't show his gross, smarmy face at the Masque?" Cat asked.

More eye avoidance from the royals, and Queen Calisa waded in again. "As Elayne said, there is what I have no doubt will be a thorough investigation already underway. We'll learn what there is to learn when there's something to know."

"Perhaps we should turn on the screen?" Mrs. Truelock suggested.

Before the queen could stop him, Tim, who was leaning against the front of the king's desk, said to the room, "Screen engage. Play latest newsfeed."

A large screen unfurled from the ceiling and a human female newsreader appeared on it.

"We've received reports of a massive malfunction of the ground level fireworks display at the Midnight Masque this evening," she was saying.

Sounded like Germaine hadn't missed a beat, as usual.

At least it was good to know she was fine and functioning on all cylinders.

"There may be casualties, but we haven't received official word," she went on. "Emergency forces were dispatched to the Sceptred Isle. We await further news on developments."

"Screen mute," the queen called.

The newsreader continued to be displayed, her mouth yapping, but we couldn't hear her.

"They can't possibly think hundreds of people who saw, and even battled, trolls are going to keep their traps shut about seeing and battling freaking *trolls*," Mon remarked.

"No, we won't be able to keep that under wraps," the queen agreed. "However, perhaps we can do it long enough the appropriate comms can go out so we'll be at the ready."

"At the ready?" Gayle asked. "For what?"

The queen turned frighteningly sober eyes to her.

And then she decreed, "My dear, I'm not certain who did it, but someone did. They launched an attack against Nights' Fall. And now, we are at war."

CHAPTER 45
INGRAINED

It was a full hour before Set arrived in the king's study to give us a brief rundown of what they knew.

Two RS agents had been killed, three guests had also been killed, and there were forty more casualties from the battle with the trolls. Of the wounded, seven were so severe, they had to be ambu-lifted to a hospital in the city.

Further casualties numbered twenty-seven. These were guests who had been injured in the stampede to return to the Palace. Luckily, only two of those were severe enough to go to hospital.

And one hundred and twenty-two trolls had been streamed dead in the gardens.

No trolls survived.

After delivering this news, Set opened the door to a phalanx of RS agents, including Fannon and Geleena, explaining we'd be escorted back to our chambers.

Obviously, Fannon and Geleena walked me to Aleksei's and my suite.

They also requested I stand outside with Geleena as Fannon preceded me and checked the space before they allowed me in. And then they took their places as sentry in the hall.

Apparently, chances were not being taken.

I was down with that.

As I entered the sitting room, I saw all three cats lying side by side on a window seat, tails swinging, attention aimed out the window.

I went to stand behind them.

Fog drones hovered, flooding the entire garden with light. There were a dizzying number of white tents set up, my guess, covering troll carcasses for investigative purposes. And an equally dizzying number of uniformed beings were moving urgently about, investigating the vast scene.

There were also dragons seated on the massive plinths I'd noticed positioned all around the perimeter of the island, but I'd thought those plinths were decorative.

They weren't.

They were sentry stations.

For dragons.

There were further dragons in sets of five flying in the air.

It seemed all the guests were gone.

Aleksei wasn't in the suite, I knew, because I couldn't feel him.

But I didn't know how much time I had before his return, so I did what something in my heart was telling me to do.

I found my tablet and video commed Nata.

She answered immediately.

"Oh my gods, are you okay?" she asked as greeting.

"I'm fine. Everyone in the family is fine. We're...it's a lot. But we're fine." Before she could reply, I went on, "Listen, I know it's late, or really early."

"That's okay," she said swiftly. "I was up. I couldn't sleep. Everyone is freaking out about what's happening."

I didn't ask her what they were saying, or what she knew, because I wasn't sure I had time.

"Thanks, but what I have to ask you to do might not be okay."

She didn't look even mildly wary. "You can ask me to do anything, Laura."

Totally picked right with this gal.

"I need you to comm my father and tell him I'm okay."

Her face shut down.

Yep.

Picked right with her.

"Okay, getting a little personal here," I began, "I'm not sure where I'm at with him, but I know he'll be worried. That said, I don't want to open up a direct line of communication again, because I'm not sure I'm ready for what he might assume from that. You don't have to get into detail. You don't even have to video comm him. Just introduce yourself in a text comm and tell him I asked you to share I was fine."

"I can do that," she said readily.

"You sure?"

"I'll be your go between, Laura. Especially if it keeps you out of his direct line."

She was so great.

"Thank you," I said effusively.

"No problem. Try to get some sleep," she replied.

I was exhausted.

But...

No way that would happen. Not until Aleksei was doing it at my side.

"Will do. See you."

"Yeah, see you."

We disconnected, and I wedged myself in next to my curious cats who were fascinated by the show outside.

I then did what I had to do next.

I returned to my pane search to pull up that article on Aerin and Iphelia.

I'd searched the True Heir with a vulnerable True Bride. There had to be something in it, especially after what Calisa said, and the new knowledge I had that night my beast was of a warrior caste, and Iphelia had been the same.

She wasn't an outlier. Throughout history, there had always been female warriors of every race and breed, and there were several elite squads made entirely of females that were famous for their heroic deeds.

I just didn't know, until that night, I was one of them.

I read, and most of what I read was what I knew of their story.

Until I got to the part where it said:

According to various sources close to the True Heir, along with what was written in Princess Iphelia's journals, Prince Aerin experienced critically debilitating lack of control due to his concern over his fated mate placing herself in danger.

This went far beyond the customary need to protect of a male mate.

It famously caused a rift between the lovers. One that tore them apart and shocked the realm.

Unfortunately, although it's known they reconciled, and nine months later the next True Heir was born, as she often did—understanding her journals would be kept for historical purposes—Princess Iphelia did not detail this reconciliation as she rarely detailed the more private moments she shared with her husband.

It is simply known that they were never apart again, in living life or in fighting wars. And there were no further indications that the prince suffered this debilitation in regard to his mate.

In fact, they became famous at the time for their synchronicity on and off the battlefield and revered as formidable opponents to any enemy.

It is also known that, from their reconciliation onward, they reigned together as partners, this being unusual to this day for any monarch, king or queen, to share this power with their spouse.

"Well, that doesn't help much," I muttered to my tablet.

"Meow?" Comet asked.

"Nothing to worry about, baby," I cooed to him.

There was a knock on the door.

"Yes?" I called.

Fannon opened it and walked in. "I'm to escort you to the prince now, Laura."

I was being taken to him?

Interesting.

I nodded, quickly taking my feet and said, "I need to throw on some shoes." *And a bra*, I didn't say.

He returned my nod.

On my dash to the closet, I tossed my tablet on the sofa. I took the time to put on some flats, a bra, and the mane-mate in order for it to do my hair in a ponytail (my fabulous chignon was long gone). Then I was hustling back out to the sitting room.

Geleena stayed behind to guard the suite, and Fannon and I descended to the first floor and then down the hall toward the admin wing.

Once there, we hit a lift, took it down two floors and then out into a hall I'd never been in and didn't know existed. It had none of the elegant trappings of the upper floors, but instead was cold and utilitarian.

There were two defense bots standing outside a door, their sight ring pulsing a lavender light, which was both creepy and cool, knowing they could use it to see three hundred sixty degrees.

Fannon was talking into his watch unit as we approached, so when we got there, the door opened.

"Mistress Laura," a male I'd never met said.

He bowed then moved back so I could enter.

Fannon stayed outside.

I entered, eyes wide, taking it all in, because all of it was *mega*.

There were a good dozen beings in there, seated around a long table.

They all took their feet (aside from King Fillion, who was sitting next to the Prime Minister, a male I'd met in the receiving line that night and who was still wearing his tuxedo, though it was dirty and had a torn lapel, but he, too, got up when I entered).

Aleksei, sitting to one side, also took his feet.

I saw Bainon and Cormac at the long table. Tanyn was standing and appeared to have been pacing before I arrived. There was a female also standing at the foot of the table, and I knew I'd arrived in the middle of her giving a briefing. But around the seats were a variety of males and females, three in uniform (one male, two females).

And Germaine was there.

Every wall in the room was a screen, and on them a variety of live vids were displayed, including the activities in the west gardens, inside and outside of tents, and the trajectory of a lone craft that was speeding through the night.

The long table in the middle had displays built in at each seat, and hovering over it was a holo map of the entire Sceptred Isle. It glowed yellow, except for a tiny area to what would be the southwest edge of the island, which was red.

Clearly, this was the situation room.

And it was insanely cool.

"Laura, if you'd be seated by Aleksei," the king invited.

I didn't ask why I'd been invited to this session. I was just thrilled to be there.

So, without hesitation or that first sound, I moved around the head of the table to sit in the vacant chair next to Aleksei.

I caught his gaze and was pleased to see he didn't look ticked at me, or anyone. There was no purple or pinprick of stars in his eyes, though the room was rather dim, so maybe I couldn't see the latter.

But he did look serious. Very much so. However, that was no surprise.

He held my chair as I sat. And once I did, he did, as did everyone else.

"Carry on," King Fillion called.

The female standing aimed a laser pointer at the little red area on the holo map.

"The preliminary breach was at the southwest dock. The boat signal was that of Baron LaFleur, who was, with his wife, to be an attending guest at the Masque. Radio communication affirmed that the voice heard after hailing was LaFleur's. However, an hour ago, the baron and his wife were found deceased in their flat in Nocturn," she stated. "Murdered."

I nearly gasped, even though I'd never met the LaFleurs.

Although I wasn't certain why I was there, I knew this was a briefing of important people (I just didn't know I was that important), so I didn't want to do something stupid, like gasp.

The holo pixilated like falling dust into the table, and a new one sprang up in 3D, full color, of a male in an elaborate mask and tuxedo alighting from a boat and going to talk to the RS agent who was guarding the dock.

"This male has been identified as Randal Tapshine, an Arnaud sympathizer," the female reported.

I had to hold back another gasp as Tapshine engaged his demon speed and snapped the neck of the RS agent. He then turned some kind of weapon on the other agent who was in the guardhouse, and faster than a blink, she went down too.

Tapshine then moved into the guardhouse, and it was sickening how matter-of-factly he yanked her body out so he could enter it.

"At this point," the female reporting said, "Tapshine hacked into security, commandeering cameras to display false images. He also jammed nautical detection beacons and the frequency sensors on the west side of the island."

That holo dropped and the island came back up again.

"Therefore, the trolls approached by boat and were able to breach the island here first." She pointed to the red area, and another red area sprang up at the western end of the island. "This was their second point of entry." A third illuminated on the northwestern side. "And this was their last. The landing was coordinated, and we found comm tech in their boats that were set to a short-range frequency to corroborate that."

She took a deep breath and gave her conclusion.

"We believe the trolls were meant to decimate the beings populating the isle and then occupy it. The boats were captained by demons, and once the drop-off had been accomplished, they made their escape."

"Considering what's been happening, and the increased security we were meant to have because of it, in twenty-four hours I'll want a report on how island security was so easily breached by a single male," King Fillion said tightly.

The female nodded solemnly. "I can already report, the digi-disk he used to hack our systems was something we've never encountered before. He took it with him, and it self-destructed when he was apprehended half an hour ago. We already have our techs working on the remnants, and any trails it left in the system, and obviously, they're treating this code red. Our lads in the lab are good, your majesty. If there's something to find, they'll find it."

"And the voice recognition that clearly did not detect a recorded voice?" the Prime Minister demanded.

"This, too, we're looking into," she replied.

"Your highnesses," a male across the table from us broke in, and he appeared to be addressing both Aleksei and Tanyn. "Arnaud approaches the border to Sky's Edge."

My eyes flew to the screen displaying the lone craft being tracked. A craft that I now knew was transporting the pretender king.

Aleksei and Tanyn exchanged a glance.

Tanyn jutted his chin.

"Send in the units," Aleksei said.

The image moved from a screen on the side to the one at the foot of the table and everyone watched as craft from all around appeared from out of nowhere, surrounding the red UtiliSport.

I could see RMI craft, Night's Fall military craft, but also others that appeared to be not only from Sky's Edge, but from Central Command (the law enforcement agency of the Center).

"Open channel to Alpha Squad," one of the uniformed females called. Then she ordered, "Report."

A voice filled the room. "The subject has been informed he's being detained due to infractions of InterRealm Statutes 1A, sections eight, twelve and fifteen, 2C, sections three and seven, 5E, section four, 9B, section two, and to be questioned regarding the murder of Tula Longshot. His craft has been shielded and locked down. Tractor beams are engaged. Reversing course."

Tula Longshot?

Who was Tula Longshot?

I watched as the formation of crafts switched directions and started gliding the other way.

"I'm out," Tanyn announced, prowling toward the door.

"Tan," Aleksei called.

The prince turned back.

"Good luck," Aleksei bid.

Another chin jut from the prince, and he was out the door.

"And you're on," Germaine said in the direction of the king and the Prime Minister.

Both males stood, so we all did, and Germaine and two of the uniformed beings left the room with them.

When the door closed behind them, we sat again, and I leaned into Aleksei, "Who's Tula Longshot?"

Aleksei turned to me. "Arnaud's fiancée."

Holy Hecate.

"She's dead?"

"She was found beaten to death in the king's suite at the Imperial."

At that, I couldn't help it.

I gasped.

"He did it?" I asked.

"Evidence gathered at the scene indicates that yes, he did. Without a doubt."

"He beat a twelve-year-old child to death?" I snapped.

"Yes."

My voice was rising. "Why would he do that?"

"Perhaps when he returns to Nocturn, we'll find out."

Good gods.

That poor child.

My eyes went to the door then back to my mate. "Where are the king and the Prime Minister going?"

"To do a live broadcast to announce the pretender king, Arnaud, launched an attack on the Celestial Palace tonight. Along with the fact that, for centuries, Sky's Edge has been clandestinely harboring and breeding trolls for military use. And Night's Fall considers this an act of war, and as such, the Edge is in criminal breach of at least four statutes of the InterRealm Accord of 1933. Further, Arnaud will be returned to Nocturn to be questioned in the murder of Tula Longshot, before he's moved to the Center to answer to charges pertaining to the breaches of the Accord. However, if Prince Tanyn is crowned king within forty-eight hours, and any remaining trolls are transported to the Center for assessment and confinement, Night's Fall will not be moved to retaliate against the realm of Sky's Edge."

I was having trouble breathing, but still I managed to get out, "Where are kings Dagsbrun and Niall?"

"They're returning to their realms to discuss with their president and prime minister respectively, making public announcements of alliance with Night's Fall in its war with Sky's Edge."

Well, one could say, while we were drinking, chatting, and I was reading about Aerin and Iphelia, Aleksei and all the rest had been busy.

My gaze drifted to the crafts gliding back to Nocturn.

And I asked anxiously, "Does this seem a bit easy to you?"

"It does and it doesn't," he replied.

I returned my attention to him.

"The defense bots are a new acquisition to Sceptred Isle," he stated.
That was surprising.
"They are?"
He nodded. "Yes. They were assigned here after the first assassination attempt on me. This was known by the military, the RS, Father and me. Not Errol."
Hmm.
"As such," he carried on, "we believe Arnaud didn't know we had an army of bots readily available to defend the island. Bots whose modern weapon capability would easily penetrate troll skin. We had agents providing security, but the additional bots doubled their number, and completely outnumbered the trolls, something he didn't envisage. However, although preliminarily, the trolls were expected to occupy the island, they were not ultimately expected to survive, or triumph, as obviously, the military would have eventually launched a counteroffensive."
When I nodded, he carried on.
"Therefore, their mission was simply to wreak havoc and make a statement. We believe Arnaud anticipated and planned for a good deal more carnage, if not the annihilation of three royal families, as well as what was perhaps his main target, Tanyn. We know he had a least one operator among the guests at the Masque. We believe this male reported back to Arnaud that his plan had not succeeded, and in a fit of rage, and the timing of death appears to corroborate this, he murdered his 'true love,' beat a hasty retreat to his craft and attempted to flee back to Sky's Edge."
"Why would he come all the way down to Night's Fall if he never intended to show at the Masque?" I asked.
"It makes no sense," Aleksei agreed. "But some killers return to the scene of the crime or involve themselves in the investigation to get some sick thrill reliving their deeds. Perhaps it's something like that."
Perhaps it was.
I took a surreptitious look around at the remaining personnel in the room, all of which were conferring, or working on tablets, the displays in front of them or their Palms, though I noted Bainon and Cormac had left the room.
Then I leaned closer to Aleksei, "Why am I here?"
He didn't answer me.
He turned to the last being in uniform and asked (but it was an order), "You'll contact me when he's officially in custody?"
"Yes, your highness," the male replied.
With that, Aleksei stood, taking my hand to pull me to my feet.

We were both silent as we walked back to the Palace, Fannon leading us.

He took his post with Geleena outside as we entered the suite. Aleksei closed the door behind us and went directly to the cabinet in the sitting room that concealed the contents of a bar.

"Want something?" he asked me.

I shook my head.

He poured himself two fingers of whisky.

He then walked to the windows, pushed a hand in the pocket of his jeans, and sipped while he stared out of them.

"Aleksei?" I called, feeling strange because his mood was strange.

I mean, obviously, it would be.

But also, he was with me, and I'd hoped he'd learned that he could lay anything on me.

"You stream," he said to the windows.

Oh dear.

"Honey."

He turned to me.

Before he could speak, I said, "Like I told you in the courtyard, I didn't know I did. It was a surprise to me as well. And I had no control over transforming. I don't know what came over me, but the instant those trolls got hold of you, there was nothing I could do. She wouldn't allow anything, but what we did."

"I know that feeling," he murmured before he took another sip and returned his attention to the windows.

I was getting concerned, because he didn't seem mad, he didn't seem remote, he wasn't being argumentative.

I didn't know what was happening.

I moved deeper into the room and encouraged, "Aleksei, talk to me."

"The most likely result of what's about to happen is that the many beings in Sky's Edge who wanted Arnaud out and Tanyn in will rejoice. Arnaud will answer for the murder, and to the UCR for the invasion tonight, the deaths that occurred, and if we can find the evidence to support it, his assassination attempts on you and me."

"Well, that's good," I remarked.

He again turned to me. "However, some of his followers are more like zealots. This spectacular fall from grace isn't unexpected, considering he's insane, and he's never given any indication he's brilliantly insane, just insane. That does not extend to his mother, who, as far as we know at this point, has done nothing. Though with the kind of female she is, none of us believe she doesn't have some hand in this if only to encourage his insanity and attempt to keep her son on the throne. Now, she'll be removed from Berg Castle. Tanyn may even be moved to strip her of the title she stole from his mother, and he'll soon have the power to do so. And she will not like either of those things. And she is far cleverer than her son."

Hmm.

This didn't sound good.

"So we're not out of the woods," I deduced.

"We're not out of the woods, and you stream."

I took another step toward him. "Aleksei, I really want to understand where you are in your head, but I'm not locking on."

"You cannot control her, as I can barely control him. This is where *we* are, darling. But for my part, I have no choice but to come to terms with the fact you are warrior caste, in a time of possible war, and that will not be easy. But the bottom line is, you are, and we are for all intents and purposes at war, so you were brought in on the briefing because you need to know what's happening."

One good thing about this (really good), he was skipping past the critically-debilitating and the rift-tearing-us-asunder parts and pushing directly into the dealing-with-it part.

Even so, I said, "I'm not a warrior. I don't even want to be."

"*Bissi*," he said softly. "You flew in formation and instinctually understood our cover fire strategy without my creature communicating that first thing to yours. Even before that, you glided low for over five hundred yards with the enemy leaping for you, and you flew evasively so successfully, not a single one of them got close to touching you. I've seen this before at Red Lair. There are those who just get it. It's natural. Ingrained. I was one. And you, my darling, are too."

All right, even though a bit of me thought this was cool (a bit), I made a face, because, no shade on kickass warriors with ingrained instincts, I wasn't all fired up to be one.

He chuckled and ordered, "Come here."

The chuckle was good.

The order to come there was better.

I went, and he wrapped an arm around me and held me close.

"Now that I'm not terrified for you, I can tell you I'm proud of you," he stated.

Aw.

My gorgeous male.

"I'm proud of you too."

That got me another chuckle.

And he took another sip of his whisky.

I waited for more.

But I guessed that was it. No knock down, drag out. No big scene.

Thank the gods.

"Aren't you tired?" I asked because he had to be. I certainly was.

"I want to watch Dad's announcement. It should have gone out by now. We can get a replay. And then, yes, we need to sleep. Tomorrow is going to be busy."

I nodded.

He took his drink and me to the bedroom. From the ceiling, he unfurled the screen that hung at the foot of the bed. We hit the bathroom and got ready for sleep, went back out, and after we settled in, me cuddled to Aleksei's side, he ordered the screen to display the king and Prime Minister's announcement.

I heard Germaine all over it, even if she wasn't on the PM's staff, and the PM did most of the talking.

So it was good. Angry. Clear. Resolute. Short. But informative.

And surprisingly, they intimated that Arnaud may be behind the attempts on Aleksei and my lives, as well as the deaths of Antheme, Naylan Biggerstaff and Richard Tayor.

When it was done, he ordered the screen to refold and reached for his Palm.

With me watching and reading as he did, he thumbed through some social tapes.

Shock. Dismay. Outrage. Disbelief.

There were some that clearly came from the Edge calling for beings to calm down and wait for more information to emerge.

But there was also a ton of footage that had been uploaded by guests of the troll attack (including, embarrassingly, of my dragon, and Aleksei's, doing warrior things—he was right, we looked like we'd trained together for years, and it was awesome, it was also crazy).

I had a feeling from the tapes and comments that our ratings were going to go up again.

But mostly, he was alive. I was alive. All the ones we loved were alive. Aleksei didn't lose it because my beast entered the fray (well, not *too* much). Arnaud would be arrested. Tanyn would be crowned king soon.

And I was shattered.

So while Aleksei continued to scroll, I passed out.

CHAPTER 46
LOVE YOU

"Darling, wake up. Cat is here."

I blinked gritty eyes and stared at the impossibly handsome, awake, vital face of my beloved.

"What?" I mumbled.

"Cat is here, love. And your Palm has some urgent messages from Gayle. I think something's happening."

As his words penetrated, considering all that had been swirling for weeks, not to mention my beast dropped an actual troll in the middle of the sea last night (among other things), my adrenaline spiked.

I tossed the covers aside, jumped out of bed and raced into the sitting room.

Cat was standing there, her coppery tresses a mess (but they still looked great), her face makeup free (and she was just as gorgeous), and she was wearing a robe and slippers.

She'd walked through the Celestial Palace in a robe and slippers with no makeup!

When there were gorgeous princes running amuck!

Was the world ending?

I dashed to her. "Oh my gods, what's going on?"

"We need to get to Gayle. Now."

I didn't ask.

I said, "Hang on a sec," raced back to the bedroom, hit the closet, slipped on my own slippers and shrugged on a robe.

I was still tying it when I dashed back.

"Let's go," I said, turning quickly to Aleksei, who was standing there, fully dressed, holding a cup of coffee and watching us.

I quickly aimed a kiss on his jaw and headed out with Cat.

"Okay, what's happening?" I asked as we moved.

"I don't know. I just got up, checked my Palm, saw I had a dozen messages from her, so I looked at them, and in all of them, she's sobbing and practically incoherent. They came in hours ago, but I put my tech on mute. I've commed and commed, and she isn't picking up."

Oh dear.

We doubled our pace, jogging around the corner and down the south hall to Gayle's room.

We knocked.

No answer.

We knocked again.

No answer.

"Gayle! It's us!" I called.

No answer.

Cat and I looked at each other.

Farg it.

I turned the knob and walked in.

The curtains were closed, so it was pitch black.

"Lights, ten percent," I called to the lightbulbs in the old-fashioned lamps.

"No," we heard said weakly from our left.

Gayle didn't have a suite, but her room was large, with a sitting area and a massive bed.

And she was huddled in said bed, knees to chest, resting her side against the headboard.

"Lights, thirty percent," Cat ordered.

"No!" Gayle cried.

But the lights geared up...and dang.

Gayle's eyes were bloodshot and swollen, her face splotchy, her hair was not a gorgeous mess, it was a tangled one.

She was a disaster.

We darted to the bed and climbed into it with her.

But it was me who pulled her into my arms, cooing, "What's going on? Are you reacting to last night? Do we need to call a doctor?"

She let out a harsh laugh the like I'd never heard from her.

Cat and I locked eyes over her head.

"Last night. Yeah," Gayle stated bitterly. "But no doctor can help me."

Cat laid a hand on her back and stroked. "Honey, what's going on?"

"Nothing," she bit out. "Precisely nothing. And it never will."

What?

"Maybe start at the beginning?" I suggested.

The instant I did, she tore out of my arms, scrambled off the bed and whirled on us with such quick energy, Cat and I were so surprised, we didn't move.

"Guess who knocked on my door last night," she urged acidly.

"Um..." I was too scared by her demeanor to guess.

"Sirk?" Cat, who was never too scared of anything, queried.

"No. Not Sirk," Gayle snapped. "I *wish* it was Sirk. I *wish* I had agreed to date him. I *wish* I hadn't been *so fucking stupid* as to wait for my mate."

Oh no.

"Did...Cormac come to you last night?" I asked haltingly.

She leaned forward and hissed, "*Yes.*"

"I take it this convo didn't go well," Cat noted tentatively.

Gayle leaned back and threw out both hands. "I don't know. The male the Earth God destined for you showing at your door in the middle of the night, abruptly and emotionlessly telling you he's aware that you're his mate, but he has no interest in mating with a half fae from Night's Fall when he's the full fae prince and one-day king of Land's End. And therefore, informing you, you should feel free to live your life and find your happiness without him. Is that good? Or is it what it seemed? Very, very *bad.*"

"Oh my gods!" Cat exclaimed angrily. "What an asshole!"

"He said that to you?" I breathed in shock.

"Stood right outside my door, didn't even bother to come in, and said just that," Gayle confirmed.

"Well, fuck him," Cat let loose.

"None of that kind of thing will be happening, obviously," Gayle returned with deep sarcasm.

And then she dissolved into tears.

I scurried off the bed, took hold of her and guided her back to it, whereupon we all cuddled together, Cat and I holding, rocking and stroking Gayle.

"Wh-when I heard the knock, and...and I felt it was him, I jumped out of bed and I was *so excited*," she wailed into our skin. "Then I opened the d-d-door and he was so *cold*. It was just unbelievably so, *so...awful*. And when he walked away, it felt like he cut off big chunks of me and took them with him."

Cat and I locked eyes over her head again.

Hers were red with demon ire.

Mine couldn't turn red, but if they could, they would.

We said nothing more, just held her and soothed her until, after a while, she lapsed into sleep.

"Turns," I whispered to Cat. "I'll go grab a shower, get dressed and come back. You do the same, and while you're gone, I'll order up coffee and breakfast."

"Plan," she replied.

Carefully, I extricated myself from my friend, smoothed her glorious hair, quietly made my way out of her room and hurried all the way back to mine.

I was in such a hurry, I ran smack into Aleksei in the sitting room.

He grabbed my upper arms to steady me.

"What is it?" he asked harshly, staring at my face.

He felt it.

"Do you have Cormac in your Palm?"

His brows went up. "Of course."

"Comm him. Video."

"What is it?" he asked again, now watching me closely.

"Just comm him, *drahko*!" I yelled.

He let me go to pull the Palm out of his inside jacket pocket.

"Video comm Cormac," he ordered it and handed it to me.

I aimed the display at my face.

Cormac's face came on it, his mouth open to greet Aleksei, but it snapped shut when he got me.

"Oh yeah," I bit at him. "It's me. And you're going to listen to me, you insufferable piece of poo. There will come a time, probably soon, when you realize you can't live without her, and you're going to want to win her back. Mark my words...*mark my words*, your highness, you will beg and you will crawl before I *ever* allow that to happen. Do you hear me?"

I didn't wait for him to confirm he heard me.

I disconnected and tossed the Palm back to Aleksei, who caught it readily.

"Would you like to explain why you're threatening a prince of a realm we need as an ally?" he drawled.

I scowled at him. "He's Gayle's mate, and before he headed home last night, he paid her a visit and told her he, the almighty prince of Land's End, had no intention to mate with a half fae from Night's Fall."

"Oh shit," Aleksei muttered.

"Dang straight!" I cried.

"You called him an insufferable piece of poo," he noted, and I had to ignore the fact he sounded amused.

"Because he is! He's worse!"

"Darling—"

"Are you close to him?"

"Mac's in the ring ice league."

Gah!

They were close.

"Is he a bigot?" I asked.

"He's never, not once, given any indication that he was."

"So what *is* this crap?" I demanded.

"I don't know," he said soothingly, pulling me into his arms. "What I do know is that it's never advised to get between mates."

"I'll consider that wisdom when Gayle hasn't just cried herself to sleep in my arms after spending all night curled into a ball, crying herself out of sleep."

The compassion in his face was amazing.

But I was in no mood.

"I need to take a shower and get back to her," I declared. "Is there something I need to be doing with political intrigue and declarations of war?"

His lips twitched. "No. I can report, upon arrival in Nocturn, Arnaud was taken into custody without incident and charged with murder. At the same time, Central Command informed him he's also being detained while they investigate crimes of engagement. The magisterial panel in Sky's Edge held an emergency meeting first thing this morning and upheld Tanyn's claim to the throne. Sky's Edge Parliament is in session and will hold a vote at one p.m. to confirm succession. If that goes as expected, he'll be unofficially crowned tomorrow morning at nine, with a coronation to take place when it can be planned."

"Good," I snapped.

"And the UTC has announced it's forming a committee to investigate the breaches to the InterRealm Accord, along with violations within the Engagement Convention. Obviously, since that was written and agreed in 1935, there was no mention of trolls. Regardless, Arnaud attacked without provocation using what could be considered an unknown weapon and this absolutely is a violation of approved engagement."

"That's good too."

"And that's all I've got."

It hit me I'd been gone awhile, and he was still in our suite, so I looked around and asked him, "Don't you have somewhere to be?"

"I do. But you and Cat tore out of here so I put it off and waited for you to return. I wanted to make sure all was well."

Ugh!

Sometimes he was so awesome, I couldn't take it.

"And someone had to feed the cats," he finished.

See?

I threw myself in his arms, kissed him hard, broke it and said, "I need to get sorted and get back."

"Do you need me to order you breakfast?"

Seriously?

I couldn't take it!

"No, I've got it." I touched my mouth to his, pulled out of his arms and dashed down the hall, calling, "I'll comm you later."

"Love you," he called in return.

"Love you too," I shouted.

Then I hit the bathroom and snatched up my Denti-Clean.

✦ ✦ ✦

An hour and a half later, Gayle was still crashed, and Cat and I were huddled at a table by the window that was covered in our used breakfast dishes, and we were having a whispered conversation.

I was filling her in with all that had happened.

She was visibly relieved the Arnaud thing appeared to be at an end, and seeing her relief, it was the first time I realized it was at an end.

He was in custody. He was in deep doo-doo with murder and mayhem to answer for. He was about to lose his throne. And if they could prove he killed that poor young female, and all the rest, he wouldn't be free, maybe for the rest of his life.

So outside of still being insanely pissed at Prince Cormac for being such a massive dick, I was relieved too.

And maybe, now that the Masque was over, Aleksei and I could go away for a week and chill the heck out before I was thrown into engagement party planning, wedding planning and the movie started shooting.

"Something happened last night with me too," Cat whispered.

I came out of my thoughts and right back into the room, because her voice was weird.

"What?" I asked.

"Well..." Her eyes slid to the side.

"Cat, really. Things seem to be going our way, finally, but only after more beings died last night. If this is bad, just sock it to me."

"I got a middle of the night visitor too."

I stared.

"Tanyn knocked on my door last night," she finished.

"What?" I whisper-shouted.

"What?" Gayle plain old shouted from the bed.

Cat narrowed her eyes toward the bed. "Were you pretending to sleep?"

Gayle pushed the covers back. "Not at first. But I could smell bacon and coffee, and it woke me up."

That would wake any gal up.

I reached to the pot to pour her a cup when she made her way to us.

I slid the cup and saucer to her at the same time watching her curl, knees to chest, into a chair at the table.

Still assuming a protective position.

Yep.

And I was still pissed at Prince Cormac.

"How are you doing?" I asked her, knowing it was a stupid question.

"I feel like shit," she replied, giving me the answer I already knew.

I loved her, but unsurprisingly, she looked like it too. She'd be under a spa-visor for an hour to get rid of that redness, swelling and those dark circles.

Totally, when Cormac came back to her (and he would), he'd better beg and crawl.

"Drink caffeine," I urged.

She reached for the cup but said to Cat, "Spill."

Cat drew in a big breath.

"Well, I heard the knock on the door, and I thought it was you with some news," she said to me.

I nodded and took a sip from my own cup.

"It wasn't. It was him," Cat went on.

"And?" Gayle prompted.

"And...I just opened the door and stared up at him, kinda frozen in shock that he was at my door in the middle of the night," Cat shared.

She was also probably frozen in shock that a ridiculously handsome prince was right there at her door in the middle of the night.

"And?" I pushed when she stopped talking.

"And, he said nothing."

"What?" Gayle asked.

"Nothing?" I asked.

"Not at first. He just hooked me with his arm, pulled me in for a deep, wet kiss, and when he was done with my mouth, he let me go."

By Lilith!

"What?" Gayle nearly shouted.

"Oh my gods!" I also nearly shouted.

"And then he said, 'Get rid of him. I'll be in touch.' And he walked away," Cat finished.

By the gods, that was *hot*.

"Holy Hecate," Gayle breathed (she thought it was hot too).

"Who acts like that?" Cat asked.

"Was the kiss good?" I inquired.

She didn't quite meet my eyes.

It was good.

"How good?" I pushed.

She shoved her plate away and flounced back in her chair. "Who cares? You don't walk up to a female's door, kiss her, tell her to dump her male and walk away. What is that?"

As I mentioned, it was *hot*.

I kept my mouth shut on my opinion since it didn't seem Cat felt the same way.

Though, she'd said, "when he was done with my mouth." She hadn't said, "when I pushed him away."

"I wish Cormac had done that to me," Gayle mumbled.

Cat took her hand on the table. "Oh, honey. I shouldn't have said anything."

"Why not?" Gayle asked. "He told me to live my life. This is part of my life. Gabbing with my gals."

Cat gave her a sympathetic look.

Gayle gently disengaged her hand and reached for a rasher of bacon, asking mock casually, "So, are you going to go there?"

"Be the plaything of a very-soon-to-be king?" Cat shook her head. "Not a chance."

If she really wasn't into Tanyn, then I hoped her dad never found out about his middle-of-the-night visit.

"Where's Monique?" Gayle asked.

"She's at the salon. Clients. Yes, even after all the chaos last night. I can't believe that female's work ethic. It's inspiring," Cat said.

"I've seen the plans for her renos, so I get why she's going for it. Her flat is going to be mega when it's done," Gayle shared.

We lapsed into our normal gabbing.

But I did it watching closely.

I noted Gayle was still wounded, but she was putting a brave face on it, and Cat was holding something back. But I knew from experience you had to let her pick her time to share, or find the right one to push, and that wasn't now.

After a while, Gayle said she needed a shower, and we all needed to find out what was happening, including if everyone was free to go home, so Cat and I left.

I walked her to her room.

"So, how good was the kiss, *exactly*?" I probed.

She sighed. "It was great. But I mean, really, Laura. Who does he think he is?"

I grinned at her. "A very-soon-to-be king who's about to move into a kickass castle."

She rolled her eyes.

I let it go, left her in her room and went back to mine.

Aleksei wasn't there, of course, so I commed him.

He picked up right away, and the display showed he was outside somewhere, the wind ruffling his hair.

Talk about hot.

"Hey," I greeted.

"*Bissi*, can I comm you back?"

"Sure."

"Are you in our suite?"

"Yes."

"Are you staying there?"

Well, I wanted to check on the queen and Aleece, not to mention Monique, and touch base with the Truelocks and Vinestrongs.

But I said, "Do you want me to?"

"Yes, I'll be there in half an hour."

"Okay, see you then."

"Love you," he replied.

I'd never get used to that. And I'd never stop melting at getting it.

"Love you too," I returned, hoping he felt the same way (about the never getting-used-to-it part, I knew my male could catch fire, but I didn't think he could melt).

We disconnected.

I made some comms.

The Truelocks and Vinestrongs were in the midst of packing in order to move back to their homes.

Aleece wasn't picking up.

I sent a text comm to Monique so I wouldn't disturb her at work, and she hadn't had a chance to text back.

And I chatted with Nata, asking her to get with Dita, the queen's aide, to ask if I could have some time with her. We further made plans to go through the clothing and accessories that afternoon to see if there was anything I wanted to wear to my upcoming events.

She also confirmed she'd gotten in touch with Dad, and he'd expressed gratitude that she'd commed to let him know I was okay.

I was scrolling through social tapes (Arnaud was seriously getting torn apart, and I was there for it—and my creature had been nicknamed "BBB," which stood for "Beautiful Badass Bitch," which I was uncertain about—not to mention, Tim's dragon was getting a lot of positive tape play, and I hoped he saw it) when Aleksei walked in.

I knew the minute I saw his face, something was up, and whatever that something was, it wasn't good, so I popped out of the sofa.

"Is everything okay?"

He said nothing.

He just walked right to me and gathered me in his arms.

Once there, he held me close.

No.

Everything wasn't okay.

I gave him some time, then whispered in his ear, "What's up?"

He pulled away but replaced his arms around me with holding my head in both hands.

"The comms were traced. The agent who was at the Masque last night, the one who'd insinuated himself with Errol, did report to Arnaud that things were not going as planned."

Oh farg.

I'd forgotten all about Errol.

How had I forgotten about Errol?

"The spy has been picked up," he continued. "The RIC will deal with him."

"Okay," I said.

"And Errol had a number of questions about why he couldn't transform last night, questions that we've answered, including showing him the vid of his interrogation before his memory scrub. He didn't take it well."

Oh dang.

"As such, I've made the decision that Rol will be quietly admitted as an inpatient at Empathy Sanctuary on Lucius Island," he announced.

Empathy Sanctuary was the go-to rehab for the rich and famous.

"We just sent him off," he finished. "And we did it against his will. He was restrained."

"Oh honey," I murmured. "That couldn't have been easy. But this is a good idea. He can get help there."

He took his hands from my head and put them to my hips. "Laura, there's a section of Empathy many people don't know about."

Oh boy.

"What's that?"

"It's very nice, and he'll get help, but it's a lockdown facility. He can't leave unless his doctors feel it would be detrimental for him to stay, but with the accommodation he'll be afforded, this is highly unlikely, considering this is an exclusive, platinum star facility on a tropical island. The other option is that I release him."

"So essentially, he's going to a resort-type mental health and rehab hospital on a beautiful island, he'll get top-notch counseling there, and he can't return unless he's convinced you he's got himself together."

"Not essentially. That's exactly what it is."

"And you feel bad about it."

He shook his head.

"He conspired to murder your beast. He nearly got you killed, my beast possibly killed. And his actions, decisions and the beings he allowed himself to spend time with opened our family to peril and took the lives of eleven people. Three of those dedicated their careers to keeping this family safe, and one of them a female I greatly respected. No. I don't feel bad about sending my brother to a facility where he'll be living in a luxury suite, waited on hand and foot, and spending his time in isolation aquariums and yoga classes. I feel bad that my mother and father are wondering where they went wrong. My sister is heartbroken that one of her brothers is such a fuckwit. And my other brother feels betrayed, and also feels guilt he shouldn't feel."

"So you're disappointed you couldn't kick his behind."

He gave me a small smile. "Yes. That."

I fit myself to him. "It still was the right choice."

"Mm."

I tucked my hands under his suit jacket to explore the muscles of his back over his shirt and asked, "What can I do to make you feel better?"

His eyes darkened. "What are my choices?"

"Do you still have that dragon mask?"

His lips hitched. "I'm sorry, love. I lost track of it when I found myself battling creatures from another age."

"Bummer," I muttered.

He turned us and started walking me backward to the bedroom. "But we can get creative."

"That sounds interesting."

"I can promise you, it will be."

I smiled at him.

He kissed me.

We both got creative.

And it was a lot more than interesting.

EPILOGUE
PORTRAIT

Aleksei

Laura clutched him with everything at her disposal, internally and externally, signaling her climax, telling Aleksei he could finally let go.

Centered on her, breathing for her, existing only because she was his, he buried himself inside his mate and exploded, as always, feeling nothing but her and seeing nothing but stars.

As he came down, he felt her hands moving on the slick skin of his back, her mouth running along the line of his neck, and in his ear she declared, "Vintage is always the way to roll. No way we could do this in a bathing pod."

He burst out laughing and took his face out of her neck to look down at her.

Humor.

Beauty.

Love.

The warm water of the shower was beating on his back, and he had her pressed to the marble, his hands to her generous ass, her arms and legs wrapped around him, and he wanted to be nowhere else.

Ever.

But that wasn't the life they led.

He kissed her and then, unfortunately, since they both had busy days, he had to pull her off his cock.

She made that disappointed mew she always made when she lost him, something that never failed to both tease and torture him, but he had no choice but to set her on her feet.

She didn't know it yet but soon.

They would have time for just the two of them, very soon.

He held her until he was sure she was steady, then he reached for the soap.

He'd taken care of that part of the shower for her before things got out of hand and he had no choice but to fuck her against the marble. Now he had to see to himself.

Laura tried to take the soap from him, but he pulled it out of her reach.

She pouted up at him, adorably blinking those extraordinary eyes in the spray.

"Darling, we both have busy days. If you lather me, we might never get out of the shower," he warned.

She appeared to be contemplating that, so he burst out laughing again. Still doing it, he pulled her close, kissed her deeply, then scooted her out of the shower.

He soaped up and watched as she toweled off. And he made quick work of it so he could exit the shower and stand beside her as she cycled through her toilette tech.

In the beginning, his driving need to be with her every second of the day alarmed him greatly. Especially since he'd never experienced anything like it before, and making matters worse, Laura didn't seem to feel that same need.

This had settled.

It helped when she showed him the article about Aerin and Iphelia.

Aleksei reasoned that his creature understood she was warrior caste before even Laura did, and this led to the intensity of Aleksei's response to her.

That need still buzzed low, always, but it was something he could control.

Now, he just enjoyed every second he had with her.

Even when she was drooling through a Denti-Clean.

"I could get you a sonic toothbrush," he offered for the third time, reaching for his own.

She pulled the Denti-Clean out, rinsed, spit and replied, "It doesn't do as thorough of a job."

She was incorrect about that, but considering how cute she was drooling through her Denti-Clean, he didn't push it.

Laura donned her cosme-mask and mane-mate while he shaved. Then together, they went into the closet.

"You did well yesterday, love," he said.

She pulled a face.

"Don't make that face, you did," he asserted.

She stopped slapping through the hangers (there was no cycling program in their closet at Spikeback, like nearly everything but her toilette tech, they had to go manual), tipped her head to the side and asked, "Do you really think so?"

"Those young were eating out of your hand."

"You're sure?" she pushed.

They'd gone to the drama department of a school in Nocturn. As it was her first official visit, and her first appearance after the horror of the night of the Masque, it had been a mad crush.

Aleksei knew it was nerves and grit that kept her head high, the warm smile on her face, and her focus on the young ones.

And she was amazing with them, attentive, openly interested, seeming to have all the time in the world for each, even if she skillfully made certain to limit that time so she could spend as much with as many as she could.

Laura was a superb princess, and she would make an excellent queen.

More importantly, he'd learned yesterday (not that he didn't already know it with the way she treated her pets), she would be an amazing mother.

He moved to her, hooked his arm around her waist, dropped a kiss on her nose, and murmured, "I'm sure, *bissi*."

She beamed up at him.

He returned her smile, feeling her pride settle into his bones.

She disliked that part of their lives, but she was in this to win it, because she was in love with him.

She wouldn't run.

She was here to stay.

He allowed himself a moment to fully feel that feeling, then returned to dressing.

They were eating breakfast at the table in the sunny turret alcove of the solar off their bedroom at Spikeback, where they found they both preferred to breakfast, when Laura's Palm vibrated.

She took the comm and smiled at the display.

"Hello, Maman," she greeted.

Aleksei felt something shift, watching his mate's face light up when she saw his mother, and hearing the form of address.

He heard his mother's voice come from her Palm. "Dearest, yesterday was a *triumph*."

"That's what Aleksei said," Laura replied.

"Well, he was correct. Your ratings are stratospheric. Germaine is beside herself. Now, obviously, you can't be visiting every school in Night's Fall. You'll need to..."

Aleksei tuned his mother out and his breakfast in.

He didn't do this because he wasn't interested. He did it because he knew his fiancée was in hands he could trust, and he'd heard his mother drone on about these things since he could remember.

When they disconnected, he was scrolling through social tapes, seeing proof that he and his mother were right. Their visit yesterday, particularly Laura's, was a triumph.

He put his Palm down, took a sip of his coffee and noted, "So, fittings with Mardel today?"

"Yes. I have him for two hours," she replied, spearing some scrambled eggs.

Aleksei preferred cooking breakfast with her, or for her, rather than having Cook send up what they ordered the night before.

But things had changed for them at Spikeback.

And when they wanted to reminisce their beginnings, they could spend a few days at the penthouse or her loft.

"So I hope I can get it all in," she continued. "Then I'll program any alterations into the Seam-Stitch. After that, I have the interviews with the applicants for the costume assistants. Directly after those are done, Nata and I have a meeting with the curator of MdV. But Nata will keep all of this on target, and I should be home around five or six."

"I'll aim to be home then too," he murmured.

"And your day?"

He already knew her schedule before he asked, as she knew his.

There was something that tugged at his heart that she asked anyway, even if, for him, it wasn't nearly as diverse and exciting as her day always turned out to be.

Nevertheless, she made a point to draw him out, and he knew it was because she worried she didn't see to him and his interests well enough.

He knew he couldn't simply tell her to relax and let it go.

He had to let her have time doing these things so he could use them as examples when he eventually told her to relax and let it go.

He was going to give it two weeks.

"They're close to opening one of the bays on Thoth. A good deal of my day will be going over those details to make certain we can make the announcement and stick to the date. And then the director of R and D at Roots Innovation will be demonstrating the new features of a Palm we hope to release in the coming year. He's promised the bugs have been dealt with, but that remains to be seen."

He had another appointment late that afternoon, but he hadn't decided if he was going to tell her about that one yet.

"Oo...a new Palm," she cooed before she glanced at her own, yelped, took one last hurried sip of coffee then sprang out of her chair, rounding the table, saying, "Gods, I lost track of the time. Fannon is waiting at the craft. I have to go."

She gave him a peck on the lips, another one, then she gave up on that and just kissed him.

Deeply.

He chuckled at the end of it and whispered, "Go, darling. I'll see you this evening."

She gave him one more peck before she bid, "Have a great day, honey."

"You as well."

She dashed off.

His creature throbbed at her departure.

Hers pulsed in return.

Aleksei watched her go.

No, he'd never known a female like her.

She loved him. She liked him. She was interested in him. She was attracted to him. He was her mate, her life, her future. She was the same in all to him.

But she was still Laura, with her friends, and her job that was her passion, and her determination to perform her duty as his princess, no matter how it cut across the grain.

He was not a satellite in her life, he was the center star, as she was to him.

But she had a universe to illuminate, and she did that.

It wasn't the first time he had this thought, but he still thought it...

The Night God certainly knew what he was doing.

✦ ✦ ✦

Aleksei landed the JetPanther in the space on the street that had been cleared for him outside the narrow, two-story Pre-Unification brownstone.

He turned his eyes right, and with interest in what he'd see, but none in what he was about to do, he took in the home where Laura grew up.

Considering the beings who had inhabited it for the last twenty-five years, he would have expected it to appear neglected. Therefore, he was surprised to see the two wide-bowled, squat urns on either side of the front door filled with healthy autumn flowers and the impeccable cast of the shiny barn-red paint on the door.

When Set was standing outside his craft, Aleksei ordered the door to open and climbed out.

Set at his back, other members of his detail in place, Aleksei walked across the pavement, up the steps, and before he could engage the announcement unit, the door opened.

A male humanoid bot stood there.

"Your highness," it said on a short bow.

"He's expecting me."

"Of course. Come in."

The bot stepped back, allowing Aleksei entry. Set came with him.

"I'll take you to him," the bot replied and moved through the house.

Aleksei looked around as they walked through the space.

It was nice, yet it had no personality. Middle of the road when it came to expense, like the bot. Though, better than most. It was clean, and in good nick, but again, if he didn't know who lived there, he'd have no idea of anything about them.

This, he didn't find surprising.

The bot led them through the kitchen at the back and Set took point when they followed it out into the courtyard.

Now this was something else.

There were fall flowers here too, as well as some late vegetables in raised beds that hadn't yet been harvested. Other beds had been turned over, readied for winter.

All of it was neat and tidy, including two seating areas, one for eating, one for lounging, both having far more personality than the living areas he'd just walked through. They were stylish and inviting.

Along the entire back of the courtyard was a greenhouse.

The bot led them there.

Set stepped in first, then stepped out and nodded to Aleksei.

Aleksei walked in, seeing a riot of green and color, more vegetables, as well as herbs. It was humid in there, warm, and standing in it, he saw Tern

Makepeace wearing a battered button down, the sleeves rolled up, and jeans, both had dirt marks on them. He was tending to some pots.

He stopped what he was doing when Aleksei came in and did a small bow, greeting, "Your highness."

"I'm uncertain why I'm in your greenhouse," Aleksei replied, not particularly liking seeing this man in what was clearly his element, relaxed, at ease.

Normal.

Makepeace had a trowel in hand, and he used it to indicate the brownstone. "It's far more pleasant out here than it is in there."

He wasn't wrong.

Nevertheless.

"This isn't a social call," Aleksei pointed out.

Makepeace nodded. "I appreciate you granting me this audience. And coming to me."

"It's an audience of ten minutes, and I don't want my mate to know I'm here," he shared this not to be informative, but as a warning. "And speaking to you here will be one of the few places she'd never guess I'll be."

Makepeace's face turned melancholy. "It's not my place to say, but I learned the hard way you shouldn't keep anything from your mate."

"It is, indeed, not your place to say. And now you have nine minutes."

Makepeace nodded. "Cetra has filed official papers for the dissolution of our marriage with the magistrate."

"I'm aware of this."

"She's living with Chevalforce."

"I know this too."

"He's a male I hate. That's why she chose him to sleep with."

Aleksei was tiring of this because he had no interest in it.

"Now you have eight minutes," he warned.

"He's a male I hate because he's not a good male. She'll learn this if she doesn't already know it. She might stay, as she did with me, so she can have the life she wishes to lead, something she can't have unless she cohabitates. But I doubt it, because he's that detestable and she no longer has the reason she had to be with him, that reason being attempting to harm me. And when she finds herself at loose ends for a partner to share expenses with, this might become a problem."

Aleksei understood what he was saying, and reminded him, "She's signed an agreement to remain out of Laura's life."

"This won't stop her because she knows her daughter, or more to the point, she knows what buttons to push to get her way, and if those don't work, she's highly adept in creating a situation where she'll get the attention she needs, even if it's negative."

"Meaning?"

The male tipped his head to side. "Have you not noted Laura's soft heart?"

Aleksei felt a muscle in his jaw tick, because he most assuredly had, in the numerous ways she displayed it.

Including her having even a hint of understanding of how this male treated her.

Makepeace gestured to the greenhouse with his trowel. "When Laura left, I attended anger mitigation classes. One of the things they suggested was to find a hobby. Spend some time each day doing something you enjoyed."

And the male chose gardening.

Aleksei didn't want it to, but he found this choice interesting, and his dedication to it telling.

"I asked Cetra to attend with me, or to sit down with a relationship counselor to try to understand if we have anything to work on. She refused both."

Aleksei was unsurprised at this, but he said nothing.

"There is no excuse—" Makepeace began.

"No, there isn't," Aleksei agreed before he could say it.

"And I know that, so I can assure you I will honor Laura's no contact order. If she wishes to keep me informed through her aide, I will gratefully accept. If I never hear another word, I'll accept that too. I won't like it, but I'll accept it, and I'll do it because that's what my daughter needs. But the matter of what I was to her and what I did to her is very different than what kind of mother Cetra was to her."

This, he was interested in.

"Explain," Aleksei ordered.

Makepeace appeared uncomfortable. "I do believe Cetra loved me, at first. This is part of my penance. That I was so lonely after my loss, I found the first female who would take me in my sorry state and marry me, not considering what it might do to her."

"And?" Aleksei prompted.

"That love quickly turned to hate. Understandable, in one sense. If it was directed at me. However, she's the kind of female who was unable to feel her feelings, find her way to something better, or find a way to work it out. Instead, she put everything into making those around her just as miserable as she was. Even her daughter. Recent case in point, Chevalforce. Cetra is an attractive female. She could find any number of lovers. She chose him specifically."

"This isn't lost on me either."

Makepeace inclined his head. "What I'm saying is, there's no excuse for what I did. But I understand I did it. I take responsibility for the ramifications of it. I know I harmed my own daughter to the point she wants nothing to do with me. And this is what I must live with. Cetra does not take responsibility for her actions. I'm no danger to Laura, not anymore, but I know I also am because of our history." A look of agony flashed through his expression before he could control it. "Now, I hurt her just by existing. Cetra doesn't understand she does the same."

"You think she'll eventually attempt a reconciliation," Aleksei summed it up.

Makepeace nodded. "For what she can get out of it, yes."

"You must know, in order to protect my mate, I'm paying attention to you both."

The male dipped his chin. "Of course. But you must understand, I know how I hurt Cetra. I take responsibility for that too. I'm relieved about this dissolution, for myself, but also for her. She needs to be free of me. So this isn't me being bitter and trying to get one over on her. I fear, if she's given half a chance, she'll connive her way back into Laura's life. And Laura may be taken in by her. There are two in each couple, your highness. You are here and she doesn't know. Laura can do things too that she doesn't want you to know. You were angry when you caught her speaking to me. What might that bring if her mother reaches out to her?"

That muscle jumped in his cheek again, and it cost him to say what he said next.

But it was the truth.

"I'm an adult, so is my fiancée. She can do as she pleases. But in the end, whatever comes of it, rest assured, I have her heart safe in my hands."

With that, Aleksei turned to leave.

"Your highness," Makepeace called.

Aleksei blew out a breath and turned back.

"I'm selling the bot, to pay back taxes," he shared. "And the brownstone. I don't need this much space anymore."

Not that he'd tell the male, but Aleksei was grateful he'd extended his warning about Laura's mother.

But he wasn't doing this.

"My coming here is about Laura speaking to you two weeks ago. It's because I wanted to assess what that might have communicated and reiterate that you are not to seek her out for any reason. What this is not is your opening to me or your opportunity to try to win me over."

"I would have made the same decision about my Laura," he murmured.

"So, we're done," Aleksei stated.

"Keep her safe," Makepeace replied.

Aleksei felt a vein pulse in his forehead and growled, "You do not have to say that shit to me."

Makepeace dipped his chin again, but he did it watching Aleksei closely...and fighting a smile.

Aleksei moved out of the greenhouse, into the garden, and he and Set walked through the house and to the craft.

Once he was inside, had requested a course to Spikeback, and as he waited for approval, he pulled out his Palm because it was vibrating.

He had a pic comm.

He opened it and it was a selfie of Gayle, smiling at the cam, with Sirk in the background, throwing a grin over his shoulder while he was cooking.

It was from Laura.

And the only communication she attached to it was *!!!!!!!!!!!!*

He smiled, even if he didn't want to get involved.

He really didn't.

But Mac had broken Gayle's heart, regardless that they barely knew each other.

And now Sirk was involved.

Aleksei had lived with the idea that Laura might not choose to be his mate for five hours, and every second of those five hours was wretched.

Gayle had been living with it for nearly two weeks. In the meantime, she'd hooked up with Sirk, likely for the same reasons Laura's father had found her mother.

Once you found your mate, the void of them was agony. Aleksei could understand moving swiftly to fill that void, even if it never felt anything but empty.

This brought him back to Tern Makepeace, a place he didn't want to be.

And with all of that, he felt compelled to forward the pic to Cormac, with an attached text comm that said, *Advice. Don't let this get any more fucked up.*

He received course approval and lifted off, and in that time (or after it), Mac didn't reply.

But his dash comp told him he had an incoming video comm from Tanyn.

"Accept," he said.

Tanyn's face filled the screen on his dash.

"How are things, your majesty?" Aleksei joked.

A ghost of a smile flitted over Tanyn's lips before he replied, "The trolls have been successfully tallied, contained and are ready for transport to the habitat that's been created for them in the Center."

"Final count?"

"Five hundred and seventy-three."

Aleksei was surprised. "That's it?"

"That's it," Tanyn confirmed. "I've been reading through centuries of reports on these creatures, Lex. It's horrifying at the same time fascinating, though I'll admit that fascination is morbid to extremes."

"So warned, tell me," Aleksei encouraged.

"Through a lot of trial and error, which means not a small number of deaths of observers and trainers, it seems these creatures have two basic instincts. Eat and kill. They don't even copulate unless they're bored."

"And this is why the numbers are so small after eight hundred years?"

"That, and it takes resources to keep them contained. The barracks they're in are extensively fortified and cost a fortune to maintain. But it's essential. For the first few hundred years, they kept getting loose and wreaking havoc. Though, another reason they aren't prolific is because, with nothing else to kill, they kill each other."

Aleksei was stunned. "Fucking hell."

"Yes," Tanyn agreed. "They tried repeatedly to create some kind of tactical unit with them. Nothing worked. They have no language, though they do communicate, mostly through frequencies of grunts. Nor do they have the mental capacity to be organized. Not even something as simple as taking formation or marching. This was discovered after most of their trainers were maimed or killed over decades of trying. Somewhere in the early 1500s, they gave up. They tried again in the 1800s, and early 1900s. No joy."

"Did they harvest the skin?"

Tanyn nodded. "Yes. We have a warehouse full of it. They also experimented on it, and unbeknownst to the general public, back in the day when weapons used bullets, our bulletproof armor was made of troll skin."

"It isn't stream proof," Aleksei remarked. "Did Arnaud know that?"

"Absolutely. And this is the important news I have to share. There are recent records about using the trolls for experiments on upgrading the PR60. And before these experiments started, the inventory of trolls was six hundred and fifty-two."

Aleksei couldn't hide his shock. "They put down seventy-nine trolls for their experiments on the PR60?"

"Another way they contained the population. These weren't the only experiments they conducted on the trolls."

"Fucking hell," Aleksei repeated, feeling sick to his stomach.

It seemed they weren't fully cognizant and they were violent, but they were still living, breathing creatures.

"I've made a recommendation to the UTC of rendering them infertile," Tanyn shared. "Allowing them some sort of natural habitat where they can live as they will, which will likely mean they'll kill each other off, and then go extinct on their own. But even if it's clear they aren't quite sentient, we treat animals better than they've been treated."

As Aleksei saw Spikeback getting closer, he nodded and asked, "Any news on Tatra?"

"After blustering through her presser about her son being unfairly accused, there's been no word from her."

Aleksei found this suspicious. "So she's fine with being exiled to Snowy Ridge?"

"Tatra is a master of lulling beings into a false sense of security. Ask my mother. Tatra was her best friend before she stole her husband."

Aleksei grimaced at the reminder.

But the good news was, this meant Tanyn was keeping an eye on her.

"Any word on the tech used during the Masque?" Aleksei asked.

Tanyn shook his head. "Arnaud's followers scurried like rats when he was taken into custody. Those in his closest circle disappeared, and they didn't leave much behind when they did. They were so thorough in this, it's clear there was a failsafe in place. We do have the docs on the PR60 experiments, which we'll provide to you for the assassination case. I'll also be sharing all that was gleaned through centuries of working with the trolls. But it's early days, Lex. We're still digging and interrogating those we think might have been involved. I'll keep you informed if we find anything further."

"Appreciate that, Tan."

"How about your techs?" Tan asked. "They get anything?"

"The self-destruct on the disk eliminated anything of use. And as far as they can tell, all traces erased themselves in the system within milliseconds of the code doing what it was written to do. They've exhausted all efforts and haven't found anything."

This didn't make Tanyn look happy, then again, Aleksei felt the same.

"More from Arnaud?" Tan asked.

Aleksei shook his head. "He maintains his innocence. Says he had nothing to do with the trolls, didn't even know they existed. Says he was framed for the murder, and he's heartbroken at Longshot's loss."

"I saw the vid on that, Lex, and it fucks me to say this, but his grief seems genuine," Tan remarked.

It fucked Aleksei to think it, but he agreed.

"He says he found her like that, noted his detail had disappeared, realized something was very wrong, and took off," Tanyn shared something Aleksei knew. "Denies any communication or knowledge of an agent embedded in Errol's orbit. Stated he came to Night's Fall to go to the Masque, found Tula as she was, tried to get in touch with his detail, they were gone, so he saw the writing on the wall, took the only one left, his aide, and headed back to Sky's Edge."

"I've had questions from the minute we locked onto that UtiliSport, and there was no security craft flying with it," Aleksei shared.

"Same," Tanyn agreed.

"Would Tatra set up her own son to take the downfall if her bid to keep him in power failed?" Aleksei asked.

"Tatra has already sold her soul to the Hell God to languish in the deepest depths of eternal flame to get whatever wealth and power she can amass. I wouldn't be surprised at anything she did."

At this, both males looked unhappy.

As Aleksei hovered over the landing bay at Spikeback, Tanyn finished it.

"That's all I've got for now."

"I appreciate the update," Aleksei replied, then to alleviate the heaviness of their conversation, he added, "Laura and I'll be up there for the coronation, whenever that's planned."

Tanyn frowned.

Aleksei laughed. "It's a bunch of ceremonial bullshit, but beings love it."

"Right. I'll see you and Laura then."

"You will. Later, Tan."

"Later, Lex."

He descended into the bay that had opened behind the castle, and once he was in and powered down, the bay doors above him slid closed.

Before he exited the craft, he stared at his Palm.

"Fuck it," he muttered, engaged his Palm and commed Allain.

"Your highness," Allain greeted.

"Quietly, I'd like you to get word to the magistrates that will be hearing

Tern Makepeace's case, and let it be known I'd consider it a personal favor if they waive prison time."

There wasn't even the slightest tick in Allain's expression. "This will be done."

They disengaged and Aleksi exited the craft, went to the lift and took it up to the first floor.

Once he was there, he tuned into his creature to find her.

And he walked through the grand hall, the waning light streaming through the tall, narrow windows and glinting against the stone columns burnished by dragon fire until he hit the parlor on the first floor.

The only thing that had changed in this area was that he'd asked, and Laura had agreed, for the shadowboxes from her loft with the pieces she'd designed to be mounted for display in the hall.

In the gothic spectacle of Spikeback, the demonstrations of her extreme talent were the perfect fit.

He stopped in the doorway to allow himself to fully process the sunny smile Laura aimed his way and then he looked down to his feet.

Nova was winding around his ankles, but she sensed the minute she had his attention. Thus, she gazed up at him with her sad blue eyes and opened her mouth in a silent mew.

Obviously, he bent and picked her up, cradling her upside down in his arms like a baby.

She instantly started purring, even before he started scratching her chest.

All three cats now had trackers, though Nova and Comet didn't need them, as they liked to be close to Laura and Aleksei.

But Jupiter had dedicated his existence to finding every nook and cranny in the castle.

One could say Jupiter had also found his happy place. Dark and cavernous, with lots of windows to peer out of, and when he was feeling his alone time, even more places to hide.

Aleksei went to his mate, bent and dropped a kiss to her upturned mouth, then he turned to their surprise (to him, Laura was drinking with them) guests.

His brother and sister were sitting with her.

"Are you two staying for dinner?" he asked.

"Hello to you too. And is that an invitation?" Tim asked in return.

"Or is it your way to tell us to get the hells out?" Aleece put in her own question, her eyes twinkling, since she knew it was not.

"Laura and I have both had busy days," he warned them, taking a seat beside his mate on the sofa.

He set Nova in his lap, where she curled contentedly, and he wrapped his arm around his mate, who settled into his side, also contentedly.

Both of these things made Aleksei content.

Completely.

"Is that your way of saying you're not cooking?" Tim asked.

"It is. We're ordering in Shape's," Aleksei told him.

Laura gasped, looked up at him and exclaimed excitedly, "Shape's? I'm getting a double bowl of their clam chowder. It's *insane*."

He smiled down at her, taking in her gorgeous, jewel-toned eyes, bright with happiness, and realizing he'd had absolutely no idea, if she'd decided differently, how wretched his life actually would be in those five hours he waited before he came to her door with Captain Jacques's.

But now, he did.

"Anything you wish, *bissi tressa*," he whispered.

Her eyes warmed with love (or, more of it).

"Blech. Before you start getting too mushy, let's get our order in. I want lobster mac," Aleece ordered.

"Baked scallops," Tim put in.

Aleksei turned to his brother. "You have a Palm."

Tim smirked. "I also have no credit."

Too true.

Aleksei pulled out his Palm, said to it "Pull up Shape's delivery," and tossed it to his brother.

Tim caught it.

When this occurred, Laura didn't hide how delighted she was that he and Tim were making progress.

Aleece didn't either.

They were doing so because Tim was making an effort.

He had lapses to the punk he used to be.

But evidence was suggesting the loss of his allowance and much of his freedom gave him time to think on things (they'd had to put him back into rotation for royal appearances with the absence of Errol—they hadn't quite agreed yet how they would explain that, but fortunately, no one seemed to have noticed he was gone).

Not to mention, it was clear Tim was still smarting from all that had happened with Rol, and he'd turned that into an attempt to rehab his relationships with his other two siblings.

"Crabcakes," Aleksei ordered. "And a lemon parfait."

"Oh! I want a parfait too. Make mine chocolate," Laura ordered.

"I want a lime tart," Aleece said.

"Hold it, hold it, bloody hell," Tim groused. "One at a time."

"That's all for me," Aleece said.

"Me too," Laura added.

Tim nodded, got up and moved out of the seating area so he could speak into the Palm.

"While you're up, open another bottle," Aleece called after him.

He waved at her and left the room.

"Please tell me you guys got a bungalow out on the water on Anubis," Aleece begged.

Aleksei blew out an annoyed breath and looked to the ceiling.

"Wait. What? We're going to Anubis?" Laura breathed.

"Yes," he muttered to his mate and shot a killing look to his sister.

"Whoops. So that was a surprise?" she asked.

It was.

He returned his attention to Laura. "Your vid starts shooting in a week. We won't have long there, but we leave tomorrow morning, and we'll be back two days before you have to be on set. Allain arranged everything with Nata."

Laura sent Nova scampering since she'd thrown herself at her mate and was kissing him all over his face.

"You keep missing my mouth, love," he teased.

She stopped fucking around and laid one on him.

He wrapped his arms around her, cocked his head and took over.

"See what happens when you don't pay attention, Tim?" Aleece shouted. "They get out of hand."

"Gods, I can't unsee that," Tim, obviously returning to the room, griped.

Aleksei ended their kiss with a quick one on Laura's nose, and she turned and cuddled into him, nestling her head under his jaw.

"You're constantly so cute, I'm going to have to do a warp trip to the Six Realms so I can visit one of their ancient vomitoriums," Aleece joked.

She then reached between her thigh and the cushion of the chair she was in to pull up her Palm.

She looked at the display, said, "Engage," and then, "Hey, Mom."

"Where are you?" his mother's voice came from his sister's unit.

"At Spikeback for drinks with Lex and Laura," Aleece answered, then turned the display around to circle the company as she carried on, "Now we're going to have Shape's with them."

When the display hit her, Laura waved.

Gods, she was adorable.

"I take it this means you and your brother won't be at pre-dinner drinks in ten minutes?" their mother asked.

"Sorry, Mom. Lex mentioned Shape's and we were all in. That just happened or I would have commed."

"Fine. I'll tell Cook. Love to all."

The last she called out to the room, and he knew she disconnected when Aleece tucked the Palm beside her again.

Aleksei let Laura go before he pushed himself up to get a drink, and as he moved to the drinks cart, they lapsed into general chitchat.

Understandably, it had been a busy time since the attack at Celestial Palace.

But now, things were settling. Laura had broken the seal on her first appearance. She was going back to work. They were ensconced at Spikeback.

This was their life. Busy. Steady. Together.

But no one was plotting their murder.

So it was good.

On this thought, his creature snapped to attention so fast, Aleksei had to let out a sharp breath as he turned swiftly.

This was because Laura was alert on the couch, her eyes to the door, and the beast in her chest was alert too.

And they were because Catla was bursting through it.

She was carrying what appeared to be a large, framed, wrapped canvas.

And her eyes were wild.

"Oh my gods! You will *not* believe what Dad has done!" Cat cried to Laura as she raced to the sofa, resting the canvas against the side.

Laura slowly stood, asking, "What's he done?"

"He arranged a marriage for me."

"Holy fuck," Tim muttered.

"By Lilith," Aleece whispered.

Bloody hell, Aleksei thought.

This was a demon thing. It used to happen all the time, but now, only occasionally. And that occasion was usually when the patriarch decided his daughter had dallied too long in finding a match.

There were no laws that forced any female into a marriage. And there were demon females who refused the matches. But if they did, they were usually excommunicated from their families.

Cat was a together female.

But he saw how close she was to her parents, he doubted she'd do anything to break ties with them.

Just as he doubted Mammon would make anything but an excellent match for his daughter.

Even so, this was extreme, and Aleksei didn't condone it.

But she wasn't his daughter.

"Oh my gods!" Laura exclaimed. "To who?"

"To who? *To who?*" Cat shouted, sending Nova scurrying right to Aleksei.

He picked her up again as Laura said, "Yes, honey. To who?"

"To *King Tanyn*, that's who!" Cat yelled.

Well...

Shit.

Laura's gaze darted to him, and he knew why.

She looked pleased and she didn't want to Cat to see.

Aleksei agreed.

So he smiled.

Slowly.

✦ ✦ ✦

They sat on the buttoned velvet bench at the foot of their bed, Laura in his lap.

"It's embarrassing."

"It is not."

"I wish he'd just sent you the one you liked."

"I don't want the one I liked. I want the one I love. That one."

Saying this, Aleksei gave her a squeeze and tipped his head across the room to the painting resting there.

It was the one Cat brought.

After the drama of her announcement (and Tim had added Cat's selections to their Shape's order, and Aleksei had made Cat a martini), they'd unwrapped it and read the note from Terrinton.

With no salutation and no sign off, it said:

> I'm keeping Marie.
> But you'll always have Laura.

That was all it said.

The painting was of Laura in a swirl of purple butterflies, mist, dragon fire and bright white stars, done in Terrinton's indelible style, which married realism and stark fantasy with hints of illusory, all of this chaotic, but fascinating.

It was remarkable.

"I want it mounted in here," he declared.

"Ugh," she grunted, rolling her eyes.

He grinned at her.

"Right there, above the bureau, across from the bed," he said, teasing, because he knew she'd hate it there, so it would not be mounted there. "That way, when I'm taking you on all fours with you facing the end of the bed, I can fuck you and look at your face at the same time."

"Gah!" she cried and attacked him.

He pretended to defend.

And as such, eventually accepted his defeat graciously.

✦ ✦ ✦

"Gardening?" she whispered to him in the dark.

Fuck.

"Yes," he replied.

She was silent.

Aleksei was on his back. Laura was resting down his side.

It took long moments, but her whisper came back.

"And you intervened about him serving time?"

Fuck.

"Yes," he replied.

She pressed into him, pushing her face into his throat, and doing it hard, before she kissed him there, settled and finished, still whispering, "Gods, I love you."

Aleksei exhaled.

Then he turned into his mate, tangled their limbs—and wound up in each other in their bed in their gothic castle—the True Heir and his True Bride fell asleep.

✦ ✦ ✦

In the end, they compromised about the painting.

Her portrait was mounted in the solar where Aleksei could gaze at it every day over breakfast.

Which he did.

When he wasn't gazing at his Laura.

✦ ✦ ✦

Tatra

Sky's Edge
  Snowy Ridge
  Hectic Royal Chateau

The female stood at the window, watching the flurries drift down, peaceful and soft.

She heard him come in but didn't take her eyes from the view.

"Is all at the ready?" she asked.

"Yes, your majesty."

She was still called that, by the leave of the new king.

And she would be that again, in her own power.

Yes, she would be.

"Tell them to commence," she ordered.

"Consider it done," the male replied and exited the room.

Tatra stared at the window, but she didn't see the peaceful fall of snow.

She saw the reflection of herself, her eyes glowing red.

And her lips forming a smile.

The End

FOUR REALMS DYNASTIES, GLOSSARY AND TIMELINE

Ruling/Reigning Dynasties and Historical Alliances

Night's Fall – Starknight Dynasty

- King Fillion Knightstar
- Queen Calisa Knightstar
- Prince Aleksei Knightstar
  - Fated Mate: Mistress Laura Makepeace
- Prince Timothee Knightstar
- Princess Aleece Knightstar
- Prince Errol Knightstar

Dawn's Break – Dayrise Dynasty

- King Dagsbrun Skybreak
- Queen Delanta Skybreak
- Prince Bainon Skybreak
- Princess Anna Skybreak

Sky's Edge – Hellsfire Dynasty

- King Tanyn Firefierce
  - Fiancée Catla Truelock
- King Arnaud Firefierce (Tanyn's half-brother, deposed)
- Queen Tatra Firefierce (deposed)
- King Rinald Firefierce (deceased)

Land's End – Earthsabre Dynasty

- King Niall Claymore
- Queen Laoise Claymore
- Prince Cormac Claymore
    - Fated Mate: Gayliliel Vinestrong
- Princess Rowan Claymore

*Night's Fall/Land's End vs. Dawn's Break/Sky's Edge – historically allies.
*Night's Fall/Skye's Edge vs. Dawn's Break/Land's End – historically enemies.

Realms in Four Realms

Dawn's Break (east) – majority population: witches/conjurers.
Land's End (south) – majority population: fae.
Night's Fall (west) – majority population: shifters.
Sky's Edge (north) – majority population: demons.
The Center

InterRealm Government

United Council of Realms (UCR) – The governing body that oversees all four realms in matters that could supersede the laws a realm made for itself. This is located in The Center.

Night's Fall Government Infrastructure

HMRD, His Majesty's Revenue Department
Royal Armory
Royal Catalogues/Catalogues of the Palace – where all the historical papers and items are held, including jewels.
Royal College of Art and Design
Royal Fire and Safety
RIC, Royal Intelligence Committee (akin to the CIA)
RMI, Royal Ministry of Investigation (akin to FBI)
Royal Ministry of Law and Justice
RS, Royal Service (akin to Secret Service)
RVPB, Royal Vulnerable Person's Bureau

Drugs/Medicine

Benzodypenes – known as "dypes." Used in prisons and hospitals to suppress shifter beasts.
Benzobytines – known as "benzos." Prescription used widely as sedatives and for anxiety.
Birth Control Serum – taken by males and females to prevent conception.
Medi-Aid – home medical device used for healing of lesser wounds like cuts and bruises.
Memory Scrub – medical apparatus that removes memories.
Porto-Ano-Scanner – portable anatomy scanner for medical uses.
Truth Serum – injected to induce subject to share facts.

Holidays/Celebrations/Parties

Dead Winter – celebration on the shortest day of the year, usually celebrated within families with a roast pork dinner eaten by candlelight and the exchanging of gifts.
Midnight Masque – formal ball at the Celestial Palace of the royal family of Night's Fall. Held on the first full moon of autumn. Known for its exclusive guest list and the elaborate clothing of attendees.
Summer Solstice – celebration on the longest day of the year, celebrated socially with festivals, dances, fayres and carnivals.

Monetary

Credit – "line of..." used for additional or secure purchasing power, same as in our world.
Mark – monetary denomination akin to "dollar," "pound," "euro," "yen," "peso" etc.

Museums

Musée de Vêtements – Clothing Museum
Musée Histoire Bestiale – Natural History Museum
Musée Histoire de Guerre – War Museum

Technology

<u>Cooking:</u>
Bev-Buddy – receptacle that can be stocked via delivery chutes and programmed to provide beverages.
Chill-Cabinet (Chill-Cupboard) – receptacle that can be stocked via delivery chutes and programmed to provide food. This is refrigerated.
Cook-Companion (Chill-Cupboard/Cook-Companion can come in one unit) – apparatus that can cook food that is stocked to provide meals.
Cool-tub (for ice) – device that keeps ice cold, at the same time it's open and available for use.
Snack-Sensation – receptacle that can be stocked via delivery chutes and programmed to provide snacks.

<u>Bathing/Grooming:</u>
Bath Pod – tub, uses light to clean hair/body.
Beard-Raze – shaver for men.
Body-Tone – workout equipment.
Cosme-Mask – device that covers face and applies makeup.
UltraPaint 5000 – the best version of a Cosme-Mask that also has facial care functions.
Denti-Clean – teeth cleaner.
Mane-Mate – hood that covers hair to dry and arrange it.
Shower Pod – stand up, uses water to clean hair/body.
Spa-Visor – apparatus that covers face and provides facial care.

<u>Other:</u>
Digi-doc – digital document.
Digi-notes – digital note.
Digi-pads – digital notepad.
Digi-pane/Panes – websites.
Digi-post – digital Post-it.
Digi-sign – digital sign, for example, on a wall by a piece of art.
Display – the screen on tech, such as phones/tablets.
Lamp Drones – drones that provide illumination by hovering where programmed, do not have cords.
Palm – cell phone.
Pics/Picced – photos/being photographed.
Privacy Shields – blinds that can be set at percentages of visibility/coverage over windows.

Scanning Tube – weapons and tech scanner.
Screen – in reference to TV/movie watching.
Seam-Stitch – makes clothes.
TechCheck – found at clubs or other venues where you leave your tech, akin to a coat check.
Vid-shopped – akin to photoshopped.

Therapeutic Practices

Isolation Aquariums – akin to an isolation tank, but with fish.
Mystic Sanctums – meditation studios.

Vehicles/Transport

Types/Terms:
Craft/Land-sky craft – vehicles.
Docking Tickets – parking tickets.
Flybys – restaurant drive-thrus.
Identi-tags – license plates.
Monorail – above ground mass transit.
Skyscreen – windshield.
Subterra – akin to subway, below ground mass transit

Specifics:
Ambu-Lift –ambulance.
BratShot 240 – personal vehicle, akin to sports car.
Combat-crafts – military vehicle, armored.
Heli-Craft – helicopter.
Hover-Cart – akin to golf cart.
Glide-cycles – akin to bicycles.
JetPanther 570 – personal vehicle, luxury, high performance, exclusive sports car.
LuxeCraft – personal vehicle, akin to limousine.
Moto-bike – motorcycle.
OpuStar – personal vehicle, luxury, high performance sedan.
Sky Yacht – large recreational spaceship.
TrailLiner – personal vehicle, sports utility.
UtiliSport – personal vehicle, luxury sports utility.

Four Realms Timeline

(1200 Years of Clan History in Night's Fall)

c. 1275 The Battle of the Chasm

1278 Dark War (in Land's End – light and good dark fae vs. bad dark fae – light/good dark wins)

1324 The Troll Invasion

- Nine realms, at the time, including Knightstar Clan, Cliff's Mountain, Day's Rise.
- The four monarchs credited as defeating the trolls divided all the lands up to the Four Realms with The Center

The First True Heir of Night's Fall (year not noted)

The Great Peace (broken by Sky's Edge, year not noted)

Battle of Peak Neige (year not noted)

1637 Demon Rift (First Families of demons leave Sky's Edge for Night's Fall)

1700s Dark Epoch

Mid-1800s The Revivalist Era

Pre-Unification/Pre Uni – all time before the attempt at unification of all Realms.

Unification – unification of all Realms (years not noted)

Crash – end of Unification (years noted)

Post-Crash (years not noted)

1920s Insouciant Riche Era (akin to Art Deco)

1932 Last War

1933 InterRealm Accord

1935 Engagement Convention

c. 2018 Weapons Banned in Night's Fall

2118 Current

Continents in the Realms World

Four Realms
Six Realms (west of Four Realms)
Three Realms (south of Four Realms)
Seven Realms (east of Four Realms)

NEWSLETTER

Would you like advanced notification about Upcoming Releases? Access to exclusive content? Access to exclusive giveaways? The first to see a new cover reveal? Sign up for my newsletter to keep up-to-date with the latest from Kristen Ashley!

Sign up at kristenashley.net

ABOUT THE AUTHOR

Kristen Ashley is the *New York Times* bestselling author of over eighty romance novels including the *Rock Chick, Colorado Mountain, Dream Man, Chaos, Unfinished Heroes, The 'Burg, Magdalene, Fantasyland, The Three, Ghost and Reincarnation, The Rising, Dream Team, Moonlight and Motor Oil, River Rain, Wild West MC, Misted Pines* and *Honey* series along with several standalone novels. She's a hybrid author, publishing titles both independently and traditionally, her books have been translated in fourteen languages and she's sold over five million books.

Kristen's novel, *Law Man*, won the *RT Book Reviews* Reviewer's Choice Award for best Romantic Suspense, her independently published title *Hold On* was nominated for *RT Book Reviews* best Independent Contemporary Romance and her traditionally published title *Breathe* was nominated for best Contemporary Romance. Kristen's titles *Motorcycle Man, The Will*, and *Ride Steady* (which won the Reader's Choice award from *Romance Reviews*) all made the final rounds for Goodreads Choice Awards in the Romance category.

Kristen, born in Gary and raised in Brownsburg, Indiana, is a fourth-generation graduate of Purdue University. Since, she's lived in Denver, the West Country of England, and she now resides in Phoenix. She worked as a charity executive for eighteen years prior to beginning her independent publishing career. She now writes full-time.

Although romance is her genre, the prevailing themes running through all of Kristen's novels are friendship, family and a strong sisterhood. To this end, and as a way to thank her readers for their support, Kristen has created the Rock Chick Nation, a series of programs that are designed to give back to her readers and promote a strong female community.

The mission of the Rock Chick Nation is to live your best life, be true to your true self, recognize your beauty, and take your sister's back whether they're at your side as friends and family or if they're thousands of miles away and you don't know who they are.

The programs of the RC Nation include Rock Chick Rendezvous, weekends Kristen organizes full of parties and get-togethers to bring the sisterhood together, Rock Chick Recharges, evenings Kristen arranges for women who have been nominated to receive a special night, and Rock Chick Rewards, an ongoing program that raises funds for nonprofit women's organizations Kristen's readers nominate. Kristen's Rock Chick Rewards have donated hundreds of thousands of dollars to charity and this number continues to rise.

You can read more about Kristen, her titles and the Rock Chick Nation at KristenAshley.net.

- facebook.com/kristenashleybooks
- instagram.com/kristenashleybooks
- pinterest.com/KristenAshleyBooks
- goodreads.com/kristenashleybooks
- bookbub.com/authors/kristen-ashley
- tiktok.com/@kristenashleybooks

Also by Kristen Ashley

Rock Chick Series:
Rock Chick
Rock Chick Rescue
Rock Chick Redemption
Rock Chick Renegade
Rock Chick Revenge
Rock Chick Reckoning
Rock Chick Regret
Rock Chick Revolution
Rock Chick Reawakening
Rock Chick Reborn
Rock Chick Rematch
Rock Chick Bonus Tracks

Avenging Angels Series
Avenging Angel
Avenging Angels: Back in the Saddle
Avenging Angels: Tenderfoot

The 'Burg Series:
For You
At Peace
Golden Trail
Games of the Heart
The Promise
Hold On

The Chaos Series:
Own the Wind
Fire Inside
Ride Steady
Walk Through Fire
A Christmas to Remember
Rough Ride
Wild Like the Wind
Free
Wild Fire
Wild Wind

The Colorado Mountain Series:
The Gamble
Sweet Dreams
Lady Luck
Breathe
Jagged
Kaleidoscope
Bounty

Dream Man Series:
Mystery Man
Wild Man
Law Man
Motorcycle Man
Quiet Man

Dream Team Series:
Dream Maker
Dream Chaser
Dream Bites Cookbook
Dream Spinner
Dream Keeper

The Fantasyland Series:
Wildest Dreams
The Golden Dynasty
Fantastical
Broken Dove
Midnight Soul
Gossamer in the Darkness

Ghosts and Reincarnation Series:
Sommersgate House
Lacybourne Manor
Penmort Castle
Fairytale Come Alive
Lucky Stars

The Honey Series:
The Deep End
The Farthest Edge
The Greatest Risk

The Magdalene Series:
The Will
Soaring
The Time in Between

Mathilda, SuperWitch:
Mathilda's Book of Shadows
The Rise of the Dark Lord

Misted Pines Series
The Girl in the Mist
The Girl in the Woods
The Woman by the Lake
The Woman Left Behind

Moonlight and Motor Oil Series:
The Hookup
The Slow Burn

The Rising Series:
The Beginning of Everything
The Plan Commences
The Dawn of the End
The Rising

The River Rain Series:
After the Climb
After the Climb Special Edition
Chasing Serenity
Taking the Leap
Making the Match
Fighting the Pull
Sharing the Miracle
Embracing the Change
Finding the One

The Three Series:
Until the Sun Falls from the Sky
With Everything I Am
Wild and Free

The Unfinished Hero Series:
Knight
Creed
Raid
Deacon
Sebring

Wild West MC Series:
Still Standing
Smoke and Steel
Smooth Sailing

Other Titles by Kristen Ashley:
Heaven and Hell
Play It Safe
Three Wishes
Complicated
Loose Ends
Fast Lane
Perfect Together
Too Good To Be True

Made in the USA
Columbia, SC
20 September 2025